By Amy Line

Published by Dreamspinner Press
www.dreamspinnerpress.com

Published by DREAMSPINNER PRESS
www.dreamspinnerpress.com

Choose your Lane to love!

Familiar Angel

"*Familiar Angel* is fantastic… a transcendent love story… Harry and Suriel are heroes to die for, and their love is a lesson… I can only have faith and desperately hope she will keep turning out more tales like this!"
—Cindy Dees, *NYT* and *USA Today* Bestselling author

"Both striking and sensual, the thought-provoking novel pays equal attention to love, sacrifice, the divine, and family."
—*Publishers Weekly*

Red Fish, Dead Fish

"Packed full of action, suspense, and of course steamy goodness, *Red Fish, Dead Fish* is the sequel we have all been anxiously waiting for."
—Love Bytes

Manny Get Your Guy

"Amy Lane can tug my heartstrings better than any other author in the history of ever!"
—Hearts on Fire Reviews

More Praise for
Amy Lane

The Virgin Manny

"I have no qualms about recommending this one. In fact, I might just insist you all go get it."

—Joyfully Jay

Summer Lessons

"This read was a sweet and snarky romance with a whole lot of funny, dirty and sassy moments thrown in for good measure."

—Gay Book Reviews

"This series is a delight! If only we were all lucky enough to find such a wonderful group of friends."

—The Novel Approach

Tart and Sweet

"I highly recommend this book and the entire Candy Man series both in written and audio-book formats… 5+ Stars!! A MUST read!!"

—Alpha Book Club

"Amy Lane has done it yet again: Pure. F*cking. Magic!"

—Diverse Reader

An
Amy Lane
Christmas

Published by
DREAMSPINNER PRESS

5032 Capital Circle SW, Suite 2, PMB# 279, Tallahassee, FL 32305-7886 USA
www.dreamspinnerpress.com

ISBN: 978-1-63533-539-2
Digital ISBN: 978-1-63533-532-3
Library of Congress Control Number: 2017916620
Published December 2017
v. 1.0

Printed in the United States of America

This paper meets the requirements of
ANSI/NISO Z39.48-1992 (Permanence of Paper).

TABLE OF CONTENTS

If I Must

AMY LANE

CHAPTER ONE

JOEL VERY carefully taped the phone list on the refrigerator, and then his itinerary, and then the magnetic calendar with the dry-erase reminders, all in bold, black, square, print-block writing.

"Ian... Ian? Ee, are you listening to me?"

Joel's roommate, Ian Cooper, pulled his head from whatever genius realm it usually occupied and aimed his slightly crossed blue eyes at the list. He nodded soberly and focused his Siamese-cat gaze over his crooked beak of a nose, and then smiled. That goofy, game smile was probably the only reason Joel had made it through five months as Ian's roommate, but it did nothing to reassure him now.

"I've got you, Joel; don't worry, mate. I've lived on my own for a lot of years now. I'll survive four days without you."

Joel wasn't so sure. In fact, he was reasonably certain that Ian's survival to this moment was a matter of sheer stinking luck.

"It's five days, and if you're so sure it's going to be easy, repeat after me: this is my itinerary in Colorado, this is where I'll be and when I'm going to be there. Here's my mom's number, my sister's number, my cell phone number, and when the returning flight gets here. Can you deal with all that?"

"I *have* your cell number, you goofy bastard," Ian protested, and Joel refrained from rolling his eyes. Yes, Ian did have his cell number, except it was in *Ian's* cell phone, and Joel knew for a fact that Ian had needed to buy at least five new cell phones in the last four months.

"This is just in case your cell phone gets lost or stolen," Joel explained patiently, and Ian interrupted him with an earnest nod of his head.

"But even if it gets lost, mate, I've got your number in the regular phone!" Ian smiled triumphantly, and Joel had to concede. Yes, his number *was* in both handsets of the house phone. Because Joel put them there. After he bought the house phone. After Ian had lost his third cell.

"Okay," Joel conceded after he looked twice at the kitchen table to make sure that both handsets were plugged in, charging, and not broken. (They'd had to replace one of them after Ian's ill-advised in-line skate parabola/hyperbola experiment. For that matter, they'd had to replace the table too.) "So, the phones are set. Now, don't forget Manky Bastard's vet appointment on Tuesday."

Ian blinked, a sudden look of panic crossing his appealing features. He had one of those faces where the cheekbones left shadows in the hollows of his cheeks. Not even a goatee could make Joel's broad-cheeked, square-chinned Hispanic face look anything better than plain in comparison to Ian's narrow, Roman-nosed, Aussie profile. Typically, Ian truly didn't seem to notice his own good looks.

"Uhm, what day is it again today?" Ian asked apologetically, and Joel squeezed his eyes shut in an attack of good humor. Of course, his own looks weren't the only thing Ian Cooper didn't notice.

"See here—this is the calendar. Today is Saturday, see? Big plane, says 'Joel goes bye-bye'?"

Ian's giggle was as endearing as his open-hearted goofy smile. "Go ahead, treat me like a child, mate! I'm good for it!"

Joel shook his head and resisted the urge to fall into that smile. "How long were you up with your paper?"

Ian blinked, and because Joel knew him, he could see the light red patina of sleeplessness in Ian's spring-blue eyes. "Haven't been to sleep yet—Riemann, he was calling me, right?" Joel nodded. He knew. Ian was a genius—a certifiable, IQ in the stratosphere genius. U.C. Davis was willing to pay for Ian's room and board, just so Ian would write them a paper and give a few guest lectures. Ian made the rest of his money working as a CPA for the faculty and their high-toned friends, which explained why he could replace things like cell phones and kitchen tables on a whim, because he was cracking good at it. It was the day-to-day that needed a little work.

"I gotcha, Ee. Now try to focus here. The cab will be here in a minute. There's frozen food in the freezer, milk, bread, and lunchmeat in the fridge, fruit on top of the microwave, and peanut butter and jelly in the cabinet. For Christ's sake, *eat!* Right?"

Ian nodded soberly. "I won't make that mistake more than once, I promise."

Joel couldn't even think about it; it made his stomach hurt. "I'll hold you to that. Now Manky Bastard has been barfing more than usual. I made her a vet appointment on Monday. You've got to take her, E. I'll give you a call to remind you, but you need to be able to find the phone and get your ass in gear, you hear me?"

Ian nodded earnestly. "I hear you, mate. She's been a good cat. I hate to see her feeling so sickly, right?"

Joel's smile softened. "Right."

And that right there was the thing that kept Joel from leaving, in spite of the chaos of living with Ian Cooper.

Ian's heart was as big as the goddamned sky. It was as simple as that. How could you desert a guy who would take in a mangy cat, give all his cash to the homeless people who abounded in the city of Sacramento proper, and who would, no matter how angry Joel got at his goofiness, simply smile that open-hearted, guileless, spring-blue smile and say, "You're right, mate. I'm a disaster. I'm lucky you're here."

There was a knock on the door, and Joel had his answer.

He could leave Ian because his mother called him and asked him to visit before the holidays.

Ian blinked at the door and the open, cheery expression he usually wore changed drastically. "Oh right," he murmured. "You're going."

"I'll be back Wednesday evening," Joel said, reaching up from his stocky five foot nine inches to embrace Ian's rangy six four. It was a quick, "manly" hug, the type with the double-thump with the fist. "Don't worry, I've got a Thanksgiving dinner ready to cook in the freezer, and I can catch a cab home—"

"No!" Ian was neither dreamy nor sleepy now. In fact, his arms tightened for a moment around Joel's shoulders. "I'll come get you."

Joel didn't want to contradict him—it would hurt his feelings—but he didn't want to be waiting at the airport for hours either. "I'll call you when I land," he temporized, thinking that if he could get Ian's attention when he landed, the wait wouldn't be that long.

Ian *was* a genius. "And I'll answer that call at the gate!" he said with dignity, and Joel grinned, rolled his eyes, and grabbed his luggage. "Have a nice visit, mate!"

"Take care of yourself, Ee!"

"If I must," Ian replied mildly, and then, as Joel disappeared out the door, he hollered "Take care!" at full volume.

Joel tried to wince while Ian could still see him. It was six-thirty in the morning, and Ian probably just woke every last tenant in their three-story refurbished Victorian. Oh well, he would be out of the city before old Mr. Pomerantz could move his ass from bed to his doorway to complain.

CHAPTER TWO

"I LIKE the goatee, *pappi,* but you look skinny. You not eating enough!"

Joel rolled his eyes at his sister—all big boobs, long stomach, and inviting hips. "You should talk, *mammi,* what? You stuff your bra with apples to keep that tummy so small?"

Melody Martinez laughed and ruffled her little brother's hair. It was late Sunday night, their mother was in bed, and they had lingered so long over dessert to catch up that they had done the dessert dishes and then just broken out the pie and sat, each of them with a fork, and finished it off.

"No, I been working out, *mammi,*" Joel said now through a forkful of pie. "That's where I met Ian."

"Your psycho roommate?" Melody took her own. Pecan, it was their favorite. Since neither of them planned to stay for actual Thanksgiving, their mother had chosen to go all out for the four days before they both boarded planes and left Denver, Joel for Sacramento and Melody for Los Angeles.

"He's not psycho, Mel," Joel said seriously. "He's just focused."

"Yeah, psychos is focused you know! He probably stalking you at that gym!"

Joel shook his head, remembering the first time he'd seen Ian Cooper. "The only thing Ian stalks at the gym is bodily injury!"

Mel laughed, but Joel couldn't.

Ian had been so helpless under that barbell.

Joel's co-worker had introduced Joel to the family gym, and Joel was grateful. There was an eclectic mix of people there—hardcore weight-lifters with tattoos and motorcycles, toned business women working the machines, spry elderly people enjoying the yoga and arthritis classes, and even children running around the ball pit in the day-care. Joel, who had grown up in a Hispanic neighborhood in South Denver, had been reassured by the diversity. It felt like a real community, and not just a place to be stalked by gym bunnies.

Those girls had never really appealed to Joel anyway.

And the bulletin board added to the community, everything from free puppies to offers to carpool and, Joel hoped, roommates.

When he'd first come to the city, he'd ended up in one of those prairie-dog apartment warrens, the kind where every apartment was the shape of a cracker tin and you could tell what your neighbor was doing upstairs whether you liked it or not. Joel might have toughed it out in one of those until he could afford to rent or buy a house, but he wanted to ride his bike to work. Since he had to move anyway, he was looking for something with... well, character. He'd driven around the city in his little hybrid, and he'd seen the neighborhoods with the Victorian-era houses. Some were high-toned, some were run-down, and some were in between, but they had seemed... eclectic. Interesting. They had character, and Joel was in a strange city on his second job. His first job had been in a cubicle; he'd made sure this one was in a big, open-air office with people who knew what the others looked like. He wanted character.

Then the first chuffing sound penetrated Joel's involvement with the bulletin board. He swung around to see a lanky man, shirtless, being crushed under a barbell that looked seriously *overloaded for such a slender frame.*

Joel dropped his duffel bag and hurried over to rescue the poor bastard, and as he pulled the barbell up and rested it in the cradle, he was treated to an upside-down version of that sweet, goofy grin that would dominate the next five months of his life.

"Thanks, mate. That 'bout buggered me." The man was in his mid-twenties, like Joel, and his curly blonde hair was a spiky, sweaty, halo all over his long skull. Joel would learn that, with the exception of the sweat, it always looked like that.

"Well, you need to make sure you always have a spotter," Joel told him seriously.

"Yeah, mate, if I must. Here, you want the job?"

Joel was going to say no—he'd actually been on the way out of the gym—but that smile appeared, and it was so winsome and so trusting that Joel found himself standing over Ian and helping him with what appeared to be a ridiculous amount of weight.

After a couple of sets, he had to admit that the weight wasn't ridiculous. The strength in that long, rangy frame was the outstanding thing.

"Thanks, mate," Ian panted when he was done. He sat up and rubbed his face with a towel. "I was lucky you came along. What were you looking at over there?" He jerked his head in the direction of the bulletin board, and Joel looked over and grimaced.

"A roommate," he sighed. "I want to live someplace interesting, but I don't have enough money for interesting. Just cheap."

The young man blinked, and his head went through a series of bird-like movements that Joel had come to associate with Ian thinking on the fly.

"A roommate, you say?"

"Yeah, a roommate. Why? You know someone who lives in a cool house downtown who wouldn't mind a broke computer programmer in their spare room?"

That grin again—except without the goofiness, it was full-on blinding. "Yeah, mate, me!" The young man had extended a long-fingered, bony-knuckled hand. "I'm Ian Cooper, and I've got a cool top-floor and a spare bedroom."

"So just like that, he offers you a room?" Mel was very carefully wiping the bottom of the pie tin with a manicured finger.

Joel shrugged and grinned at his big sister. Mel was a buyer for a department store in L.A. On most days, she was one hundred percent Vogue, one hundred percent of the time. But during holidays, for family, she wore ratty sweats and piled her hair on the top of her head and ate whatever she wanted. In return, Joel wore his accent in his voice like a badge of honor, and together, they could be themselves.

"I think he just doesn't like living alone," he told her honestly. Ian certainly didn't need the money.

Somebody's phone was ringing, and Joel couldn't find the damn thing. With a sigh, he started picking through the disaster in the living room. He'd just moved in the day before, and although Ian had made a good-faith effort to clean up, Joel had found him, a pile of dirty clothes in his lap, typing feverishly after about an hour of housecleaning. The man said he got distracted by his work, but until that moment, Joel thought it was probably just a charming personality quirk, not an impediment toward health, living quality, and good hygiene.

With a grunt Joel tripped over a free weight and landed on all fours in a pile of blankets that smelled like sex and beer. The ringing got louder, and Joel reached under the oxblood leather couch to be rewarded by the tiny cell phone buzzing in the palm of his hand.

"Jesus, Ian," he griped, "don't you have a house phone?"

"What?" Ian looked up from his room blankly and then turned back to the paper he was typing—something about imaginary numbers and Riemannian geometry, and Joel was damned if he could follow half of what Ian said when he was talking about it.

Joel rolled his eyes and sat on the floor, leaning against the couch, to answer the phone.

"Hello. Ian Cooper?" The voice was educated, older than thirty, and female.

"No, I'm sorry. This is his roommate."

There was a subtle pause. "Roommate?"

"Yeah, roommate." As if! "What can I do for you?"

"This is Florence Kohl from U.C. Davis. I was just calling to remind Dr. Cooper that he has a lecture tomorrow."

"Does he know where it is?" Joel asked, looking around the spacious top-floor apartment a little desperately for a pen and paper. He'd already started a grocery list in his head: laundry hampers, vacuum cleaner bags, Swiffer, sponges, dish soap. He added "pen and paper" to it now, so he didn't have to make the next list in his head.

"Oh yes." Florence laughed appreciatively. "Just get him to the campus around ten o'clock, and he'll probably show up by ten-thirty."

The nice woman with (presumably) Ian's paycheck in the palm of her hand rang off, and Joel took a deep breath and looked around. The apartment was gorgeous: oxblood leather furniture, hardwood floors, cream area rugs and a burgundy accent with white trim. And it was huge; the rent was a steal. The fact that it currently looked like a thrift store clearinghouse because of the sheer volume of clothes on the floor, in the corners, on the couches, and over the coffee table, and that it smelled like a monkey's ass notwithstanding, the situation had potential.

But first, there had to be some semblance of order. That was okay. Joel was good at order.

"Ian," he said, standing up and dusting off his hands, "buddy, you have a lecture to give tomorrow."

The effect on Ian was electric. He stood up abruptly, left his computer, and started running around his room, rifling through clothes, throwing items from the pile on the bed onto the pile on the floor, and digging through stuff in the pile on the floor and tossing it to the lone basket at the foot of the bed.

"Oh fuck," he was muttering. "I don't have anything to wear!"

Joel had to suppress a laugh. "Then what is all this shit on the floor?" he asked with good nature, and Ian sent him a panicked look from his wild-blue eyes.

"It's not funny, mate. All this shit, it's wrinkled! I've got to do laundry! I've got to find a laundromat! Jesus, I've got to get quarters!"

He was so distraught that Joel couldn't laugh anymore. "Ian... Ian... Ian!"

Ian stopped so abruptly that he tripped over a dress shoe and fell sprawling on (what else?) a pile of clothes. Joel was over to him before he could pick himself up, crouching down to see if he would live.

"Ian. pop... buddy... you okay?"

Ian blinked up at him like a startled child. "I'm fine," he said softly, and a troubled version of that smile appeared. "I hadn't meant for you to see me lose my nut quite so soon. I'm sorry. I just- I completely forgot...."

Joel looked carefully at his roommate, saw the bloodshot eyes and the dark bags, and recalled that Ian hadn't slept the night before, he'd been so intent on his work. Joel took a deep breath, snagged a paper and a pen off the clutter that was Ian's desk, and sat down to put his tidy mind to work.

"All right, Ee. Here. This is a list of shit we need. I can pay you back for my half..."

"No worries," Ian assured carelessly, and Joel had rolled his eyes. He'd pay the guy back. He didn't like being in someone's debt. "No, really!" Ian assured him. "You're helping me out of a jam here. Let me pay, right?"

"Ian, it's no big deal," Joel laughed, and he was surprised when Ian's long-fingered hand wrapped around his wrist and stopped him from writing. Joel looked up and met those spring-blue eyes. They were intent and laser focused, and Joel's breath had caught in his chest.

"It's a very big deal," Ian said seriously. "You didn't sign up to be my keeper. I've made a piss-poor showing here. I appreciate it."

There was something naked in his eyes, something stripped bare. Ian was afraid of what Joel would think of him.

Joel tried a tentative smile, although there was still something in his chest that wanted him not to breathe. "Yeah, well, I wasn't doing anything else." This was true. Christ, when was the last time he had a date?

"Well, if I get in the way of you getting laid, let me know, right, mate?" Ian grinned, and Joel blushed for no good reason he could think of.

"Whatever. Look, man, just get this stuff." He had a thought. "Do not stop, do not pass go, do not get anything but what's on that list."

"What about some takeout for dinner?"

"And dinner. And by the time you get back, I'll have clothes ready to go in the washer, and we can go together."

Ian blessed him then with the widest, sweetest, most grateful smile. "Well, if I must do laundry, I couldn't ask for better company."

"So," Melody said seriously while washing out the pie tin, "you keep his life for him, and he pays for dinner. Sounds like you're his houseboy or something!"

Joel had to roll his eyes. "Not even that glamorous. And it's not like that. He just… he loses track of the world so thoroughly, you know? All those clothes on the floor? It was just easier for him to go out and buy new clothes than it was to find what he needed in what he already had. I went through and organized, and he had, like, three pairs of the same jeans!"

Melody laughed for a minute and then looked at him thoughtfully. "Doesn't that get old though? You know, keeping someone's life for them?"

Joel shrugged. "He's kept it up since I organized it. And trust me, he's got his own life. In fact, I think he fucks anything with a pulse!"

"Oooh… lots of hot women coming in and out of your pad?"

Joel flushed. "Like I said, …um, *anything* with a pulse."

Melody turned to him in titillation, her well-crafted eyebrows reaching her hairline and her mouth making a little moue. "*Really.* An equal opportunity kind of guy?"

Joel's blush intensified. "Yeah, um, I can't say much for his taste, though."

The boy with the unbuttoned jeans and bare chest was pretty, Joel would give him that. The kid's hair was tousled, carefully streaked, and his little heart-shaped face and brown eyes were truly charming.

Joel would have been more impressed if he hadn't found the boy rifling through Ian's pants and palming his credit card.

Christo! Joel had to shake his head. On the nights that Joel worked late, he would sometimes find Ian gone when he got home. In the morning there would be a stranger doing a red-faced walk of shame out of Ian's room. Usually the stranger was female, but not today.

"Hey, you, what the fuck you think you doing, punto? *You get the hell away from shit that don't belong to you!" Joel's accent—the product of being brought up in a mostly Spanish-speaking home—only came out when he was back at home or really, really pissed off.*

The kid started guiltily and dropped the jeans and wallet, scattering the credit cards on the (clean!) floor. "Hey, baby, don't get mad at me because your boy got takeout last night!"

It was probably the ingratiating smile on the kid's face, but in about two seconds, Joel had him pinned to the pretty purple wall with his forearm at a slender, corded throat. "I could give a shit what he sleeps with, as long as it doesn't take him on the twinkie express when it's done."

"Yeah?" the kid hissed. "What're you gonna do? For all you know he liked what he got!"

Joel rolled his eyes. "Yeah? For all you know, he thinks you someone dead who was doing some sexy math in his dreams."

In less than a minute Joel had hustled the kid out onto the landing and slammed the door in his face, ignoring his cry of, "But I don't even have my shoes!" Then, in as quiet a huff as he could manage, he tiptoed into Ian's room. He tried to ignore Ian's sprawled, naked body on top of the covers as he began to quietly pick up the clothes on the floor he knew for certain weren't Ee's.

"Mmmmm," Ian groaned, just as Joel was about to close the door and let him sleep, "Joel? S'that you?"

"Yeah, popp, uh, Ee. What you... what do you want?"

"What're you doing?"

"Saturday chores?" Joel tried, and Ian sat up sleepily. God, his chest and abs really were cut! And his... never mind. Joel wasn't going to look at that. It was huge, but he wasn't gonna look.

"Saturday?" Ian murmured. "Don't we usually get breakfast on Saturdays?"

Joel resisted the temptation to say something catty, like Well, yeah, did you want to take your Friday Night Special too? *And instead concentrated on the fact that Ian seemed to have forgotten about Twink Lightfingers who was standing half-naked on the landing.*

"Yeah, Ee," *he said with a sigh,* "but first I've got to take out the trash."

Later, over pancakes at IHOP (because it was Ian's favorite, that's why) Joel read him the riot act.

"For Christ's sake, Ian, he was stealing your cash! I hope you at least wore a raincoat, you feel me?"

Ian blinked. "Why would I want a raincoat, Joel? I was having sex."

Joel put his face in his hands, closed his eyes tight, and prayed that when he looked up and opened them Ian would be kidding.

He wasn't.

"A condom, *Ian, I hope you used a* condom!" *Oh God, he was not having this conversation with a twenty-something bisexual college professor. It was not possible.*

"Why would I?" *Ian asked seriously. He looked anxious. It was as though he understood he'd done something wrong, but he couldn't for the life of him figure out what it was.* "It's not like either one of us can get pregnant, right?"

"Disease, Ee?" *Joel realized he was on the verge of tears. How had this man managed to live on his own and be this innocent?* "You know, HIV, herpes, shit that'll make your dick fall off?"

Ian's eyes were suddenly saucer-shaped, and his mouth was wide open. Oh yes, now the light bulb was on. "Oh, well, shit, mate, I never thought about that! I just...." *He cocked his head, something suddenly occurring to him.* "And how would you know about that? I didn't know you swung that way, do you?"

Joel shook his head. "I want to Catholic school, where they teach you everything with a healthy dose of 'God will hate you if you do that, but if you want God to hate you go ahead'. Or maybe that was Sister Margaret." *Joel tried a laugh, but Ian was looking more and more distraught, so he tried some kindness instead.* "Look, Ee, we'll get you tested. It'll be no big deal."

"Do you believe that?" *Ian asked suddenly, a pinch around his eyes.* "You don't believe that God hates me, do you?"

Oh crap. Heaven save Joel from literal mathematical geniuses.
"No," he said softly, trying to do anything to take that pinched look from
those Easter-sky eyes. "I think as long as you care about the person, and
you're being good to each other, God's all fine with it. But that's why this
worries the hell out of me, Ian. You don't even like these people. I mean
hell, I don't think you even remember that kid's name!"

"Benji," Ian supplied helpfully, and it was all Joel could do to not
make gagging motions with his fingers.

"Yeah, whatever, it's like when I'm not there, you wander out and
bring back a warm body. You deserve better than that, Ee. What you're
doing is dangerous, and you could get hurt, and I don't want that to
happen."

Ian shrugged and looked away. "I don't know, mate. I used to be
okay, but now... you're not there. It gets lonely in the place, right?"

Joel did laugh now. "Jesus, Ian! Get a cat!"

That lost look went away, and Ian looked across the table and
grinned back at him. "That's an idea. I like cats."

They were sitting near a window, and Joel found himself fascinated
by the way the light hit that halo of curly blond hair and brought out the
reddish hints in Ian's eyelashes. He stopped himself and thought of a way
to keep Ian safe.

"Okay, then, you look for a cat, and I'll promise to call when I'm
going to be late, deal?"

The look on Ian's face transcended "pleased" and bordered on
"sublimely happy".

"Right, mate. If I must!"

Joel and Melody made it to the couch, each one sitting on the
end and tangling their legs companionably in the middle. Melody was
channel surfing with the sound off, listening avidly to Joel's latest story,
and when he was finished, she leaned her head back sleepily. Joel was
pretty tired himself, but, well, he missed his big sister. They'd bickered,
like most children, but he'd always loved knowing she had his back—
bullies at school, his first broken heart (a girl from public school their
father hadn't approved of)—she was Joel's own personal pit bull, and
really, until Ian, his best friend.

"Honey, that's sweet and all, but really, don't you think you got
enough to take care of with this Ian person? You really want a cat?"

Joel felt his expression go soft and a little dreamy. He couldn't help it—he knew how it must look, but...

"Ee actually takes care of the cat," he said truthfully. "Ian feeds it, and he's the one who took it to the vet when we first got it."

Melody snorted, her eyes half closed in sleep. They'd talked until nearly one in the morning. "So he can't take care of himself, but he can take care of the cat? How's that work?"

Joel shrugged. "I think he thinks the cat's more important."

A week after their little sex-ed discussion, Joel came home to find a little tin of high-priced cat food on the landing.

The thing eating out of it and snarling through spittle-covered whiskers barely passed for a cat.

"Ian?" Joel called, jostling his bike and his backpack over his shoulders and hoping they could co-exist for just a few more steps. He'd just come from work and was wearing his bike shorts. "Ian?" Gingerly he reached over to open the door (Ian rarely remembered to lock it) and swung a leg over the threshold. The cat—a dark brown short-haired behemoth with pale tortoise-shell stripes on its side—stuck out a massive paw and clawed his bare ankle.

"Ian!" Joel screamed, not wanting to kick this new development off a three-story landing and not wanting to lose any more blood, either.

Ian popped out of his room—shirtless, as usual—and trotted over to help Joel through the door.

"He got you? Why would he get you?"

Joel glared at the cat who looked at him and growled some more. "Because I interfered with his evil plan to rain destruction down on mankind," he said sourly, and the freaky thing licked its whiskers and damned near smiled.

Ian laughed, and now that Joel was safely inside, he sank to his haunches and scratched delicately under the cat's chin. The feline monstrosity had the balls to purr.

"Hullo, you manky bastard," Ian murmured. "You giving Joel a hard time? You can't, you know. He was here first."

Joel looked at the cat in a mixture of humor and horror. "Well, it's nice to know I rate!"

Ian's grin appeared again, and Joel wondered why the cat suddenly looked more like a cat and less like a refugee from a zoo. "Rate? Brother, you're more important to me than Riemann!"

Joel had to blink. Wow—Riemann was like the guy's god—or at least the subject of his latest paper. Joel took a big breath and realized most of his irritation with the animal was gone. All that was left was his perpetual good humor.

"Jesus, Ian! I said get a cat —I didn't say to just let one wander up to the house."

Ian turned that sunny smile up at Joel one more time, and although he refused to admit it, Joel's heart stuttered in his chest. "I don't know, brother. That's sort of how I got you, isn't it?"

Joel's mouth went sober. He met Ian's gaze and flushed, and Manky Bastard (as the female *cat would forevermore be known) sank her pointy, street-cat teeth into the ball of Ian's thumb.*

Ian shouted and stood, and the little opportunist took that moment to run inside the apartment and sit, snarling, in the corner of the bathroom between the toilet and the tub. Joel, still a little dizzy from that long look he'd shared with Ian, went out and got cat litter, a box, and a pooper-scooper, and they put it where the cat seemed to want to stay. Ian had already bought enough food to last the damned cat a year. (They still hadn't gone through even half the Fancy Feast under the counter.)

Joel made two appointments the next day: one for the cat, which Ian kept, and one for Ian, because his thumb turned blue and doubled in size. Joel took Ian to that one. While they were there, he made Ian take a blood test too.

The results were negative, and Ian had promised to go back after the window period was over. "Well, if I must!" Whenever he said that, Joel had no doubt he'd do it.

Melody seemed to have gotten her second wind. She sat up on the couch and was staring avidly at Joel's face. Joel wondered if she could see something he couldn't.

"So now you gots a cat?" she asked, her face soft in the glow from the television. Joel had no doubt his sister could be hard as nails when she was driving a bargain or running her staff, but with him, she was all Little Mommy.

Joel nodded and grimaced. "You should see Ian with her. He brushes her, feeds her shit that cost more than my food, and she thinks he put fish in the damn ocean. But she's sick. I think she's just old." He shuddered. "I hope she's okay. Ian really loves her."

"Mmm-hmm." Melody's voice went up at the end of that, and Joel found himself sitting up and looking at her funny.

"What was that for, *mammi?* It sounds like you thinking something you shouldn't!"

Melody shook her head. "I'll tell you when I'm ready, little brother. So, you think he'll take care of the cat when he can't take care of himself?"

"I know he will," Joel answered softly. That was one story he *didn't* want to tell Melody. For some reason it just hurt too much.

Joel had been gone for a two-day seminar. He'd asked Ian repeatedly, "You going to be okay, Ian? You going to be okay?" But he had to go— what, he was going to tell work he was going to turn down free training because his roommate was a flake?

He got back to find a mound of open, empty cat food tins on the floor, and Ian sitting shirtless on the couch. (He was always shirtless. The man would have clients come over to get their taxes done, and he'd meet them in cargo shorts, flip-flops, and sweat.)

He was eating cat food out of the tin, and he was stinking drunk.

"Ian?" Joel asked, dropping his luggage on the floor inside the door. "Ian, what the hell? You said you'd meet me at the airport! I had to take a cab!"

"I'm sorry, mate," Ian said, sounding more than distraught. "I was gonna." He nodded solemnly. "I was gonna... but I woke up this morning, and there was nothing in the fridge but beer. And cat food. There was lots of cat food. So first I drank the beer, and then, when I threw up, I ate the cat food!" He sniffled a little, sounding pathetic, and then he had what looked to be an attack of clarity.

"What kind of asshole lets a friend down like that?" he asked himself cruelly, and he sniffled again.

Joel stared at him in blank horror.

"Jesus, Ian," he said softly, walking to the refrigerator and feeling lost. "There's corndogs in the freezer, you know that, right?"

Ian started to giggle softly, and he put the cat food down on the floor next to the couch. "Thank God, mate. I thought I was going to have to puke again!"

Joel told himself it was anger as he threw the corndogs on the plate and broke out a can of corn to nuke with them. Jesus. He and Mel had been fixing themselves dinner since the third grade; you'd think a certifiable genius with an IQ of 170 would be able to fix his own goddamned lunch, would be able to….

Joel turned to Ian, who was sitting on the couch looking so dejected that Joel's heart lurched.

"I'm sorry," he muttered, not even trying to meet Joel's eyes. "I'm sorry. I'm a pain in the ass. I know I am. I- I'm up all night and I never wear clothes and… I just… when you're not here, all I am is the stuff in my head. I've got curves and hyperboles and Riemann and Gauss and they're sayin' shit and the world looks clear but time… it just passes, and I don't see it. How come I know mathematical theory, but I can't count to sixty? What kind of right is that? And the only thing that makes me more than the shit in my head is doing something for Bastard or…" Ian swallowed, hard, "or when you're here. You're the only one who makes me… real."

Joel realized that helpless tears were running down Ian's face. Oh God. He hadn't even said a word—not one goddamned word—and here he'd gone and made Ian cry.

The microwave dinged in the silence between them, and Joel grabbed a towel and brought the plate over, not forgetting the fork for the corn and the ketchup.

Ian took a bite of corndog and seemed to pull himself together, smiling that sunshine smile through his muddle-headed misery, and Joel wanted to do something, stroke his face, pet his wild hair, do something that would reassure him.

He thumped him heartily on the thigh and hoped that worked okay. "Look, Ee," he said softly. "I'm mad at you because you're my friend here. I come home, and you're falling apart. How's that supposed to make me feel? I can take care of you for you, but you can't take care of yourself for me? C'mon, Ian, I worry about you."

"I was just fine before you came along, I swear!" Ian nodded eagerly. "I pay bills. I've got money. I make it to my lectures." He smiled

for a moment, shaken out of his despondency. "You should see me give a lecture, mate. I sound... smart, you know?"

Joel nodded seriously, because he actually had seen Ian lecture one day, when Ian hadn't known he was there. Ian had been poised and intelligent, and even funny, but that man was hard to see in the lost soul Joel was feeding now. Something in Ian's handsome, sweet-natured face haunted him. Ian may have stayed alive, he may have made it through school across an ocean and into a job, and he may even have managed to pay the bills (he was, after all, an accountant), but whatever he had been before Joel got there, Ian had obviously not been "just fine." No amount of thinking about teaching the guy to take care of himself would ever assure Joel that he would be "just fine" without Joel, himself, personally, to help in the task, and he just didn't want to think any further than that.

Instead, he cleaned up the cat tins, helped Ian into the shower, and then pulled out a T-shirt and some jockeys for the guy. When Ian was dressed, Joel made absolutely sure he lay down in bed. He slept for sixteen hours, and Joel thought he'd probably been up for the seventy-two before that. He woke up apologetic and sheepish and more than ready to accept any crap that Joel wanted to ladle out for him being (his words) a manky arse, but Joel didn't want to bring up the incident again.

"Just do me a favor, Ee. Feed yourself, okay?"

"Right, mate!" And then, to make it a promise, "If I must."

CHAPTER THREE

JOEL AND Melody actually fell asleep on the couch, probably in the pause between "Ian stories," but Joel couldn't be sure.

They staggered to their own beds in the wee hours of the morning and slept late, which was what you got to do over your Thanksgiving break, wasn't it? But Joel didn't sleep too late. As soon as he was awake enough, he snagged his cell phone from the end table and remembered to call Ian.

"Hey, Ee." Oh geez did he sound like he just woke up? Did he sound like he was calling from bed? Suddenly the inappropriateness of calling from bed hit him, and he swung his legs over the side of the mattress and sat up so he would feel less self-conscious.

"Joel, you having a good time?" Ian sounded happy to hear from him, and just hearing his voice on the other end of the line eased an ache Joel hadn't known he'd harbored in his chest.

"Yeah, mom's trying to make me fat, and me and Mel are catching up. You staying sober?"

Ian laughed. "I should be. You left enough food in the freezer for a horde of wild barbarians. I even went out and bought vegetables. Aren't you proud?"

Joel thought about his sweet, brilliant roommate, who would probably go down in history as the guy who… well, whatever it was Ian knew that the rest of mankind didn't, he'd go down in history as the guy who figured it out.

"I'm always proud of you, Ee," he said sincerely. "I just miss you is all." Oh God. That must have sounded…. In his mother's little house in the Denver suburb, Joel fought the urge to tuck his head under his pillow in embarrassment.

But if he sounded like a weepy asshole, Ian didn't seem to notice. "Miss you too, mate. Here, I'll call you after I get home, how's that?"

Joel doubted he'd remember, but it sounded promising. They spoke a few more moments and then rang off, and Joel showered and prepared to face his family. He couldn't think of why, but he thought he should be embarrassed to say good morning to Mel. Had he really talked all night about Ian? What an asshole! This morning he needed to ask her about her job. Mel being Mel, there would probably be a quiz later.

But Mel being Mel didn't want to talk about work. As their mother bustled about in her flowered housedress and apron, pouring coffee and cleaning up the last of the breakfast dishes (corn pancakes—Mommy was definitely trying to send them both home fat!) Mel made it perfectly clear that what she wanted to talk more about was Ian.

"Ian?" Mommy asked, sitting down to drink her coffee with them. "Isn't that the man you share a house with?"

"More like an apartment, Mommy," Joel said, telling them about the vast top floor of the Victorian that dominated the block.

"His roommate is a real character," Mel said, looking over her coffee at Joel. "Seems like he couldn't find his ass with both hands if Joel didn't hand it to him all labeled and neat, you know?"

Lucia Martinez nodded. "That's Joel—even as a *niño,* he kept neat—you remember his room? He used to save his shoeboxes to keep his toys straight."

"I liked knowing where to find them," Joel said with dignity, and then, because he couldn't stand that his sister thought badly of Ian, "and Ian's brilliant." *Lost, but...* "Don't let me give you the wrong impression. He's just eccentric."

"Eccentric?" Mel had what Joel always thought of as her "evil" look now. She was teasing him, trying to get him to say something that she could get him with later. "You told me the guy once forgot his own birthday!"

Joel regretted telling that story. It was a fun, glib story you could use to get someone to laugh, but now it felt wrong. Now it felt like Mel was getting to know Ian, and Joel wanted his big sister to like the guy.

"He remembered his birthday," Joel corrected seriously. "He just forgot how old he was!"

"Well, it must be nice to get so wrapped up in your work you can't remember you's getting wrinkles, eh *papi?"*

Joel shivered, and the mood at the kitchen table grew inexplicably sober. "No," he said quietly. "No. No. Nothing nice about it at all."

On the days Joel didn't bike to work, he dragged Ian to the gym. Ian usually went willingly, but, if left to his own devices, he forgot how long it had been since last he went. On this day, Joel got home a little early and breezed through the living room shouting, "I'm gonna get my stuff, Ee, are you ready?"

"Ready? For what?"

Ian stuck his head out of his room and turned that lost-Siamese-cat gaze toward the calendar on the wall. "What are we doing again?"

Joel came out of his room wearing only his work khakis. "The gym? Working out? It's Wednesday, remember?"

"Wednesday? Wednesday the what?"

"Wednesday, September twenty-fourth," Joel told him patiently. He was unprepared for Ian to stand up off his rolling chair and peer at the calendar closely as though the damned thing had lied.

"Really? The twenty-fourth?"

"What's the matter, Ee? You miss a lecture?" Joel didn't think so. Since that one phone call from Ian's supervising professor, Joel had put all of Ian's guest lectures on the calendar and taken to giving him one reminder the night before and one reminder as he left the house. Florence Kohl had sent him a case of really good wine, but mostly, Joel did it so Ian wouldn't have to look lost and miserable the way he had the last time he'd been caught unaware.

"No, I just...." Ian turned around and squinted at Joel in that way that told Joel he hadn't looked away from his computer in a while. "I think today's my birthday."

Joel's face split into a grin. "Well, awesome! Fuck the gym, let's go out!" Ian had treated Joel to a gigantic steak and a nice bottle of wine in Old Town when Joel turned twenty-seven. The least Joel could do was get him out of the house.

"How old are you, anyway?"

He was unprepared for the dismay this question seemed to cause.

"I- I don't know," Ian murmured. "Twenty-five? No. Maybe? Twenty-six?" He looked up at Joel in a panic. "Oh God, what if I'm thirty?"

"Ian." Joel should have been used to this feeling by now, this jarring, violent make-fit between Ian's world and the real world, but it never seemed to get any easier.

"I don't remember." Ian held out his hands and started counting on them. "Let's see, I was fourteen when I left the orphanage and went to University..."

Oh God, Joel had known he was an orphan. He'd even known he was a genius, but he was unprepared for the idea of a fourteen-year-old Ian, turned loose on college life.

"... and I must have been twenty or so when I got my doctorate, and then I came over here. How long have I been here? I renewed my visa last year... or was it the year before? Or do I have to do that every year?"

Ian's gaze went from inward to outward, and he looked up at Joel with open palms. "I don't know. I- you need to have people to tell you that's important, don't you? I- I guess I don't have any people? How old am I? Jesus."

There was a certain panic to Ian's voice, and Joel felt it, right in his gut, how adrift this man could be without a person in his life to care for him. He could live, yeah, but what a vague surfing of the years, without any markers like birthdays or holidays, without any solid, real moments to anchor him to the here and now.

Joel took Ian's hands in his own, feeling calluses from weightlifting and the softness from not doing much else, and made sure Ian had his attention.

"Don't worry, Ian," he murmured. And then, grinning a little bit self-consciously, he leaned forward and reached around Ian toward his back pocket, making a little whiffle of disgust as he did so. "Christ, Ian, when's the last time you showered? You smell like monkey ass!"

Ian laughed, which was the point, because in reality he smelled a little sweaty but very human, and not bad at all. "Yeah, I'm a little ripe, mate. What do you have there?"

Joel held out Ian's wallet and grinned triumphantly. "Your wallet, genius. You've got your driver's license in here."

Ian's smile was brilliant, blinding, as excited as a child's. "Excellent! So, don't keep me in suspense. How old am I?"

Joel looked at the date on the driver's license and grimaced. God, Ian really had been young when he'd been cut loose on an unsuspecting world, hadn't he?

"You're twenty-three, boy, which makes you four years younger than me and seven years younger than thirty. Congratulations and happy birthday!"

"Outstanding!" Ian crowed, practically knocking Joel over with the force of his hug. He held the hug for a moment, crushing Joel's face up against his bare chest, and Joel had to wonder that his heart seemed to

be speeding up and that Ian's scent was seeming less and less a liability with every passing second.

Joel pulled back with difficulty and kept his smile bright. "So, you ready to shower and go out?"

Ian made a little strutting motion with his shoulders and his head, his whole rangy, lean, man's body showing a child's happiness. "If I must, mate—if I must!"

"Oh, *papacito!*" Joel's mom still used the endearments she'd used when they were children. "It's so nice you finally found someone!"

Joel stared at his mother as though she had two heads. "Mommy, he's my roommate. I'm not gay."

"Oh honey," Lucia Martinez smiled sweetly, "of course you are. You just remember to wear your rubbers, you know?"

Well, maybe growing another head would have been an improvement. "Mommy, he's my friend!"

And now Melody laughed, throwing her head back and letting the coffee-rich sound roll from her stomach. "Oh right. He's your friend and I'm a virgin!"

"*Mel!*" Because even their mother knew *that* wasn't true. "Have I said *anything* that would—"

Mel shook her head. "Joey, *pappi,* it's not what you've said. It's how much you've said it! Three days, you been here three days. In five minutes you told me about work, your boss who's okay, and the receptionist who had the world's cutest baby. The rest of the three days? It's been Ian Cooper. I know more about that man than I know about your last three girlfriends, including the fact that I think I like him better already."

"You liked Penny—"

"I liked to shop with her. I didn't want her in my family."

Joel hadn't thought he could blush anymore than he already had, Shows how much he knew! "Melody, he's a friend! I'm not... you know... I can't be...."

His mother stopped his stuttering with a quiet pat to the hand. "I know, baby. Poppa would have told you, Mexicans, they can't go all gay. But Poppa was an asshole, and we all know that."

Joel wondered if he'd eaten something poisonous and then gone to sleep on it. His stomach was starting to hurt, that was for damned sure.

"Mommy!" he objected, and Melody took pity on him.

"Mommy, we're starting to freak him out. You need to leave for a minute, so we can talk, okay?"

Lucia rolled her eyes. "You kids. You think we don't know anything. Gay was a thing in the eighties too, you know!"

"I'm gonna throw up," Joel muttered to himself, and he hid his face in his crossed arms.

"Why, Joey?" Melody asked him softly. Just like she'd done when they were kids, she crossed her arms too and looked at him from about six inches away, eye level.

"You think I'm gay, Mom says Pops was an asshole—"

"What's so wrong about being gay, *pappi?*" Melody asked seriously, and Joel grimaced.

"I don't know. You know, Pops used to—"

"He used to say faggots should be burnt at the stake. I know. He also used to say sending a girl to college was like teaching a dog to read, and you know what? I said fuck him. I know he's dead, and you want to think the man was perfect, but he wasn't. He loved us, but fuck him. I do what Pops said, I be a mommy for real now, and I wouldn't be any good at that, *pappi,* I really wouldn't."

"You'd be great at it, Mel," Joel said softly. "You took good care of me when Mommy was at work."

Melody's hand came out and ruffled his hair. "You were the best kid in the world, Joey. In fact, you were too good. Nothing get you riled. Nothing make you too mad. Nothing make you cry. I worried 'bout you. I thought, 'He's a good kid, but he got no passion', you know? And I still think that. You go get your degree in computers because that's what you're good at. But it's not what you love. No, I stand by it. You do what you got to in your heart to make it right, because this Ian, you got more passion in your voice for him than you got in your life for anything."

"He's a friend," Joel insisted, but his argument was weak, even to his own ears.

"You always love your boyfriends more'n your girlfriends, you know that? In grade school it was one thing, but in high school and college? Joel, *pappi,* why you got to lie to yourself?"

Joel didn't have any answer to that. As much as he didn't want to think about it, it was probably true.

Melody sighed and continued to stroke his hair. "I taught you that stuff you know."

"What stuff?"

"That putting the calendar on the fridge, making lists, how to do laundry."

Joel managed a pale grin. "You done good, *mammi*, it come in handy."

"Yeah, well, I tell you. I could have done it all pissed off and all. You were my little brother. I had better things to do, that what you think when you young, you know?"

Joel frowned thoughtfully. "You didn't. You were a good teacher."

"Yeah, Joey, 'cause that's the sort of thing you do for family."

Joel closed his eyes tightly and fought a very real temptation to cry. "I- I never let myself think about it, you know?" he admitted at last.

"I know, Joey. You got Pops in your head, telling you it's wrong. We seen it, Mommy and me. We seen you—every time you set your sights on a girl, it was like watching you wage brain warfare in your own head. I want you to do something for me, can you do that?"

Joel closed his eyes and ignored the stiff hair of his goatee getting slick with salt water. "Yeah?"

"Yeah. Think about him in the dark, *pappi*. When no one's looking, close your eyes and hear his voice in your head, see his face. You don't got to tell no one what happens next, but you think about him in the dark and see what happens. Then you forget all about things like being Mexican and being gay, and you tell me what you want more than anything, yeah?"

Joel managed a weak nod. "Yeah," he mumbled, too tired to even object to what she was suggesting. "Yeah."

"I'll leave you alone now. Me and Mommy, we won't talk about it none, it make you feel bad. But you already know we love you, so you don't worry 'bout that, 'kay?"

Joel managed to pull himself up straight like a real man and look at his big sister with watery eyes. "I love you, Mel."

She bent and kissed him on the cheek. "Love you too, little brother." And then she moved gracefully out of the kitchen, like she was dancing.

THINK OF him in the dark.

There was a story that Joel hadn't dared tell anybody, not even Melody. That night, he lay in the narrow twin bed from his childhood, looking at the walls painted beige with navy trim, and allowed himself to remember the sound of Ian's voice, the look in his eyes, the smell of his skin, on Halloween.

Their Victorian was in a nice residential area, and everybody decorated for Halloween. Joel bought a bunch of spooky purple and orange face lights, and he strung them around the window facing the landing. He bought plastic pumpkins and a carving kit and made Ian leave his computer to carve the faces and put the flashlights in. He even bought eight pounds of chocolate in spite of the fact that only the really brave would trundle up a three-story walk-up in search of candy, and together they strung spider webs and one of those funky-scary motion-activated ghost things on the front porch.

It was hot that day. Sacramento sometimes gave fall a complete miss and went straight into winter sometime around November, so they opened their door for the ventilation, turned off their lights, and sat and watched Poltergeist *while they waited for their ghost to go off so they could give out candy.*

They got a surprising amount of traffic for being so high up, and one of their last groups of kids had a little girl of no more than three with dark hair, dark eyes, and a little witch costume with a pointy hat and a broom. When Joel gave her an extra big handful, she thanked him in rapid patter Spanish, and Joel returned with his own greeting.

He left the doorway and came and sat down on the far side of the couch, stretching his legs out as far as he could without kicking Ian. He was just about to press play on the remote when he realized Ian was looking at him in the dark.

"What?" he asked, puzzled.

"You speak Spanish." Ian's voice was as full of wonder as though he'd said, "You glow in the dark!"

Joel shrugged. "Yeah? Lots of people in California speak Spanish."

"But you're from Colorado."

Joel scrubbed his hand across his face and smoothed down his close-cropped goatee. "Yeah, they got- have- there are Mexicans in Colorado."

Ian tilted his head, like he was listening to faraway music. "You... you translate, don't you? You suppress your accent. Why do you do that?"

Joel shrugged and let his accent coat his voice when he spoke next. "I don't know, Ee. You get told, you know? They tell you not to sound Mexican or you not get no job. It's called 'code-switching', you just know, you talk Mexican at home and white at school."

"But you don't talk- speak 'Mexican' at home." Ian sounded hurt, and Joel couldn't figure out why.

Joel shrugged, wishing he'd pressed "play" so he could get lost in the movie instead. "Unless I'm talking to someone else who speaks Spanish, or I'm at home, I just... I'm just comfortable speaking like this, you know?"

"Oh." With that little word, Ian stood up and moved down the hall, and Joel wondered again what he'd done wrong.

"Ian, hey, Ee? What's the matter?" Joel caught up with him in the hallway in front of his room. Ian stopped, and Joel stopped short, arrested by the Ian's hurt, shiny eyes in the dark. "What?" he asked, kidding, "you not like me anymore 'cause I'm Mex?"

"That's not funny," Ian said softly.

"Then what, pappi?" The endearment came so naturally. He'd been fighting it for months, and now, in the forced intimacy of the dark, it sounded like what he'd wanted to call Ian since they'd met.

"I thought this was your home." Ian swallowed and then looked away. "Forget it. I'm being stupid. Let's go finish the movie. I've never seen it before."

Joel chuffed out a sigh, and they were standing close enough for Ian to close his eyes from the passage of their breath. He put what he thought was a companionable hand on Ian's shoulder and squeezed. "Tell you what, Ee. I won't fight it here, okay? I can't promise I'll suddenly sound like I do in my Mommy's kitchen, but I won't fight it. It might be sort of a mindfuck, you know. I could suddenly start swearing in Spanish and blow your mind."

Ian grinned then, and as always, the expression made Joel's stomach do a little drop-flutter. He sort of just... forgot... that he'd been touching Ian for longer than American male protocols strictly called for.

Ian leaned closer. "You're too good for me, mate," he said softly, and Joel's heart thumped in his ears. Ian was wearing a T-shirt tonight— surprise!—but it had been warm, and they'd worked quickly getting the house ready, and he smelled like clean sweat. Like Ian. Earthy, warm, real. Human and kind.

"You're a good man, Ian," Joel rasped. Ian's face was looming a little nearer, and he was close enough that their chests brushed, and

his skin buzzed in anticipation of more contact. Joel closed his eyes and breathed in that earthy, human smell, and he was disappointed when Ian's warmth suddenly disappeared.

He opened his eyes and Ian was laughing self-consciously; his smile was the goofy one that said he was laughing at himself because he knew he wasn't like everybody else.

"I'm sorry. I know, I know, I probably smell like monkey ass."

Joel gasped out a laugh and opened his mouth to say what? *To say "No, you're actually really turning me on?" To deny the monkey-ass thing and tell him they should go watch the movie?*

The fact was, Joel had no idea what he would have said, and right then their little motion-sensitive ghost thing went off, and the last group of kids for the night called out "Trick-or-treat!" from the landing.

Joel's hands roamed his own body. His chest buzzed from the remembered contact, his hand tingled from where the heat of Ian's shoulder had warmed it. His nipples were pointy and sensitive under his pinching fingers.

His cock was hard enough to joust with.

His eyes were closed, and in his mind's eye, he'd stopped Ian, he'd buried his nose in Ian's throat and breathed deep and licked the skin of his neck. In his mind he pushed Ian back against the wall and ground up against him, tangling his hands in that blond halo of curls and pulling Ian's puzzled, open face down to his in the dark and opening his mouth for their kiss.

In real life, he grasped his prick so hard the head was purple and the skin of his palm was skating on pre-come. His thumb came up to smear the thickness of the pre-come over the sensitive head and around the crown, and in his mind, Ian had whirled him around and against the wall and was grinding up against Joel too. In fact, he'd worked his hand down Joel's jeans and was fumbling for a good hold, a firm grasp, and a stroke so rough it was almost painful—

Joel gasped and spattered a thick jet of come up against the inside of his underwear and along his stomach and over his chest under the covers. His eyes opened in the dark of his old room, and what he'd been thinking and doing hit his arousal zones, and he shot again and again and again.

He stopped, gasping, suppressing a groan, panting in the narrow light, so in awe of what he'd imagined to happen that when his cell phone went off next to his bed, it was all he could do not to jump and scream.

Ian's voice on the other end of the phone was so welcome, it made him hard all over again.

"Ee?" Joel murmured, wondering if Ian could hear the sex in his voice. Oh God, what if he could? What if he didn't want it? A thought intruded on Joel's panic: maybe Ian had wanted Joel all along? When Ian started speaking though, he sounded so lost that all of Joel's designs on his roommate's body faded away.

"I had to leave her at the vet's, Joel," Ian said, obviously upset. "They said she was old, and they didn't know what they could do for her, and…" deep, shuddering breath, and the obvious suppression of a little boy sob, "… and we may have to put her down tomorrow. I- I just came home and sat, and there's no one here, you know?"

Oh God. "I know, Ian. Look, *pappi,* I tell you what. I'm getting my laptop right now. I'll find a flight out tomorrow, right?"

An audible sniff. "Joel, no, that's wrong. You're home with your family. I can't ask you to just ditch out on them for this idiotic albatross you put up with for cheap rent—"

"Shut up, Ian!" Joel snapped, anger washing over him even as he pulled out his laptop and booted up. "Shut up. I'm with my family, sure, but you're my home, Ee. You got to know that, right, *pappi?* You, that damned cat, no worries, right?"

Another sniff, this one sounding relieved. "You'll never get a flight out. It's some sort of holiday, you know?"

"Yeah, Ee," Joel replied dryly. "I know. You sit tight. I'll be out by tomorrow, I promise."

CHAPTER FOUR

MELODY LOOKED at Joel in bemusement. "Well, that was a damned fool promise to make, *estupido*! It's Thanksgiving. Have you not noticed all the damned planes is full? And it's snowing. It's not like they gonna get any less full, you know?"

Joel tried not to roll his eyes. He'd changed his clothes and showered, but the lapse of time hadn't done anything to make the ticket situation on the computer look any better.

"Look, Mel, I don't know what else to tell you. Ian has to put the damned cat down, and the cat was the only reason I thought I could leave him alone in the first place."

Melody put her hands on her hips. "Is this the roommate that's only your friend?"

"No, Mel," Joel snapped, a little desperate. "This is the roommate that I'm totally in love with and I'm afraid for, because all he has in the world is me and a soon-to-be-dead cat! And I'm too stupid to hold on to him, and did I mention the dying cat?"

His face felt taut and cold, and he tried to tell himself that he was overstating things, but he couldn't. If only…. Ian had needed to know that, if nothing else, Joel would always come home. Even if they weren't going to be lovers, even if they were *never* meant to be lovers, Joel had become home to Ian, he'd become time, he'd become Ian's anchor to reality, and he'd just- just left. Without a "I love you, man," without a "Look, you know I'm coming back," without even letting his guard down, even a little, and telling him face to face, "Take care of yourself for me, *pappi*. You what I'm coming home to, okay?"

Mel put her hand on Joel's shoulder and interrupted what he dimly realized was a full-out spin into panic.

"Easy, Joey," she murmured. "No worries, right? My ticket, it's for tomorrow night. I stop in Sacramento. I'll spend the day trying to get a flight from Sacto to L.A. right?"

"It shouldn't be too hard," Joel said out of a dry throat. "There's a lot of commuter flights in and out. You should be good."

"Yeah," Mel said, giving him a long hug and a laugh. "Wait 'til I tell the girls at work my brother is gay. I swear, my coolness will shoot up like a rocket!"

"Yeah," Joel muttered into his sister's shoulder, "you got cooler the minute I was born."

"I knew that, *pappi*. You know I did."

JOEL CALLED Ian in the morning and told him when his flight arrived. He called him from the airport and told him when it left and how long it would be in the air. He called when he landed, and Ian answered, "I know you're here, mate. I'm at the baggage carousel, waiting for your shit."

He sounded happy, Joel thought. He hoped it was true; he'd feel like a first-class asshole if he'd stolen his sister's ticket and left his mother's home early for a guy who wouldn't even notice he was there.

But any doubts he would have had faded away when he saw Ian, slouching near the back of the baggage carousel, looking towards Joel's gate.

Joel had the curious sensation of the chaos of the airport fading to a dull swish in his ears, and suddenly, the only person in the world was Ian. He was unaware that he was trotting at all possible speed, dodging luggage, children, and reuniting families, just so he could get there and see Ian smile.

It was blinding.

Their hug went on longer than was probably appropriate, but Joel didn't give a ripe shit, not when Ian was there, warm, needing, and grateful.

They released, but Ian kept his arms around Joel's back, and Joel didn't pull away. "You know," he said, looking somewhere else, "you didn't have to do that. You did tell your sister thank you for me?"

"Tell her yourself. She's sleeping on the couch for Christmas," Joel said with a soft smile.

Ian blinked, befuddled. "Why would she want to do that?" he asked. Together they saw Joel's bag and moved toward it, Ian's arm still looped around Joel's shoulders. Joel refused to comment about the arm. Ian's casual touch was sustaining him, anchoring him to the world, making all those revelations he'd had about Ian when he was alone in his child's bed seem real and solid and true.

"I'll tell you later," Joel said, hoping that by then, Ian would still want it to be true. Ian snagged his bag—those amazing muscles managing the entire case without benefit of wheels—and together they headed outside and across the street to Ian's little Prius.

When they'd loaded up, Ian hesitated for a minute before turning the keys in the ignition.

"How's Manky Bastard?" Joel asked quietly into the silence. It was the one thing Ian hadn't talked about, and the one thing Joel was pretty sure he knew the answer to.

"In a vase on the mantel," Ian replied, his voice catching.

Joel put a hand on his shoulder and squeezed. "I'm sorry, *pappi*. I'm sorry she had to die. I'm really sorry it had to be when I was gone."

Ian nodded, looking determinedly to outside his window. "It wasn't your fault," he said softly. "I just... I just hope, you know... you don't... you won't think...." Ian looked at him, helplessly, waving his hands and sniffling, wiping his face on the back of his hands and looking embarrassed about that.

"Ian—"

"I took care of her, Joel. I can take care of another one, honest! I can take care of myself, I swear. I just don't want you to...." He trailed off, and Joel unbuckled his seatbelt and turned, grabbing Ian's shoulders and shaking him a little.

"Ian... *pappi,* you need to calm down. I know you can take care of yourself. I know you took care of her. Why is this so important? You're not—" Oh Christ! This thought didn't even bear thinking about but he had to say it anyway. "You're not thinking, you know, that you don't need a roommate no more, are you?"

Ian shook his head. "No, no, mate. I'm just worried...." Ian's face crumpled like a little kid's and suddenly he was sobbing in Joel's arms. "I just thought the only reason you stayed was because of the *caaaaaaaaattt*...."

In spite of himself, Joel found he was laughing quietly into Ian's hair. "No, Ian. No. I'm not leaving, I promise, *pappi.* You can't shake me that easy. Shhh. Shhhh."

Ian pulled himself together eventually, but not before Joel got a wonderful muscular armload of despondent Aussie genius.

"I'm sorry," Ian sniffled, wiping his face on his shoulder and pulling on his belt again. "You're going to think I'm some sort of hormonal poofty queen. I'm not like this. I- I think the only times I've ever cried in my life are around you."

"Lucky me," Joel said softly, meaning it. "Look, Ee, let's get home, eh? I'm tired, I been stuck in that tin-can most half of the day, and I probably smell like monkey ass. I want to sit on the couch witchu, talk some." He wanted to lean on him, stroke his chest, kiss his blond, stubbled cheek, feel his heart under a circling palm. "You know," Joel finished weakly, "reconnect, right, *pappi?*"

"Joel?" Ian said, after he'd started the car and maneuvered to the freeway on ramp.

"Yeah, Ee?"

"You know you're wearin' your accent on your sleeve, right, mate?"

"That's 'cause I'm home witchu, *pappi.* Don't ever doubt it."

The twenty-minute ride home was pretty quiet after that, the rain that had threatened the skies as Joel landed staving off until they arrived. Eventually Joel was bathed, wearing a pair of sweats and an old T-shirt, and sitting on the couch with a new afghan his mom had sent home with him. Ian grabbed him a soda from the fridge (Joel had taken pains to not keep any beer in there) and sat down on the opposite end of the couch. Together they looked at the little black vase over the mantle on the purple colored wall, and Joel nudged Ian with his bare toe.

"Can I say I'm sorry again?"

"No," Ian replied with a self-deprecating smile. "I might cry again, and that would suck for us both, now wouldn't it?"

"Can I tell you I'm really glad to be home?" Joel poked Ian's thigh again and was rewarded when Ee slid his long-fingered hand up Joel's calf.

"I'm glad you're back." Ian's gaze—that spring-blue, wild-sky gaze—was suddenly very sharp and very focused on Joel, sitting back in his worn T-shirt and his gray sweats. Outside, the rainstorm that had threatened since Joel got off the plane suddenly spattered the windows, and Ian looked away from Joel's searching eyes and turned that way.

"It threatens to get nasty out there," he said inanely.

"No worries, *pappi.* All we need to do in the next two days is go get milk tomorrow. I got all of Thanksgiving in the cupboards. I even bought some new placemats and napkins and shit."

Ian's next look was simple and direct, pure and full of gratitude. "It sounds nice, but you know. Why? I- I'm dying to have Thanksgiving with you. And Christmas, too, if you must know the truth, but why? You take such good care of me, and I can't even keep...." He looked up at the mantel, and they both knew how he'd finish that sentence.

If Joel had expected Ian to simply pick up on all his unspoken cues, he'd been living with the wrong man for the last five months. With a sigh, he swung his legs over, sat up, and then moved in closer to Ian than they usually sat. "I like taking care of you, Ee," he said into the rain-spattered quiet. "I like knowing you're going to be happy. I like knowing I'm, you know, your anchor to the world."

"I'm a colossal asshole, brother. I've got all this high-level shit in my head, and nothing real," Ian said, rolling his eyes at himself, but Joel wouldn't listen to that.

"No, no, Ee. You're amazing. You're smart, and you're funny. You've got a heart as big as the sky, you know that? You don't need a roommate. You just took me in 'cause I liked the apartment—"

"I took you in because I wanted to get in your pants," Ian supplied crossly, and Joel's grin made Ian blink.

"Yeah? You never made a move!"

Ian shrugged. "You don't swing that way. And besides..." Ian looked at his bedroom, with its king-sized bed and it's jumbo cluttered computer desk, and then he looked back, meeting Joel's eyes with a resigned expression. "Everybody I slept with ran away in the morning. I- I'd do almost anything to keep you from running away."

Oh God. Joel leaned close and rubbed his thumb on Ian's lean bottom lip. "Brother, I've got news for you," he said quietly, hoping he could treasure the awestruck, worshipful expression on Ian's face forever.

"Yeah?" Ian leaned closer, and Joel could smell him underneath shampoo and deodorant and... was that cologne? It didn't matter. He still smelled earthy and human and real.

"I do swing that way. And I just invited my sister to stay with us for Christmas so she could meet you and make sure you were worth her plane ticket. I have no intention of running away from you, Ee."

"Why would she want to meet me?" Ian asked, and he was close enough to bump noses with, so Joel did, rubbing the smooth part of his cheek along Ian's stubbled one, feeling the silk of Ian's breath on his face.

"Because I love you, and she wants to welcome you to the family." It was bold. It was probably insane. But it was the truth, and if Ian kicked him out for it now, Joel would know it was never meant to be.

Ian kissed him.

Their lips met, met again, and Joel opened his mouth, letting Ian inside. He tasted like Dr Pepper and… and just like Ian. All of that joy, all of the kindness, all of the earthy humanity, all there on Joel's tongue for the tasting.

Joel groaned and pulled Ian closer, tangling his fingers in that halo of blond hair just like he'd imagined doing, pulling Ian on top of him, loving his friend's weight, pinning him to the couch.

Ian moved his kisses to Joel's neck, and Joel's head fell back as he made an "ahh ahh" sound, and then that mouth, eager, questing, fascinated by the texture of Joel's skin, continued on. With some shifting Joel found he was bare-chested, and Ian's big hands were spanning his chest, rubbing his nipples, stroking the tender flesh of his abdomen.

Ian paused for a minute then and peered into Joel's face owlishly. "Mate, uhm, just how long have you swung this way?"

Joel's smile was a little embarrassed. "Probably forever," he muttered, thinking about his sister's astute assessment of his love life. "But I've only really known since I jerked off in my old bed, dreaming of you," he finished. Ian grinned and then looked thoughtful. "Why?"

"Because now I know what you've done and what you haven't, and what I'm going to do next."

"Ian, you don't even know how you're going to get to work."

Ian shook his head. "This is different, mate. I've been dreaming of this for months. I'll be damned if I bollix it up now."

And then, as though he couldn't help himself, he lowered his head to Joel's chest and opened his mouth over a tanned nipple and suckled, and Joel arched against him, hard and needy.

"Oh God, Ian, Ian?" Because Ian kept kissing down to Joel's tender stomach. He kept kissing while Joel arched his hips to give better access to pull down the gray sweats, and then he kissed down the trail of black fur from Joel's navel to his— "Oh God… *Ian!*"

Ian was a lot of things, but subtle wasn't one of them. With an open mouth, he engulfed Joel's cock and pushed his lips all the way down until they touched the dark, curly hair at the root, and he stayed there for a moment, swallowing to make it fit.

Joel's fingers stayed tangled in that surprisingly soft hair, and he moaned in the back of his throat and tried not to squeeze his eyes shut in pleasure. Ian pulled back up his shaft, sucking as he went and swirling his tongue around the broad, purpling head. Joel thought his eyeballs were going to pop out of his skull, and then he thought he was going to scream, and maybe die, and love every minute of it.

"Mmmmm... *God... oh fuck oh fuck oh fuck...*" and then he didn't have anything to say at all, because he was coming, spurting into the back of Ian's mouth, and Ian was still swallowing, letting just enough hot spend dribble out of his mouth to make Joel's prick sloppy and slick and sexy.

Joel's head flopped limply on the back of the couch, and Ian pulled himself up and peered down with as smug expression as Joel had ever seen.

"You're looking pretty damned proud of yourself, you know that?" Joel chuckled, stroking the hair back from Ian's temple.

"It's a limited skill set for a bloke," Ian said with dignity, and Joel laughed.

"Well, you're a master of it, *pappi*. If I didn't love you already, I'd stay with you for the blow jobs alone."

Ian's eyes grew anxious, and Joel cupped his face, glad that he could. Ian looked anxious far too often. Joel's new job was going to be to erase that pinched look from his eyes as often as possible.

"You do love me? Really?"

Joel lifted up and kissed him, tasting his own spend and not caring. "Yeah, Ee. I do."

"I think you could be the only person ever to love me. And I love you back." Ian kissed him again, deeper, stronger, and Joel lost himself in the kiss, in the knowledge that Ian needed him—not to keep his house or buy his food or set his schedule, but just to love him. Maybe it was all Ian had ever wanted.

It had been a long day, and they went to bed shortly after that. Joel lay in Ian's arms and kissed him again, and again, and harder, until Ian pulled back and said, "No. We're not doing that tonight."

"We're not?" Joel asked, a little amused and a lot tired.

"It needs to be good. I want to be awake, and I need to know you'll be here in the morning."

Joel might have been hurt at that, but then, so many people had failed Ian. Joel understood the impulse to make sure this was real before they took it all the way. He settled down in Ian's bed, feeling strong arms wrapped around his shoulders and listening to a man's breathing in the dark and smiled a little to himself.

It was real. And it would be there in the morning.

Chapter Five

Joel knew exactly where he was when he woke up in the morning. He knew Ian's smell, he knew the feel of the arms around his shoulders, and he had a good guess as to what that thing was poking him in the ass-cheek.

He shivered and swallowed a little, and then he scuttled quickly out of bed.

"Where you going?" Ian asked sleepily.

"Gotta brush my teeth, Ee," he muttered. "My breath smells like—"

"Monkey ass?" Ian supplied, pushing up on one arm, and Joel turned around and went in for quick peck on the lips before pulling back.

"That monkey, he gets around," Joel quipped against Ian's mouth. "I'll be back in a sec," and then he trotted off.

When he got back, Ian was scrambling back into bed, a little bit of toothpaste on the corner of his mouth, and Joel grinned.

"Ian, do you think people who've been married for a couple of years kiss with morning breath?"

Ian blinked. "I dunno. Maybe we'll find out, you think?"

Joel moved in closer, so all he could see were those spring blue eyes. "Yeah, that'd be nice." But then Ian kissed him, and Joel was suddenly in Ian-land: there was no future, there was only the now.

Ian took charge again. Joel had two brain cells, maybe, to be amused that Ian could be in charge in the bedroom when he couldn't organize his own sock drawer—and then his sweats were down around his ankles again, and Ian's mouth was on his cock.

"Ahhh... *Christo, pappi,* you good at that!" Joel groaned, and Ian grinned at him from his position at Joel's groin. Then, very deliberately so Joel could see him, he stuck a finger in his mouth and pulled it out, slick with spit. He took that finger and traced it down the underside of Joel's erection, down, between his darkly furred balls, to the ticklish space underneath. Joel knew where he was heading, and he gasped as Ian stroked his taint and gasped again when that finger teased his entrance, circled... tested... invaded....

Then Ian's mouth was on him again, and Joel came so hard his vision blacked behind his eyes.

Ian chuckled around him, the vibrations getting him to being hard again, and then he swallowed and pulled back. "You keep coming like that, I'm not ever going to get to fuck you proper."

Joel blushed and found he was stammering. "I... honestly, Ee... I don't think it'll fit."

Ian laughed again, his mouth open, his slightly crooked teeth flashing in a clean smile, and then he moved sinuously against the bed. Joel realized that his new lover had gotten him off twice and not gotten off himself at all.

"You want to see it?" Ian asked ingenuously. "You get to know it for a bit, maybe it won't be such a bugaboo, you think?"

Joel's mouth went dry, and his cock, which was still wet and semi-hard in Ian's hand, got a little harder. "I think," he rasped.

Ian reached down one hand and wriggled right out of his briefs, and then he swung his hips up over the bed and crooked one leg up over Joel's head. Joel found himself face-to-face with the most tender part of Ian's body.

He swallowed. It was amazing. Tentatively he ran his palm from the curly blond hair at the base to the flared head the tip, and then he wrapped his hand more firmly around it and pumped.

Ian gasped, his breath tickling Joel's own erection and making it just that much harder. "You can be a little rougher there, brother," Ian breathed. "That thing won't bite!"

Joel laughed and stuck out his tongue to taste Ian's pre-come. "Yeah, Ee, but it sure does drool!"

Ian sucked in a hard breath, and Joel tried his tongue again and licked that broad head firmly, and then under the crown, and then, fascinated by the way Ian's body jumped and throbbed in his palm, he opened his mouth and engulfed the thing, stroking his hand down to the base and pushing his mouth to his hand. Ian groaned and pulled Joel into *his* mouth, and Joel sucked harder because, well, because, oh God, it just felt so good!

He focused for a minute, not wanting to come again, not before Ian, and began to pay attention to details. Like the way Ian grunted when Joel touched his blond, furry testicles. He took his other hand and massaged them. He heard Ian's gasp when his lips brushed the sensitive little harp string on the underside of the purpling head, so Joel tried, very gingerly, to brush that with his teeth.

Ian pulled back then and started to beg. "Not yet, mate, want to be inside you."

Joel made a negative sound in his throat. He didn't want to give this up. He loved the taste and the power and the noises Ian made when Joel pleased him.

There Ian's fingers joined Joel's cock inside Ian's mouth, getting them slick at the same time they slid around the sensitive head. Those wet, slick fingers slid down, to Joel's backside, and then—

"*Gaaaahhh*! Ian!"

Ian's reply was garbled, and then those fingers moved again and stretched, and Joel found his mouth was slack and open and Ian's cock was bobbing lightly on his cheek as he tried not to blow his wad with his mind.

Ian took advantage of Joel's complete submission, and in a moment Joel found he was on all fours and Ian, the bastard, was using his strength and his height to haul his ass in the air, and then, oh God, was that his tongue?

Joel whimpered into the sheets and concentrated on his breathing because it felt *soooo* good. "Jesus, Ian… it… wait… condoms…."

Ian was suddenly over his back, nibbling his neck and his ear, and Joel turned his head to meet his kiss, which was musky and spicy and not like monkey ass at all. Ian pulled away and murmured, "I got tested again this week. I'm clean. You?"

Joel had gotten tested after his last girlfriend, who had been a skank ho, and he might tell Ian that story later, but right now, "I'm clean," he gasped.

Ian reached over his shoulder now and fumbled at the nightstand and came up with a little bottle. There was a click and then— "S'cold!" Joel shivered, and then Ian was using his two thumbs to stretch and pull and stretch some more, and Joel was dimly aware that he was gibbering into the sheets again.

"*God, please, Jesus, Ian, fuck me!*"

One of Ian's arms came around Joel's chest to pull him up, and Ian's other hand disappeared. Joel was stretched again, and he whimpered in pleasure, and then Ian slid home, and Joel swore again. "*Fuck me, Ian, oh God, please!*"

"If… I… must…." And then his hips started pumping, and Joel lost all words, all coherent thought. Ian's hand came around to his cock, and he damned near lost consciousness. He came, spattering up his stomach and on the sheets, and then Ian grabbed his hips and both hands and thrust and thrust and thrust.

"Gaaaaaaaawwwwd," Ian swore, and his hips jerked against Joel's even as Joel fell forward.

They stayed there for a moment, face down, Ian's body still spasming. Joel thought he could probably stay there and feel Ian's pleasure forever.

"Ian?" he murmured, and Ian grunted, "Am I crushing you?"

"I'm good, Ee. "

"You're awesome, mate."

Joel laughed, but not hard because he really couldn't breathe that deep, and Ian put a long-fingered hand over Joel's shorter, blunter one as it clenched the sheets.

"I really love you, you know?" Joel gasped, because, dammit, the guy was *heavy*.

Ian kissed the back of his neck, and his ear, and he shifted so he could kiss down Joel's jawline. The shift pulled him out, and Joel closed his eyes and savored the feel of Ian's spend trickling down the inside of his thigh.

"I love you too."

Joel closed his eyes. "Good, *pappi*. That's good."

"SO YOU got tested this week?" Joel asked later, when they were both dressed and in the kitchen. Joel had put Ian to work spreading the piecrusts in the tins, and he was fixing the pumpkin pie filling over the stove. He was planning on pecan, too, having gotten the recipe from his mom before he left, but he was a little nervous about that one because he'd never made it before.

"Yeah," Ian muttered, and Joel gave him a glance and then laughed as Ian blushed.

"What?" Joel gave the filling a final stir and then moved up to wrap his arms around Ian's waist and rub his cheek on his back. "No, you can't get all embarrassed and not tell me!"

"I hoped," Ian mumbled, paying scrupulous attention to ready-made piecrust. "I wasn't sure, but, you were so close. I just hoped that maybe someday, and even if it didn't happen you...."

"What?" Joel asked softly. He had to move in a minute to stir the pie filling again, and they had lots of work to do if they were going to have dinner ready the next day, but this was worth hearing.

Ian stopped and looked Joel in the eyes, smiling a little at their closeness. "You cared for me, Joel. Even if we were never lovers, you cared for me. It made it seem worthwhile, you know? To care for myself." Ian grinned. "Now go stir that. You're dying to, I can tell!"

"Oh, fine," Joel murmured. "If I must."

CHAPTER SIX

THANKSGIVING WAS a success.

They ate too much, and had leftovers for a week, but that was fine, because Ian had never had the full Thanksgiving works before, and he had become extremely fond of stuffing and gravy.

They made love a lot—but not every night. Some nights they just brushed their teeth and went to bed together. Joel started to wonder, in a very real way, if he'd ever be able to go to sleep again without knowing Ian was next to him, breathing in the dark.

They still talked over dinner and worked out on Monday/Wednesday/Fridays and watched every science fiction show on television. *Supernatural* was still their favorite, only now when they watched it, Ian confessed to a long-time crush on the shorter actor who played "Dean." Joel wished he could have claimed a crush on the taller guy who played "Sam," but really, "I've only got eyes for you right now, Ee. We can crush on other guys later."

Ian flushed then, and Joel enjoyed watching that *very* much.

Joel told the story of his last girlfriend, Rachel, the "skank ho" who had slept with most of his dorm before breaking up with him.

"Everyone else had to get shots for chlamydia," Joel muttered, shaking his head. "Brother, I was never so grateful for Sister Margaret in my life!"

Ian heard the story with wide eyes and the sudden shock of someone who realizes he'd had a near miss. "I never thought of that," he confessed. "I- I guess I just wanted… a person there."

"Someone to love," Joel supplied, rubbing Ian's calf as it rested on his lap. They were "handsy" lovers—the kind of people who didn't do a lot of public kissing, but once they were alone, in their sanctuary, were always touching. Joel liked it like that; Ian close was good. Ian closer was wonderful.

And really, that was the wonder of becoming lovers. The good things didn't change, they only got better. And the best things, like choosing a Christmas tree and buying decorations, well, those became amazing. Fun. Intense. Anything Joel could do to make Ian's days different from each other, to make reality as compelling as the rabbit hole in Ian's brain that he still disappeared down, well, that was Joel's favorite thing.

Unfortunately, Joel didn't realize that this meant the bad stuff got worse until he walked smack-dab into their first major fight.

Joel was early. At Ian's request, he'd given up riding when it got dark early, and for once, driving actually got him home before his bike would have. As he opened the door, he heard voices coming from Ian's bedroom, and then the door opened, and Ian appeared—sans shirt—talking to the person inside.

Logically, Joel knew it was a client. Logically, Joel knew this was Ian being Ian, completely unaware of his surroundings, including the weather, which was cold enough to make his chest goose-pimple and his nipples pebble, even inside. Logically, Joel knew it was no big deal.

Emotionally, the glare he cast Ian's way was enough to make his "roommate" trip over his own toes and fall down, right there in the hallway as his client came up behind him.

The distinguished, middle-aged woman was sleekly dressed in a pantsuit with pearls, and she smoothed some of her silver-tinted hair back from her face and smiled at the man sprawled at her feet.

"Ian, good Lord! I always knew you were eccentric. I had no idea you were clumsy!"

Ian started to pick himself up and cast Joel a wounded look. "Sorry, Professor Kohl. My roommate sort of took me by surprise."

"Oh!" The professor's eyes lit up, and she extended a hand towards Joel. "Mr. Martinez, I'm so glad to meet you in person! We sure have appreciated your efforts in the department, that's for certain."

Joel smiled and hoped it looked sincere. "Anything I can do to help Ian, Professor," he said through a dry throat, and he winced as Ian threw him a glare that said plainly the he didn't need any help if Joel was going to look at him like he just did.

The professor looked from one man to another and took in the undercurrents. "I'm sorry, Mr. Martinez," she said with a sophisticated smile, "you do realize we were just going over accounts."

Joel inclined his head. "Absolutely. I knew that."

"Well, next time I'll be sure to remind Professor Cooper to put on a shirt before I come in. Now that I know he has a…" her eyes lit up ironically, "… 'roommate', I think that's more appropriate."

Joel didn't even try to disguise his relief. "Thanks, Professor. That would be great."

The woman excused herself then, even as Ian finally scrambled off the floor and stood to open the door for her, and the two of them were left in the silent, suddenly cold apartment.

Joel sighed and flopped down on the couch, gazing sightlessly at the Christmas tree. They'd gone to a craft fair, and damned near every ornament was handmade—carved tin, quilted, sculpted, crocheted—you name a craft, and it was on the tree, but Joel might as well have been staring at a blank wall.

"Jesus, Ian, you couldn't remember to put a shirt on in December?"

Ian scowled at him. It was an unaccustomed expression for Ian, and it looked more hurt than anything else. Joel tried to not feel like shit. He failed.

"Look, Ee, I'm sorry. I know better, I do, but- but that's your room, and she was in it, and you weren't even dressed!"

"She's twice my age!" Ian pouted.

"I *know* that, Ee! She could have been anyone. I didn't know who you had back there! Can't you, I mean, I can't do this! I can't just walk in and not know what I'm going to see in your room!"

"It's *our* room!" Ian shot back. "You haven't slept in your own bed in a month!"

"Okay, *our* room. *Our* bed. But, can't you see that you being in there with someone when you're not even dressed is *bad?* "

"Don't you trust me? You're going to just throw this in and break up with me and leave me because you don't trust me and I didn't even do anything—"

"Wait a minute—"

Ian stood up and shouted, his face twisted by anxiety and unhappiness beyond anything the situation warranted. "You *promised,* dammit. You *promised* you wouldn't leave!"

Joel stood up and shouted back. "I'm not leaving, asshole! I just want some sort of promise from you that you're not going to change your mind in the middle of this and go back to being roommates!"

"Well, it's not like I can go out and buy you a ring—not in this manky-assed state!" Ian said, sounding completely baffled. "What am I supposed to do? What do you want?"

"Just a promise, that's all. We've said all sorts of 'I love you's, but not once have we said 'only you'—all I want is a promise!"

Ian's entire demeanor changed, a light going on in his face that was brighter than the thin December sun. "Oh," he said equably. "I'll be right back!" And to Joel's surprise he took off for the front door.

"Ian! Your keys, maybe? Shoes? A jacket? A *shirt*?"

Ian's unbreakable grin answered him. "Oh yeah, mate. Right. If I must!"

Ian was gone in less than thirty seconds, looking very odd and very, well, *gay* in one of Joel's T-shirts that left his navel bare, cargo shorts, and a pair of leather loafers without socks. Socks, thought Joel in complete exasperation, would have interfered with whatever stroke of genius that had sent him bolting out of the apartment.

Joel looked around the empty apartment and closed his eyes. What had possessed him? Here he was, sleeping with a man for less than a month, and he'd just thrown his first overblown hormonal bitch queen tantrum.

Well, shit.

He scowled and looked over at Ian's room, like the location itself had caused all the commotion. *It's our bedroom, dammit!* Ian's words rang in his ears, and suddenly he got an idea of his own.

When Ian returned, nearly two hours later, Joel was covered in dust. He had two cuts on his hand from disassembling Ian's computer desk and a swollen thumb from putting it back together. He also had a bruise on his hip from running into his bureau when it was in the hallway, and another on his shin from tripping over one of the drawers on the floor of Ian's bedroom after he'd decided the damned chest couldn't be moved by just one person when it was full.

But he was done. In fact he was sweeping up the dust buffalo and spare pen caps that had littered the floor under the desk even as Ian walked in.

"What are you doing?" Ian asked, and Joel looked up and grinned.

"I'm fixing our bedroom... wait. What is that?"

Ian looked down at the little fawn-colored fuzz-bundle in his arms, and the thing looked back at him and mewed.

"It's our new cat." Ian licked his lips nervously and ducked his head and then powered through. "He's a boy, but they chopped off his balls, because at the vets I guess that's what they do. He's had all his shots, and he's a baby. So he'll be around awhile. So, you know. You need to stay, at least as long as he does." There was a hopeful look from those wild-sky eyes. "He's my promise, right? I even had a tag made for him."

Joel closed his eyes, opened them, felt them burn a little and squeezed them tight again. Carefully he set down his broom and walked over to the fuzz-bundle and stroked it between the eyes.

Unlike Manky Bastard, who had never really warmed to him, this one started to purr.

"He's awesome, Ee," Joel said softly, wondering what he was going to get Ian for Christmas now. Didn't matter. This meant the world to Ian. Joel wouldn't take it from him for the world. "I think he even likes me."

"He's your color too!" Ian said out of the blue, stroking the light-brown fur.

Joel choked on a rather weepy laugh. "Are you telling me you went out and got a Mexican cat, *pappi?*"

"I don't think so," Ian said with a rather shy smirk. "He doesn't meow with an accent."

Joel laughed and wondered when he'd become such a cat person, and Ian reached around the little neck and pulled out a tag. "See, it's got our names on it."

Joel read the tag and smiled, and his eyes burned some more. "*Joel and Ian's Manky Bitch. If lost call…*"

He raised up on tiptoe, leaned over the kitten, and kissed Ian's cheek. "It even has my cell phone on it."

"Yeah, in case I lose the handsets again." It had happened the week after Thanksgiving in an experiment involving radio vectors and Lobachevskian geometry that Joel never did understand.

"I actually found them," Joel said with a smile. "They were under your desk. Here, want to see what I've done?"

Ian blinked and stepped gingerly over the pile of dust on the floor. "You're moving out?" he said with enough uncertainty to make Joel thwack him on the back of the head.

"No, genius, I'm moving in. See, there's your computer desk in the guest bedroom. And that's my drawers, in our room."

"But that's your bed!"

"Not after I get a new comforter, and that way Mel don't have to stay on the couch, because that girl can *sleep!*" Joel was nervous. His accent, which he let slip more and more these days when he was at home, had suddenly gotten even thicker. "Anyway, here's your desk, in here. Even if you don't remember a shirt, it's like an office now. No sex happens in here, I don't pitch a big queenie fit if you forget shit, you know?"

"You didn't pitch a fit," Ian said softly. "You got mad. I'm the one who pitched a fit. I'm sorry about that."

Joel shrugged. "I wouldn't have gotten that mad if I wasn't sort of committed here, you know?"

Ian put the kitten down to go chase dust buffalo and wrapped his arms around Joel's shoulders. "I know, Joel. You've got to believe that I know."

"So, now we've got a cat and an office and a bedroom that's ours together. Can you relax about me leaving? I'm not planning on going nowhere, *pappi*. I like it here. And I really love you. So, you know, can you just believe in me?"

"Yeah," Ian sighed, resting his chin on the top of Joel's head. "If I must, mate, if I must."

It was the best promise Joel could ask for, the only one he wanted to hear.

Christmas
with Danny Fit

Amy Lane

FANTASY AND FICTION

KIT ALLEN moved out of his mother's house one week after he started his new workout regimen, two months after he got his new personal assistant at work, and six weeks before Christmas. He was thirty years old, and these events had more in common than first meets the eye—all except the Christmas.

Jesse, his new assistant, was a beautiful man, with hair the color of dark honey and sloe brown eyes. He keyboarded like the wind, understood the internet like a prodigy, ran interference when Kit was getting work done, and prodded him to get up out of his seat and move around when he'd done too much work and had to force himself to remember to breathe. He was constantly trying to anticipate Kit's needs, and since Kit didn't seem to need much, he was constantly trying to bring Kit things—coffee, water, a funny YouTube.com video he'd never seen—that Kit hadn't known he needed but apparently couldn't live without.

Something about Jesse made Kit supremely aware of the fact that he was forty pounds heavy and had never gotten laid.

It wasn't that Jesse *tried* to make Kit feel uncomfortable. In fact, just the opposite. Jesse went out of his way to be friendly, and since Kit had always been a shy, awkward sort of boy and then a reserved, awkward sort of man, overtures of friendship were foreign to him.

"Would you like me to get you coffee, Mr. Allen?"

"Uhm...." And suddenly another cup of coffee sounded both wonderful and frightening.

"How about some water? Water's good for you, you know."

"Uhm...." It was the first time in his life he'd ever felt that something good for him would actually seem good for him.

Jesse would offer to eat lunch with him when he worked at his desk, and Kit would freeze, absolutely stunned. Should he make conversation? Should he work on the tables and figures he'd stayed in his office to finish in the first place? Holy crap! How was he supposed to behave when Jesse sat and chatted to him about television and movies and....

Wait a minute.

"Yeah," Kit said in bemusement, "I thought David Tennant was the best Doctor Who. *How could you not? But I think Matt Smith has a lot of potential—he's got this wise thing about him that makes him seem a little older, you know?"*

Jesse's face lit up, and he looked a little surprised as well. "Absolutely—and I think Amelia Pond is adorable. Donna Tate seemed like a lot of fun too—probably less likely to try to get into my pants, which would be more comfortable. So tell me, do you like Torchwood *too?"*

As it turned out, both of them shared a deep and abiding love of science fiction television, starting with *Doctor Who* and moving on to *Torchwood, Being Human, Firefly, Dollhouse, Stargate (SG-1, Atlantis,* and *Universe!), Battlestar Galactica, Babylon 5, Warehouse 13, Eureka,* and even that most holy of holies, *Star Trek,* all five incarnations, including the only spin-off not to make it seven seasons, *Enterprise.*

After that first week, lunch became less and less about doing work at his desk and more and more about talking about sci-fi with Jesse.

It was at the end of the second month that Kit saw Jesse with some of the other men from his building, playing basketball in the yard across the street from their accounting firm in the slanting November sun. He'd waved, and Jesse had waved back, but after a couple of months of working together—and eating lunch and yearning, at least on Kit's part—Kit was not quite sure if he was comfortable enough to go up and say anything.

"Hey, boss-man! Come join us!" Jesse called, his breath steaming in the sharp November air. Kit looked up, feeling helpless again. Jesse was wearing an old sleeveless T-shirt, and sweats, and tennis shoes with socks that did *not* go up to his knees, and he was casual and sweating, and the razor-gold sun glistened off his shoulders, and the muscles in his biceps looked firm and hard and defined and, well....

Kit was Kit. Short for Christopher. Had played the tuba in the band, but had nearly hyperventilated from carrying all that weight during the parade.

"Maybe next week!" he called desperately. "Got dinner plans!"

Well, sort of. His mother expected him home for dinner, but he didn't feel any compulsion, really, to make it there on time. He'd been dodging his mother's dinner table since high school—she tended to cook with cheese, butter, and bacon, and Kit was fully aware that some of what he carried around on his ass came from that table and nowhere else. But he thought that maybe, with a week of preparation, he could find a way to play basketball and not feel like a marshmallow in a tracksuit.

So he went to Borders and bought some workout videos and went home and introduced himself to Danny Fit.

Danny Fit was beautiful.

He spent that first evening in his room getting to know Danny as the fitness guru on the DVD took Kit through strength training, cardio, and finally (thank God!) ten minutes of yoga and cool-down.

Danny was tall, early fortyish, with toffee-brown hair and pebble-dark eyes and a blinding white smile in lean tanned cheeks. Danny had a long, lithe, perfectly trained body where every muscle popped out like an anatomy poster, except covered with golden smooth skin.

By the time Kit was done with the yoga video, he had such an aching erection that he brought himself off in his pants as he writhed on the yoga mat.

He hadn't masturbated since he was fifteen, when he realized he was jerking off to the jocks in his gym class instead of the pretty girls in French, and that his mother *must* be right—playing with himself was sick and wrong, and he shouldn't do it.

But since then, Kit had been to college. He knew what gay was, and he knew he was it, and he knew that he'd never settle down with a nice girl like his mother kept telling him to do before he moved out. His mother was older and ill and cranky. Nobody liked her. She had no friends. If he left her, she'd have no one. Kit had been unwilling to have the "gay" discussion with her, so he had simply sat on his sexuality, squashing it down with creampuffs in the morning and potatoes at night. He'd sat on it, and it had lain there, flat and uninteresting and pretty much playing dead.

And then Jesse had looked at him with sloe eyes and said, "You know, David Tennant doesn't look like a llama at all."

And then Danny Fit had worn loose pants during a warm-up, and Kit had seen his junk flopping heavily under his shorts.

And now Kit's cock—which had mostly been used for taking a leak before that moment—woke up and screamed *I WANT! FEED ME ASSHOLE!* And Kit had given it a good handshake until it threw up.

As Kit lay facedown in a puddle of his own come, his vision fastened hungrily on the lean, fit man making Downward Dog look like a porn video, he realized two things.

One was that his body felt like it had been hit by a tractor. He was *really* out of shape.

The other was that he needed a sex life, even if it was an imaginary sex life with a guy who was probably straight. (At that point, he wasn't sure if he was imagining Danny or Jesse—but he didn't think it mattered.)

Then his mother started banging on the door. "Christopher! Christopher! I'm going to bed now! I need you to turn the television down! For chrissakes it's almost nine o'clock! What the hell are you listening to? I won't put up with no fornication videos, you know that, Christopher!"

Kit rolled over to his back and pushed himself heavily off the yoga mat, wiping his hand on the inside of his shorts. "Ma?"

"What?" The smell of tobacco wafted through the door. Oh yay— another Virginia Slims bit the dust.

"I'm moving out next week."

"I'll believe that when I see it! Don't be stupid, Christopher. You don't have anyone to take care of you! What the hell are you going to do in your own place?"

Kit thought about it and pushed up his meaty body. "Go on a diet and get a cat. Now go away, Ma. I've got to take a shower."

The next day was Saturday. By the end of the day he had a nice little house lined up, not too far from the accounting firm he worked at in downtown Sac. It was brick, in the thirty blocks (so, pretty damned nice, since he'd saved up a lovely fat down payment while living with his mother), had hardwood floors in the living room and two bedrooms, and green tile in the kitchen and bathroom. It had a small front yard and a backyard big enough for some hydrangeas and a cat. It had a one-car garage, central heat and air, and decorative wrought iron around the windows.

Kit figured he could be an aging gay man in there with considerably more personal space and comfort than he had in his mother's home.

And the only thing that smelled like cigarette smoke was him.

On Sunday, after surprising the hell out of a real estate broker— and thanking the gods that the previous owners had already moved and were waiting for a quick sale—he went shopping for some furniture. He bought nothing with flowers, nothing with a lever that reclined, and nothing in pastels. It was all deep colors—a dark-brown couch, a dark-burgundy loveseat, and a dark-navy stuffed chair, in corduroy, even though he was pretty sure a cat would shed all over it.

He didn't care. His furniture. His cat.

He tied it all together with a black throw rug with all the dark colors tumbling about the dark surface like blocks. He was pleased with the results. He was particularly pleased that it looked like a man's furniture. His mother's constant bitching about "those girlie faggot boys, taking over the whole goddamned world" didn't seem to have rung true for him.

He got the furniture on sale, because it was three weeks before Thanksgiving, and he was mildly surprised—for once he didn't have to think about frozen turkey and potato buds. For once, he would have something to be thankful for. The quick sale of the house coincided with the furniture delivery—*oh my God and holy crap.* He would be moving in the Saturday before Thanksgiving.

The thought made him a little dizzy, and he flopped down on the showroom model of his newly purchased loveseat and sat there, just beaming, until he was pretty sure he made the salesgirl uncomfortable.

It didn't matter—he'd already put the money down. He was safe.

When he got home from all that, his mother asked him where he'd been.

"Buying a house and ordering furniture, Ma."

"Real fucking funny, Christopher. Seriously. The neighbor's dog's been yapping all fucking day—I need you to tell it to shut up."

"Tell it yourself, Ma."

"It doesn't listen to me."

"Neither do I. Excuse me, Ma. I want to work out before bed."

He'd worked out the night before—really worked out, not worked out and jerked off—and he felt like shit. His shoulders kept cramping, his legs kept tingling, and his stomach ached in odd ways from the yoga. But then, he'd felt like shit for so much of his life, he figured this was just a higher-quality shit.

This night he did cardio twice and skipped the strength training. The strength training made him sore, that was true, but that wasn't why he skipped it.

He skipped it because of the girl.

Danny had two girls, a sweet little girl in green leotards with red hair, and a dark-haired dynamo with a *big* smile and fan*tas*tic tits. The girl in the green leotards looked nice, like someone's mother or sister or best friend, and she helped Danny on the cardio video.

The girl with the dark hair and fan*tas*tic tits looked like she and Danny had been making out in the closet right before the strength-training video was shot. It was offensive. It made him not want to pull on the big green rubber band and stretch all sorts of painful things in his chest that really shouldn't be stretched.

Both those women should *know* that Danny was his!

So he skipped strength training and ran around in circles attached to a rubber band attached to his wall. It hurt like hell and made him blow like a busted car exhaust, but at least he didn't have to look at that bitch with the dark hair and know she'd had his man.

At the end of the yoga session (which he welcomed, breathing hard), he fell asleep on his yoga mat in full workout kit. It had been a helluva day.

THE NEXT day, he could hardly pick himself up off the floor and get to the shower. And the floor was drafty—he'd managed to pull his coverlet off his bed and onto his body while he'd been sleeping, but he still had a stuffed nose and a clogged head at work that morning, and lunch with Jesse was just awkward.

"You got a cold how?"

"I dob wab bu talk aboub ib," he answered miserably.

Jesse sighed and said, "Okay, boss. Tell you what. You stay here at your desk, and I'll be back in half an hour with lunch."

"I'b nob thab hunwy," Kit replied. He should have gotten some cold medicine on the way to work. There was some in his mother's medicine cabinet, but somehow taking it just seemed to violate all the rules of self-emancipation.

Jesse patted him on the head, and Kit knew that his careful water-comb was probably a bit of a mess, but he didn't care. He found himself looking limpidly up at his assistant as though this pretty, dynamic person held the keys to the universe.

"Don't worry, baby. I'll get you something that'll work."

Kit nodded helplessly and put his head on his desk. He had his own office, but it was small, and certainly not big enough for a couch or a comfortable chair. His whole body ached anyway—what was a cramp in his neck from spending his lunch hour asleep?

Jesse was back in half an hour, and he felt a little bit better after the nap. Unlike Friday, which had been hard and bright with sunshine, this November day was sad with fog. Jesse came in with his honey-colored hair lank from the fog and his sloe eyes bright from the cold.

So. Not. Fair.

In fact, it made Kit want to crawl under his desk for the rest of the day.

But Jesse pulled out some sort of magical soup that was spicy enough for the smell to penetrate Kit's sinuses, and then he pulled out a cup of hot water and tea and some Theraflu, and in ten minutes or so, Kit felt almost human.

And his worship of Jesse had in no way diminished.

"God!" he said from a suddenly clear nose. "That was wonderful. What was it?"

Jesse preened. "Thai soup from La Bou. Pretty up there in calories, but nothing beats it when you're sick."

Kit looked stricken. "Calories. Oh shit. Calories. I should be counting them, shouldn't I? I started the workout, but I forgot the diet." Suddenly his time with Danny Fit seemed tainted, somehow, with this omission, as though he'd cheated on Danny with the big mayonnaise-covered hamburger he'd eaten after he shopped for furniture the day before.

Jesse looked at him, repressed curiosity radiating from every line of his fit body. "You started working out? When?"

Kit felt like a deer in the headlights. If he told Jesse about the workouts, he might have to tell him about moving out, and maybe about being gay, and all of it was just so embarrassing. He wanted Jesse to look at the new him— or at least the new him projected sometime after New Year's, the one with his own house and the smaller waistline and the cat.

But then, if he didn't tell Jesse, who would he tell? The lady at the counter of Barnes & Noble? It was true, they'd developed a rapport as he'd bought his sci-fi novels, but they weren't on a first-name basis. He could tell one of the other senior accountants, but those men all had families, and he wasn't sure they'd go for the new, gay Kit. (He wasn't sure if they liked the old, gender-neutral Kit either, but, well, that one was at least safer.)

Maybe he'd tell part of it. He'd keep Danny a secret. And Ma. Or at least the parts of her he hadn't wanted friends to visit in high school (which sort of explained why he had no friends either).

"Friday," Kit said, aware that he'd sat there like a frog in the road while Jesse waited for an answer.

Jesse's lips quirked up, and he didn't look hurt at all. "I thought you had a dinner date Friday."

Kit flushed. At first he thought it was some sort of by-product of the cold and cold medicine, but as his eyes got round, and his mouth made a little O, he realized it was sheer fucking embarrassment.

"I'm not graceful," he muttered helplessly into Jesse's amused silence. "I didn't want to embarrass you." Oh, and *that* wasn't too much information?

Jesse's amusement went away. "It was just a pickup game, boss—no worries."

Kit shrugged and tried to smile it off. He dealt with the takeout trash in a distracted way and attempted to say something that would make it no big deal. "If the working out starts doing its job, maybe next time I'll take you up on it."

The grin on Jesse's face was blinding. It made dimples pop out. It made the sun shine through the fog. It made Kit's cock jump up and down like a horny Scottie dog yipping to be petted. Kit managed to keep all that inside, though, and simply sit through the grin like a mere mortal sat through the searing blast of heavenly grace.

Jesse shrugged. "It's getting cold—probably our last game for a while. You've got time."

Kit managed a hopeful smile, and as he sat up straighter, that pinched nerve in his neck twinged and he grimaced.

"Ohmigod!" Jesse said it all as one word, like a college student, and Kit wondered how much younger the other man was. "What did you do to yourself?"

Fuck. "I fell asleep on the workout mat?"

The sound Jesse made then wasn't a laugh, really, or a snort, and if Kit had to classify it, he'd say it was a nonverbal exclamation point, with a question mark thrown in.

"For the love of…. Holy shit, boss—how long did you sleep there?"

Kit's neck was tied up in a little question mark, too, so he had an excuse for screwing his eyes shut when he answered. "All night. It's how I came down with the cold."

Jesse stood up and moved behind him, and then there was a heavenly warmth, and a pressure on his neck and on his shoulders. It stroked and kneaded insistently, and Kit sat up a little straighter and made an embarrassing purring sound in his throat.

"Feel good?" Jesse asked, massaging a little harder right… right… right….

"Nnnnhaaaahhaaa," Kit managed. Oh God. His cock ached—but let it. Jesse was *touching him.* Suddenly Kit understood that college word. *Ohmigod ohmigod ohmigod ohmigod ohmigod….*

Jesse chuckled a little and kept squeezing the muscles in his neck. He bent down then, and his breath tickled Kit's ear as he spoke. "You should come work out at my gym," he said softly. "I swear, we'd never let you fall asleep on the yoga mat."

"Nnngg?" Oh good. A college degree and obviously some advanced communication skills.

"Promise?" Jesse said softly, and in spite of the warmth and the arousal and the *ohmigod human touch*, there was, as always, Kit's whole problem with Kit Allen.

"I don't know if this body is ready for prime time," he muttered, and Jesse chuffed softly in his ear.

"You let me know." But he didn't move. His hands kept moving, but the rest of Jesse stayed still, inappropriately, wonderfully close.

"Besides, I'm gonna be busy," Kit choked out, unable to stop himself. "I'm moving at the end of next week."

"Moving?" Jesse stayed close, and Kit managed to nod. Those wonderful hands—and the cold medicine, and the craptastical night's sleep—were beginning to take their toll all over again. Kit felt another nap coming on.

"Out of my mother's house and into my own." Kit was so tired. His head dropped, and he put his arms up on the desk, disregarding the crumbs from lunch, and rested it there. He couldn't remember feeling so… so… so *safe* in his entire life.

"Wow," Jesse breathed. "When did you decide to do that?"

"I should wake up," he mumbled. Kit was almost asleep, and lunch hour was over, and that was easier to say than *When I saw you play basketball and wanted to touch you.*

"I'll watch the door for you while you nap some more. A little more sleep and you'll be all better." The words were real. Kit was pretty sure the words were real—but he must have imagined the kiss in his hair.

AGE AND INEXPERIENCE

THEY DIDN'T talk about the backrub.

Kit was unsure how to bring it up.

Hey, I know I'm an overweight loser who still lives with his mother, but, uhm, you touched me, and I'm probably making a big deal out of this because I haven't been touched since I was, like, in day care, but I'm thinking that it was a special, very awesome sort of touch, but you're beautiful, and you bring me soup, and you love the one thing that's kept me sane as a thirty-year-old virgin, and I can't help wondering if maybe you're not straight and maybe, just maybe, you like me a little.

And please don't sue me for sexual harassment.

That last line was the kicker right there.

Kit was pretty sure that if Jesse was actually Jessie-short-for-Jessica, he might be able to bumble his way through a *your job does not depend on this, I swear* come-on. It would suck, and Jessie-short-for-Jessica would probably quit out of sheer embarrassment, but he could do it.

But coming on to a male assistant, one he'd done all but bare his heart to? Uhm, no.

He slept for an hour that day, and when he woke up, he rubbed his face, reflected that, hot damn! Did he feel better!, brushed the crumbs off his desk, and went back to work. Jesse left before he did (per usual) with not much more than a wave and a "Hope you feel better, boss!" and Kit didn't have much of a chance to do more than wave back and say "Thank you!" before he disappeared down the sterile beige hallway.

The next day, it had been business as usual—he'd tried to insist that he pay for both their lunches, since Jesse had sprung the day before, but Jesse had simply shaken his head and smiled.

"No—and we're not eating out. Here. I brought us something."

He'd proceeded to produce two chicken sandwiches—the kind made with chicken breasts and tomatoes and lettuce and pickles, on plain old wheat bread—and Kit had almost wept.

"These are really good!"

"Yeah—and they're pretty low-cal. The chicken's easy to cook...." And he'd proceeded to write the recipe down for Kit.

Kit said, "Oh crap! I have to buy pots and pans and shit!"

Jesse smiled a little. "That didn't occur to you until just now?"

Kit's blush covered his entire body. He was going to have to explain this now, or at least part of it. "I'm having all my furniture delivered new. All I have to move is my clothes and some other stuff. It'll probably fit in my car. I hadn't thought about cooking stuff—I guess I should have."

"Okay—man, I haven't wanted to pry, but that's just... uhm...."

The blush got worse. Jesse was furrowing his perfect brow at him, and Kit could only stammer through the rest.

"She's not a nice person, but... my dad walked out on us, and she didn't have anybody. I just"—*edit edit edit*—"reached a point where I needed my own life." He shrugged. "I've got plenty in savings—I just...." *Don't know how normal people live. Never had enough imagination to think about a real life on my own. Was asleep, like a giant squishy possum until you looked at me with a basketball under your arm, and I woke up thinking I had to be a better man.*

"I just needed to get my grown-up on, I guess."

Jesse smiled, and it was brilliant. "My home life sucked too. You stuck around, you know, to make it better. That's nice. I bailed. I've been living in shitty apartments since I graduated from high school. That's why the assistant job—tech school got me out quicker, and I wanted to, you know, have a *life* and not just be in school."

Kit blanched. "How old are you?"

"Twenty-three," Jesse said through a full mouth, and Kit couldn't decide whether to blow out a sigh of relief or not. "I worked for another firm for a couple of years but...." He shrugged as he let the sentence trail off. "They moved you from person to person, you know? Sort of assistant-by-slut, right? And I had enough moving as a kid. I just wanted to find a good boss, someone I could work for and have fun with and...."

Inexplicably, Jesse blushed.

Kit blinked, transfixed, but Jesse was looking down at the desk and couldn't see how that one moment of embarrassment started a terrible hot/cold chain reaction of hope in Kit's chest, like a BENGAY (or Jesse-might-be-gay) poultice around his heart.

"I just wanted to make a connection, you know?" Jesse said at last, looking up, and Kit nodded, in that moment completely understanding. Their eyes met and caught, and Kit had some more trouble breathing. Christ—this was a kid, and Kit didn't even know if he was gay.

When he heard his own voice, he thought someone might have taken over his body.

"I need to go shopping for cooking stuff this week, but I wanted to go to a movie on Friday. Anything good out?"

The smile that bloomed across Jesse's face made Kit glad he'd gotten up that morning. He'd been tempted to call in sick and nurse his aching muscles, and maybe watch Danny Fit videos until his cock was sore, but he'd decided that was too pathetic, even for him.

"*The Fifth Element* is playing at the UA—Friday night only."

Kit's own smile was suddenly not hesitant at all. "Best. Movie. Ever."

Jesse shook his head, and his smile turned subtler and almost sly. "*Serenity. That* was the Best. Movie. Ever."

The intimate and thrilling moment was over, and they were back talking about science fiction, and Kit was relieved. They would go to a movie as friends. They both seemed to need friends—it would be good. Kit could have Jesse as a friend and Danny Fit as a lover. The mathematical ease of that formula made Kit feel good all day.

It wasn't until Jesse was leaving that Kit realized people weren't necessarily as neat and tidy as the figures he used to make his living.

"Uhm, boss?"

Kit looked up from his computer, and Jesse—who always seemed so natural and graceful—was actually fidgeting at the door. "Yeah?"

"Uhm, what do I call you? I mean, it's not the fifth grade—you're not my teacher. But all I know you as is Mr. Allen. You go by Chris? Christopher? Topher?"

"Topher?" Were there people actually named Topher?

"There's an actor that goes by that…. No, seriously. What do I call you?"

He'd die—literally shrivel up and die like a salted slug if this beautiful young man ever called him "Christopher" in the same irritating smoker's-gravel twang his mother used. "Kit," he said. He didn't know how not to make his voice go soft.

"Your friends call you Kit?"

His colleagues called him Chris. "My dad, uhm, called me Kit, before he took off." His dad had been a good guy, really, but not much could have stood up to that determined, seething nerve bundle of sourness and despair that was currently sucking down Virginia Slims courtesy of her alimony check.

Jesse just stood there for a minute, those big brown eyes wide and limpid, and his mouth set in a half-smile. "Kit," he said after a moment. "See you tomorrow, Kit."

Kit nodded, not sure when his mouth had gone so dry. "See you tomorrow."

That night he made it through forty-five minutes of workout without hyperventilating or falling asleep on the floor. He even managed to take a shower and start going through his clothes for the move. He'd ordered a dresser and a bed from Sears—he could leave his mother the stuff in his room (old and battered anyway) so she could have a guest room, and he could masturbate in a bed that didn't reek of his own childhood.

While he was packing, his mother wandered by. She was wearing one of those big, all-purpose dresses and flip-flops, with a scarf over her brightly dyed platinum hair. He'd seen a variation of this outfit every day of his life, except a couple of blissful weeks of band camp that his father had paid for.

"What in the hell are you doing?"

"Packing to leave. I told you—I'm moving out on Saturday."

"You're moving out the week before Thanksgiving? What kind of bastard does that?"

"I can still come by for dinner, Ma," he placated. The thought gave him the hives.

"Don't fucking bother. What? I support you for thirty years, and you just bail on me? Who's going to take me to the market? Who's going to take me to church? Don't you have any fucking courtesy?"

Kit stopped packing and thought about it honestly. "I don't know, Ma. You're the only person I see, and you're not exactly a stellar example."

His mother blinked at him through poisonous green eyes. Kit had green eyes too—but they weren't that bright. He thought the green might have been a contact.

"What the hell does that mean?"

Kit sighed and walked over to close his door. "It means that if you wanted me to take you to church or to the market, all you had to do was ask me for my new phone number and pick up the phone. Since you'd rather bitch at me for being ungrateful, I'll take that as a no."

The door snicked shut (he didn't slam it—and was very proud of himself for that) and Kit was left alone, in what used to be a claustrophobic room. It was the secondary room of the house, with a bed, a bookshelf, and an old television, the kind with the regular screen that weighed two and a half million pounds.

Now, with his clothes folded and put in suitcases and his books in boxes around him and his posters (including a *Serenity* poster signed by Nathan Fillion that he'd had framed) down and in a neat stack in the corner, he felt a curious sense of freedom. The walls were all white—it was like he could stand on the bed and leap and fall into the sky and never land.

Then he thought of painting the walls of his new house (he drove by it every night, opened the door and walked into the echoing space of it, just to dream of what it would look like when all the furniture was delivered) and he thought landing might be very nice too.

When he slid into his bed that night, all showered and clean, thinking of good things for the future, he started thinking about Danny Fit.

He imagined his body, slimmer, fitter, his muscles defined, and his chest waxed (now that he was thirty, he'd started growing a small sized chest pelt, right between what he was hoping would someday be pectorals but were now man boobs). He imagined Danny climbing in next to him, and the way that perfect body would feel. Danny looked to be about forty—Danny would know what he was doing. He would tell Kit all of the mysterious things about sex with a man that Kit didn't seem to be able to get off the internet, and he would show Kit what to do to make things feel good. Kit allowed himself to wonder what it would be like to run his hands down another man's firm, taut ass and grasp a hard (thick, long) cock in his hand. He was sure Danny's mouth would be soft against his, and Danny's hands would be hard, and his breath would be minty fresh.

He couldn't imagine much after that. He'd never experienced the giddy feeling of skin against skin; he could only rub his own body— his padded ribs, soft stomach, tender nipples—but it was enough. He thought that Danny's mouth might be hot and wet on his cock, and the thought alone was enough to make it start oozing pre-come. He slid his hand under his shorts and started playing with his new favorite toy. His fist tightened on it, and his thumb rubbed the head while he thought of that toffee-dark head bobbing up and down while the lean hands touched him voluntarily.

And then he thought of nothing, saw nothing, just fell into the white-blindness of orgasm like he'd fallen into the freedom of his four white walls.

A few minutes later, after washing up quietly, he was back in bed and trying to imagine laying in someone's arms, and if that would be like seeing the walls painted in his new house—would it make being gay real? Would it make sex real, to touch someone without the one specific goal? What was touching like, really, when sex was out of the way (temporarily)?

It was a lovely thing to daydream about, and he tried to picture Danny's face as he pillowed that dark head on Kit's shoulder and rubbed his chest.

What he saw instead, just as he dropped off to sleep, was Jesse's young, narrowly pretty face with the big dark eyes and the fall of honey-colored hair, and the expression he had of being desperately eager to please.

JESSE CAME shopping with him for pots and pans. Kit didn't expect him to, and almost canceled the trip to the movies altogether.

Jesse left at his usual time that Friday, with a "Meet you there at eight, okay?" and Kit agreed, and left shortly after Jesse. When he got outside, Jesse was leaning against the wall, leaning against the shiny granite of the outer wall and smoking casually in the twilight.

Kit's heart completely fell to his knees.

Jesse looked at him—that pleasant, eager-to-please expression on his face. "You're leaving early? I thought you usually stayed an hour."

Oh God. Calm down. He's not your mother. This is a stupid thing to get upset over.

"Yeah," Kit said, trying hard to keep his face neutral. This man had been nothing but nice to him—treating him like a pariah over one bad habit was not something a good person would do. "I thought I'd go shopping first. You smoke?"

Jesse grimaced, and his look at Kit was full of sloe-eyed contrition. "Yeah—old bad-boy habits die hard." He exhaled then, ground out the butt in the sand tray outside the building, and fell in step next to Kit.

For some reason, not *seeing* Jesse smoking made it easier to bear. It was like the filthy, disgusting, embarrassing reek of his mother's tobacco habit disappeared if Kit could only smell the smoke in his own clothes.

"You were a bad boy?" he asked, finding that hard to believe.

Jesse shrugged, tucking his hands in the pockets of his denim jacket. It was chilly—Kit had brought a flannel lined camp jacket, which was probably not what the other accountants wore, but he liked it. Jesse had a denim jacket without gloves or a scarf, and Kit looked at him worriedly. He was going to get sick if he didn't stay warm.

"I was," Jesse confirmed, oblivious to Kit's contrary attack of revulsion and worry.

"What makes you a bad boy?" Kit was honestly curious. He had so little experience being bad himself, he really wanted to know.

Jesse gave him a sly, slanting look from under his eyelashes. Kit was a few inches taller than the younger man, and the expression made him extraordinarily alluring.

"I snuck alcohol in my water bottle," Jesse said airily. "Snuck cigarettes in the bathroom. Made out under the bleachers when I should have been in English. Lots of stuff in a high school for bad boys to do, you know."

Kit's heart tripped over itself. He sounded flirty—and young.

"Who'd you make out with?" *Great, Kit. Sly.* They were walking toward the parking building on the corner of J Street, and Jesse seemed intent on staying with him, so he assumed the guy (boy—he was a boy, right?) had parked there too.

Jesse's grin turned coy. "Anybody who'd make out back. Soccer players, cheerleaders, theatre majors, band kids—I was sort of a man whore back then... but since I mostly stopped at third base, it was all fun."

Oh shit. All those answers were gender neutral! And wait—wasn't third base oral? How many blowjobs had he given? Gotten? From whom?

They started walking up the parking garage and got into the elevator together. Jesse asked him what his high school had been like, and while he was fumbling an explanation of why the fucking Sousaphone was *not* sexy, the door opened, and they both got out and headed for Kit's little blue Honda Hybrid.

They got there, and Jesse went to the passenger side, grinned impishly, and said, "So, boss. Where are we going?"

Kit gaped at him, completely caught off guard. He was a bad boy? He smoked? Kit had a fleeting moment of disdain—*Danny* wouldn't do any of these things. *Danny* kept his lungs and his nose clean, and, in his dreams at least, *Danny* was 100 percent hella-fucking-gay. The silence grew awkward, and Jesse looked away, his hurt unmistakable.

"I…. You know, since we're going to the movie and everything. Never mind. I didn't realize you had other plans before…."

"Shopping!" Kit said quickly. Jesse's hurt was terrifying. The idea that Kit could wipe the easy smile off that pretty face completely boggled him. "We're going shopping for cookware."

Jesse turned one of those shining grins toward him, and Kit smiled back gamely. He'd just ask nicely for Jesse not to smoke in the car.

TURNS OUT, Jesse didn't ask, and his help with the cookware thing was invaluable.

"What's that called again?" Kit asked. It was a pan with a slotted cover. All he really knew was that it was shiny.

"A broiler pan." Jesse was holding back a smirk, and Kit realized he must seem pretty silly to someone who'd been cooking on his own for five years.

Kit looked at the thing doubtfully, but when Jesse added, "It's so you can cook meat without grease," Kit dropped it into the basket so quickly it clattered, and both of them hunched their shoulders and grimaced as the echoes died down through the expensive cookware store in the K-Street Mall. The basket already weighed a ton, and Kit wondered if he did a couple bicep curls with the thing, would it help make up for the fact that he wasn't going to work out that night.

He must have grunted, because Jesse said, "Oh Jesus—here, give it to me and go look at plates and stuff. You'll need a place setting for eight, at the least…."

"I don't know eight other people!" Kit protested, not realizing how pathetic that sounded until it came out.

"Yeah, but I know at least three, so plan on that!" Jesse shot back with good humor as he trotted the basket up to the front so they didn't have to carry it.

Kit had a fantasy, then, as he looked sightlessly at seven different, brightly colored sets of stoneware. Him and Jesse, sitting at the kitchen table he'd just ordered, having cooked a dinner that was healthy and good, with an open bottle of wine and Jesse's as-of-yet faceless friends. A part of him tried not to choke on the sap in this vision, but most of him was swooning at the perfection of it. It was… it was like his fantasies of Danny Fit, going down on him. It was grown-up and happy, except, unlike Danny Fit, this one seemed as close as the man (kid) chatting up the sweet young thing at the cash register.

The fantasy changed, and now it was Jesse and the sweet young thing, over for dinner, and Kit's misty vision changed, and he was their lonely gay friend with the cat.

He sighed and settled on the stoneware in the different dark colors—burgundy, navy, forest, and earth. Well, at least he was in his own home and Jesse had helped him cook.

Jesse came up behind him and bumped shoulders. "So, boss—you got something in mind? Cause I want to get to the theatre in time to buy popcorn!"

Kit realized his stomach was grumbling too. "Crap," he muttered. "I was going to stop and get something to eat."

"Popcorn," Jesse said decisively. "You can eat healthy any other time, but movies demand popcorn. Now let's go ring this up and schlep it to the car."

"Schlep?"

"Yeah, schlep. My history teacher used to say it all the time. Great word. Now come on."

Jesse made friendly with the checkout girl, and Kit had to admit she was pretty cute. He had a friend now—a friend with a past, sort of, and even Kit knew that was more fun to deal with in a friend than a lover.

Again, it was all mathematical in its simplicity. He could have his grown-up cake, his friends, his wine, his something-not-fried dinner, and he could have Danny Fit give him imaginary blowjobs on a regular basis. It was good. Nobody would get hurt, and Jesse would be happy. He liked that.

Of course, he would have liked the new and improved body he had planned even more—especially when he and Jesse each took an equal share of the pots, pans, and stoneware to "schlep" back to the car.

"Oh God," he panted. "I've got to stick to that workout thing!"

"How's that going?"

Kit gave him a sour look. He sounded revoltingly perky.

"Every night!" Every night Kit turned on the DVD, and Danny Fit made him hurt. Then he jumped in the shower, climbed under the covers, and Danny made him hurt so good.

Jesse gave him one of those sideways looks again, and if Kit wasn't sweating and out of breath already, the look alone would have done it.

"It's showing, trust me."

Kit almost walked into the concrete pole at the parking garage, and Jesse laughed good-naturedly while he tried to orient himself. He was too embarrassed after that to speak until they got to the car.

But then they were heading for the movie theatre, and that was all good. Popcorn, sodas, talking about how Luc Besson must have had a very active knight-in-shining-armor complex as a child—and *The Fifth Element?* Enough said.

Or it should have been, but they kept talking—just like they talked at work, except longer. They talked through coffee and through the ride in the darkened city to Jesse's car. They talked in the car for a while, in the dark, and Kit could study Jesse's features—could drink in his expressions, the way he tilted his head, the animation that took over his eyes when he was talking about science fiction and computer games and World of Warcraft and the things he loved.

At one point, as the conversation finally wound down, Jesse gave him one of those sideways looks. "So, what are you doing for Thanksgiving?"

Kit smiled a little. "Unpacking. Learning how to cook a little tiny turkey. Thinking about getting a cat for Christmas. Why?"

Jesse looked away. "I'm actually visiting the evil ex."

"The evil ex?" *Ex-what? Ex-boyfriend? Ex-girlfriend? Ex-cat or ex-turkey? Jesus, Jesse—can I buy a pronoun?*

"Yeah… a cheating slut bag, if ever there was one—but the slut bag's got a little sister who's sick."

Seriously, Jesse. A pronoun. Would it fucking kill you? "How sick?" Kit asked instead.

Jesse shrugged and looked away. "Leukemia sick. Pat's a bad person, but Emmy—she's the best. Odds are good she'll get better, you know? But she asked me to come visit, and as much as I hate home, I'll go."

"Where's home?"

"Truckee."

Kit whistled. Truckee was a small town/area between Sacramento and Tahoe—it was a long drive and an even longer culture gap. "Hope you have your cold-weather gear." It was already snowing in Truckee. Truckee was, in fact, where all the news people went during ski season to tell you how cold it was and how impossible the snow was to get through. It was like the last stop between where things got shitty and things got too shitty to drive.

"Yeah," Jesse sighed, looking out the window. "In more ways than one."

"You staying with your parents?" Jesse had mentioned them briefly—"mom and step-fuckhead du jour" being his exact words.

Jesse shuddered. "Hell no. Emmy asked her parents to put me up—they've always loved me, so I get the couch."

Kit couldn't help it. He put a hand on Jesse's shoulder, just to sort of take up some of the melancholy he saw there. "Sounds dire."

Jesse turned to him with a suddenly brilliant smile. "It's all good. I can tell them I've got a new job, and a new friend—and he's a little bit weird, but, you know, so am I. It'll be fine."

Kit dropped his hand and ducked his head a little, embarrassed and pleased. For a moment, he forgot all about his private arrangement with Danny Fit and concentrated on squashing that little zing that thrilled under his skin at the idea that Jesse thought he was worth mentioning.

The zing traveled straight to his groin, and all the social easiness that he'd had for the last few hours started gasping for breath as all his blood rushed to his cock.

So much for squashing a damned thing.

The silence stretched between them, and Kit looked up, realizing it was his turn to say something. "I hope you enjoy your visit." The answer scored zero points for originality, interest, or even relevance. He was going to see a little girl sick with cancer—how much fun could Jesse have?

Jesse's mouth quirked, wry and somehow disappointed. "Well, I'll see you at work before then. I hope you enjoy your move." He'd moved a little, leaned forward, maybe to see Kit's expression in the dark.

Kit nodded and swallowed. The swallow didn't take, because his mouth felt like a sandbox, and he had to try again. He found that his smile, though, was incredibly sincere.

"I've been looking forward to *that* for most of my entire life!" He managed to say fervently. Jesse laughed, and the strange, awkward moment was broken.

"See you Monday!" he called, getting out of the car, and Kit waved and watched him unlock and start his little yellow Corolla.

Suddenly work on Monday sounded even more fun than getting out of his mother's house on the weekend.

FULL AND EMPTY

As IT turned out, moving out of his mother's house was a lot simpler than living with her had ever been.

She sat on the couch and smoked in silence, studying the shopping channel while Kit loaded up his car with his clothes, his posters, his books, DVDs, and music. At the very end, he was hefting the television down the stairs, and she snapped, "That's mine, moron."

Kit stopped and put the set down. "Dad gave it to me when I turned sixteen." Dad had been good on gifts and college tuition—not so good on cards or phone calls. Kit consoled himself with the thought that guilt money from Dad and guilt imprisonment from Ma allowed him to skip the crappy college apartment stage and go directly to the dream house.

"Bullshit. I let you have it when he left it on the stoop."

Happy Birthday, Kit had been Sharpied on the box. They were lucky it hadn't been stolen before Kit got home from school.

But it wasn't worth fighting about. Kit was minutes from freedom. He took two steps up and put the television on the landing. He'd buy a smaller flat screen for his bedroom on the way to his new home.

He got to the bottom of the stairs and looked at his mother, who refused to look at him. He was tired already—but not, he hoped, as tired as he would have been three weeks earlier, before he'd met Danny Fit.

"I'm cooking on Thanksgiving, Ma. I could bring you something. You could come over—"

"Don't bother. You're going to leave me here alone?"

"You don't like me to talk when you're watching television anyway." It was the truth. And the television was always on.

"Don't be a smartass. Don't you care about me at all?" Her voice broke a little, and he realized she was actually hurt a little by his leaving. He decided he owed her the truth—she was manipulative, and not a nice person, but she was his mother.

"I'm gay, Ma. I'm moving out before you kick me out, because I'm tired of not having a life." He turned away then, so he didn't have to see her process this and didn't have to see her revulsion when it finally sank in. "Give me a call if you want to get together for Thanksgiving, okay?"

The door closed on absolute stunned silence.

He got to the little house right before the movers came. He had a chance to open the doors, to carry in his stuff and put it in the corner by where the bed would go. (He'd ordered a bed from Sears, along with the washer and dryer and refrigerator—all of it was due today. It was actually pretty wonderful—all the fun of moving in, none of the stress of getting the stuff in and out of trucks. Kit thought seriously about never moving out of this perfect little house.)

The movers arrived, and suddenly Kit was ass deep in people ripping off plastic covers from pristine furniture. Within two hours of chaos and big trucks in front of his tiny house, he had a house that looked like a showroom and a shopping list as long as his forearm.

After a trip to Lowe's, a trip to Sears, and a trip to Target, and a trip to the grocery store, he had a bunch of bags in his kitchen, some groceries in the fridge, a new small television in each bedroom as well as the giant plasma one he'd had delivered, and no energy at all to do anything else.

He hooked up the small television to the new cable box, took a shower, realized that he had to go back to Target for towels, and used an old T-shirt instead. He fell asleep on a brand-new mattress and brand-new blue flannel sheets, with his old desk lamp still on and the television playing a *Star Wars* marathon.

He had never been happier.

The next day he went to the store for what he hoped was the last time for at least a week. The sheer bulk of things he needed to survive was astounding: toaster, microwave oven, shampoo, liquid soap, hand soap, dish soap, clothes soap, toilet soap and toilet brushes—all of it came from someplace. He sighed when he had the last grocery bag unpacked, then called his mother's house and left a message.

"Ma, just so fair's fair, I wanted to say thank you for all the stuff you bought to make things run smooth. I appreciate that now. Thank you."

She didn't call him back, but then, the message was more for his conscience than because he thought she would. At five o'clock at night, when the last razor-edged shaft of light was shattered by the darkness, he had, for the most part, the home of his dreams.

It was really, really quiet in there.

He had a spare bedroom, and he'd bought a rubberized carpet for it and set up his small television on a shelf in there, and suddenly he had all the room in the world to work out, and not just a yoga mat. The cardio left him breathless, the strength part reminded him that he'd been unusually active, and the yoga relaxed all those tight muscles, but none of it, surprisingly, made him horny.

He showered, set up his computer and computer desk in a corner of the living room, and then started dinner. At Jesse's urging, he'd bought a cookbook, and tonight, it was mushrooms and onions cooked in chicken broth on top of a baked potato—no butter—with a breast of broiled chicken and a small salad.

It wasn't bad.

He went to bed early, thinking of all he'd have to tell Jesse at lunch.

IT WAS the telling that made it worth it. Jesse laughed—*a lot*—when Kit recounted the conversation the movers had about the couches. ("I never realized that 'fuck' was a noun, verb, adjective, adverb, and article!") He giggled when Kit told him about the six zillion shopping trips. ("You know, it didn't occur to me until the next day that I could have gotten *all* that shit at Target!") And he was gratifyingly supportive about the cooking. ("Bagels and low-fat cream cheese, tomatoes, salad, canned vegetables. It's weird how much shit I *didn't* know a grocery store had in it until I shopped with a cookbook in my hand.")

They finished lunch (Kit brought it this time—chicken breast on wheat with apple slices and two yogurts for dessert) and Kit said, "So, when are you leaving for Truckee?"

Jesse sighed. "Wednesday afternoon. I hope it's okay if I leave early."

"No worries. I'll probably be the only one in the office anyway—everyone else sort of just doesn't show up. You could take the morning off if you wanted to. I'm good."

Jesse gnawed on his lower lip, the gesture making him look charmingly (terrifyingly) young. "You know, I hate to think of you all alone during Thanksgiving. I've…. Even when I moved out, I always had people to eat with."

Kit colored. He must have seemed so pathetic—it was embarrassing. He stood up to get rid of the lunch mess so he didn't have to look Jesse in the eyes. "Are you kidding? Thanksgiving with*out* Ma? It'll be the first time I have something to be thankful for." He stopped for a moment and then added, "Besides my new assistant, of course," with complete candor, even if he couldn't look at Jesse when he said it.

"I'm a 'thankful'?" Jesse asked, and Kit managed to get a glimpse of dimples and bright brown eyes before he concentrated fiercely on the hand sanitizer on his desk.

"Best friend I ever had," Kit said, appalled at his own truthfulness. Oh God. Better say it now, so Jesse could run off and sleep with his ex-whatever in Truckee and giggle over his weird boss.

"Nice," Jesse said, nodding thoughtfully. "I'm honored." There was a silence, and then Jesse stood apologetically. "Time to get back to work. Can't keep my crappy apartment without my crappy paycheck, right?"

Kit imagined that Jesse's "crappy" apartment looked like it had been lived in, probably had old furniture, with real dents in the walls and scuffs on the floor, and a haphazard mess in the bedroom. There had probably been sex in Jesse's crappy apartment, the kind that involved two people, and probably laughter as well.

"I'll bet your crappy apartment is fun place to be," Kit said a little wistfully.

Jesse stopped at the doorway, and the look in his eyes was wise and old. "Anyplace can be fun, Kit, when you're not alone there."

"Yeah." Kit tried hard not to sigh, and then remembered the other part of his plan and brightened. "I'm going to get a cat."

"Can I help you look? I like animals—I just never have apartments where they can stay."

The strangely empty hollow in Kit's chest suddenly warmed and filled, and he knew his smile gave too much away, but he couldn't make himself care. "That would be awesome. Before Thanksgiving or after?"

"After," Jesse said regretfully. "I've got packing and cleaning tomorrow night, and my bestest bestie is in town tonight." Kit must have looked puzzled. "My best friend from high school," Jesse clarified. His expression softened, got dreamy. "I wouldn't have survived high school without her. Anyway, I promised her a night of talking and a crash on the couch, so if you can wait until Saturday? PetSmart has adoptions on Saturday—I'll meet you at your place, if you give me the address, and we can go then!"

It was a date, one that made the rest of Kit's day bearable, especially when he went home to his empty house.

He got used to the empty-house noises, though. He cut cardio out of his workout program and walked around the neighborhood Monday and Tuesday, enjoying seeing the other people around him, the happy families, the places where kids played in the yard and adults had porch swings or benches to sit on. The neighborhood was nice—but not too nice. You could still see people, unlike the really pricey places where they all huddled inside or "went somewhere" for recreation. He waved at the guy who lived next door as he helped his daughter on a bicycle, and the guy waved back. He went home, did his workout, fixed his dinner, watched some sci-fi, and surfed his computer. It was a lot like living with Ma, except....

Better.

It was still a lonely existence, he figured as he walked in to work Wednesday, but it was his, and that made it better. (He'd also managed about six loads of laundry and some dry-cleaning. His clothes already smelled less like tobacco. He tried to tell himself that this was yet another reason to wish that Pat was short for Patricia, but it sounded hollow, even in his own head.)

To his surprise, Jesse was at work, waiting for him.

He was dressed casually—no slacks and button-down work shirt, but jeans and a sweater, and his hair, instead of being carefully blow-dried back, was gelled and a little spiky. Kit literally found it hard to talk for a moment. God. Just... God. He was beautiful. He was so beautiful. For a moment, Kit knew his eyes got bright and shiny. He was beautiful, and Kit was... Kit. Even if he lost a zillion pounds, he had sandy hair, muddy greenish eyes, and an unlovely rectangle of a face. He could never have Jesse, even if Jesse were gay, even if Jesse stopped smoking, even if... even if....

"Kit?" Jesse said softly, and Kit took a breath. Spots were flooding his vision, so he must not have done that in a while. He took another one.

"I didn't expect to see you today," he said, trying to be bright and breezy. Oh God. He was so fucking bad at bright and breezy.

"I wanted to say bye on my way out of town."

Kit couldn't look at him. He made a business out of walking past Jesse to take off his jacket, then hang it on the hook inside his office. "That's nice of you," he said, meaning it, but unable to make eye contact. "It is. I mean, I know I probably seem sort of sad, by myself on the holiday, but I'll be fine. You never told me about your time with your friend the other night. You'll have to fill me in when you get back. Saturday, right? You said you'd be back by…."

Oh God. He was babbling, and he'd taken off his jacket and put down his briefcase and booted his computer and arranged his pencils, and he didn't have anything else to do to mask the fact that seeing Jesse right now completely unhinged him. Jesse was so beautiful, bad boy in high school (and that was actually starting to be a turn-on) or not.

"Saturday," Jesse said from right next to his chair.

Kit was so startled that he gasped and flipped the pencil right off the desk.

"Here. I'll get it." Jesse's voice was very gentle. He knelt down and stood halfway up, eye level with Kit. Their eyes connected, and Jesse straightened but kept one hand on the back of Kit's chair and the other on the desk, so that he was leaning over, and Kit was looking up at him, flustered and helpless.

"I'm looking forward to Saturday," Jesse said softly. "I really want to see your new dream house."

"It's a little lonely," Kit confessed, embarrassed.

"Well, we'll make it not so lonely."

Jesse was leaning into him, close enough for Kit to tell he didn't use aftershave, and his soap was subtle and clean. His eyes gleamed with an intent that Kit had never seen and could barely recognize. "Jesse?"

Jesse's mouth was a precious little bee sting of a pout, and he quirked up one end of it. "Yeah?"

"What's 'Pat' short for?"

The quirk became a full-blown grin. "Patrick."

Kit's mouth made a soft little O, and Jesse's grin disappeared, and then their lips were touching, and it was…. Oh God. Jesse took advantage of his complete and total bemusement and invaded with his tongue, and he tasted… like coffee, faintly of cigarettes, but not enough to matter. He just…. He tasted like human contact and warmth, and that ever-present laughter. He tasted of sweetness. Jesse was the boy (man) who made Kit's days sweet, and he tasted just exactly like that.

Kit was breathing hard when Jesse pulled back from the kiss, and his body felt like the Fourth of July, without the heat, stickiness, and smell of sulfur.

"I'll see you Saturday," Jesse said softly, kissing his forehead.

"Sbulahbhay." Oh God. Kit's brain had done it. It had scrambled itself and would never be useful again.

"Yeah. Saturday." He kissed Kit again, quick and hard, and then stood up and flashed that killer, *let's suck Kit right down the rabbit hole again* grin, and turned around and left.

Kit stared after him for what must have been half an hour before he realized that he was never going to get any work done at all, and that maybe he'd have a better day if he either went home and masturbated repeatedly or went shopping for his small Thanksgiving dinner and caught a movie.

He went for option B, mostly so the anticipation of option A could grow painful and delicious for the rest of the day.

While he was shopping, he saw a flier for the local soup kitchen, asking for volunteers and supplies. That night, after getting a small, fresh turkey, potatoes, greens, a box of Stove Top, and a fresh box of bakery cookies (instead of pie), he also threw in half the canned-good section of his local grocery store. After he got home, worked out, and got ready for bed, he took a moment to actually think about the kiss in his office.

It had been… soft. That was his first thought, and he savored it. Jesse, whose ex was Patrick and not Patricia, had kissed him, and it had been soft. It had just been lips and tongue and the taste of Jesse's smile, and he'd come by just especially to tell Kit bye and to… to kiss him.

He found the thought was too wonderful even to masturbate to. In fact, lying there, thinking about all the years he could have been kissing but hadn't been, it made him want to cry. Then he thought that maybe it was worth it, not kissing anybody, just so Jesse could be his first kiss, and then he really did cry.

He was glad nobody got to see him, weeping in the dark, mourning a youth spent in a cocoon of fantasy and science fiction and smothered in the bitterness of his mother and an eternal, voiding sort of loneliness.

He pulled himself together after a minute. He had the possibility of a real life now, and he didn't want to be a loser in it. He could no longer say he'd never been kissed, and he could no longer say he'd never been in love. He had been—although, whether it was with Jesse or Danny Fit, the vote was still out.

He told himself firmly that either way, he had a life, even an inner one; then he wiped his eyes on his new sheets (which weren't as stiff as they'd been when he moved in) and then set his alarm early.

It was hard getting up at four a.m. to prep his turkey and put it in the oven, and it was even harder to dress in jeans and a sweatshirt and go out into the smoking cold of dawn.

But it was worth it when he drove up to Loaves and Fishes with cans of everything from green beans to Spam and asked one of the volunteers where they needed it. They helped him park his car safely (a big if, off of Richards Boulevard) and the woman—in her fifties with frizzy gray hair and a warm smile who was there because, she told him, her kids were in college and her husband was sleeping in—took him to the back, showed him where to leave his jacket, and put him to work peeling potatoes.

He peeled potatoes for two hours, listening to the sounds of the soup kitchen, the forced happiness of the volunteers, the remorseful gratitude of the people who'd had it too rough this year to do for themselves. When he had half an hour left to get his bird out of the oven, he told his volunteer (Margaret) that he had to leave, but he'd return sometime if she liked.

She hugged him. No "personal space," no "you're a stranger and I barely know you"—she just hugged him, told him warmly that she would love to see him whenever he had the time, and wished him a happy holiday.

Kit thought he might show up at the soup kitchen a lot after that— if there were people there who would adopt him and be kind, well, then, he probably had lots of charity in his heart to give.

He went home, and the turkey smelled great. The sides weren't too difficult, and he lit candles, put a vase of flowers on his table, and set music, then sat down and had himself dinner.

He imagined that Jesse was there. He imagined that Danny was there. Danny would be a perfect host and a good lover. Jesse would be a perfect guest and a lot of fun. And maybe, if Kit was lucky, Jesse would gift him with more kisses like the one in his office.

At the end of the meal, he couldn't decide who he'd rather have at his table in reality, but he was aware that a little bit of reality was necessary. He packed up a small tray of food, complete with cookies, and took the ten-minute drive to his mother's tiny Victorian on R Street.

He knocked on the door with conviction, and when she opened it—in nothing but a house coat, red eyes, and a dangling cigarette—he thrust the package into her hands.

"Happy Thanksgiving, Ma. Enjoy."

He turned around, not expecting a lot of thanks or even recognition, and he reached the top step of the porch before she said, "What? You're not even going to eat it with me?"

He contemplated ignoring her, but then it hit him. That was the closest thing she'd ever expressed to an actual desire for his company. He turned back around.

"Sure, Ma. What's on TV?"

"Crap. Nothin' but crap. But *Wizard of Oz* is on right now. You used to drive me crazy with that one when you were a kid."

Kit blinked. He didn't remember this. "Figures," he said philosophically. "Yeah. I might have a cookie." He'd packed all the extras with the meal—why not?

He stayed through the rest of the movie, while his mother ate her little impromptu meal, balanced on her lap. The dining room table was dirty, still—lots of bowls full of cereal and a few empty beer bottles. To his memory, she'd always had food on the table for him. He thought about the people in the soup kitchen that morning—the same couldn't be said for them, could it?

"How's the food, Ma?" he asked, hoping he didn't sound needy.

She swallowed a bite. "It doesn't taste like shit. But you need more damned cheese in the mashed potatoes."

He smiled, practically swooning with the compliment. "I'll remember that next time."

"You'll come visit again?"

"Yeah. How 'bout Monday night?"

"Why not Saturday?"

"I'm getting a cat."

His mother took a bite of turkey and potatoes and prodded the green beans experimentally with her fork. "I could come over and see it sometime. I like cats."

Kit nodded. "No smoking in the house, okay Ma?"

"Be fucking picky. Yeah, fine. Whatever. Just make sure your fucking cat has all its fucking shots, okay? I don't want rabies."

"Yeah, Ma. Germ-free cat. It's a deal."

"You got a faggoty boyfriend yet?"

"Got a hope for one."

"Just don't do no ass-fucking while I'm there."

Kit swallowed, thoughts of sex with Danny *or* Jesse suddenly fleeing his mind like rabid bats from a ghost-shrieking cave. "I guarantee it."

He left at the end of the movie, after clearing up the takeout mess and sharing a cookie. He kissed her cheek firmly before he left, and although her smile would never light up the world, she wasn't calling him a fucking faggot and throwing him out on the lawn.

It was a start.

MAIDENS AND MAIDENHEADS

HE SPENT Friday painting one of his bedroom walls burgundy, and he liked the effect so much, he painted one of his living room walls blue. He would have gone out and bought some more sci-fi or comic book prints to hang after that, but he understood that Black Friday was sort of a nightmare, so he figured he'd done good.

Saturday, he was shocked to hear knocking on his front door at six o'clock in the morning. He stumbled out of his bedroom in sleep pants and a T-shirt and threw open the door before he even looked through the peephole to see who it was.

Jesse launched himself into his arms, wiggling and breathless like a puppy, and kissed him full on the mouth, morning breath and all.

Kit stumbled backward and managed to find the couch in the front room by luck so he could tumble backward over the arm of it. Jesse kissed his morning breath away, and he smelled like coffee and tobacco, and Kit didn't care. His mouth was warm and wet and soft, and his body on Kit's was hard and lithe. Oh… oh *God*. There was a man's body, wiggling around on top of him. Seriously! And he didn't mind that Kit was rubbing his back and cupping his ass. In fact, he was arching against Kit, and their groins were hard and mashing together imperfectly, and it felt… oh damn… even better than his own hand on his cock.

The thought was enough to make Kit come, just a little, and he groaned and pulled back, because he was trying not to embarrass himself by coming in his pants after a little bit of necking.

Jesse perched up on his chest and grinned. "Sur-prised?"

Kit tried to reply and could pretty much only manage a stupid grin. He nodded and then reached up for a little peck on Jesse's lips. Jesse pecked back, and Kit remembered something to say.

"Did you drive all night?"

"Yeah, pretty much. It was slow coming off the summit anyway. I…." He yawned. "I caught a couple of catnaps at the chain stops, but…." He yawned again and sagged against Kit comfortably. "You don't mind if I nap with you, do you?"

Kit blinked. Why not? He'd been hoping to sleep in until nine. This way he could sleep in with Jesse next to him. A part of him wanted to dance and sing—or go catatonic with shock—and he ruthlessly squashed it. He wanted to enjoy this, dammit, and not spend all his time being stunned that it was happening.

"Yeah," he said, and then pushed Jesse off of him playfully and scrambled to sit up. Jesse gave him a hand, and they both went into the bedroom. Jesse looked around appreciatively, letting out a low whistle.

"This is pretty swank, Kit, new paint smell and all! You sure you want to squander it on a lowly assistant?"

Kit shook his head. "It's missing personality and warmth," he said seriously. Then he smiled, liking Jesse all sleepy and disheveled, smelling of the car and the caffeine and fast food and, yes, the dreaded smoking habit that Kit hated, but still looking beautiful and perfect. "That's where you come in."

Jesse turned half-lidded eyes toward him and blinked. "That could be the nicest thing anyone's ever said to me," he said softly, and Kit blinked back.

"You need better compliments…. Here, do you want some sleep pan— Never mind." Because Jesse had stripped down to blue boxer-briefs and a T-shirt, leaving his jeans, hooded sweater, boots, socks, and denim jacket in a puddle on Kit's floor.

He scrambled into Kit's new bed like a child, tucking under the comforter into Kit's spot. "Oh, God, it's warm," he sighed, and his teeth were chattering a little. "Something about being up this time of morning and outside, it makes me so cold! What are you doing?"

Kit straightened from laying Jesse's jeans over the chair in the corner. "Straightening your things…."

"Well, stop it!" Jesse ordered crossly. "Get in here and be the big spoon! I'm freezing!"

Alrighty then. Kit abandoned all attempts at straightening and crawled into bed behind Jesse, using his height and the width of his shoulders to pull the smaller man back into his arms. Jesse wiggled and chattered, and Kit held him closer and tighter, until both of their bodies tightened and relaxed with sort of a sigh, and they melted into the mattress.

Jesse felt so good. Kit closed his eyes and rubbed his cheek against that smooth, honey-colored hair.

"How was your Thanksgiving?" Jesse mumbled, already close to sleep.

"I missed you," Kit said honestly. He could do that, since Jesse was there in his bed. "What made you decide to come back so early?"

"I almost slept with the evil ex." Jesse's voice was matter-of-fact, and Kit tried hard not to kick the first man who'd ever wiggled into his bed right back out.

"Waaaah?"

"See," Jesse didn't sound so close to sleep anymore. He sounded very… very careful, actually. "The thing is, his sister is dying."

"Oh, Jesse…."

"Emmy didn't tell me when she called. She didn't want to depress me—or even pressure me into visiting—but the whole family knew. She won't make it until Christmas. I brought her a book, you know, since I wasn't going up for Christmas, and it just hit me that she'll never have a chance to read it."

Forgiven. Kit didn't realize he could forgive something like cheating or almost cheating. He'd never even thought of it. His dream guys never cheated, period the end. Danny Fit never cheated on him—unless it was on those days Kit skipped strength training, and he was getting it on with the red-leotard girl on the DVD behind Kit's back—but Kit doubted it. But here, in the real world, with a heartbroken Jesse in his arms, Kit didn't even need to hear the rest of the story to see where this was going. An "almost" lapse, when he and Jesse had been nothing more than a kiss in the office? Forgiven. As simple as that.

"I'm so sorry," he said quietly, and Jesse took his hand and kissed it with so much tenderness Kit didn't think he could say anything else for a while.

"See"—Jesse kept talking like he hadn't just shorted every fuse in Kit's brain—"there Pat and I were last night, out on the couch, and I was trying not to just lose it, because the whole family was being so strong and so brave for the whole two days, and I didn't want to be the big, bawling baby in the middle of them, and Pat put his arms around my shoulder, and there we were. You know. Pity sex—it was going to happen. And then Emmy called me into her room—she'd been out and about all day, but she was too tired and needed to be hooked up to oxygen and shit, and I got up so fast I think I elbowed Patrick in the chest."

Kit chuffed a little bit of laughter into Jesse's hair. Apparently Jesse was enthusiastic like a puppy in his natural state.

"Anyway," Jesse continued, "I go in there, and she tells me to sit down, and then she just starts talking. And she's only sixteen, but I used to talk to her about everything—like one of those kids in the movies, who seems to know more about adult shit than adults do? And she tells me that she knows what gay is, but she always used to imagine me as a knight in shining armor, and that I'd be the one to come pick her up and put her on my horse and take her away to do icky forbidden things to her when she turned eighteen. She made me laugh, you know? There she is, and she's skinny and she's dying and she's got me cracking up, and then she says, totally serious, 'Baby, please don't sleep with my brother'. I almost choke on my tongue, because I still don't expect shit like that to come out of her mouth. I'm like, 'Sweetheart...' and that's all I got."

Jesse's voice was cracking now, and his shoulders were trembling, and Kit realized with some awe that Jesse had driven all night to come here, to his little, cold house, and fall apart in Kit's arms. He tightened those arms and nuzzled Jesse's hair and held on.

"So then she starts going on about how she's going to die a virgin, right? And that's a girl's worst nightmare. I crack a joke. I'm like, 'Well, sweetie, if you thought *I* was going to be your knight in shining armor, I don't think you were going to lose that soon anyway'. She laughed and then told me I was an asshole, and I'd missed the point."

Jesse was quiet for so long that Kit wondered if he'd fallen asleep, shaky breathing and all. "What's the point?" he prompted gently.

"The point was that she would rather die a virgin than just give it away and have it mean nothing, and that even though I was a guy, that didn't mean I couldn't feel the same way. And I thought about it, you know? Pat and I—we fucked each other, and then we went out and fucked anything that moved. When I said 'enough', Pat just didn't take me seriously, you know? That's why I broke up with him and moved out here and got my tech thing after high school. Did I really want to just up and have pity sex with someone who didn't take me seriously, when I had a guy in a place I'd sort of made mine, who kept looking at me like I made his heart beat?"

Kit couldn't even blush in embarrassment. He hadn't realized how transparent he'd been—but he couldn't regret it now.

"So I told Emmy thank-you for the set-straight, and she smiled a little and asked me if I had someone I liked better than her slut-bag brother—her words. They love each other a lot, you know, but they give each other shit too. Anyway, I told her about you, and she told me to go home and go pick out a really good kitten for her, since they hadn't been able to get her a new one when she got sick. And I told her I loved her, and kissed her goodbye, and said bye to her folks, and left at midnight and came here."

"I'm glad you did," Kit told him, feeling weak and stupid. He was crying a little, like a big pussy, and he was really glad that Jesse was turned away so he didn't have to see Kit come unglued from a story. Then Jesse turned around, and there Kit was, naked with his clothes on, but Jesse had been weeping too. He used his thumbs to clear Kit's cheeks and kissed him softly on the mouth.

"So I just drove all night to see if it's true. Are you going to tell me if it's true?"

Kit looked at those shiny brown eyes, limpid with grieving, and wondered if he'd ever had any courage at all. "Does my heart beat for you?"

"Yeah."

Well, it certainly didn't beat for Danny Fit, now, did it?

"Yeah."

Jesse smiled a little, obviously exhausted, and snuggled into Kit's arms like a child—or a lover—and raised his face for a quick, sweet kiss. "Good."

KIT DIDN'T think he'd sleep then—it was such a new sensation, having someone in his bed, touching his body. But Jesse fell asleep almost in the middle of their kiss, and Kit didn't want to move. Jesse needed comfort. Jesse needed *him*. The idea was extraordinary, alien, and amazing. If Danny Fit had walked out of the television one morning and sank to his knees to take Kit's cock in his mouth, Kit could not have been more dumbstruck—or happier.

What was strange was that Jesse's misery—and the fact that Kit felt miserable with him—didn't seem to make it worse than he imagined. There was no disappointment in the real-world pain that Jesse brought with him. There was only joy that it brought Jesse too.

It was on this thought that he actually closed his eyes and fell asleep.

He woke up a little cramped from being wrapped around Jesse, and went to wash his face and brush his teeth and shower, not thinking that anything more extraordinary than Jesse sleeping in his arms could possibly happen.

He came out of the shower with a towel wrapped around his hips and was surprised to see Jesse, awake, lying on his side, the cover pulled up to his waist.

His T-shirt and boxer-briefs were in a puddle on the floor in front of him.

Kit was not quite surprised enough to drop his towel—but it was close. Jesse dropped his head a little, shyly, and said, "I, uhm, used your toothbrush when you were in the shower. I guess you didn't hear me."

Kit blinked and looked at him again. His chest had no hair at all, and his muscles were small but well-defined. His chest wasn't broad, but his waist tapered anyway, and his abdomen wasn't a six-pack like Danny's, but it was stringy and taut as it disappeared under the blanket.

"Didn't hear you," Kit repeated, his mouth as dry as baby powder. "Uhm...."

Jesse's eyes met his unexpectedly. "You wanted to, didn't you?"

"God yes!" Kit burst out with so much passion that he startled himself.

Jesse grinned. "So, uhm, do you like to top or bottom?"

Blink. "Wha?"

"You know, do you wear the condom or not?"

Oh God. Kit needed to correct a very basic assumption right here and now. "Uhm, Jesse?"

And now Jesse was looking both uncertain and a little bit hurt. "What?"

"You're making this really big assumption—"

"You just said you wanted to!"

"I do! I do! Oh God, I do! I just haven't yet."

"Haven't had sex with me? I thought we were, you know, going to... going to do that...."

Oh God. Suddenly hiding his face was more important than hiding his soft belly and hard private parts, and Kit pulled the towel up to bury his face in it.

"I haven't had sex *at all, ever!*" he confessed piteously, so embarrassed he thought his penis might fall off with the pure shame of it all.

The silence in the room was so profound that Kit found he had to look over his hands to make sure Jesse hadn't killed himself laughing.

Jesse had swung himself up in the bed and kept the sheet around his waist, and was regarding Kit with absolute sobriety. When Kit met his eyes, he said, "Really?"

Kit nodded and shrugged at the same time. "It was just easier," he rasped, feeling like some sort of explanation was demanded from him. "I lived at home, with my mother. I... I wasn't a catch, you know? I'm a pudgy accountant, right?" He shrugged again and tried to look anywhere but Jesse's wide, sympathetic eyes. "I don't know if I like to top or bottom. I don't know how to"—oh God—"touch things, or what feels good to someone else or... etiquette, or...." He trailed off and then manned up. This could be the worst thing he had to confess, ever, and he'd done it. Finish strong or not at all, right? He looked Jesse in the eyes.

"About all I really do know is that I probably don't need a condom. Which is good. Because I don't have any."

And that last part seemed to prompt Jesse into action. He stood, and for a second he struggled with the sheet like he was going to take it with him, and Kit struggled with the towel to put it back around his body, and then Jesse dropped the sheet and came over to Kit and took his hands.

The towel flurried to the floor.

"You didn't even hope for me?" Jesse said softly, and Kit avoided his eyes. He'd pinned all of his hope on Danny Fit, really, because he had absolutely no expectations of that one ever coming true.

"It hurts to hope." It was a painful admission. He wondered if he could ever tell Jesse about Danny Fit and decided that maybe, just maybe, *that* would be harder to do than confessing to his overripe virginity.

Jesse nodded. "I know that," he said. "I *do* need a condom, okay? Because you don't want to wait for someone who might be special, because it hurts to hope for something like that. And then you just sleep with anyone who might make it hurt less, and not with the right someone who won't make it hurt at all." He kept his head down and seemed to stare at Kit's hands, his soft accountant's hands, as he stroked the backs of them with his thumbs. "I'm not a virgin," he said with a sardonic smile. "I've done lots of things... lots of *men* that I'm not proud of."

He looked up at Kit then, and he grimaced, and Kit thought maybe he was fighting tears too. "Do you remember the first day at work? You were showing me how to use the copy machine?"

Kit shook his head. He'd spent the entire day dazzled. There was no single moment he remembered, just Jesse, big eyes, sweet smile, all of it.

"Well, I was feeling a little out of my league—that thing's a monster, and it's all hooked up to the computer and everything, and you showed me how to use it, and you were like, 'No worries. Just think of it as the helm of the Starship Enterprise—you're like, Chekhov, right? We won't make you wear the red jumpsuit, I swear'."

Kit couldn't look at him. Were they both just standing there, naked, staring at each other's hands?

"Look at me, Kit."

Apparently not. Kit looked up, and Jesse smiled into his eyes.

"It was the nicest thing anyone ever said or did for me on the job or at school or anything. And you were nice every day since. You said 'please' and 'thank you' and put aside your work to talk to me. You were funny—when you let yourself talk. And I kept thinking, 'God, if he liked me, even a little, I would so totally risk my job to hit on him'. And I did—and it was worth it. It was worth it to drive all night because you weren't going to try to nail me when I felt like shit. The look on your face when you opened the door and saw me? I don't know how I lived my whole life without someone looking at me like that, okay?"

Kit looked at him now and let his dazzle shine through. "Okay. Okay." He nodded and said it again, because suddenly being naked wasn't a scary thing; it was an exciting thing. Jesse wasn't going to hurt him—not on purpose. He wasn't going to laugh at him or make fun of him. Something in Jesse was just as dazzled by Kit as Kit was dazzled by Jesse, and it just might be all right.

Jesse straightened and reached, and they kissed again. Kit encircled Jesse's shoulders, feeling the urge to protect him. He'd been hurt by life, Kit realized, and Kit was afraid enough of life to want to keep him safe—and to think he was incredibly brave.

Their skin rasped together, and Jesse tasted like Kit's toothpaste and raw enthusiasm. Kit loved that, and he returned it, pushing Jesse backward, steering him toward the bed. Jesse stopped when the backs of his knees hit the bed, and he sat down abruptly, then scooted back and stretched out, patting the space next to him for Kit.

"Want to start again?"

Kit grinned. "Are you kidding?"

Jesse grinned back. "Not even a little."

Kit crawled in and lay on his side, and Jesse started the kiss back up, and this time, their hands were free to roam.

Jesse's skin was smooth. He had tight, stringy little muscles, and Kit could feel his ribs under a shallow layer of them. The hollow where the small of his back dipped to his buttocks was silken, and the slightly furry tops of his thighs were soft even under the coarse hair. Kit was erect again, except now his cock was mashed up against Jesse's groin, and Kit could feel the ridge of Jesse's cockhead right by the crease in his thigh.

Kit whimpered.

"Let me touch."

Jesse smiled against his lips. "Me too."

They backed up a little, and Kit took Jesse's actual throbbing cock in his hand. It was not as large as his own, which both surprised him and didn't bother him at all. Jesse, on the other hand....

"Holy God." Jesse's fist tightened around Kit, and Kit gasped. "This thing.... Jesus, Kit—it's a fucking thing of beauty!" He stroked from Kit's base to his tip, and Kit had to remember to keep his own fist wrapped around Jesse. He stroked again, and Kit groaned and threw his head back against the pillow and let go of Jesse's body, which sucked because he wanted to explore, but... but....

Jesse stretched up and kissed his cheek. "Easy there, buddy. I've got this, okay? You're primed to go off here—trust me, I get it."

Kit was about to say "But...", and then Jesse scooted down the bed and engulfed Kit's cock in his mouth, and Kit let out a sound that he didn't know a human could make. He stroked Jesse's hair back from his face, and Jesse hollowed in his cheeks and sucked hard, pulling back until Kit popped out of his mouth. Then he turned his head and grinned up at Kit, and Kit's breath just trammeled up in his chest and stayed there.

"That felt good, right?"

Kit couldn't manage real words—about all he could do was groan and thrust his hips up, so his cock slid through Jesse's spit-slick grasp. Jesse's grin widened, and then it went away entirely as he took Kit in again. He was doing a swirly thing with his tongue on the upstroke and using his fist at Kit's base, too, and his other hand (oh, how very sneaky!) came to play with Kit's balls and to finger the cleft of his bottom. Oh God. That was unnecessary. That was too much. That was going to.... Not so soon.... No no no no no no no no....

"*Gwwwwaaaagghhhhhh!*" Kit didn't even have a chance to warn him, and Jesse swallowed quickly and again and again, until that precious, bee-stung mouth was just gulping Kit's come, and the way that felt on Kit's cockhead was.... "*Gwwwaaaaahhhhhgggg! Jeeeeee-sus!*" Kit's knees came up, and he turned sideways, dislodging Jesse, who scooted up the bed, wiping his mouth while Kit curled up into a little ball and shuddered.

Suddenly Jesse was there, arms around Kit's shoulders, gooey kisses in his hair, and tender strokes against his shoulders. He smelled like Jesse and sweat and Kit's come, and Kit wanted to kiss him worse than he wanted to breathe. He captured that sweet little mouth and demanded, and Jesse gave in to him so free and easy Kit could almost believe that sex, all of sex, would work.

Kit's breathing subsided, and Jesse thrust against his thigh and grunted, just enough to let Kit know that his friend (lover? They were lovers now. Fan*tas*tic!) was still in need. Awesome!

Kit pulled back and said, "Can I?" and Jesse smirked at him.

"I thought you'd never ask!"

Kit kissed his way down Jesse's body, feeling giddy as he suckled on a nipple and felt Jesse's hands tighten in his hair. Oh God... his skin tasted so good. It was sort of honey colored, like his hair, and Kit wondered what he'd look like tan in the summer, and then he kissed his way to the vulnerable skin of Jesse's stomach and nibbled, just to hear that throaty giggle that he'd heard Jesse make on occasion.

Jesse made the sound now, and Kit grinned up at him before turning his attention to the one part of a man's body that all things seemed to center around.

Jesse was right—it was a little smaller than Kit's, but it was gold with a flushed pink head, and the skin felt soft and tight against Kit's hand. Kit squeezed and the head turned purple, and Jesse moaned a little and thrust up inside the cave of his fist.

The first slide of the thing between his lips felt awkward, even when he made sure his teeth were safely covered. He kept going, though, because the sound Jesse made was... sweet. Begging. Cock-stiffening. Kit squeezed the base again and slurped down until his lips met his fist, and then he moved his fist to see how deep he could take it down his throat.

Almost all the way, he discovered, and Jesse groaned harshly and then gave Kit's hair a little jerk until Kit pulled back.

"Just use your hand, okay?" Jesse panted when Kit had pulled off it and was meeting his eyes. Kit must have looked disappointed, because Jesse touched his cheek. "I haven't been tested recently. Just to be safe, okay?"

Kit nodded. Even a thirty-year-old virgin had heard of HIV. He propped his chin up on his arm and started stroking Jesse's shaft, and then he sat up a little and switched arms, stroking with one hand and moving his other hand to explore a little. Jesse's balls were hard (at the moment) and the skin around them was soft and covered with dark-brown fur. Jesse pulled his knees up and spread his thighs, and Kit looked at him, asking permission.

"Feel free," Jesse grunted, squeezing his eyes shut as Kit thumbed the pre-come on the mushroom head of his cock. "Explore at... oh God... will!"

Kit grinned, but Jesse didn't see it; then he stuck one of his fingers in his mouth and sucked, slicking it up, because he'd read a little about this and wanted to see what would happen. Then he stroked again while he took that slick, naughty little digit and finger-walked it to the entrance of Jesse's asshole.

Jesse keened, begging, and Kit grinned again. Oh God—in all his imaginings, he'd never imagined how much fun it would be to hear Jesse make those noises begging him to play with his body in carnal ways. He slid in one finger and wiggled it around, and Jesse clenched against him and thrust forward some more, and Kit was delighted enough to slide in two fingers and then grasp and squeeze and stroke some more.

"Oh Christ!" Jesse gasped. "Now!" His come was hot on Kit's fist, and some of it was white and some of it was clear as it spattered across his stomach and his lean chest with its vulnerable ribs and the tiny mole up next to his right nipple. Kit longed to taste the fruits of orgasm, like Jesse had tasted his. Jesse's face was contorted without any self-consciousness at all. He looked fierce and almost in pain, and then, as Kit kept pumping, he relaxed a little and reached out a hand to stop Kit's pressure.

Kit pulled back and reached over the bed to where he'd dropped his towel on the floor. He used the towel to wipe off his hands and clean Jesse up, his movements patient and reverent, while Jesse watched him with wide, limpid eyes. When he was done he moved up next to Jesse and claimed that mouth again with so much tenderness aching in his throat he just knew Jesse would laugh at how young he was, a virgin, in love with the first guy he laid.

When he pulled back, Jesse's eyes were shining, and he wiped the back of his hand across them with a rough movement.

"You're pretty good at this sex thing, you know that, Kit?" His voice was rough and wobbly, and Kit felt his eyes get bright too. He kissed Jesse softly and stretched out next to him, and thought that maybe it wasn't the sex he was good at, it was the love part, but he didn't say that.

It just may have been too real.

They lay quietly for a while after that, and Kit spent some time running his hand up and down Jesse's chest and arms, skimming his fingertips over youth-prominent clavicles and stroking his deceptively strong-lined jaw.

Jesse tried to do the same thing to Kit after a few moments, and Kit remembered that he was naked, and he was imperfect. The thought sent him diving for the covers, and Jesse's laugh had the ring of hurt to it.

"Come on, Kit.... I like your body too!"

Kit clamped the comforter over his chest with his arms. "You'll like it better in six weeks!" he said adamantly, and Jesse's eyes narrowed.

"I'm not waiting six weeks to see you naked, you moron! Jesus— we just.... You just let me go down on you—do you think I didn't see it then?"

Kit turned red. "Well then, you know," he said, because anybody would know after that.

Jesse prodded gently at the arm nearest him. "Know what?" His voice was as gentle as his touch, and Kit allowed his arm to be moved for no other reason than it was Jesse.

"Know that I'm the size of a Volkswagen," Kit grumbled, and Jesse laughed. He actually laughed.

"You're thick, all right. You're thick in the head and you're thick in the cock, but your body is not nearly as bad as you think it is."

"Fine." Kit grabbed the comforter and threw it down to his hips, and Jesse laughed some more. Suddenly, Kit thought he might run naked through their little office building if it would make Jesse laugh just like that, warm and throaty and kind.

"Nice," he murmured appreciatively. "You can see where the workouts are doing their job.... See?" He poked Kit in the stomach, and Kit tightened reflexively. "Look at that. Voila! Definition."

Kit smirked a little. "You could bounce a quarter off your stomach— don't bullshit me."

"Well, you want that tummy, you need to go to my gym!"

Kit colored. "Nah. I think I'll stick with Danny Fit, thank you."

Jesse grimaced playfully. "Oh God! How's a mere mortal going to compete! Danny Fit! God of gay fitness!"

"I didn't know he was gay," Kit said, wide-eyed, and Jesse saw the hero worship and rolled his eyes.

"Jesus, Kit, pop culture isn't just for sci-fi—read a magazine at a checkout stand, whydontcha!"

"Oh." Kit looked away, embarrassed, but not for long. Imaginary, gay Danny Fit was tucked away on his DVD player, and live, cute-as-hell, willing-to-touch-him-and-like-him-for-who-he-was Jesse was *in his bed,* and getting ready to go down on him all over again.

Danny who?

THEY MIGHT have played in bed all day, but Jesse stretched at around one o'clock and said, "There's a lot more we could do here, buddy, but I'm about all come out." He rolled over onto his stomach and propped his chin on Kit's. Kit smiled at him and stroked his hair back from his face. It was a little bit greasy, because, hey, the guy had driven all night to see him, and him alone, and that was a reality Kit could live with.

"Did we want to try the, uhm," Kit blushed, but he kept stroking Jesse's hair.

"The thing?" Jesse supplied drily, and Kit nodded. Penetration. Condom. Lubricant. The big A. The *thing.* Top or bottom, Kit was looking forward to it.

"Can we wait until after we get the kitten?" And Kit was a little stunned. He'd forgotten all about the kitten, and his expression showed it.

The face Jesse turned toward him was tragic. "You said we were going to get a kitten—you're not going to go back on that, right? It was a promise!"

Kit blinked and saw a whole new Jesse. He put things together, about Jesse not wanting to visit his mom, and strings of boyfriends, and a slut-bag ex.

"Lots of people have broken promises to you, haven't they, Jesse?" he asked, actually amazed at his own perceptiveness, and Jesse looked away.

"I…I just really wanted to get that kitten. I told Emmy I'd call her and tell her what kind we got."

Kit nodded and sat up, and pulled Jesse closer to kiss his temple. "Absolutely. Adoption day at PetSmart. You shower, I'll cook, you eat, I'll shower. It's a plan.

Jesse's grin returned. "You don't want to shower together?"

Kit looked away and blushed. "I'm, uhm, trying to keep that promise, remember?"

So they showered and ate breakfast instead.

CONCERTS AND FUNERALS

IN THE end, they got two kittens, a brother and a sister, a boy with gray-and-white patches that they named Mal, and a girl with black-and-white patches that they named Zoe. Jesse had approved and helped Kit pick out the bowls and the cat boxes and the collars, and together they made the appointments for shots. They took the kittens home, and Kit had made what was now a very rare stop for takeout. They ate while the kittens played with their toes (and their sweaters and their hair) and they watched old *Firefly* episodes on DVD and tried to introduce the kittens to their namesakes.

The kittens were unimpressed, but the men who already loved them had a good time.

When dinner was cleaned up, Kit told Jesse to call Emmy.

Jesse made Kit stay in the room.

It was hard—even harder because although Jesse's voice was all rainbows and lollipops, his face was all mortal wounds and broken bones. Jesse made it through, though, after a thorough description of black-and-gray patches and pink paws, rough tongues, and animals so thoroughly ensorcelled by their humans that they purred on command.

He finished because Emmy was tired, but before he hung up he said, "Yeah, Emmy. He's the best. Thank you, sweetheart—I'm in good hands. Yeah. I love you too. Night night."

He cried all over Kit then, and there had been no lovemaking that night. Kit didn't mind, not even a little.

They stayed in bed the next morning, though, after a shower and a quick breakfast. Jesse was not a morning person, and Kit made a mental note to buy a coffeemaker, because Kit thought it might help. (It would also have helped if the kittens hadn't spent all night purring on their heads and kneading their hair, but that was beside the point!)

Kit got his second, more thorough education on what two naked male bodies could do together. Kit leaned patiently on his hands and knees and allowed Jesse to invade his body, and the feeling had been… odd, at first. Stretchy and full and vulnerable, even.

And then Jesse had started to move, and it had become tingly, and then it had become pleasant, and then Jesse had nailed his prostate, and it became explosive. Jesse came first, moaning and sweating onto his back, and Kit found he was aroused and unfinished and aching.

"Good," Jesse panted into his shoulder. "You can do it to me now!"

The condom was another first, and Kit frowned as Jesse rolled it on. (Jesse had put his own on as well, and Kit thought it was something he should practice. It looked sort of tricky.)

"I'll get tested," Jesse promised. "And I'm always careful, so it should be good. And then we won't need them. How's that?"

That sounded great, and Kit said so, but inside he was reminded: he had waited thirty years for a good thing, but Jesse's friend Emmy proved that some people didn't even have that long.

Jesse started out on his hands and knees, like Kit had, but Kit frowned some more. "Can we do this face-to-face?" he asked, pretty sure the mechanics would work. "I want to see you."

Jesse turned over then and blushed. "You don't ask much, do you?" His tone was edgy and impatient, and Kit realized something else about his young lover.

"I have to be naked, you have to be," he insisted. Jesse's grin was a little bitter and a little embarrassed, but then Kit took the lubricant and started doing what Jesse had done—squirting it on his fingers (it had been in bed with them, so it was warm) and then thrusting the fingers inside Jesse's bottom.

Jesse's ass came off the bed, and his head threw back and he moaned. "Oh, God... Kit... that's good...but... oh... damn... you have no subtle... *shit*!"

Kit had thrust deep inside, and he'd found it—the walnut under the skin. He'd read about it, and Jesse had brushed against it, and he found he wanted to see what happened when....

Jesse's hands scrabbled on the blankets, and his feet pressed hard into the mattress. "Kit?" he whined, managing to fasten his eyes on Kit's face. His eyes were wide, and his cheeks were flushed, and he looked... eager and begging and soft.

Kit hadn't known his cock would *get* this hard.

"Kit, buddy, is there any way you could... uhm... fuck me hard anytime soon?"

Kit grinned at him and moved his cock into position. For a moment, it looked… threatening. Jesse's entrance, even stretched by Kit's fingers, was still small and vulnerable, but Jesse whined, and Kit placed the flared head of his cock against that tight ring and thrust slowly in.

Jesse's ass clamped down on him tighter than anything he could imagine, and Jesse's body was *so* hot. Kit groaned and pulled back until his cockhead was stretching Jesse again, and Jesse groaned and begged, "Please, dammit, Kit, *please!*" His eyes were half-closed now, and Kit thought it was totally worth it to look at his face. He'd never seen anything as breathtaking as Jesse, abandoned to Kit's body inside his own.

Kit felt a total sense of the moment as he drove his hips forward *hard* and watched Jesse throw his head back and howl. That worked so well that he did it again. And again. And again. He started thrusting harder and faster and made sure that every time he did, he at least brushed that little nerve bundle that Jesse liked so much until Jesse started begging for something very different.

"Let me touch you," he panted, leaning up enough to fondle Kit's stomach. "Want to touch you!"

Kit's technique would go all to hell if he did that, but technique wasn't what Jesse seemed to want. Kit fell forward onto his elbows then and kept moving erratically (he was close, so close, and this new angle was odd, but he was almost there…), and Jesse kissed his neck and stroked his shoulders and whispered wonderful, terrible, obscene things in his ear.

Kit would admit later, while Jesse was lying with his head on Kit's very sweaty shoulder, that it was the dirty talk that did him in. The words were filthy and erotic. In fact, the things Jesse was saying were…. Oh God… the images were *exactly what Kit was doing*! And it was that reality that sent Kit heaving into orgasm, shuddering, groaning, lunging for that impossible peak and free-falling off it with a grunt and a howl and whoop of triumph as he went.

They laughed softly into each other's arms then, and Kit collapsed on the bed and fell out of Jesse so he could pull Jesse right on top of him.

"Kit?" Jesse panted.

"Yeah?"

"You're not a virgin anymore."

"Fucking awesome."

Jesse giggled and kissed the corner of his mouth, and Kit kissed him back. And it really was fucking awesome.

IT WAS hard telling him goodbye that evening. In two days, they had managed to turn themselves into a little family, complete with kittens for babies.

"I can get you tomorrow night," Kit said as they were kissing at the front door, afraid to go outside. "I have to come home and work out and then go visit Ma, but then I can pick you up."

Jesse pouted. He did that sometimes—he'd done it that morning when Kit didn't have oatmeal, and he'd done it at the pet store when Kit had wanted a boy and a girl kitten instead of two boys. It was not the best side of Jesse—and it charmed Kit completely.

"Why can't you come work out with me? The gym is a few blocks from my apartment. I can bring extra clothes—that'll work fine!"

Kit blushed and shook his head. "I, uhm, don't think I want to work out in front of all those people, Jesse."

Jesse sighed and blew out a breath, but he didn't press the point. "Well, how about you follow me home from work, and I can come here and work out with you?"

Oh Jesus. Jesse in the same room with Danny Fit? That would almost be like a threesome. It sounded dangerous—and vaguely icky. Fortunately, that didn't solve the fact that Kit still needed to visit his mother, and Kit said so.

Another sigh, and Kit felt like shit, even though it was the truth. Jesse shook his head. "I swear, it's like you don't want me to meet the guy, you know?"

Kit shrugged and said, "Well, what Danny and I had together is very private," with enough dignity to sound like he was kidding.

But Jesse wasn't stupid. His eyes got big, and he put his hand over his mouth like a little schoolgirl. "Ohmigod! He's your jerk-off buddy!"

Kit wondered if he could will himself to die of a heart attack on the spot. He knew his blood was certainly thundering in his ears enough.

"I… uhm…."

"He is!"

"Well. Uhm…."

Jesse shook his head and chortled some more. "Never mind, baby. You keep, uhm, working out. Anyone who waited for thirty years for the right person to come along gets to have imaginary sex with as many people as he wants!"

Kit could do nothing but stand there with Jesse in his arms and blush. Jesse was Jesse, though—he could laugh like the kid he was, but he picked up on Kit's discomfort after a moment.

"It's okay, Kit—I swear. Every boy has an imaginary stroke buddy—no worries."

A part of Kit got indignant—he objected to hearing Danny referred to as merely a stroke buddy—but most of him got it. Jesse was being supportive. Jesse was being kind.

Kit kissed him, because, dammit, that's what you did when the person who had just made love to you for two days straight tried to tell you that your weirdness was not terminal. Jesse kissed him back and then hurried out to his car.

The next day was surprisingly… normal. Kit and Jesse were good at their jobs, and they'd worked well as a team for a couple of months. Jesse didn't shut Kit's door during lunch and go down on him for a quickie, but he sat and talked to him instead. The companionship, Kit had realized long ago, was very much as important as the sex.

Kit picked him up after visiting his mother that night and got a chance to see Jesse's apartment. He was surprised to find that he did not envy it—Jesse was right. It was a low-rent apartment occupied by four men (two of them straight) who (in Jesse's words) went home to change, fuck, or drink beer. The posters were tacked on the walls, and the beige carpet was appalling. Jesse's room was roughly the size of Kit's hallway, and while Jesse had literally covered the walls with sci-fi posters—many of them cadged from local movie theaters—it didn't seem to have Jesse's warmth. It certainly didn't feel warm enough to keep Kit's Jesse safe.

Kit wondered at the lag time before sleeping with someone and living with them. He wanted Jesse in his home. He wanted him in his bed every night. *What do you know? You were a virgin seventy-two hours ago!*

I know that I love him. I know I don't want anyone else—not even Danny Fit.

Kit took Jesse home that night and proved it.

They developed a pattern, a system, and it worked. Jesse was at Kit's house more nights than not, and that was good with both of them. Kit always managed to get his Danny Fit workout in—sometimes when Jesse was at the gym, and sometimes when he was in the living room, reading or playing with the kittens. (Mal, it turned out, was a terrible troublemaker. Zoe was stoic and responsible and occasionally ate Mal's head to keep him in line.)

Kit realized that he hadn't been turned on by Danny Fit since Jesse first kissed him. That kiss had been his real-life switch—once Jesse was activated, Danny Fit became just another fitness guru, putting Kit's body through some twisty-puffy cardio-strength pain.

They went and got a Christmas tree—a small one, so they could put it up on a bookshelf and the kittens wouldn't wreak havoc with it. Jesse had never had a tree—he said something about his mom always promising and never delivering and left it at that. Kit took him to Target, and they picked out ornaments—Jesse made sure they matched Kit's décor.

And then Kit took his courage in both hands and called his mother. "Ma, we've got a Christmas tree. Come see it."

"Who's we?"

"Me and my boyfriend. You have to be nice to him, or I'm taking you home."

"I'll be Mary-fucking-Sunshine. Don't gross me out or anything. You two fags neck, and I'm out of there."

The words were harsh, but she actually managed a pair of jeans and a Christmas sweater to meet Jesse. She brought some smoke-flavored cookies, and Jesse ate one politely, and she played with the kittens for half an hour while bitching about the neighbors behind her and how their goddamned Christmas lights would flash to music until eight o'clock at night.

Kit considered the visit a success—especially when Jesse stopped at the drugstore the next day and bought a box of nicotine patches.

"Anything inspire that?" Kit asked innocently, and Jesse shuddered.

"I have seen my future, and it's wearing a reindeer sweater and espadrilles," he said back, and Kit nodded seriously. He was very conscientious about supporting Jesse's efforts after that, and two weeks before Christmas, Jesse was proud to announce he was patch free.

Three days later, they got a call from Emmy's parents, and Jesse cried all night. Kit called up the office and told the girl in personnel that neither of them would be at work until after Christmas. Jesse listened to him take charge with liquid eyes and lashes spiked with tears.

"What if I can't make rent?" he asked, his voice clogged and listless.

"What's wrong with living here?" Kit said, trying to keep it light. Jesse sobbed on him again without answering, and Kit wasn't sure if that was a yes or a no.

The funeral was two days later, and they drove up together, listening to Jesse's alternative rock music, which Kit had never really heard before.

They had just passed Auburn when Jesse started to talk, seemingly at random.

"You're going to meet my mom—she'll be there. She'll have my little brother with her. See, she never kept promises. Like, she'd always promise to have a tree, or that the next boyfriend or husband wasn't going to suck and hit on me or Jakey, or that her next job would last longer than it would take for welfare to cancel the check. So, you tell me that you want me to move in, and that's a promise. You can't just say that because it's easy. You've got a home, Kit. A real home. You want me to be a part of that, I'm going to take it serious, and I don't know how serious you can be when we've only been together for a month, you know?"

Kit opened his mouth to say he was serious, and Jesse cast him a sideways glance over the steering wheel. "Man, you still have a crush on Danny Fit—how serious can you be?"

Kit didn't want to argue with him, but short of burning all the guy's DVDs, he didn't know what else to do.

The funeral was… was sad. A child had died in a small community—most of the town turned out to the little roughhewn funeral home off the main drag of Donner Pass. When the service was over, Jesse grabbed Kit's hand and tried to drag him out before anyone could see him, but a woman—spit-whip thin with Jesse's sharp cheekbones and a mouth as sour as Kit's mother's, came up to them, a sulky boy in her wake.

"Hi, Mom," Jesse said weakly. Kit put his hand in the small of Jesse's back and was proud when his back straightened. Jesse looked up, and a real smile thawed the pinched expression around his eyes. "Hi, Jakey."

Jakey smiled back, and both of them looked unhappily at their mother.

"You coming for Christmas?" the woman asked, and Jesse shook his head.

"I'm staying with Kit."

Jakey gave him a real smile then. "Can I come with you?" he asked eagerly, and Kit was opening his mouth to say, "Christ yes!" just to make Jesse smile again when Jesse's mom sneered and shook her head.

"Come along, Jakey—we'll have a real nice Christmas at our place this year. I promise."

Jakey cast a forlorn look over his shoulder, and Jesse held up his hand, thumb and forefinger extended in the universal "call me" gesture. The two of them disappeared into the crowd, and Jesse said it was time to leave.

They went so Jesse could embrace Emmy's parents and hug his ex—an extremely handsome, fit young man with beautiful blue eyes, who looked so thoroughly devastated that Kit couldn't even think about him being Jesse's ex and could only hope the poor man's heart healed sometime soon. After Jesse's murmured promises to call, he grabbed Kit's hand and dodged people who seemed to want to talk to him, and they slipped out the back.

"You don't want to stay longer?" Kit asked cautiously as they pulled out of the parking lot.

"That's my past," Jesse said resolutely. "Jake and Emmy were the best parts about it." Kit was driving back, but he could still see Jesse's chin tremble. Maybe when things didn't seem to hurt so much, Jesse would go back there. Maybe he would get his little brother out of a home that obviously hurt to live in. But right now, all Kit really cared about was that Jesse was still hurt, and Kit needed to find some way to convince him that Kit could keep a promise, new lover or not.

"Jesse...." Kit reached out and took Jesse's hand, keeping his eyes on the road.

Jesse didn't say anything back, but he clung to that hand until Kit needed it to drive. Randomly, Kit remembered that he'd asked Jesse if he wanted to go to the soup kitchen Christmas morning. Jesse had flushed and looked away and said it sounded too much like the community Christmas breakfast at the Elks Lodge that had been meant for the poorer families in the community. "We were there a couple of times," he said through a tight mouth, and Kit resolved to go alone on another day.

Then Kit remembered that moment in November, when Jesse seemed wondrous and perfect, and unattainable. That bony hand, tight and uncomfortable, was so much more important than the imaginary Jesse that Kit couldn't figure out how he'd had the courage to love at all with only the illusion to hope for.

They went home—Kit's home, but it was becoming Jesse's too—and sat on the couch sideways, Jesse pulled back into Kit's body, and played with the kittens and didn't speak for a long time.

THREE DAYS later, Kit spotted the announcement on a flier in the newspaper.

"Look!" he said, trying not to sound like a schoolgirl. "Danny Fit is going to be in town!"

Jesse looked over his shoulder and smacked Kit in the arm. "Yeah, but you can't go—it's in two days!" Kit looked and sighed. He'd bought tickets for the Trans-Siberian Orchestra that night—he'd never been. In fact, until Jesse, he never would have had the courage to go, but they'd been looking forward to it for two weeks.

Kit looked back at the flier. "But it's only downtown—and he'll be done by two o'clock. I can get here in time to get ready—totally easy."

"Right," Jesse snapped, abruptly angry. "Yeah—you do that. You go ahead and risk plans you've had with me for weeks so you can go meet your imaginary crush. Peachy. I'll meet you there—I'm going home."

It was late afternoon—they'd been planning on dinner and a movie.

"Jesse!" Kit stood up away from the computer. "Wait a minute! You said this was no big deal! 'Stroke off to who you want to', remember?"

"Well yeah!" Jesse snapped. "But look at you—you find out he's, you know, real, and you can meet him, and you slobber all over yourself to go shake the guy's hand. It's like, I'm what? Second choice? You really wanted Danny Fit, but you ended up with me? Fucking awesome!"

"Fucking wrong!" Kit snapped back. He thought with wonder, *Oh—this is a fight. Now I know. It sucks. I'll try not to do this often.* "I really wanted you...." His voice broke, just that suddenly, because he'd never said this. "I *really* wanted you. And you were so... so beautiful, so kind, and it just broke my heart. And I thought that getting you would be the one thing that never would happen. So I got the workout stuff, and I felt so pathetic, like here I was, trying to make myself perfect so I could get you…."

"I'm not perfect!" Jesse looked appalled, and Kit had to stop him, or he'd get hysterical about the wrong thing.

"I *know* that! You're better than perfect. You're you. You *never* hang your jacket up, I have to beg you to do the dishes, and your car is almost as disgusting on the inside as your roommate's refrigerator. I don't care. I *love* the real you! But if I hadn't been stroking off to Danny Fit, I never would have had the courage to… to do *any* of it. To move out, to ask a friend to the movies, to… to…." Kit's face softened, and he tried not to sound maudlin. "To let you kiss me. To open the door and hold you when you needed it. You went back home and said, 'I'm going to put my past behind me' and walked away. I think part of that was a mistake, because any idiot can see you miss your little brother like crazy, but not all of it. Don't you see? Danny Fit is the only past I've got. I want to say hello to the human so I can say goodbye to the fantasy. Is that so goddamned bad?"

There was silence between them, and Jesse fidgeted in the middle of it. It was the first time in a while that Kit was reminded of how very young he was.

"I'll clean my car," Jesse muttered, and Kit tried not to laugh.

"I could give a damn about your car. I want your trust."

Jesse's head snapped up. "I trust you…."

He was so transparent—but Kit wasn't going to quibble. "Then let me go visit my pathetic fantasy ex-boyfriend, Jesse. I promise—I'll come back to you."

God, those brown eyes were expressive. The hope in them was awful—as though it had been Jesse who had been holding back hope the entire time. "I'll hold you to that," he said, and smiled as he moved into Kit's arms, but his voice was as sober as a child's funeral.

Kit woke up early the day of the concert and dressed while Jesse was still in bed. He looked… vulnerable in Kit's bed, that honey-colored hair in disarray, his bee-stung mouth all swollen with kisses. He'd gotten his HIV test the week before, clear as expected, and since it had been three months since Jesse had been with anybody, they'd gotten to have sex without the condoms.

It had been good—really good—but the best part had been that Jesse had felt safe in Kit's arms, safe with Kit's body. Kit's stomach was getting flatter, and his biceps and shoulders were becoming more muscular and less bulky, but mostly Kit was starting to think that the wonder of his body was that Jesse sought shelter in it like an unanchored boat in a harbor.

Being needed was a wonderful thing. Kit wouldn't trade it in for all the Danny Fits in the world.

Kit started the coffee maker and left Jesse a note: *Had some errands to run. Open the presents under the tree in blue paper. I'll be back by two.*

The boxes in blue paper had a coat and gloves and a hat—there had been a cold snap, and Sacramento had suffered temperatures in the thirties for the past week. All Jesse had was his denim jacket and hooded sweatshirt, and it just wasn't enough.

Kit took care of his errands in time to get to the bookstore a little early, but it didn't matter: the line was still really long. Kit grabbed the book on nutrition that Danny was selling and leafed patiently through it, thinking the recipes sounded good but that he'd have to get Jesse to look at it to see there weren't any pictures of Danny besides the one on the front.

The crowd was not all gay men, Kit was happy to see—there were plenty of pretty, plump, engaging women who seemed to find Danny Fit's warmth and style appealing. He wasn't sure why, but for some reason, this made him feel much less perverted about his celebrity obsession. Kit watched Danny eagerly through the crowd so he could look for clues as to who he really was when he wasn't the uber-positive workout buddy.

He seemed nice enough.

He smiled charmingly at people when they handed him their books, and cracked jokes with them if they looked nervous. A slightly younger man was sitting next to him, making sure he had water and being generally attentive. Kit, who had to admit he probably had the worst gaydar of any gay man in history, had no doubt that they were lovers.

When it was finally Kit's turn, he found that he stammered, because what he wanted to say was so maudlin, so corny, and so awfully true.

"You probably hear this from about a thousand people," he said, feeling inept and dumb, "but seriously—man, you really helped me get my act together."

The handsome man with the toffee-colored hair looked up and gave Kit a tired but sincere smile. Kit realized that he was working—it was a job he loved, but he was tired too.

"That's good to hear!" Danny said, making his voice warm and encouraging with an obvious effort. Kit was suddenly glad for the younger lover—Danny would have someone to go home to, someone to take care of him. "That's awesome—how long have you been working out?"

Kit shrugged, embarrassed. "Only about six weeks. But I'm sort of committed now." *In a lot of ways, actually.*

Danny nodded, and something about Kit's quiet enthusiasm seemed to calm down the ragged edges in the sports superstar, and his next smile was less tired and more sincere. "Well good. The commitment is all you can hope for, you know? People fall off the wagon all the time, but if they've got a goal in mind, then I have faith that they can do it. Who do you want me to make this out to?"

Kit's smile suddenly lost all hints of self-consciousness. "Could you make it out to my boyfriend Jesse?" He gave Danny an inscription, and Danny blinked and then laughed.

"I'm sure there's a story there somewhere," he said with an honest grin.

Kit nodded. "Yeah—but right now I have to go give Jesse the book so it ends happy." He met Danny's extended hand and shook it firmly, a meeting of equals. "It's been an honor to meet you."

"Likewise. Thanks for letting me into your life."

His hand was warm and firm, and his tanned fingers were hard-boned and soft-skinned with moisturizer, and Kit was proud to shake hands with the man.

But that was all.

When he got home, Jesse was sitting outside. He'd been raking leaves (Kit's yard didn't have a tree, but the yard next door had a fruitless mulberry, and the yellow leaves were everywhere) and the lawn was now clear of them, and there were big full black bags in Kit's green-waste can by the garage.

Jesse was wearing his hat and his gloves in the chilly December light, and he was drinking what Kit assumed was coffee, but when he got closer and could smell it, he could see that Jesse had made hot chocolate and poured coffee in it.

He sat down next to his lover, not minding that the concrete of the porch was cold as hell, and took the mug from him for a drink. Without a word, he handed Jesse the bag in his hand.

"What's this?" Jesse asked, his voice not as hostile as his expression had been when Kit had pulled up.

"Presents," Kit said between blissful sips of the chocolate coffee.

The sulky turn of Jesse's mouth relaxed a little more. "You already gave me presents. It's not even Christmas yet."

Kit grinned at him and tweaked the brim of the forest-green skater's beanie that Jesse was wearing. It matched the gloves. Green may not have been an average color, but it looked so nice with Jesse's coloring, and Kit was besotted enough to see it on him.

"You like?"

Jesse's smile was sweet and very, very soft. "I like that you're back on time."

"Good! Now open your presents!"

Jesse looked at him dubiously, then reached into the bag and grimaced. "The book? Seriously? You got me the Danny Fit book?"

Kit grinned. "Now read the inscription."

Jesse's eyes narrowed, and then he laughed a little, as though he was embarrassed. "*Jesse, Kit says you have nothing to worry about. Danny'.*" Jesse kept giggling and aimed those good-natured, narrowed eyes at Kit. "You didn't."

"I did."

"What'd he say?"

"He said there was a story in there, and I said yeah, but I had to get home and give you the book so it would end happy." Kit was practically dancing as he sat, he was so pleased with himself—and so nervous, too, because the book wasn't the only thing in the bag.

Jesse leaned forward finally and kissed him on the mouth, and Kit opened for the kiss, and they scooted closer to each other to share some body heat on the chilly-assed porch. Kit pulled back and nodded to the bag. "There's more in there! Look!"

The next item Jesse pulled out made him laugh helplessly. "A membership card to my gym?"

Kit nodded, still bouncing as he sat. "Uh-huh. We can go together now. You know, because...." He flushed and looked away. "Because, well, we'll be together, so I can't look that bad, right?"

Jesse kissed him again and pulled back with dancing eyes. "Are you saying I make you look good?"

Kit's grin was blinding. "Yup! Absolutely. Best workout buddy ever!"

Jesse chortled some more and then looked surprised when Kit said, "But there's more!" Jesse dug in the bag for a minute, because this next item was smaller, and when he pulled it out, he frowned.

"It's a key."

Kit nodded, absolutely sober now. "It's your key."

"My key?" There could be a lot of ambiguity here, Kit knew, but he'd meant it that way.

"It's a promise," Kit said earnestly. "And proof, you know?"

"A promise of what?" Jesse searched Kit's face, his eyes very bright, and Kit tried very hard not to screw this up.

"A promise that whenever you're willing to take me up on the offer, it will be there." Jesse sucked in a sharp breath, and Kit kept talking. "You see? The key is yours. You can come by anytime. It's like the place is yours. But better, because if, you know, one day, you want to come in and bring your stuff, you can do that too. But it's a promise that it's open to you, you know?"

Jesse looked at the key in his palm like he was afraid to touch it. "Jesus, Kit. What if I fuck this up?"

Kit remembered a tired man giving some good advice. "People fall off from good intentions all the time, Jesse. What matters right now is the commitment. This is my commitment, you know? You and me, we're going to be real. All we have to do is commit that it's real. It's something. If we have that as a goal, we should be good, you think?"

Jesse's hand started shaking, and Kit's came up to cover it, closing his fingers on the key. He let out a big sigh of relief when Jesse's hand clenched, and he cupped his other hand over it, like it was something precious.

"We're good," Jesse said through a rough throat. He slipped the key in his pocket and wiped the still shaking hand over his cheeks, and then took the coffee from Kit and set it down on the porch.

Then he threw himself into Kit's arms and held on so tight, Kit thought maybe this moment would freeze in time, like their asses were about to freeze to the concrete porch. They held each other as long as they could, and then a moment longer, and when they backed off, Jesse was all dimples and bright, bright eyes.

"You dork! How are you supposed to impress me on Christmas if you give me all of this today?"

Kit grinned back and stood up, giving Jesse a hand up, too, and snagging the coffee mug to go inside. "Are you kidding? We're spending Christmas in bed!"

Jesse practically choked on his own snicker. "You think you've got that much stamina?"

Kit opened the door and pulled Jesse through. Their home echoed with their footsteps and their laughter, and with the two kittens who came running with bells on their collars to greet them.

"Of course I do! I've been working out!"

Jesse was still chortling as the door closed behind them.

Puppy, Car, and Snow

AMY LANE

CHAPTER 1
FIRST ROUND

"HEY, RYAN, give me your hand."

Ryan made sure his aching foot and calf were firmly anchored on the brake and the car was completely stopped before he looked over at his boyfriend, trying not to yawn. Five hours. They'd been trying to get up the hill to Donner Summit for five hours. God—were they the only people who could put chains on before it got critical?

The smell of exhaust was making him queasy; he'd started up and killed the engine about six times to conserve gas while they were at a standstill; and Blitzkrieg, the world's most massive not-poodle, had needed to be walked on the side of the road three times. She'd also eaten some of Ryan's luggage. Ryan didn't want to look. It was a new set, and it was just too painful.

The look he shot Scotty was annoyed at the world at large.

Scott grinned back.

Scotty Davidovich had high Russian cheekbones and longish, if carefully cut, hair. (It was black and yellow this month—dyed specially, Ryan thought, to piss off Ryan's mother at the holidays. It was a worthy endeavor. Ryan approved.) He also had blue-gray eyes with dark lashes that glinted wickedly when he looked sideways and full, smiling lips that looked like sex in a shot glass when he licked them and parted them just so. He was Ryan's first male lover, and the love of Ryan's life.

And right now, in the car, the look he was shooting Ryan was pure, one-hundred-percent, unadulterated, give-it-to-me-baby, fuck-me-without-mercy-in-front-of-the-dog sin.

That look was so incongruous with the little Honda stuck in traffic on the way up to visit Ryan's parents for Christmas that Ryan had to look twice.

He put the car in park and turned off the ignition just in time for Scott to grab his hand from the keys and put it under the blanket he'd thrown on his lap the last time they'd turned the car off.

Ryan's eyes got so big the chilled air from the windows dried them out. He blinked rapidly and squeezed, listening to Scotty's grateful "Ah-ah-ah… ooooooohhh…" with a little bit of shock.

"Scotty, is that your…?" Stupid question. He squeezed Scotty's cock—stiff and warm and peeking out over Scott's underwear, yet still under the warm fuzzy blanket. Scott whined a little and bucked his hips and thrust deeper into Ryan's hand.

Ryan's heart started roaring in his ears, and he took a rabbity little look around their vehicular neighborhood to make sure no one was watching him give Scotty a hand job in the front of the car.

People in front of him in the big SUV? Little kids apparently enthralled by a new Dreamworks film featuring a fifty-foot woman with a nice rack. Check. Pouty teenage girl with iPod to the left of him, asleep against a pillow on the window? Check. People behind him still blocked by the luggage sharing the back seat with Blitzkrieg? Check. Rowdy frat boys on Scotty's side surreptitiously passing a joint from person to person in the traffic? Check.

Operation Hand Job was a go!

Ryan loved the feeling of Scotty's prick in his hand. It was hot, and the skin was soft, and the veins throbbed against Ryan's palm. He watched Scott's face as he stroked, loving the way Scotty threw his head against the headrest and started moaning softly in complete abandon. Traffic? Scotty didn't see no stinking traffic; all he knew was that Ryan was jacking him off, rubbing his pre-come over his cock-head and murmuring hot things into the cold space of the car.

"You like that?"

"Mmmm…. Yeah…."

"Want it harder?"

"Ohhh… please, Ryan!"

"Harder?"

"God yes!"

Ryan let his grip slack to nothing, and Scotty's cry of denial was almost a howl of pain.

"Ry! Please, Ry… please… lemme come… I wanna come… God… please…."

His hands were on the armrests, holding them tightly, and Ryan recognized the game; Scotty wouldn't touch himself right now, because that was Ryan's job.

Ryan worked hard to be good at his job. He tip-toed his fingers up Scotty's slender length, listening to the hitch in Scott's breath tell him that his teasing was just right. When he got to the tip, he rubbed his fingers in the pre-come that was drooling out of the slit. Scott whimpered, and Ryan used two fingers and two fingers only to slick Scotty up. He knew that the air leaking in under the blanket would serve to titillate Scott even more.

Scott wasn't gibbering anymore. All of his concentration was on keeping his ass locked in his seat and his hands clenched on the armrests. So when he turned to Ryan with his eyes large and pupils dilated, his hips squirming and his full lips parted in mute appeal, Ryan knew he was about at the end of his rope.

"Please?" he murmured. "Please, Ry? Please finish me off?"

Ryan took one more look around and, after twisting his body in the unforgiving space of the car, dropped his head, grateful when Scotty pulled the blanket back and then covered him up with it. In the warm cocoon of come-scented dark, he fumbled for a minute, then found Scotty's cock with his mouth and swallowed him down.

Scotty grunted, the sound reverberating against Ryan's ear, and then Ryan grunted, because after three years together he loved this, loved taking Scotty's cock into his mouth and sucking hard, and loved the sounds that Scotty made when clenching his hands in Ryan's hair and bucking up, unashamed, completely lost in Ryan's mouth on his body, in being tended to and waited on and loved.

Scotty groaned, the sound starting in his toes, vibrating in his thighs as they sat under Ryan's cheek, and bouncing around his stomach for a while, and then Ryan was too busy swallowing, swallowing, not letting himself gag on the taste even a little, or it would make him spit up and Scotty would need to change his pants.

Scotty stopped coming, and there was quiet then under the fuzzy blanket as Scotty rubbed his hands on Ryan's head and Ryan let Scotty's cock fall out of his mouth and pulled back far enough to breathe.

Then Scotty's whole body stiffened. "Oh shit, Ry! There's a news camera three cars up. They're interviewing people. Sit up, quick, before they spot us!"

Ryan sat up so suddenly the blanket came up, and then there was a frantic scrabble as Scotty pulled his loosest pair of jeans up and did the fly and Ryan wiped his face on the edge of the blanket while Scotty was using it to cover his crotch, just in case.

Ryan let go of the blanket, and Scotty pulled him forward for a kiss that suddenly stopped time and panic and all sorts of things, including Ryan's heart. When Scott pulled back, his smile was gentle, even though his eyes were still dancing wickedly.

"Thanks for helping me get my perv on," he said, that mobile mouth stretched into a smile.

"God, I love you!" Ryan blurted, because there was one person in the world who could have convinced Ryan to commit vehicular fellatio in a traffic jam.

Scott's smile faded, and his hand came up to cup Ryan's cheek and rub his lips with a tender thumb. "The news crew is about to knock on our window, Ry. Don't make me get all sloppy stupid right now, 'kay?"

Ryan laughed and then almost jumped out of his jeans at the knock on the window. He clicked the keys, pressed the button, and turned around and flinched back from the blast of cold air and the fucking camera that damned near pushed its way into the car.

"Hi, I'm Suze Bachman from FOX News. So, what brings you up the hill in the middle of the crush?" Her hair was blonde and stiff under the fashionably soft red hat, her teeth were brightly veneered, and her voice was sort of scritchy-bright, and Blitzkrieg gave a muffled "ooof?" from the back seat. Ryan smiled and tried to sound like a lawyer and not a sexual deviant.

"Hi, Suze. We're just going up to visit my parents for the holidays. I got caught up in work, and we left a little late. We were trying to beat the rush."

"So, you and your roommate are staying in the family cabin for Christmas. That's sweet." She didn't trip over "roommate," and he didn't see a reason to correct her—until she put her manicured hand on his shoulder through the window. He flinched back and Blitzkrieg, being the good guard dog she was, sensed the tension, skipped the "ooofing," and let out a for-real bark.

Scott and Ryan both cringed as the entire car shook until the windows rattled. Suddenly, Blitzy wasn't just a hidden monster in the luggage. She was a giant, black, curly head with ears long enough to fly, thrusting her narrow muzzle between the car seat and the window and biting like Suze Bachman was a new flavor of Alpo and she was gonna get her some of that.

Suze gave a little yelp and tripped backwards, and Scotty leaned over Ryan's lap and called out, "Sorry about that. She's jealous of strangers." Ryan shot him a droll look that Scotty returned blandly, and then they both smiled at the camera and waved when Suze and her camera man took the "How Miserable Are These People In Traffic" show down to the next car in line.

Ryan rolled up the window, and he and Scott looked at each other and giggled like the stoned frat boys in the next car. (And why weren't they getting interviewed for the six o'clock news, that's what Ryan wanted to know!) Blitzkrieg whined, and Scotty pulled her forward, rubbing those fantastically silky ears and crooning, "Good dog! Who's the bestest good girl in the world, oh yes! Driving off that nasty, mean reporter who wanted your other daddy's body! Good girl!"

Ryan rolled his eyes. "She was just being annoyingly friendly—no lust needed." But he joined Scott and petted the dog, because she was warm and she liked to lick their faces, and because she was their baby and had been since Scott had brought her home from the grocery store six months earlier and said, "Isn't she a sweetheart? She's supposed to be a toy poodle, and she was free!"

They'd learned a couple of things since that day in the summer. Thing the first: the dog wasn't a toy poodle. She was maybe a cross between a giant poodle and a Clydesdale horse. Thing the second: They both loved the rapidly growing kibble disposal unit with an almost frightening intensity. Thing the third: There was no such thing as a free dog.

It was a thing Ryan had known when he put her in the backseat with the new luggage and the reason he could forgive her for slobbering all over his best suit right after he'd had it cleaned. It was the reason he'd risked his credit for a little house in the suburbs and the reason for the exclusive "Yes, I make house calls because your idiot canine ate garbage with a chaser of shoes" veterinarian, and generally one of life's big lessons that didn't hurt at all when Blitzy was licking your face after a shit day at work.

And now, as Ryan's hands tangled with Scott's in the curly tornado of Blitzkrieg's fur, he realized that the dog might not be free, but that didn't mean she didn't pay you back.

"Yes," Ryan said softly, squeezing Scott's hand. "The dog saved me from the predatory heterosexual female who was horning in on your turf. Are you going to give her a treat now?"

Scotty flushed. "Sorry, Ry. It's not the female that got me, really. You know that, right?"

Ryan knew. Scott usually wasn't jealous at all—mostly because he kept saying that Ryan was the most trustworthy man he'd ever met. But usually they weren't going to meet Ryan's family.

"Look," Ryan said reluctantly. "If you really don't want to go, we can always take the next overpass and turn around."

Scott rolled his pretty gray eyes. "For another five hours of traffic? No. We have to visit with them eventually. I mean, they do love you."

And it was true. They did love Ryan. It was Scott they weren't so crazy about, and not because he was the reason their son came out of the closet, either.

Ryan sighed, and then flashed a grin at Scott. "Just shows they're biased—doesn't mean they're smart."

"Yeah? How smart are they going to have to be to figure out that we were fooling around right before that news camera showed up?"

Ryan shrugged. "It wasn't like it was written on our faces. Besides, that Suze person didn't even see it, and she had to have read the vanity plates." SCTSBOI was what the plate actually said. "Scotty's Boi-Toi" was what the plate frame around the plate said. Scott had bought them for Ryan's Christmas present the year before, and Ryan loved them.

Scott gave Ryan a purely male shove on the arm. "For all she knew, you were Scott, and the plates were about the car! And as for written on our faces...." Scott finished the sentence by pulling his hand up to Ryan's lips and rubbing his thumb across the bottom.

Ryan looked in the rearview mirror and groaned. He'd wiped off his mouth, but his lips were both swollen and red. He'd been doing something with his mouth, that was for sure.

"Oh shit," he mumbled. "God. I do. I look like I've been blowing someone with a cock the size of the Chrysler building."

Scott smirked. "Well, I don't like to brag...."

Ryan was aware that the cars around them were starting up in preparation to move, and he did the same. But no one was moving quite yet, so he turned around and smiled gently at the man he was pretty sure he couldn't live without. "It's not bragging, sweetheart, it's the truth. Besides, what are the odds that'll actually show up on the news and my folks will see it? Best way to kill time in traffic ever."

Scott's smirk softened, became the rather vulnerable smile that Scott saved for Ryan and Ryan only, and then the car in front of them moved and it was time to move on.

CHAPTER 2
WELCOME TO THE FAMILY

WHATEVER HAD been going on in the front of the traffic jam, it was gone by the time Ryan and Scott got there, and the next three hours went smoothly—or as smoothly as they could go when Ryan white-knuckled it all the way.

Scott had a way of respecting his stress, though. He always had. He'd respected Ryan's stress when he'd been working all of the long hours for the law firm a year and a half before, and that right there was exactly why Ryan had risked his job by insisting that his firm cut his business trips in half. It had hurt—he didn't pretend it wouldn't—and he might never make partner in his law firm, ever, but he'd decided he didn't give a shit. He and Scotty had made do. Scotty's quick mind had formed an e-business, and on weekends they worked together to get it off the ground. Ryan had realized that the time spent with Scotty—talking, laughing, working toward a common goal—that wasn't anything he could get with boundless ambition. That was something he could only get with Scott. It was his second real lesson that the perfect vision a person has of life can't compensate for the thousands of perfect moments a person has when he's not planning it.

His first real lesson was falling in love with a man in a bathroom when he'd thought he was straight.

So Scott was good at respecting his stress inside the car, but it was freezing on the side of the road, so Ryan couldn't exactly pull over and de-stress at the moment. He had to keep going until he found the little cabin that his parents kept for family holidays so that he and Scott could get the fuck out of this godforsaken car. Scotty knew this—he just kept a quiet conversation going, the kind that could lapse at any time, while Ryan kept the car on the road and his eyes on the snow-laden dark.

When the car finally found the snow-buried road and sailed into the driveway with a controlled fishtail, Ryan killed the engine and thumped his head against the steering wheel in relief. Scott's hand came up and rubbed the big knot between his shoulders, and Ryan whimpered from the touch.

"We're here," he muttered, and Scott's soothing hand just kept rubbing. "You did great, baby. I didn't fear for my life once."

Ryan chuffed out a little breath. "You were awesome. You really were. I'm sorry I was such an intense asshole, but I probably would have skidded off the road just to break the tension if you hadn't been so awesome."

Scott leaned his head on Ryan's shoulder and sighed. "Well, I guess there goes the idea about the leaving if things get shitty." He was right; the roads were going to be blocked by morning, and Ryan looked at him unhappily. He hadn't complained—not once, even when Ryan had tentatively broached the idea of them spending the holidays at Ryan's parents' cabin—but just the fact that he said it now meant that he was having doubts. Ryan had a plan, though, the sort of grand, romantic plan that would work in all of the super-sappy movies Ryan had ever seen, but he wasn't sure would work this time in front of his family. He was hoping, though. He really wanted to make that grand gesture for Scotty, if for no other reason than to make time with Ryan's family a little less of a pain in the ass.

Ryan looked down at his lover's fancy hair and the artificially tanned skin and wondered if anyone but him saw how very much Scott wanted to be liked.

"If things get really shitty," Ryan said gently, wrapping his arm around Scott's back and abandoning all of his grand gesture plans in one offer, "then we can come out here. We'll bring blankets, and I'll run inside and get a space heater and run you hot food and hot toddies, and we'll just cocoon out here for six days and stay completely shitfaced until this is over. How's that?"

Scott's grin was pure joy. "For a guy who'd do that for me, the least I could do is face the dragon lady." And then Blitzkrieg woke up and started panting at them, and they both separated and sighed.

"I'll get the bags, and you get the dog," Ryan said, the better to spare Scott the first introduction with his mother, and Scott nodded gratefully.

"I'll take her around back so she can take a dump and no one will step on it until it freezes, okay?"

Ryan laughed—sue him. The idea of frozen dog crap really was funny. "Have her put it next to a tree so none of the kids will pick it up in a snowball fight, okay?"

Scotty brightened. Ryan's family chafed Scott raw on a number of levels, Yvonne and Walter included, but geez, did Scotty adore their four children. "I almost forgot they were here. I'll make it quick!" And with that, he put on his parka and opened the door, snapping Blitzy's lead on almost before the dog knew it was time to go out for walkies.

Ryan decided to schlep all of the luggage up to the porch before knocking on the door, which gave him time to stretch out his arms and legs that were cramped and sore from the drive and really gave him time to contemplate the difficult, unfortunate relationship between the family who had always loved him and the beautiful, amazing, perfect Scotty Davidovich.

RYAN AND Scott had met three years before at a party. Ryan had been dating a girl at the time, and Scott had attended the party with another man, but Ryan had dodged into a bathroom to take a leak and Scott had been there, hiding from a predatory office secretary with scary-tall high heels and something of a psychotic smile. She'd also had an amazing rack—and the fact that Ryan had neither noticed nor appreciated this should have clued him in to what happened next.

Scott had stepped out from behind the shower curtain and made one flirty comment about Ryan's (impressive) equipment, and Ryan's breath had caught. They'd met eyes then, and suddenly—

Just that. Suddenly. Suddenly Ryan's life made sense. Suddenly he knew why his perfectly acceptable girlfriend wasn't doing anything for him, and why his whole driven life in search of the perfect career hadn't been doing anything for him either. It turned out Ryan wasn't interested in women as a whole.

After one night with Scott, he wasn't interested in men as a whole either. He was mostly just interested in Scott.

And Scotty—funny, irreverent, irrepressible Scotty—had returned that interest with his whole heart.

Unlike Ryan, Scott had known he was gay—and had been enjoying the hell out of his gayness and any man who flirted back—for pretty much his entire life. Ryan had been so in love with him after that first night he could hardly believe Scott wanted him back. Scott told Ryan that he had been so in love with Ryan after that first night he couldn't even imagine a world in which Ryan wouldn't want him. He said that when he tried, the sun went black. Ryan swore that there would never be a time when he made Scotty's sun go black.

It was a gay fairy tale, unreal, surreal, and bizarre: a man steps into a bathroom and steps out of a closet he never knew he lived in. But it was also Ryan and Scott, their lives, so entangled by now that they hardly knew whose clothes were whose.

Ryan wouldn't have it any other way.

And at first, his parents were thrilled for him. He'd been lucky; he still thought so. There had been no unhappiness over Ryan's sexuality—there had mostly been happiness that he had found someone who made him happy. And then Ryan's parents had actually met Scott, and the fairy tale had met its first dragon.

Ryan's mother, Taylor Connors, was an interior decorator who had built her business from the ground up. In a crap economy, Taylor's business was thriving; she'd just opened another branch in Los Angeles, and Ryan's sister and her husband both ran it. Yvonne was winning awards and being featured in *Better Homes & Gardens*, and Walter had just won some sort of prestigious humanitarian thing for his landscaping, and generally?

They were just reeking with the perfection of ambition made real.

And Ryan's father was a liberal circuit court judge.

So Ryan's sexuality? Not such a big thing.

Scotty's mercurial, butterfly mind?

That was what had caused the first visit from Ryan's parents to chill to sub-frozen-tundra in a matter of three days.

"So nice to meet you, Scott. Ryan's told us a lot about you!" Ryan's father, Gordon, was always hearty and warm, just like his handshake. Ryan liked that about him—he always had.

"He has not, however, told us what you do," was spoken over Taylor's narrow-framed glasses, like a school librarian. And that was Ryan's mother, like a snowball on a campfire.

Scotty's open, happy smile never wavered. "Mostly, I just go to school and try to figure out what it is I want to do," he said, and invited them both to laugh with his wicked eyes alone.

Ryan's father had laughed.

Ryan's mother had not.

Let the games begin.

So when he hadn't been squinting into the dark, watching the snowflakes dart around like ice-moths, he'd been rehearsing his lines in his head, like he rehearsed a deposition with a witness or a presentation to a judge. He wanted his family to be under no illusions where his loyalties lay, and he never, ever, ever wanted Scott to see the sun turn black.

But he also didn't want to alienate anybody forever, either.

His stomach whined, and not just because he and Scotty had eaten nothing but a bag of Chex Mix for the last eight hours. But that hunger thing also kept him from standing on the stoop too long, either—not that Ryan was ever one for hesitating. Once he had their luggage on the porch, he only paused for a moment, smiling a little when he heard Blitzkrieg barking and Scotty swearing as he ploughed through the snow in the back yard. It was okay—Scotty was here. Ryan had never felt like he needed anyone in his life until he'd turned around and looked into Scott's eyes. But if Scotty was here, all was good.

Ryan knocked on the door and smiled broadly when his father opened it.

"Dad!" The embrace that followed put paid to a lot of family anxiety, and in a moment, Gordon Connors had helped Ryan grab all of the luggage—and the big bags of presents for the kids—and haul them in.

"Where's Scotty?" Gordon asked, and Ryan grinned.

"Out back with Blitzkrieg. She was going totally nuts in the car."

Gordon grinned and looked a little bit like an excited kid himself. Ryan's dad had the same all-American-boy looks that Ryan did, except older. His freckles had mostly faded into tanned skin, and his auburn-brown hair was gray at the sides, but his brown eyes could still crinkle with joy when something made him happy.

Dogs definitely made Ryan's dad happy. Ryan and Scotty had been scrambling to find a place to take Blitzkrieg during the holidays, and it had been Gordon (against Taylor's objections, Ryan was willing to wager) who had suggested bringing the dog with them. Scotty—sensing another ally in an uncertain house—would have wagged his tail if he'd had one.

"I'll go say hi!" Gordon said now. "Your bedroom is the upstairs one in the corner!"

With that, Ryan's dad turned around and trotted outside, leaving Ryan to schlep his bags up the stairs by himself. He didn't mind, really. The upstairs bedroom in the corner of the "cabin" (the house Ryan and Scott were looking to buy had half the square footage and none of the luxury) had a nice view—and no bedroom on either side. Which meant that Ryan and Scott didn't have to be celibate, and that was always a plus.

The living room was dominated by a twelve-foot Christmas tree set back against the window, twinkling with red, silver, and gold lights, ornaments, and tinsel garlands. The television was off, which made Ryan assume the kids had already been put to bed, but Ryan's mother, sister, and brother-in-law were sitting at a card table in the living room, playing dice. Taylor looked up and gave her son a genuine smile.

"Ryan—we were so worried. We're so glad you got here safely, especially after we saw you on the news."

Ryan flushed. "Oh crap! Was that really on the news?"

Walter shot him a disgusted look. "Yeah it was on the news. You looked like you'd been kissing a walrus. Is that all you did for five hours?"

The cabin was snug and cozy, thanks to a propane heater and a gigantic propane tank that Ryan's parents had filled before every winter visit. Taylor's glare at Yvonne's stocky, balding husband lowered the air temperature at least ten degrees. Which was fine, because Ryan was suddenly sweating under his collar.

"We were bored," he said cavalierly, figuring what the hell? That blow-job had been the best part of the trip! "We all have our diversions."

Walter's mouth was open, but Taylor cut him off.

"Walter, could you help Ryan up to the bedroom? It looks like he bought out Toys 'R' Us for your kids—it's the least you could do."

Ryan smiled gratefully at his mom. "Scotty did, actually. I just nodded and said 'sure!'"

Walter stood up heavily and came to grab the biggest bag right out of Ryan's hand. "Wouldn't want you to strain your delicate little wrist," he muttered, and Ryan rolled his eyes and took the bag back.

"Wouldn't want you to strain that stick in your ass," he retorted. "How about getting the bags of presents? They're awkward but not too heavy."

Ryan started up the stairs, happy for the help even if it was Walter, only to be brought short by his mother's voice.

"I hope he didn't spend too much money, Ryan. Since you're not really going anywhere in your company, you can't afford to get too badly into debt."

Walter snorted behind him, and Ryan said, "I just got a raise, Mother, and Scotty's business is booming. Don't worry; we'll spoil who we want to!" and then he took off up the carpeted stairs, taking them two at a time in an effort to get to his room before his mother could reply.

They got up to the room, which had been aired out and had a thick comforter on the freshly made queen-sized bed, and Ryan set the luggage down and took the packages from Walter.

"Thanks for the help," he muttered, and Walter rolled his eyes.

"I'm not a complete douchebag," he snapped, and Ryan sighed.

"Only sometimes."

"Yeah, well, my family wouldn't be all sweet about the whole fag thing, you know?"

Yes. Ryan was well aware that had he been born to Walter's family, he would have had, in Walter's words, "The straight beaten back into him." But Ryan had to spend six days in a cabin with this guy, and calling him a homophobic bigot to his face was not going to make that go any easier—not on the first day at least. Ryan would sort of hold that in reserve as a reward in case things got really bad.

"Walter, every family has its little problems, okay? Now did you want us to put the presents under the tree or wait until Christmas morning?"

"Put 'em under now," Walter told him. "The kids have been going on all day about you and Scott. This way, when they wake up in the morning, they'll know you guys were here. How bad was the trip?"

Ryan grunted, feeling the ache of being in the cramped car and the cold in every muscle down to his very marrow. "Let's just say that kissing a walrus was the only bright spot."

That managed to make Walter laugh. "Well, I'm glad someone's got one. Excuse me while I go downstairs and get my ass kicked in dice by your mother."

Ryan managed a smile as they called a Christmas truce. "Don't get too devoted to that. When Scotty brings the dog in, Mom is going to have a better target."

Walter nodded with a little bit of relief. "Not just in dice, either, thank God. I'll admit, I don't get the whole fag thing, but she really does have it in for poor Scotty."

With that he turned and trotted down the stairs with the bags of gifts, and Ryan took his time opening the suitcases and putting their stuff into drawers. They hadn't had to pack too heavily—there was a washer and a dryer down in the mudroom—but Ryan's mom liked them to dress nicely for Christmas Eve dinner, so they had suits and good shoes and everything. They shared a size, so their casual and sleep clothes all got shoved into one drawer, but Scott's jeans and T-shirts tended to be tighter and brighter than Ryan's. He got two drawers all to himself.

Their toiletries went into the small adjoining bathroom—Ryan's on the left and Scott's on the right—and when everything was done, Ryan took off his boots and put on his fleece-lined moccasins and went downstairs just in time for Scott and the dog to emerge from the mudroom.

Blitzkrieg bounded up, putting her paws on Ryan's shoulders, and Ryan was grateful that Scott had toweled her off or he'd be covered with snow. Scott came in for a brief kiss, and his familiar smell, sharpened by the cold, was enough to make Ryan pull him a little closer and make the kiss a little longer. Scotty was simple: he was all about loving Ryan. The rest of the family was complicated, and Ryan had always been a bigger fan of simple.

They pulled back, and Scotty smiled into Ryan's eyes before giving a grimace. "Hey, is there any food? I'm starving!"

"Wish I had your metabolism," Gordon said cheerfully, coming in and closing the mudroom door (which, in turn, led to the unheated garage). "There's leftovers in the refrigerator and some frozen stuff you can microwave if you like. The pantry and the outside refrigerator are stocked to feed an army. Make yourself at home!"

"Thanks, Dad." Ryan moved to the kitchen with alacrity; he was damned hungry himself. "And he works for that metabolism. I keep trying to get him to buy a car, but he rides his bike, rain or shine. Scares the hell out of me!"

Scotty grinned. "Hey, it's environmentally sound. Besides," Scotty preened a little, showing off his narrow, fit body, "it's good for me!"

"Shoot, Ryan—feed this kid! That's no way to treat the guy who walks your dog!"

Ryan nodded, pulling out sourdough bread and spaghetti sauce and noodles and went about throwing everything into a pan to heat and buttering the sourdough. "Doing my best! Want some?"

Gordon shook his head. "No thanks. I don't get nearly that much exercise. So, Scotty, how's the business going?"

Of all of Ryan's family, Ryan's dad was the only one who seemed genuinely interested in Scotty's Internet business and the only one who thought it was a good idea. Scott loved him for it, and Ryan loved watching him talk about it.

"It's going wicked awesome!" Scott gushed. "We tracked down some Neil Gaiman copies that a guy wanted to give his girlfriend as a birthday present, and she loved it so much she proposed! The guy wrote me a letter and everything—and Neil Gaiman was so sweet when I e-mailed him. That one was a real rush!"

Scotty specialized in tracking down signed copies of books or artist prints for fans. It had started when he'd tried to get a signed Dan Skinner print for Ryan for his birthday two years before, and he'd had so much fun doing it that he'd done the same thing for a few friends. He'd gone back to school around the same time and had encountered an instructor in a business class who specialized in e-businesses and who believed that the start of every successful business had its roots in a really fun idea. His professor had given him pointers, and Signa-Story had been born.

"Wait, can't you buy that stuff off the Internet?" Walter asked from the dice game.

"One would think," Taylor said dryly, but Scotty either didn't see their contempt or just chose to ignore it.

"Well yeah, you can—and sometimes people will e-mail me and I'll tell them how to do that. For people who do that a lot, I've got a list with all sorts of companies who have directions to get signed copies. They pay me a subscription fee, and I update it monthly. It's all public information, but I organize it by artist and keep it in the same place—for some people, that's worth the fee, you know?"

Ryan's dad nodded, and Ryan put a bowl of spaghetti in front of Scott while listening avidly. Of course Ryan knew how the business worked—he'd drawn up the paperwork, and applied for Scott's business license, and made sure they had the copyright on the name and everything. At least one weekend a month was spent helping to organize incoming merchandise and ship it off to Scotty's clients, and he always had so much fun sharing the origin of each signature with Scott that it felt like time well spent.

"Well, that will hardly pay the rent," Taylor said with a shrug, and Ryan glared at her.

"That's not all there is to it," Ryan said quietly. "Tell her, Scott."

Scott's look at Ryan's mother was searching, hoping for approval but afraid of being smacked down. It was a little like Blitzkrieg's look at them after she'd broken something or chewed up something or crapped in the house, and that pissed Ryan off. If his mother shot

Scotty down on this, Ryan swore he'd smack her in the nose with a rolled-up newspaper.

"Well, in a way, it's sort of like being a detective. I try to contact the author, go through used bookstores, put out ads in the paper, do a lot of research on the computer, talk to publishing houses. It's like when I was doing it for friends, I started this list of contacts, and then it just built. It all depends on the year the thing was published or painted, and that means looking through the Library of Congress or talking to art specialists—it gets really complicated sometimes, but it's a lot of fun!"

Taylor's look was skeptical. "Does it pay well?"

Scott grinned. "Well enough. Ryan and I are going to buy a house this month!"

Oh fuck. Ryan had been going to talk about that quietly in the kitchen with his mother, so she could keep her nasty remarks and sarcasm to herself.

"In this market?" Her voice dripped incredulity, and Ryan threw himself into the fray.

"We could do it even without the second job, Mom. That just makes it a hell of a lot easier. Besides, we need more room. Between Blitzkrieg and the office space Scotty needs, the apartment feels like the size of a walnut!"

Taylor raised her eyebrows, and Ryan cringed. There would be words later—but not now, not in front of Scott. Ryan was grateful. Let his mother work on him all she wanted as long as she kept her negativity the hell away from Scotty.

"I'm sure we'll discuss this in time," she said now, her voice so pleasant it knotted Ryan's guts like fishing net. He looked at her helplessly. She was the epitome of the stylish, understatedly beautiful, fifty-ish matron with ash-blonde hair parted in the middle and a svelte, cream-colored, casual pantsuit. Was Ryan the only one who saw the steel frame underneath that sweet exterior?

"I can't wait," Ryan said with a bold smile. "How's the dinner, Scott?"

Scotty took a sloppy bite, wiped his mouth, and beamed at him. "Amazing. Why aren't you eating yours?"

Ryan sighed and looked at the plate of spaghetti he'd dished up for himself while Scott had been talking. He took a bite and tried not to show that the conversation with his mother had pretty much shriveled his stomach like a prune. He swallowed anyway and smiled.

"Awesome," he said, and looked down. Six days. Well, he needed to lose weight anyway.

They went to bed shortly after cleanup. Walter helped them schlep more packages down the stairs again, and Scotty spent some time organizing them under the tree. Ryan had his gifts for Scott upstairs still, and was planning to add them—one box in particular—later. While he did that, he fielded Walter's shit about how much fun he'd had shopping for their two girls. Of course, he'd had just as much fun shopping for the two boys, but that wasn't what Walter wanted to talk about.

"You bought them a what?" Walter was looking at the big package like there was canister of nerve gas inside.

Scott smiled at him—that same big, eager smile he'd used when he was telling Ryan's mom about his job—and said, "A doll house. You remember, Yvonne? We were talking that one day about Julia Child and following her recipes, and someone came to the door, and you handed the phone to Ella-Jaye?"

Ryan's sister was a tiny, younger version of his mother, right down to high-cheek-boned face and pale blue eyes. Yvonne ran the market on "quietly competent," and she actually looked surprised when Scott singled her out and spoke to her.

"Oh my God—Scotty! You remembered from that? I'd just taken them shopping, and the girls couldn't stop talking about it! The big dollhouse with the little... oh no—you didn't!"

Scott grinned, truly pleased with himself. "Yeah. Yeah we did. Ryan helped me pick out the furniture—it didn't all come with the house—and we got two dolls so they can play while they're here. I'm sure they'll steal their brother's action figures and make do—kids do that."

He set the large package toward the back of the tree and a bunch of smaller ones around it, and Ryan put the swag for the boys on the other side of the tree so it would be easier at passing out time.

"Yeah, you probably played with your little sister's dollhouse yourself!" Walter crowed, and Scotty waggled his eyebrows.

"Absolutely—with my big brother's action figures. You don't even want to know the things that G.I. Joe did."

Walter gaped at him, apparently stunned that G.I. Joe had homosexual leanings, and Yvonne clapped a hand over her delighted smirk.

"You did that too?" she giggled when she could speak, and her mother said, "Yvonne!" with so much shock that Ryan and Gordon had to laugh too.

"So Yvonne wasn't always perfect?" Ryan asked, winking at his big sister, and she stuck her tongue out back. He remembered a time when she would have given a disgusted sniff and not played with him at all, but time and children—and Scott—apparently had brought out some little kid in her as well.

"Don't give her shit, Ry," Scott said with his own wink. "We all know what you played with."

Ryan didn't rise to his bait at all. "Yup. Cars!"

You would have thought Ryan's mother would have laughed at that, but she didn't. Everyone else did, though, including Walter and, most importantly, Scott.

Shortly after that they made their way up to their bedroom after Blitzkrieg, who ran up the stairs and curled up on the big area rug on the hardwood, happy as a big furry clam. (Ryan said that out loud, actually, and Scott shuddered. "Not in my bed!") They put on soft-knit pajama pants and T-shirts and crawled into bed, where Ryan lay for more than half an hour, stranded between awake and asleep like a dying codfish on the shore.

"Close your eyes, Ry—I can hear your eyeballs drying out."

Ryan blinked in the foreign darkness. "That's both gross and impossible," he mumbled, and Scott sighed, shifting in bed and scrambling up on his knees.

"Roll over."

"Scotty—"

"Don't give me the 'Scotty-I-don't-want-sex' whine. It's not sex; it's a backrub, you perv. You need to do something. You can't sleep. You can't sleep, I can't sleep, so roll over like a good little corporate lawyer... there you go."

Ryan rolled onto his stomach and mumbled, "I'm not a corporate lawyer anymore, remember? I'm a grinder. I like being a grinder."

"You're still a corporate lawyer," Scott told him, putting both hands on the muscle of his shoulders and pushing unmercifully. "You're just a human being too."

"Mmmmm...." Scotty's hands were long-fingered with big knuckles, hard, capable, and strong. He could have been a masseur or a physical therapist or anything really, but he'd chosen to be Ryan's everything, and that was his best talent of all. "I'd rather be a signature tracker, a detective. That's unbelievably"—oh God... right there... the twinge in his neck...

Scott had found it and was rubbing it just... so—"sexy," Ryan finished, warm and fuzzy and babbling into the pillow. Against his backside, Scott's cock was growing steadily harder, and Ryan made an effort to come out of his stupor.

"You're unbelievably sexy."

Scott leaned over and kissed the back of his neck with an open, warm, mouth and then nibbled down Ryan's neck and whispered in his ear.

"So are you. You're also almost asleep. Tomorrow, baby. I promise, okay?"

"Better."

A minute later, Scott's weight shifted and he slid in bed again, pulling the comforter up over their shoulders and backing into Ryan's body space. Ryan had just enough presence of mind to wrap his arm securely over Scotty's waist before drifting off to sleep.

CHAPTER 3
PUPPY!

SCOTT WOKE up the next morning to a pair of brown eyes a lot like Ryan's, only smaller and set widely behind a pert, freckled nose. He blinked and then opened his eyes again, and those eyes were still there, looking gravely at him.

"Heya, Ella-Jaye," he murmured. Ella had Ryan's brown eyes and her mother's blonde hair and a divot in her chin that she might have gotten from Walter but that Scott didn't want to give him credit for because Walter really was sort of a douche.

"Heya, Uncle Scotty," the little girl said avidly. "No one's awake yet, but there's a really big present downstairs for me and Kylie and some more for Tommy and W.G. I knew you'd be here!"

Scott grinned at her. His sisters had kids—he loved them as a whole and individually—and Ryan's nieces and nephews seemed to reciprocate. Suddenly Ella's voice dropped and she leaned really close. "Uncle Scotty, there's a dog in your room."

Blitzkrieg, apparently knowing that this meant her, gave a low "whuff!" and Scott hurriedly sat up.

"Shh, Pumpkin. Tell you what. How about I put on my slippers and a sweatshirt and we go downstairs, okay? Uncle Ryan drove up last night; he's real tired, okay?"

"Can you bring the dog?"

Scott slid out and found his moccasins and a hooded sweatshirt over by the drawers. He knew where to find them because they were neatly put away, because that's what Ryan did for him and then shrugged and said it was no big deal.

Together Scott and Ella-Jaye tiptoed out of the bedroom, and Blitzkrieg preceded them out the door.

Ella, eight years old and comfortable in her grandmother's cabin, ran straight for the tree, plugging the lights in, before she ran to the drapery cord on the other side. The drapes swung back—twelve feet long, off-white, and stately as hell—and both Scott and Ella gasped, because outside it was dark and the trees were harshly silhouetted by the snow. Over the horizon, in the twilight gray of dawn, they could see Donner Lake surrounded by mountains. And beyond that, the pale gold winter sun was turning the sky to fire and then watching as the snow reflected the sky.

Ella put her hand in Scott's, and even Blitzkrieg sat down respectfully until the light in the big double-paned bay window was pure enough to light up the living room and kitchen area. Ella turned to him and smiled.

"That was great, Uncle Scotty. That was like God smiling."

Scotty grinned back. "Absolutely. Here, you want some chocolate?"

Scott was actually the cook back at home. Ryan had served him the night before because Ry knew that Scott wasn't that comfortable in front of Ryan's mother, but once that disapproving librarian stare was gone, Scotty did know his way around a kitchen. It was never just hot chocolate with Scott. It was hot chocolate with a little bit of eggnog and some cinnamon and nutmeg with a marshmallow smiley face, whipped cream hair, and chocolate chip bows—or at least when he was making hot chocolate for Ella-Jaye and Kylie.

Kylie had woken up when he was heating the water, and for a minute, it was just Scott, the two little girls, and the big, silky, slobbery dog. The girls kept it down, but they also scratched Blitzkrieg's ass until she whined, groaned, and collapsed to her side with a whump and then rolled over on her back looking for more. Kylie, who was a younger, brown-haired version of her sister, had to be forcibly pried away from the Christmas tree to come sit down and drink her chocolate, but he made them both sit up on the stools at the counter while he started cooking bacon to go into the omelets for breakfast.

"Oh, eww! Are we having eggs for breakfast?"

Scott wrinkled his nose at Kylie. He'd done this last year, and he'd forgotten about how picky Yvonne's kids could be. "Okay, sweet thing, I give. What do you want for breakfast?"

"Oatmeal!"

Scott laughed softly to himself and went to work. After a couple of minutes of girl-chatter ("And Uncle Scotty, did you know that Barbie has a toy that has a toilet! It's for her little sister and it has pee and poop in it. It's so disgusting. Ella-Jaye wants it for Christmas." "So do you!"), he was relieved to hear that the boys were up.

"Uncle Scotty! Uncle Scotty! Uncle Scotty!"

Eleven-year-old Tommy hurtled down the stairs, holding his four-year-old brother by the hand, and ran directly into the kitchen to hug Scott around the waist. Scott dodged fast to get the kids out of the bacon-spatter-zone and set them up on the remaining two counter stools so he could listen to them talk too.

By the time he'd been caught up on the ins and outs of fifth grade, preschool, and when four-year-old W.G. would be old enough to ride a big boy's bicycle, Scott had managed to assemble a build-an-omelet platter with bacon, cheese, sautéed onions, mushrooms, and chili con carne (not Scott's idea, but Tommy seemed to think an omelet with chili in it was high cuisine, and since the cabin had a plethora of canned chili, Scott didn't see the harm).

He'd also managed the same thing with the oatmeal, except the oatmeal platter had sugar, brown sugar, walnuts, honey, and some pureed peaches that he'd found in the freezer. The kids ate their breakfast at the counter while Scott set the table for the adults, and yes, Tommy actually ate the chili con carne omelet. Scott was suitably impressed—and also a little nauseated. He was glad that Ryan padded down as he started to eat so Scott didn't have to watch the kid dig into it. Apparently Tommy thought eating was a full sensory experience, and by the time Ryan came up behind him and made nom-nom noises into his ear, Tommy had chili on everything in his immediate vicinity—including his little brother.

"Oh geez!" Ryan laughed from around Scott's head. "Tommy, who taught you to eat?"

Scott leaned back into Ryan and closed his eyes while Tommy said something about how his parents had been arguing about that very thing the week before. Scott had dated (term used loosely) a lot of men before Ryan had wandered into that bathroom, but none of them—not the ones in the closet or the ones proudly out of it—had ever held him with the ease and absolute possession that Ryan showed him. Even when Ryan hadn't known the first thing about sex as a gay man, he'd known how to hold Scotty to make him feel loved. Scott had never forgotten the wonder in Ryan's brown eyes when he'd turned around and seen Scott as... well, Scott never had been able to figure out what Ryan saw in him.

He just knew he never wanted Ryan to stop seeing it. He never wanted that wonder to go away. He might be Scotty-the-rebound-guy-who-worked-at-Starbucks to the whole rest of the world—including a lot of guys he considered friends—but to Ryan, he was Scotty-the-everything. The nom-nom noises in the sensitive hollow of his neck were icing on the cake.

"Wow," Ryan was saying now to his nephew. "Tommy, that is way more than I wanted to know about how you got peas up your brother's nose. How about you go get rid of some of that chili, and if you're dressed by the time Uncle Scotty eats, you can help him take Blitzkrieg outside for her morning walk."

"I'm taking the dog for a walk?" Scott asked, bemused.

"Since I'm doing dishes," Ryan told him with a kiss on the temple. "Besides, you're the one who'll get cabin fever if you don't go out and play for a while."

"You're not coming with us?" Scott couldn't keep the disappointment out of his voice. He had never been a clingy boyfriend. In fact, quite the opposite—if the guy he was dating had other plans, very often, Scotty would find another boyfriend. But not with Ryan. With Ryan, it felt like all time spent in Ryan's company was good time, even if they didn't say anything.

"After the dishes," Ryan said. "But first, c'mon—lookit what you did! Let's eat!"

Well, first they had to wipe W.G. down with a washcloth pretty much from head to toe, because the parts not covered in his brother's chili were covered in his own oatmeal. The girls needed hardly more than a napkin delicately applied to little Kewpie-doll mouths, but the boys apparently needed a pressure wash and a sandblaster with every meal. But finally all the kids were sent off to dress, and Scott had poured the omelet mix into the pan and started making an omelet for the both of them.

"I don't get to choose?" Ryan asked, leaning against the counter, laughing.

"I know what you want," Scott said, sprinkling some Swiss cheese, chopped spinach, and artichoke hearts onto the almost perfect circle. "The only thing you switch is mushrooms, and since we just had to pull one of those out of W.G.'s nose...."

Both men shuddered, and Ryan had to agree. "No mushrooms."

Scott flipped the omelet and neatly planted it, and then grabbed two forks. "How long do you think we've got?" he asked, and both of them winced as they heard somebody yelling loudly "Mah-ahm! Ella stole my sweater!" on the upstairs side where Ryan and Scott didn't sleep.

They exchanged pained glances as they sat down to breakfast and coffee, and Ryan said, "Um, I'd say eat fast!"

But Scott didn't want to rush. He forced Ryan to slow down by tucking one of the forks under the plate and feeding him instead. Ryan didn't complain, though—he never had. All of that self-assurance and burning ambition, and Ryan had no problems setting it all down to take a moment to make Scott happy. Scott had no problem asking him to do just that. Ryan ate his omelet at Scott's discretion, making cracks about the kids in between mouthfuls, and Scott hung onto his every word.

"Where's my sister?" Ryan asked bemusedly as he used his finger to get the last of the cheese on the plate. "Geez, her kids are loud enough bring the snow off the mountain; you'd think Vonnie could wake the hell up."

Scott rolled his eyes. "You think she hasn't gotten a little kid-deaf by now? When I was growing up, we were expected to get our own cereal by the time we were five. That meant Saturdays were Momma's day off!"

Ryan winked at him. "Your older sisters waited on you, and you know it."

Scotty grinned and nodded. "Totally true." He had no shame at all at being spoiled. Especially because it meant he knew how to spoil Ryan when he needed to.

"Yeah, well." Ryan stood and sighed. "If no one's getting up, breakfast is going to spoil. How about I'll put everything away and—"

"No, no, don't put it away." Taylor's voice made her son jump, but Scotty had a lot of practice keeping his eyes wide and his expression neutral. A boy could not dangle multiple lovers on multiple strings and still call them friends after the fallout if he didn't know how to be disingenuous on command.

"Of course not, Mother," Ryan said. He shot his mom a look that was part willingness to please and part caution. "I'll make you an omelet."

"I thought Scott was cooking?" The look Taylor sent Scott was warm and kind, but Scott was not fooled. Taylor had been warm and kind before, but Scott had never left her presence feeling taller than a foot and a half at the outside. If Passive met Aggressive, had an offspring, and groomed her for prep school, she still wouldn't have met Ryan's mom's approval.

"Scott needs to take the dog outside. I'm taking the adult half of the program." Ryan grinned at his mom, and Scott looked at Ryan, feeling a terrible pang of guilt. The Adult Half of the Program—apparently, Scotty was excused from that forever and ever, amen.

But Blitzkrieg had just started to get really hyper, running back and forth between the two staircases and barking her black, curly ass off, and sometimes being an adult meant walking the dog literally as well as figuratively.

He ran up the stairs quickly and dressed in record time, including thin gloves topped by a charming pair of fingerless mitts that Ryan had bought him at a craft fair. They were very manly—dark blue topped with a thicker neutral color with an interesting design on the back. Scott had given Ryan a hard time about buying him something that wasn't bright and flamboyant, but he had to admit, those gloves and half-gloves looked damned handsome. Besides, they kept his fingers really warm without being bulky or irritating.

By the time he got back down, a matching blue and beige hat pulled on his head (none of which matched his parka), Ryan was serving up a passable omelet to his mother. Scott could hear her "praise" it as he snapped Blitzkrieg's lead on and started calling for the kids.

"Nice, Ryan, but we can tell you're not the cook of the family, can't we? Well, that's just as well, since you're at work, grinding away."

"I like being a grinder," Ryan said sunnily. "I do my job, I do it well, and no one expects me to perform miracles and die of heart disease at forty-five. It's a decent trade-off, you know?"

"Very convincing—almost like cutting that artichoke heart really fine almost convinces me there was enough of it to put on this omelet."

Ryan's smile thinned and flattened. "That's my fault—it's my favorite. I'm afraid most of it went on my omelet."

"I could have sworn I saw you and Scott eating off the same plate."

"Yup. But we were eating my omelet. Otherwise Scott's would have had bacon." Ryan's tone was pert, and Taylor's return was straining to be in kind.

"Of course it would. Scott's not old enough to worry about cholesterol yet, is he?"

And that's when Scott started calling for the kids. "Tommy! Ella! Kylie! W.G.! If you don't get down here now, Blitzkrieg's gonna blow up! It'll be gross but not nearly as much fun!"

The kids gave what felt like a collective shriek and started pounding down the stairs, pulling on scarves and gloves and thick coats as they went. The only one who was fully dressed was W.G., and he was such a little bundle of clothes that Tommy had to carry him or he would have rolled down the stairs like a snowball.

Everybody followed Scott out into the mudroom, where a little stair-step progression of rubber boots was slid on over small-sized tennis shoes, and Blitzkrieg, fueled by the hope of finally getting to go outside and relieve herself, hastened everyone along by lots of barking and bouncing.

When the kids were all wrapped, Scotty opened the door into the garage and then led the way out into the snow. He and the kids stomp-tromped-trudged their way through the new-fallen powder around the front yard and into the back, where the snow was just a little bit shallower. The kids were shrill and happy as they got to the back, and as Scotty unsnapped Blitzkrieg's lead, he indulged in the pure physical relaxation of doing something fun on vacation.

He sighed and looked behind him at the cabin/mansion and wished that Ryan was out here in the snow with them. Because odds were whatever Ryan was doing with his vacation, it was not fun, and he was not indulging in anything but another stiff neck and some serious regret for driving up here in the first place.

CHAPTER 4
RYAN
COOKING WITH KEROSENE AND C-4

AT LEAST Ryan's dad liked the omelet. And Walter and Yvonne were both happy with the spiced oatmeal—Yvonne waxed rhapsodic about the charming presentation of the different spices on the lazy-Susan until Walter cut her off with a snort.

"Vonnie, I don't know why you're so excited about it. It's not like you ever cook!" He looked at Ryan, inviting him to share the joke. "Her idea of cooking is putting pizza bites on a pan and not burning them. It's why we had to hire a housekeeper."

Ryan's father spoke up from a mouthful of bacon-chive omelet. "I thought you hired a cook and a housekeeper because she was putting in fifty hours at the office and you could afford one. If she's going to spend any time with the kids, expecting a clean house and food on top of that—it's insane!"

Walter rolled his eyes. "I don't know what she does with the kids exactly. It's like they spend all their time in the car!"

Yvonne grimaced. "Soccer season. W.G. started this year. It's like four different teams, six days a week. Geeyawd! Talk about insane!"

Gordon looked at Walter with jovial curiosity. "Why aren't you in on any of that action, Walter?"

Walter blinked, and Ryan grinned, going in for the kill. "Yeah, Walter. My dad used to coach our soccer games. It was great!"

"But I've got—I mean, work…," Walter sputtered, looking truly uncomfortable, and Gordon continued, completely oblivious to having just shattered Walter's smug little bubble.

"So did I. God, it was just nuts. You remember that, Tay?"

Gordon smiled at Ryan's mother, and her own expression grew soft. "Oh yes, I remember. You'd coach on Tuesdays and Thursdays, and then I'd take Yvonne to dance on Mondays and Wednesdays. There was piano and competitions—hectic and completely exhausting. I don't know if we could have done it if we hadn't both pitched in. And you were wonderful with the team."

Gordon smiled reminiscently. "Best fun ever. Kids are awesome, you know?"

Walter looked like he was going to swallow his tongue, and his flushed complexion could be seen in the thinning spots on the top of his head. Ryan knew because he had to stand up and start clearing the table for this part. He also wanted to mask the sort of a hidden pain, one that only Scott was starting to suspect. Scotty promised him fervently that someday, someday, they would have a taste of that madness, and Ryan—who knew that Scott rarely made promises and so took them seriously—was content to wait for the right time. He certainly wasn't going to make a big deal about it right now.

"Not to hear Yvonne talk about it," Walter mumbled, and Ryan finally turned to him in exasperation.

"Well, maybe her break from the kids could be your break from your golf game, okay, Walter?"

"Ryan!" Taylor admonished, and Ryan took a deep breath.

"You know," he said with a forced smile, "Scotty cooked the first half, and I cooked the second half and cleared the table. I think someone else here is good for the dishes."

His father, God love him, stood up and said, "That's my cue!"

And Ryan took his opportunity to escape upstairs and get dressed to go out and play.

THE AIR was like a slap in the face, and he didn't have to look at the thermometer on the side of the garage to see that the temperature was in the low twenties. His gloves were fleece-lined leather—because that's the sort of thing Scott would get him because he thought that's what lawyers should wear—and he'd made sure to put long-johns on under his jeans because he hated being cold.

But he'd hated being in that kitchen even more.

He found Scotty and the kids in the back, making twin forts—one for the girls and one for the boys—and getting ready to launch a snowball offensive of the first order.

"Wheee!" Ella-Jaye called when she saw Ryan stomping out. "You're here, Uncle Ryan! You can play on the girls' side now!"

"No he can't!" Tommy said logically, looking up from where he was tamping snow down into a three-foot wall with his heavily mittened hand. "Daddy says that Uncle Scotty is the wife. Wouldn't that mean he's on the girls' side?"

There was no rancor in the words. In fact, there was nothing but the guileless expectation that his father would know what he was talking about because he was a grown-up—but that didn't mean Ryan's eyes didn't get so wide they dried out in the frigid air before he could even blink.

Scotty met Ryan's eyes with a wicked glint in his own and a shocked hand clapped over his mouth.

"Ohmygod! Tommy!" He seemed to be as much at a loss as Ryan was.

Tommy looked up. "What? Dad told my mom that Ryan would be the husband and Scotty would be the wife. Is that bad? And then something about baseball, but I asked you if were a pitcher or a catcher, Uncle Scott, and you said you'd never played, so he must have got that wrong. Is Dad wrong about the wife thing too?"

"Yes," Ryan answered, because Scott looked like he was going to just drop into the snow, fetal with laughter, at any time. "Yes, Tommy, your father is wrong. Wh…. If Scotty and I are ever married, we will both be the husband."

Tommy looked up, mildly surprised by that, and then shrugged and went back to helping his brother scoop snow out from behind the snow fort, the better to build his arsenal of snowballs, and to condense the snow for them so it would smack instead of *pffft*. "Okay then, well, if that's true, who is going to be on the girls' side in the snowball fight?"

Ryan grinned wickedly. "I am—all the better to beat you and your Uncle Scotty, okay?"

Scott laughed and bent down and scooped up W.G., who flailed his stubby arms and legs and squealed deliriously. "You can't beat me! I'm using a human shield!"

Ryan lofted a couple of really soft handfuls of snow at the little boy, who squealed some more and wiggled until Scott was forced to drop him into a snow drift. The boy scrambled out of the drift to gather back with his brother and hurl snowballs at Scott. Suddenly, it didn't matter if there was a boys' side or a girls' side. Scotty and Ryan were in between the forts and were therefore the targets, and after a few moments of "Ouch! Geez, Tommy not in the—*whoooot!* Ella! That went right down my shirt!" and

"Get 'em, Ry! You can throw harder than that! I know he's little, but he's fierce," the two men were hunkered in the center of the trench, back to back, throwing snowballs at the little hellions as fast as they could.

The fight ended when they ran out of snowballs and W.G. started to whimper with the cold. Ryan figured they'd earned themselves a snack and maybe worn Blitzkrieg out enough for her to sack out in front of the fireplace for a few hours. He picked up Ella-Jaye, who had taken off her mittens sometime in the fight and was now crying from the cold, and Scott picked up W.G., and together they tromped back around the house and through the door in the garage. Ryan and Scott had the kids form an assembly line where Ryan would take boots and Scotty would take jackets before the child went into the mudroom and started to remove wet outer garments and hang them up on the drying rack by the washer and dryer.

They folded an old towel up for Blitzkrieg, and she was content to spend her time panting and warming up in the corner while the snow melted off her coat. The kids would take turns, when they weren't being undressed and sent upstairs to go change, wiping her down and making sure she was warm. She was. Even though the room was slightly cooler than the house, it was still much warmer than the garage or outside, and by the time the mudroom was clear of little kids in their underwear, she was fast asleep. Ryan and Scotty were left pulling off their own clothes, still laughing from the frantic activity.

"Oh lordy!" Scotty was shucking off his vest and his sweater, leaving on the long-sleeved shirt underneath. "I haven't had that much fun in ages!"

"Really? It's not a club with strippers, you know." Ryan pulled his own sweater over his head so he could shake off the snow. His shirt rode up, and his exposed skin puckered in the chilled air when suddenly two ice cubes snuck up under his shirt and clamped themselves under his arms. The scream he let out was two octaves higher than his speaking voice and shriller than a middle school student dancing away from a spider, and Scotty kept his damned freezing hands up in Ryan's underarms, wiggling his fingers as he giggled.

"Have I ever taken you to a strip club?" he demanded, trying to be stern, but his usual wicked grin had cranked the naughty up a good notch or two, and he moved his body up to catch Ryan's as Ryan doubled over with helpless laughter.

"No! No no no no no no no… oh God! Scotty! No! You've never! Oh geez! Scott—*eeeeeeeeee!*"

Scott kept tickling him until his knees went out from under him, and suddenly Scott was holding him, and Ryan's chest was mashed up against Scotty's, and he could hardly catch his breath with how wonderful it felt to be this close, this intimate, with this man, his mate, the love of his goddamned life.

He looked into Scotty's eyes and giggled, and Scott's own grin grew unusually serious. "God, Ry," he said softly, "I really love you, you know?"

For a moment, there was a burning weight on Ryan's chest involving the brightly wrapped box that he hadn't yet put under the tree and a present that they couldn't really afford on top of the house but that Ryan had wanted desperately to give. He opened his mouth to say "I love you," back, and the thousand other things as well, but he hesitated just that fraction of a moment too long, and Scotty claimed him instead.

Scott's mouth was hot, blindingly hot, and after the bitter cold of outside that had seeped into Ryan's hands and feet, he just wanted to fall into that warmth and feed on it. He opened to his lover, and Scott moaned in the back of his throat, and Ryan felt himself shoved up against the washer as Scott bore down on him with uncharacteristic aggression.

Ryan always loved it when Scotty tried to top.

He moaned and opened his mouth wider and bunched Scott's shirt in his hand so he could palm the soft skin of Scotty's back. Scott was wearing snow pants, and Ryan slid his hand down under the waist band and grabbed himself a hot, tight little handful of Scotty's well-worked ass.

Scott seemed go limp, because that's what Scott did—he went paradoxically limp and tense, like a feral cat, and Ryan loved petting his baby. He gave a little hop until he was sitting on the washing machine, wrapping his legs around Scotty while he kneaded Scott's bottom with enough force to make Scott groan and hump his groin hard against Ryan's.

They very well might have gotten off like that—Ryan was blind to everything but Scott's taste and the feel of his hands and the rising, delirious pressure in his cock and his balls as Scott ground up against him—but there was a sudden chill of air.

"You guys coming in for lun—" Walter began, but he got one look at them and groaned. "Oh God, no homo necking, you two. That's just so gross!"

The door snapped shut, and Scott and Ryan were stuck clenching their butt cheeks together to try to get over the terrible squirming sensation caused by a hard-on that was all dressed up with nowhere to go. Ryan rested his forehead against Scotty's collarbone and struggled with a combination of panting and laughter that threatened to take over.

"Yeah," Scott panted. "Like he would know about gross. Doesn't know the difference between a husband and a wife, the stupid asshole."

Ryan looked up at him and nodded, remembering how tired Yvonne looked and how clueless Walter had been. "Like being his wife is so much fun!" he snorted, and then pounded his forehead against Scott's shoulder. "Forget I said that. Will. Not. Drag. Scotty. Into. Bad. Family. Drama." Scott laughed and Ryan looked up at him hopefully. "Sorry about that."

Scott shook his head. "Ryan... man, drag me into anything you want. Drag me outside again naked, drag me to Alaska and make me work on a fishing boat—hell, drag me to Six Flags with those kids. I'll go. I'll go, and I'll love it, because it's with you." Scott's mouth thinned then, and Ryan reached up to cup his cheek because he wanted that happy, glowy, I-was-making-out-with-Ryan look back on his face.

"Hey," Ryan murmured, "who else would I drag with me, right?"

Scott shook his head. "It's not that. It's just... you don't have to throw yourself on the mom grenade for me, okay?"

Ryan sighed and hopped off the dryer, and then pulled his overshirt over his head, leaving his T-shirt on. His long-sleeved overshirt was wet too, mostly because Tommy had been lobbing his shots and a few of them had slid between his fleece-lined flannel coat and his shirt.

"She's a good mom," he murmured, knowing it was true. "She loves us a lot."

"Just not me," Scott said dryly, and Ryan grimaced.

"She'll love you," Ryan told him, hoping. "She's just... demanding, you know? No one's good enough for her kids." He rolled his eyes. "Well, in Yvonne's case, she might be right, but not with you. Not even a little bit with you, okay?"

Scott laughed a little. "Maybe you're just biased." He was going to walk away, and Ryan put a heavy hand on his shoulder and yanked him back.

"Damned straight I am! Look, Scott. I didn't drag you up here just to torture you, okay? I mean, it sucks—I get it. You woke up, took care of the kids, fixed everybody breakfast, and your reward—well, besides my complete adulation, mind you—is shit. Walter's a douche, my mom's being the ice queen, and you had to spend your entire morning out in Ice Planet Zero, trying to get away from it all."

"I enjoyed myself!" Scott protested, and Ryan reached out and pulled Scott closer until they were touching below the waist, even if they had to lean back to look in each other's eyes.

"And that's one of the many reasons I love you. Look, Scotty. Yvonne and I used to get up in the morning here, and we'd turn on the Christmas lights and pour ourselves cereal and then wait for Mom and Dad to wake up so we could sit and play Yahtzee. It was fun—and we loved it—but it wasn't omelet bars and that amazing hot-chocolate thing and oatmeal with happy faces on it. It wasn't snowball fights and a big dog that wakes me up on Saturdays by licking my toes." He'd started shivering, and he pulled closer to Scott and burrowed, and Scotty, whose outer shirt was still on—and still dry—wrapped his arms around Ryan's shoulders because that's what they did. They partnered, and Scott was good at it, even though he'd always claimed to be way too narcissistic to be a good partner. "It's not you, Scott. You don't know it, but just dragging your gay ass into this place made it better. And even if you just made it better for me, that would be all I needed. But you make it better for everybody, and even if no one else sees that, I do, and it matters."

Scott shook his head, his carefully dyed hair falling in a mess around his face and his eyes darting around the little white mudroom like fish. "You're so going to make me queen up, you dick. Now let's go change and wipe the floor with Walter in Scrabble or something, you think?"

Ryan grinned at him with a little bit of shared malice. "How about Trivial Pursuit. Teams."

Scott nodded. "Oooohhh, yeah. Babe. We can so make him eat snow."

Scott's eyes were steady now, and his pointed chin with the little divot in it wasn't quivering, and neither was his full, mobile mouth. Scotty was good to go, and Ryan would let him—after one last kiss.

This one was sweet and tender, and Ryan gave as much comfort as he could, and Scott smiled gamely and stroked Ryan's cheekbone with his thumb when it was over.

"No mercy," he said soberly, and Ryan nodded.

"Let's go kick some weenie ass."

It was pure optimism on their part—but that's how they'd gotten through the first hour of their relationship, and then the first week, and then the first three years. Pure optimism that as long as they were side by side, they really could kick the world's weenie ass. Hell, wiping the floor with Walter at Trivial Pursuit was not even a problem.

But that didn't mean that Ryan wasn't counting the hours until he could give Scotty the little gift he was about to put under the tree that might make a whole lot of this headache go the fuck away.

CHAPTER 5
SCOTTY
HEADACHES AND CURES

"PSST, SCOTTY!"

Ryan's voice was coming from right next to Scott's ear in the night, and Scott grumbled. He'd been fast asleep in the comforting dark, but now Ryan was snuggling right up to his back and wiggling his hard groin up against Scott's backside, and Scotty, dammit, was getting all squirmy with need. He hadn't gotten off for three days, not since that hand-job in the car, and he and Ryan were usually a helluva lot more active than that!

And it hadn't just been the other people in the house that had caused the dry spell, either. It was the one specific person that was drying up Ryan's libido like a freeze-dried hot dog. Scotty couldn't blame him in the least. If he had to hear one more refrain of "Scotty, you know, spending money on your tan is a little frivolous if you're thinking of buying a house," followed by Ryan's brave charge of, "Nothing's frivolous if it makes Scotty feel good," or any of the other debates about Scotty's spending habits and their plans of the future, Scott's thing might get limp and twisted too.

"What?" he asked, straining back against Ryan. His eyes opened a little, and he felt back under the covers. Oh God. Ryan wasn't wearing any sleep shorts or any underwear…. Oh God. He totally meant business. Scott's hard-on went from limp biscuit to porn star in one brush of his fingers on Ryan's bare hip.

"Do you still have a headache?" Ryan whispered furiously, and Scott cringed. The only really bad thing about that lie was a boyfriend who might hold back on sex because of it.

"That depends. What's your mother doing?"

"Hanging upside down in her cave, I think. Why?"

Scott giggled a little and fumbled for the waistband of his sleep shorts. "Because if she's in her cave, my headache just got cured," he said truthfully. Ryan slid up against him, his already full cock nestling just right there between Scott's cheeks, and they both groaned.

"Oh God," Scott muttered. Ryan's warm hand wrapped around Scott's chest and found his nipples with lover's sonar and then pinched, but that's not what really turned Scott's key. What really flipped his switch, sparked his chassis, made his blood flow, turned him on, was the fact that Ryan—handsome, confident, don't-take-no-for-an-answer Ryan—had already greased up his cock with lube.

Scotty loved sex, and he loved being the bottom, and although he loved foreplay, sometimes when Ryan just totally took charge, he loved being fucked quick and dirty, and now was one of those times. He raised his leg and propped up on his toe, and Ryan took his cue and positioned the head of his exceptionally large cock.

Scott bit his lip and whimpered, his breath coming in fast pants with anticipation only, because he needed it so bad... oh God... he needed it... he needed it....

"Fuck me, Ry... oh God...."

He didn't need any preparation. Ryan was lubed, and Scott didn't mind a little rough at the beginning. Ryan had been inside him so often in the last three years he was practically pre-stretched. So when the head of Ryan's cock brushed his rim, he didn't move forward, waiting for fingers or foreplay; he wriggled, he thrust backward, he whined, he begged, he pleaded, and Ryan loved him, Ryan would do anything for him, and Ryan obliged. He slammed forward and back as hard as he could from this angle and kept his hand around Scott's chest, playing roughly with his nipples.

"Stroke yourself," Ryan commanded roughly, and Scott whimpered and complied. It was difficult. Scotty didn't used to get hard when someone was stretching his ass, sliding inside him, pounding on his prostate. He used to just flail on the bed, whimpering, loving this particular sex act but not really getting hard from it, not really coming. But Ryan didn't let him do that—not after he got the hang of things. Ryan made sure Scott stroked himself hard, made sure his cock was worked, gave Scott a place to focus. Ryan was fucking him hard and sure, but Scott didn't just get to flop around anymore: he needed to be active while he was being dominated, and he was. He wrapped his hand around himself, stroked hard, rubbed his thumb over the head and gave a vicious twist at the end of the stroke, then did it again. Oh God, was Ryan good at fucking him hard. He looked like the boy next door, and he had the kindest heart Scott had ever known, but he could fuck like a dom with a whip.

"You stroking yourself?" Ryan asked, his voice gruff in Scott's ear. Scott felt the rasp of teeth at the joint of his neck and shoulder and then a hint of tongue. He made a sound, torn between the stretching in his ass and the sensual pain of Ryan's fingers on his nipples and the glorious twisting of his own hand on his cock.

"Yeah," he panted. His hips bucked, wanting to take more, but Ryan bit harder and moved his hand to Scott's hip, keeping him in place while he kept thrusting. He changed his angle, pushing up on an elbow while Scott leaned forward so Ryan had more leverage, and Scott was practically bent over his erect cock and oh geez. It was beautiful, the pressure in his groin, his stomach, behind his balls, the stretch, the fill, the edge of pain when Ryan brushed his prostate, and most especially, Ryan's hand, possessive and hard on his hip.

That beauty built up, rushed his spine, shattered behind his eyes, and he turned his face into his pillow and cried out, exploding in a mess of come and trying not to double up with the convulsions of orgasm, because that would throw Ryan out of his ass.

Ryan held him still, though, and kept thrusting for another couple of pushes while Scott continued to shudder from those expert brushes over his gland. Finally Ryan groaned loudly and collapsed over Scott's shoulder, enveloping him in his heavily-built, freckled shoulders as they both trembled in aftermath.

Scott had to crane his head around to reach Ryan's mouth, and Ryan had to loom over him, resting some of his weight on Scott's arm, but it didn't matter. Touching lips while Ryan slid—wet, veiny, and barely deflated—out of Scott's backside made Scott shiver. He closed his eyes and, heedless of the mess and the chill, rolled into Ryan's arms and kissed him hard and solid on the mouth, and Ryan moaned into him, and then even the kiss broke off, and it was just them together, cuddled against the chilly dark of the strange room.

Ryan was the responsible one. He pulled away and dropped a kiss on Scott's cheek before trotting to the bathroom and coming back with a washcloth—warm!—and a drying towel. Scott reclined on his elbows as Ryan washed him off, looking at Ryan with amused eyes because he took the job of cleanup so seriously. He moved the washcloth down to his own groin and then looked up and caught Scott's eyes on him. Even in the darkness, Scott could see his blush and the embarrassed grin, and Scott had no choice but to lift a hand to his forehead and run his fingers through the little auburn forelock that came loose when he tugged.

"I've seen that thing before," he chided. "Up close and personal, even."

Ryan looked up and then looked away, blushing harder. He pulled away and wiped at his groin with his back turned. "I can't explain it," he mumbled. "Before and during, I'm all He-Man, fucking with decision." His voice got fainter as he moved to the bathroom and rinsed out the washcloth. He came back and kept speaking like he'd never left. "I'm all done, and I'm like, 'God, I can't believe he fell for that!'"

Scott laughed and held out his hand. "No," he said when Ryan went for the sleep shorts crumpled at the foot of the bed. "Don't put them on—we can dress later. Come to bed now."

Ryan raised his eyebrows—Scott could see the expression in the dark—and it was his turn to blush. Scott was not usually that assertive, he knew. But the little death of sex had turned him melancholy, and three days of dodging Ryan's mother's game of pin-the-barb-on-Scotty's-ass had worn down his usual cheerful good will.

But even if Ryan was surprised, he still crawled into bed with a naked Scott and pulled the comforter and wool blanket up to his chin, and then pulled Scott so that his head rested on Ryan's wide chest. Scott wiggled, making himself at home, and turned a little on his side so he could run his hand over the little nest of cinnamon curls that rested right between Ryan's pecs.

"What?" Ryan said gently, and Scott struggled for words.

"You know how you blush after sex?" Scott said softly, and Ryan's sound was embarrassed. Scott took it for a yes. "I love that," Scott said. "That's the reason I fell in love with you, you know. I mean... I was pretty sure I loved you in that bathroom, right? But...." Scott stopped petting Ryan's pec and looked up to see those adorable brown eyes looking at him seriously. "Anyone can be arrogant, Ry. It's why there's so many assholes around. But you—you go for what you want, and I love that. But then you make sure it's what I want too, and I'd never had that before. I know you're stuck, okay?" Scott had to rush this part or he wouldn't say it. "I know you're stuck, and your mom's being—" God, how did he say this?

"A snide bitch," Ryan substituted dryly, and Scott sighed, because that was pretty much how you said it.

"Yeah. Anyway. I know that, and I know it sucks. But you keep making sure I'm okay. Every time she says something, you make sure I'm okay, and even though this is the worst Christmas ever, and I miss the hell out of my sisters and my folks' place and that gawdawful borscht shit that my grandmother brought over from the frickin' old country, I'm still not sorry we came."

Ryan dropped a kiss in his hair and wrapped his arm even tighter. "There's a reason we're toughing this out, you know," he said, semi-seriously.

"Besides the fact that the roads are crap?" This was true—the radio said they might be able to leave on schedule, but right now, a new coat of snow had made driving a nightmare.

"Yeah," Ryan said softly. "Let's just say I've got a plan, Scott. I swear. I'll make this trip worth it, okay?"

Scott's eyes were closing, and he was settling in on Ryan's chest dreamily. "With you, babe. Always worth it."

Of course it was. Everything with Ry was worth it—and with what Scotty had in the small box he'd hidden under the tree, he hoped Ryan would agree.

THE NEXT day he wasn't so sure.

Taylor had planned to cook. Scott was not exactly sure the woman knew how.

Since that first morning, Scott had been the unacknowledged cook of the family. The kids would come ask him for sandwiches and soup because they knew he'd do fun stuff like cook parmesan into the bread with the grilled cheese sandwiches and dress their vegetables into things that looked like cars and kittens and Mickey Mouse.

Yvonne or Ryan had started dinner for the prior three nights, and both of them had asked his advice and followed it in matters of cooking time, seasoning, and side dishes. He'd enjoyed that time. He sat at the counter and drank a beer while Ryan and Yvonne moved like things were choreographed. He remembered Ryan talking about how he and Yvonne had woken up as kids and made their own cereal and sat and watched cartoons together. He could see that here in the way they moved, in the way they talked in shorthand, and the way they told effortless stories about each other as they moved.

Those were the times he was happiest about coming up to see Ryan's family at the cabin instead of staying back in Sacramento to spend Christmas Eve with his own and then Christmas morning sleeping in like he'd planned. He'd had other plans, too—a midnight mass, hot chocolate on their couch, Ryan's expression when he got his Christmas gift, and really hot sex including some Christmas gifts that hadn't made the cut for the trip up to Tahoe. But those plans seemed small and selfish (well, not the hot sex—he'd planned to give a lot for that) compared to watching Ryan be quietly happy with the sister he rarely got to see.

But Christmas Eve. Shit. Scott had seen the flank steak and the frozen vegetables and the olive oil and the wine—he'd been the one to bring everything out of the outside freezer the night before. He'd gone into the kitchen and had started marinating the steak and sautéeing the vegetables and suddenly….

Suddenly there was Ryan's mom, looking hurt, like Scott had stolen her favorite pair of earrings or was putting his big stinky man-feet into her new pumps or something.

"Oh, but Scott, I was going to cook." Her eyes were blue and she was petite and blonde, but that didn't mean Scott couldn't see Ryan in the shape of her mouth and her nose and even the little line between her eyebrows when she was hurt.

Like now.

"Oh," he said swallowing. "Uhm, Italian flank steak—there's sundried tomatoes in the fridge. Uhm… unless… uhm… what were you planning to cook?"

Well hell. It was her cabin and her stocked refrigerator and basically her hospitality, and Scott had been stepping on her toes. He knew that. But he hadn't seen the woman in the kitchen once, even to clean up when somebody else had cooked (and in Scott's parents' house, that was the rule,) and he'd been so good about staying out of her way. The kitchen seemed to be the safest place to do that!

"I can make flank steak," she said pleasantly, and then shooed Scott to the other side of the counter, where he debated whether to sit on the stool and offer what was probably unwanted advice or run away and let her destroy his dreams of Italian stuffed flank steak without his supervision.

"How long were you going to sauté the veggies?" she asked pleasantly, and Scott kept his sigh to himself. He was going to have to stay—if she even needed to ask that question, he was going to have to help her if this was going to be at all edible.

"Until there's only a little crisp left," he said. "The onions went in first, so they should be caramelized by then. And I was going to simmer the baby potatoes—"

"Don't mind that," she said confidently. "I was just going to skin them and mash them."

"But they're red potatoes… baby ones. Why would you…?"

She looked at him, nonplussed. "Because that's what you do to potatoes, Scotty—at least in our house. We don't have time to cook fancy when you're running a business with kids."

Scott tried to make his vision opaque beyond the countertop and vainly wished he'd managed to get his beer before he'd sat down to be tortured.

"I know," he said instead. "I started cooking when my mom needed help. She'd be so tired when she got home—it only seemed fair."

Taylor looked surprised at that, and she looked up from ruining some perfectly good baby red potatoes to ask him, "What does she do for a living?"

"She works in the family salon," Scott said. "She was a first-generation immigrant, and my dad was already established. His family had a bunch of businesses. She was groomed for one."

Taylor's eyes opened wide. "Um, Russian?" She asked the question delicately, as though Scott's heritage was a secret or something.

"That is one of the big immigrant groups in Sacramento," he said with a shrug. There were Russian businesses all over the suburbs. Even Ryan's mother, who lived in L.A., must have seen them.

There was an awkward silence, punctuated by the big chef's knife clumsily cutting the cute little baby potatoes ruthlessly into fourths. "So why don't you work for one of the businesses?" she asked politely. "Ryan always wanted to be a lawyer. I knew he'd never be a part of the landscaping, like Walter, or the interior decorating, like Yvonne. What was your excuse?"

She said it with a playful smile, but that didn't keep Scott from trying to smooth down his chafed feelings. He looked out into the living room again and realized that Ryan and his father had taken the dog and the kids outside into the last of the afternoon sunlight so they could work off some energy before changing into their Sunday best for dinner and games.

"My mom always said she didn't work in a nail salon for thirty years so we'd have to do the same, and my dad pretty much agreed with her. Two of my sisters followed Mom's footsteps because they liked it— they liked the color and the style, and they loved doing hair and wearing the clothes. My brother, the oldest, he went to business school to help Dad manage everything he got from my grandpa, and Mama always told me to go my own way. I ran with that, you know?"

"Well, you're awfully good at cooking. Why not do that?"

Scott shrugged and grinned, the same grin that seemed to melt Ryan no matter what Scott was doing, but without the sexual wattage. Taylor Connors was not amused, so he gave her an honest answer, but it wasn't as much fun as the smile.

"I like to do a lot of things," he said, and it was true. "There's just not a lot of things I like to do for money." Oh God. Taylor was looking at him like he was a wayward sixth grader who had cracked a dirty joke. He took a deep breath and tried to explain better than that.

"It's like my mom. My mom does this thing with a needle and sewing thread—it's called tatting. It's gorgeous. She makes some of the most beautiful stuff—she made the wedding veil for my oldest sister's wedding, and all four of the girls have worn it because it was so beautiful. It's in mothballs waiting for my nieces to grow up. It's amazing. It's something she really loves to do. And she made this... I guess it's a doily or a decorated runner, that she keeps in the salon to make the place look more homey, right? And all these rich women come in, and they're begging Mama to make them something, and she flat out refuses."

Taylor really was looking at him now, and he was glad she was done massacring the potatoes; otherwise he'd be off to fetch the first aid kit. "Why would she do that?"

Scott shrugged again. "Because we have enough money, and tatting is something she loves to do for fun. Once people start paying her for that, it takes all the fun out of it. She loves doing the hair and the nails now, but she started out knowing it was a trade, so she can love doing it and it's not going to get ruined. But tatting is something she does just for her. She makes stuff for other people, but it's the stuff she wants to do. That's cooking for me—and shopping for people and helping them pick out their furniture or their clothes. It's something I could do for money, but that would take all the fun out of it. So I work at Starbucks for the money, and I go to school to learn a trade, and I work my business because it's sort of a meld between the stuff I learn at school and the stuff I'm interested in anyway—it's got trade all over it, so it doesn't feel ruined when I do it for money."

Taylor was looking at him as though this was a totally foreign concept, and he was really glad that she'd never met his mother. Sofia had been raised to be a good Russian woman, and although she was strong enough to raise six children, she was also sensitive enough to have her feelings hurt when an idea that was dear to her was popped under the pressure of that glare like a summer strawberry under an icicle.

"So if you're not going to do any of the things you really love for money, how do you expect to keep making your end of the house payment?" she asked after a moment, and Scott blinked slowly.

"Well, there never really was a 'my end'," he said truthfully. "There was a 'combined income' thing—you know, like married straight people without the functioning uterus, right?"

"Well, doesn't that feel like you're freeloading off my son's bigger income?"

"No," he whispered, hurt in a way he hadn't really thought about. The house had been a bone of contention between Taylor and Ryan for the last three days. Taylor thought it was a risky venture in such an uncertain market, but Ryan had been confident in that same way he'd been confident in bed the night before. They could make it. Scott had taken the business courses. He knew the extent of their income, and he'd developed some of Ryan's confidence too. They could do it. They could have a home and a yard and a place for Blitzkrieg to run where she couldn't eat all the garbage when she was left alone for the day. Scott had known Ryan was paying a bigger portion, but that wasn't the way they did things—it never had been. Ryan hadn't once suggested they do it any different.

"No," he said again, trying to find his way past that word "freeloader." "Ryan and I… we… we didn't think that way. We just added up what we made, you know, and together it was enough. It… I mean, it didn't matter who made more. It just mattered that we could make it togeth—"

"But you're getting a business degree, Scott. You do know Ryan could pay for that house by himself, right?"

"But he doesn't want to," Scott said, hearing his voice rise childishly at the end. Scott knew that. He knew he was right. Ryan had said it with words, with his body, with the way they laughed their way through everything from Ryan's cut pay to Blitzkrieg's outrageous vet bills. "He doesn't want to. He keeps saying the only way the house would be a home is with me."

Oh geez. Scott's voice was as hurt as a socially mauled second grader's, and his chest literally ached with the idea that Ryan's mom would think so poorly of him. It wasn't fair—Walter's business had just been starting out when he and Yvonne had married. Ryan had told him that. That's why it had made so much sense for Walter's landscaping business to become a part of Taylor's decorating business. Walter did the outside, and Yvonne and Taylor did the inside. But no one had ever accused Walter of freeloading.

Taylor's hurt from earlier, when Scott had been taking over in the kitchen, seemed to have dissipated completely. Her pale blue eyes—so different from Ryan's warm brown ones—looked at him composedly, and not a strand of her silver-blonde pageboy seemed to have moved from place. "That's really romantic and everything, Scott, but it doesn't pay the bills."

Scott nodded and shot his one volley in the war. "Ryan can pay his own bills. Your lover shouldn't be the thing you do for money." And then he stood up and walked to the Christmas tree to snatch the tiny present he'd hidden among all of the kids' stuff and crammed it in his jeans pocket before going out to the mudroom to find his parka and his gloves, scarf, and hat. He wasn't foolish or emo—he wasn't planning to go outside and freeze—but just for a minute, he needed to be far, far away from Ryan's family, and, hell, even from Ryan himself, or he'd never be able to go back and look Ryan in the eyes ever again.

CHAPTER 6
RYAN
PAPER, GOLD, AND FLIGHT

RYAN SAW Scott tear out of the house, walking fast toward the road, and scrambled to follow him. He couldn't. He had the kids, who were ready to go in, and the dog, who needed to be toweled off. Dammit, the angle of Scott's shoulders and the dejected droop of his head did not speak well for a lover who had his shit together and was happy about Christmas Eve. Ryan had plans for Christmas, fuck it all, and Scotty's happiness was of preeminent importance.

He totally ditched his dad in the mudroom, buried in a flurry of zippers, scarves, and rubber boots. He didn't even take his own boots off before walking into the kitchen to ask his mom where Scotty was going.

She was looking disconsolately at something that might have been mashed potatoes but that had too many sharp angles in it, and the look of unhappiness she sent him over her shoulder was eloquent, even if her words were evasive.

"I don't know where he went, sweetie. We were talking, and he just left."

"What did you say to him?" Oh God, four days of careful dancing to keep the two of them from spending too long in the same room, and it was all ruined because his mom had decided to cook! Why had she decided to cook? Most Christmases, Ryan's dad cooked. When Ryan saw Scott get the stuff out of the freezer, he'd asked Gordon quietly if it was okay if Scott took over this year, and Gordon hadn't had a problem with that.

"Nothing in particular," Taylor said evasively. She was prodding what looked like Italian stuffed flank steak with a fork, and Ryan groaned.

"Bullshit," he muttered. "Complete and total bullshit."

"Ryan?" Ryan cringed as his dad came up in time to hear him swear at his mother—but that didn't stop his temper from ramping up.

"She said something to him, Dad. I don't know what it was, but that's Scotty's flank steak she's poking and Scotty's potatoes she's screwed up, and Scotty is outside with his feelings hurt, and I don't even know how to fix it."

Taylor turned to him bitterly. "Wonderful! That man sat here and explained to me how he didn't have the focus of a butterfly and that was okay with him because you would pick up his slack, and he gets his feelings hurt when I ask him if that's fair!"

Ryan shook his head, resisting the urge to kick the counter. "You're the one who's not fair, Mom," he said, and then turned around right back to the mudroom, wading through kids saying, "Where are you going, Uncle Ryan?" and not paying any attention until he ran headfirst into Walter.

"'Scuse me," he mumbled, and Walter put out a hand and steadied his shoulder, then spoke over him.

"Hey, Taylor, what did you say to Scott? He just apologized for being a freeloader, and he was almost in tears."

That got Ryan's attention. He whipped his head around and glared at his mother. "Don't bother serving us any of your slop, Mom. Scott and I will be heading home. I'd rather drive off a cliff than let him deal with any more of your crap!"

With that he ran in search of Scott.

Blitzkrieg was game to come with him, but she was still panting from the run that the kids had given her and still shivering from the cold. Ryan left her drying off in the mudroom. He grabbed his parka and pulled his gloves on as he walked, shivering in the change of temperature even from ten minutes earlier. The sun was almost horizontal over the edge of the valley. In a few minutes it would be completely gone, and the frigid edge of twilight would cut through the air and his parka and his long johns and probably sever his balls right off and let them roll around like hairy marbles.

He followed Scott's direction—easy to spot because of the lone set of footprints going toward the main road—and trotted as fast as he could, panting with the effort. He was in shape, but Scotty rode his damned bike all over creation and could probably leave him in the dust when it came to hauling ass through snow. He resisted the urge to call Scott's name—besides being melodramatic, he was half afraid of hearing Scott telling him to fuck off, and that wasn't their style, never had been, and it would probably break his heart.

Scott's parka was bright cherry red, which was not Scott's best color but it did match his playful heart. He'd had it before he met Ryan, and it was one of those ultimate mountaineering things that was lined with Gore-Tex and something else space-age. Scott's balls would be just fine, and Ryan was glad, because by the time he spotted that cheerful, happy color against the snow, the only reason his own weren't freezing off was that, under his long johns, he'd worked up a bit of a sweat.

"Scotty?" he asked cautiously, and Scott shrugged his shoulders and turned away, the gesture particularly adolescent. Ryan's heart sank. Oh no. He and Scott were gay men—about as gay as it got, that was true. They wore their emotions on their sleeves, easily accessible. Hell, they blew most women Ryan knew right out of the water when it came to emotional availability. But Scott was happy, playful, maybe the most cheerful person Ryan had ever met. They'd suffered through the flu together and hard finances and Ryan's decision not to set the world on fire if he could be Scotty's world instead, but for the most part, their lives had followed a gentle curve. They hadn't lost so much as a goldfish or mourned a grandparent in the last three years.

Ryan had never seen Scotty cry.

"Scotty?" he said again, his own voice cracking a little. "Babe...."

Scott let out a breath, the deep, painful kind that shuddered like wind through a broken window, and let out a little not-laugh. "Don't tell me that dinner's ready. I watched her try to cook it, Ry—we're better off with tinned soup."

"I was going to tell you to warm up the car," Ryan said gruffly. "You warm up the car, I'll throw our shit in a suitcase, and we can be home in...." He trailed off painfully.

"Twelve hours," Scott supplied with grim humor, "but I appreciate the thought." He looked up then and wiped his face with his wrist, but he was trying a smile, and it gave Ryan the courage to take a few steps in and wrap his arm around Scott's shoulders. There was no resistance in him— there never had been, not in Scotty. He went where the wind took him. He'd said once that after he'd met Ryan, all winds seemed to sweep him to Ryan's door. That was right before they moved in together, because Ryan said Scott didn't need the wind to ever be pushed into Ryan's arms.

"We can get the camping gear and sleep in the garage," Ryan said. He was completely serious, and Scott gave a tortured little laugh.

"We're going back inside and fixing some soup and having Christmas with your family," he said quietly. "You know it, I know it. We're stuck, Ry."

Ryan nodded, feeling heartsore. "I'm sorry she's being such a bitch. You know I don't believe any of that shit, right?"

Scott looked down at Ryan's chest, but Ryan could still see the trembling lip. "I'm not a freeloader, am I?"

Ryan grasped his faintly stubbly chin. (Scott didn't grow a good beard, so he didn't shave a lot when he was on vacation or someplace where he couldn't be seen and preen like the lovely peacock he was. Ryan liked it when he started getting the Shaggy whiskers like the guy on *Scooby-Doo*.)

"Scott, you remember when I told my boss I couldn't take so many business trips, and even though that meant less money, you were really happy?"

Scott nodded and snuggled his head against Ryan's shoulder. "You missed your own birthday," he mumbled. Ryan laughed a little, because Ryan hadn't missed his own birthday actually. He'd come home on his birthday when Scott hadn't been expecting him, and it had ended up being probably his best birthday ever. But Scott would always remember it as the year Ryan missed his own birthday, because as much as Scott tried to hide it, he'd been hurt beyond words, right up until Ryan had showed up on the porch, naked, with a bow around his waist.

"Yeah," Ryan agreed, even though it wasn't true. "Yeah. And you didn't bat an eyelash over the money. You said my being there was more important than anything else. And because of that, that decision made me really happy. Do you think it's different with me? Yeah, sure—you're smart. You could have had your business degree two years ago, or you could be running one of your family's businesses, but would that have made you happy?"

"No." It was so true Scott may as well have bought a T-shirt and a matching tattoo.

Ryan laughed a little and squeezed Scott even tighter against the encroaching cold. "Me neither," he said, directly into Scotty's red-rimmed blue-gray eyes, because Scott needed to know this was the truth. "I love you exactly the way you are. And the way you are is happy. You and me. It's always been you and me. Why would I want to change you? You're the man that I fell in love with in a bathroom. I mean, geez, Scotty—I can't imagine not loving you. I would do anything to see you happy, and the real miracle is that all I have to do to see you happy is love you just the way you are. I'm not going to change that. Not for all the money on the planet."

Scott nodded and smiled. Scotty was vain on his best days. He would not be pleased at how he looked. His face was blotchy, his nose was red, swollen, and running, his eyes were red, and his chin kept crinkling as he fought the urge to cry over hurt feelings. Even Scotty, comfortable with his sexuality as nobody in the world could be, felt too manly to cry.

But his smile on that wide, pouty-lipped, mobile mouth was still a miracle—a pure-as-snow, one-hundred-percent-unfiltered-joy miracle.

"Can I give you something?" he asked, his voice still clogged.

"A stomach pump if we have to eat my mother's cooking?" Ryan asked dryly, and Scott shook his head, then stopped and grimaced.

"Maybe your dad can salvage it. As long as we don't have to eat the potatoes. But that's not what I wanted to give you." He reached into his pocket and pulled out a small gift box wrapped in gold foil with a burgundy velvet ribbon, because Scott had a sense of presentation like no one Ryan had ever met.

"My Christmas present? Wasn't tonight early enough for you?"

Scott shook his head. "The whole family is going to be opening gifts tonight, and then the kids are going to be opening presents from Santa tomorrow, and it's going to be loud, and it's going to be fun," beat "sort of, but it's going to be… in front of everyone, you know?" Scott wasn't great with subtext. Ryan easily translated that to *I don't want to give this to you in front of your mother*, and he grunted in agreement. Anything, anything to keep Scotty from running out into what was now evening and crying in the snow.

"So here," Scott said nervously, hopping from one foot to the other. "Open it while you can still see inside."

Ryan's gloved fingers were clumsy, and Scott's were only a little less so as he helped to get the bow off and get under the foil, and then they both popped the lid of the box open.

Ryan gasped and then giggled and then, wonder of wonders, felt his eyes burn a little, even as he squinted them against the darkening twilight.

"For us?" he asked, stroking a covered fingertip reverently on the plain gold.

"Yeah," Scott said. He was gnawing on his lower lip and there was a little horizontal bar between his eyes, and Ryan had to laugh that Scott would be anxious about this.

"So we can be husbands, right?" he asked, feeling his voice wobble, and Scott looked at him with shining eyes and nodded.

"I mean, we're going to sign the cohabitation papers and everything," Scott said. "But that's not really romantic. It should be romantic, you know?"

Ryan nodded, touching the rings again, for a moment lost in the stillness of the woods at night and the gleam of gold, the smell of pine and snow, and the closeness of the other half of his heart. "It's totally romantic," he whispered and then kissed Scott's upraised face. Scott straightened and answered the kiss full throttle. Ryan snapped the lid of the box closed and stuffed it in his pocket and then opened his mouth and launched an out-and-out incursion into Scotty's mouth, because in that moment, he wanted Scott, all of him, wanted him naked, wanted him spread out, head back, bare and completely at Ryan's mercy. Scott was his, all his, and not a soul in the world could doubt it or question it or accuse Scott of being anything but the other half of Ryan's soul.

Scott groaned and backed up against a tree—something not pine, with bare branches and no threat of snow falling on their heads—and Ryan kept up the kiss, taking the long, deep, wet kiss to a series of voracious, quick, deep, attack kisses that he knew would make Scotty crazy until Scott bucked his groin up against Ryan's thigh. Ryan felt Scott's erection through the fabric of his jeans and underwear and thought that if he didn't touch it or taste it somehow, he'd die.

It was dark now, and the temperature was dropping damned fast, but Ryan knew his lover, knew his kinks and his quirks and knew what would make Scotty come so quickly things would not even start to think about freezing off.

Without preamble, feeling sheltered by the night, he dropped to his knees in front of Scotty and undid just the fly of his jeans. He shucked off his gloves and tucked them under his arm, then took Scott's hardened prick in one hand while he scooped up a small handful of snow with the other. While Scott made muffled, strangled moans above Ryan's head, Ryan opened his hot mouth and took Scotty in as far as he could go.

Then he pulled back and took that little chunk of virgin, powdery snow, and traced it on Scott's length as he pulled back.

Scott gasped, whined, shuddered, and Ryan threw his head forward again, feeling his hat slide down his back as Scott's fingers knotted in his hair. Scott made his "I'm gonna come!" sound, and Ryan did the same trick a few more times. He pulled back, back, keeping only the ridge of Scotty's erection wrapped hard within his lips, and traced the shuddery, edgy length with cold as he retreated. Then he swallowed Scott down as far as he could go, all the better to squeeze Scott's cockhead with everything he had.

That was all. A little bit of exposure, a little bit of snow, and a whole lot of boiling love, and Scott gave a muffled scream and came, shuddering, gasping, moaning over Ryan's head—but not crying. Not crying and not doubting and not worrying.

Ryan swallowed and swallowed (because spitting would make his mouth wetter, and that would be cold and uncomfortable), and finally he leaned his head against Scott's stomach for one brief moment to catch his breath.

And heard Walter call their names from over Scott's shoulder.

"Hey, guys, is that you? What are you doing? Taylor and Gordon are worried to death—oh, geez, are you guys… oh ew!"

Ryan had buttoned up Scott's fly and threw his gloves on from Walter's first word. He looked up at Scotty in horror, and Scott pulled his cotton sleeve out of the cuff of his jacket to wipe Ryan's face. His eyes darted to Ryan's pocket and he mouthed, "Ring!" and Ryan read his mind.

"Cool your jets, Walter," he said, marveling at how composed he sounded. He reached into his pocket and pulled out the rings, where they gleamed under a clear rising moon. "We're not doing anything dirty in the woods—I'm proposing."

"Well?" Walter demanded, walking up but keeping a respectful distance, which was fine with Ryan, who, once again, felt like he had "I just blew the Chrysler building!" stamped on his forehead.

"Well, what?" he said with a private smile to Scott.

"Well, what'd he say?"

Scott took Ryan's chilled face between his wool-covered hands, looking down at him in the gathered dark. "There's only one answer, you know that, right?"

Ryan grinned and got to his feet, and gave Scotty a quick, soft kiss, with just enough tongue for Scott to taste himself, because he knew that would turn Scott's key.

"Yes," Ryan said softly. "He said yes."

"Awesome!" Walter congratulated, and then clapped Ryan solidly on the back. Ryan turned toward him with a rather surprised look on his face, and Walter gave Scott a fully developed, full-body bear hug. "My God!" Walter said with some fervency. "You have no idea how glad I am to not be the only one Taylor can bitch at!"

Ryan couldn't help it. He had to laugh—pained laughter, yes, but laughter, because Walter had a point. His mother was protective, exacting, and demanding, but one thing was certain.

Getting on her bad side apparently meant you were family.

He wrapped a protective arm around Scott's shoulders, and the two of them fell in step beside Walter while Walter congratulated them with more sincerity than Ryan would have given him credit for at the beginning of the week.

Well, maybe being a douche didn't necessarily mean he was stupid or a complete asshole. And maybe family was just complicated, a subtle little dance of old prejudices and new expectations and behaviors, and the real beauty of it was that everyone was stuck with each other and had to make it work.

"So how are you going to do this?" Walter wanted to know. "Vermont? Canada? Aren't there some other states you can get married in?"

"New York," Ryan said with certainty. "In the spring."

Scott rolled his eyes when Walter couldn't see. "Nice touch!" he mouthed, and Ryan grinned.

"Thank you," he said mockingly, thinking of the box he'd snuck under the tree the night before, the one that Scott really needed to open with witnesses. The rings? Those were special. Scott was right—those needed to be opened in private. Ryan's gift to Scott?

That was something Ryan's mother needed to see in person.

"So," Ryan said, feeling well and truly like Christmas for the first time since he and Scotty had thrown all their stuff in the back of the little outdated Honda and pulled out of Sacramento for the hills, "what did my parents do with dinner? Do we have time to dress?"

As IT turned out, not only had Gordon put a ban on dressing for dinner, the flank steak was actually salvageable, even if the potatoes ended up in Blitzkrieg's bowl. Ryan's dad had worked some sort of subtle magic and put the flank steak into a Dutch oven for half an hour until it fell apart, and then threw in the sautéed veggies, pulled out some fresh tortillas, grated cheese, and sour cream, and served some absolutely awesome (if unconventional) fajitas.

The family started the meal as soon as Ryan and Scott washed up and then ate as though nothing had happened. Gordon talked happily about how good the steak marinade was and how that had saved the entire works for them while Taylor looked pointedly at her plate. Scott stayed out of that conversation, but the kids were so wound up about opening their two allotted presents that the din at the kitchen table probably carried over the lake anyway.

That was especially true when dinner and dessert were over. (Dessert was a kind of homemade tapioca that Scott had made the night before and chilled in the refrigerator in the garage. Taylor ate it with a look like sour lemons, but the rest of the family thought it was delicious.) The kids circled the Christmas tree, chattering like magpies, choosing exactly the right gifts to open.

The big mysterious package for the girls figured large in their plans—as it should have—but Yvonne, using some canny bargaining skills and some exasperated looks at Scott and Ryan, managed to talk them into opening their new pajamas and one toy to play with before their dad took them upstairs and read *'Twas the Night Before Christmas*, which was their own family tradition.

Tommy and Ella-Jaye, the two oldest, were both insistent that the adults open a present, and Ryan seconded the motion. "I'll get yours," he told Scott quietly. "You open last."

Ryan felt a little bit of cold anticipation shiver through him while the other grown-ups got their Christmas Eve gifts. Taylor was pleased with the tennis bracelet that had her grandchildren's birthstones on it, and Gordon was pleased with the golf club covers for his favorite set of clubs. Walter had given Yvonne a spa day—and Yvonne had given her husband two tickets to a baseball game that she insisted she wanted to attend with him.

And then it was Ryan's turn. Ryan grinned and said, "I already opened my present from Scott. When Scott opens my present to him, I'll show it to you."

Walter made a little kid's sound, like "Heeeeeeeeeeeee!" bouncing next to Ryan on the couch, and Ryan turned to him in mock exasperation.

"Geez, Walter, calm down! You've already done this!"

Walter's grin was beatific, and the look he gave Ryan's sister put paid to a lot of douchey insensitivity. Ryan could tell by Yvonne's expression that she thought so too. "Yeah, but it's really awesome, and I'm happy you get to do it too."

Taylor and Gordon didn't hear him, but Yvonne did, and she clapped her hand over her mouth in suppressed excitement.

Scotty, on the other hand, had never suppressed excitement in his life. Ryan watched his open, pretty face carefully as he turned the wrapping paper on the shoebox into confetti, and then started rifling through the contents. His excited squeal brought the kids gathering around in a tangle and sent Blitzkrieg jumping up and down and barking excitedly into the general chaos.

"New York? New York!" Scott flew to his feet and started bouncing on his toes. "Ohmygod, Ry! You're taking me to New York! And we're gonna see *Camelot*!" He pawed through the box for a moment to get to the last envelope, the one with the cool, dry legalese proclaiming the most romantic thing in the world. "Ryan! Ohmygod, Ryan! We're gonna get married! And…." The realization hit Scott in one breathless rush, and Ryan stood up too so he could capture that full look of awe with a kiss. He pulled back, his eyes closed, Scotty's wonder on his lips, and Scott put his fingers delicately on his mouth.

"You planned this," he said in wonder. "You… I bought the rings because I wanted a… a… token, but… oh, God, Ry! We're going to have the real thing!"

Ryan smiled and took him into a bear hug of joy, and Scott sob-laughed into his shoulder for what felt to be the rest of the night.

Things did calm down eventually—at least, they did after Ryan pulled out the rings and he and Scott slid them on in the midst a jumping excited throng of squealing children. Eventually though, the kids were hustled off to bed with their story, the wrapping paper was cleaned up, and the special gifts from Santa were placed beneath the tree.

The adults were left lounging on the couch, Yvonne sitting on the floor between her husband's spread thighs, resting her cheek on his knee. Ryan was leaning back into the corner of the couch with one leg propped up, and Scott snuggled into his arms where he belonged. Their left hands were intertwined so they could admire the plain gold bands on their fingers, although Scott had insisted that he take them back after the wedding to get the date inscribed on the inside. Blitzkrieg was passed out so completely at their feet that Ella-Jaye could probably lie on her back and the poor thing wouldn't so much as breathe heavier.

Gordon was sprawled on one end of the love seat across from them with Ryan's mother sitting primly next to him, drinking coffee mixed with something that smelled heavily alcoholic even from where Ryan was sitting.

The quiet was soft and easy, in spite of Taylor's apparent tension, and Ryan was rubbing his cheek dreamily on Scotty's hair, watching Scott's tanned, long fingers play with the ring on Ryan's blunter, paler one. Him and Scotty—it was the only Christmas he wanted to have.

"New York," Taylor said bluntly into the silence, and Ryan nodded happily. Scott was the born romantic of the two of them. It was nice to have a win in that department every now and then.

"Yup," he said softly, "New York."

"That's awfully final," she said, her tone still a little stiff, but Ryan was too cozy and warm to take offense.

"Marriage usually is," he said evenly, and Taylor's sigh was a concession.

"Indeed. Welcome to the family, Scott."

Scotty never could hold a grudge. "Thanks, Mrs. Connors." He gave a happy sigh back into Ryan's arms. "I'm really happy to be here."

Ryan's mother's expression relaxed a little, and then a little more, and then her posture on the sturdy leather love seat became a little mellower, like a happy matron, surrounded by her family on Christmas Eve.

"We're happy to have you," she said at last.

Ryan angled his head to get a good look at Scott's expression.

"Thank you," Scott said softly. "Merry Christmas, Mrs. Connors."

"You've always called me Taylor before," she admonished mildly. "Merry Christmas, Scott."

Sometimes Christmas was just like life. It was all about the little moments. Ryan determined that he'd carry that one all the way to New York with him and Scott, wrapped up in his pocket with two gold rings.

ALL THE DRAMA

"BUT YOU said we can go make cookies!" Josie was trying to be patient, Henry Calder knew, but it had been a long day for him too. He swung his four-year old niece up into his arms, threw his gym bag over his other shoulder, and shut the door to his brand new hybrid with his knee.

"I know, Bunny," Hank said, trying hard to keep his voice from ratcheting toward irritation as he wove around the cars in the parking lot. "But if your Uncle Hank doesn't get his workout in, he gets *cranky*!" He made his voice low and growly, and since she was in his arms anyway, he blew a bubble through her puffy pink jacket, just to make her laugh. It worked, and he held her close and kissed her blonde head. He'd done his best at a braid today, and he thought he was getting better.

"I promise, Bunny. If you can let Uncle Hank get in a little bitty workout, we'll go home, and make some cookies and we can eat some mac 'n' cheese while they're baking. How's that?"

Josie nodded adamantly. "Good. 'Cause Mommy's not going to come back unless we make Christmas perfect."

Hank smiled and nodded, and tried not to clutch his stomach and bury his face in her shoulder and cry. The odds of his sister coming home for Christmas—or any day, for that matter—weren't great.

"We're doing okay, aren't we?" he asked as he wrestled the gym bag and Josie and the door, coming in from the Sacramento cold into Cal-Fit, his happy place. "We managed Halloween and Thanksgiving okay, right?"

Josie wrinkled her nose. "That princess dress was too big!" she told him, and he nodded. It was true, the costume would fit her again next year. Well, sue him. His sister had left her daughter with him the week before Halloween. He'd managed a princess dress, candy for the door, and a friend to give the candy out while Hank took his niece trick-or-treating throughout his neighborhood. The fact that the only dress he could find at the Halloween store had been two sizes too big was extraneous. He'd come through.

"I know it was," he said, taking it on the chin. "Next year we'll do better."

"Next year Mommy will take me."

Hank held out his pass for the nice lady at Cal-Fit, who scanned his card and smiled warmly at Josie. Cindy had curly blonde-gray hair pulled back in a pony-tail and faded blue eyes. Hank felt bad—she was the closest thing to a woman in Josie's life at the moment, and Josie lit up whenever she saw her.

"Hey Josie," Cindy said, her voice sweet and grandmotherly. "You gonna go visit Justin today?"

"I like Justin," Josie proclaimed, and Hank nodded. Of course she did. The guy drove *Hank* banana shit, but no, Josie liked Justin.

"That's good, Bunny," he said, and took the name tags from Cindy before giving her an absent smile and turning down the hallway to the daycare area.

"Do you like Justin?" she asked, and he smiled. For her, he'd love Justin, marry him, take the guy into his house and give him foot rubs.

"Yeah, of course I do!"

He *hated* that guy.

Of all the flame-outs Hank had ever seen, in college and after, Justin was by far the most dramatic, over-the-top boy-princess in the entire northern half of the state. Oh God. Even as they got near the playroom enclosure, Hank could hear him squeal. And of course, the kids *loved* him.

"Oh my God! Do you guys think... did I hear... is *Santa* going to be coming to Cal-Fit? Did you *know* that? *Santa* is coming to Cal-Fit! Are you all going to be here?"

"*Yes!*" The cheer was deafening, and Hank actually *looked* at the door before he opened it and saw that there was going to be an event on Saturday. Oh wonderful. *Santa.*

"Santa?" Josie said, her voice all excited, and Hank started doing his mental schedule all over again.

"Of course," he said. "Santa." Oh God. Please God. Just let him get to the treadmill. Twenty minutes on the treadmill so he could clear his head. Twenty minutes on the free weights, and a five-minute shower, and he could do this. Just please please please please *please* let him have his happy time before he figured out how to fit Santa into redoing Josie's room and dealing with the child welfare services who were going to visit on Monday and who insisted that he show that she would have her own space and—

"*Justin!*" Josie squealed as he opened the door, and Hank looked up to see the cherry on his headache smiling so wide, Hank was surprised the top of his head didn't fall off.

Justin was young—in his second, maybe third year of college, with widely spaced blue eyes, surrounded by a fringe of dark lashes. He had one of those Irish fair complexions, the kind that showed color easily: straight black hair, a heart shaped face, and a nose that tip-tilted on the end. The first time Hank had ever seen him, Hank had thought he was one of the prettiest young men on the planet Earth, ever. And then Justin had opened his mouth.

"Josie!" Justin trilled, opening his arms and doing a little dance. Josie squealed, trying to get to Justin as he held court at the end of the coloring table. He'd apparently been inspiring all of the young artists to put glue and green sparkles on their Christmas tree masterpieces.

"Justin!" Josie squealed, throwing herself at him after wiggling out of Hank's arms and almost getting her tiny bunny butt dumped onto the floor of the gym's daycare room.

"Omigah, Bunny, you will *never* guess what I just told everybody!"

"Santa!" Josie squeaked. "You said it was going to be *Santa!* Uncle Hank said we could come, isn't that right Uncle Hank?"

Oh God. Commitment time. Hank wondered desperately who he could call to be at his house while the movers delivered Josie's little white twin bed, so she wouldn't be lost in the big queen-size that took over what used to be his guest bedroom. But Justin was pouting at him like he was being a big meanie and Josie was glaring at him like he was depriving her of this one and only childhood experience because he was determined to suck at this whole parenting gig, and, oh, hells, even *Hank* remembered that Santa was important.

"I'll try, Bunny," he said quietly. "Is that good enough?"

"*Mommy* would make sure I got to see Santa," she said spitefully, and Hank nodded. Yup, that was the truth. Amanda would have taken Josie to see Santa for the photo op. Amanda would have shown a picture of Josie sitting on Santa's lap while wearing a red velveteen dress she hadn't been able to afford, and then shown all of her friends just to listen to them coo, and then she would have told Josie to go away, couldn't Josie see that Mommy was talking to her friends? And then she would have dropped Josie at a friend's house while she, Amanda, went out to party because why was a girl her age at home with a child anyway? Didn't she *deserve* to party? Hadn't she *earned* that right? She'd had the kid's picture taken with Santa, after all.

"Yeah, Bunny," Hank said, needing the freedom of the treadmill like he needed nothing else in the world. "Your mommy would have made sure you got to see Santa."

He wasn't sure what was in his voice when he said it, but Justin flinched back, and Josie stuck her tongue out at Hank, and Hank signed his name on the roster. "I'm going to have my earbuds in," he muttered, because this was something they had to know. "If you need me, you need to come get me."

And with that he fled the gym childcare, leaving Justin, who was probably going to cry about what a big meanie Hank was to tell Josie that he was a big loser and that any uncle who couldn't sprinkle glitter on Christmas trees was obviously not going to be a good bet as a parent.

Yeah, well, until the better mommies and uncles lined up to take her, Hank was all she got.

HE CHANGED quickly and queued some Linkin Park up on his iPod, putting it in the handy little case that wrapped around his bicep. He'd always been an active kid, and since becoming an adult he'd learned when you worked your body a lot, it tended to protest when that sort of activity stopped. He'd also always liked this gym—it was designed specifically for families—and he liked it even more now that he had a family to bring here.

But at the moment, with Linkin Park queued up, he wasn't thinking about the daycare, or the nice supportive vibe or the kindness of the staff. He was thinking about nothing more than warming up and pushing his body to the point where all the stiffness got worked out, and then cooling down responsibly—and getting it all done before daycare closed. He didn't want to impose.

Oh, gods! It felt so good! There was no worrying about keeping custody of Josie, no worrying if Amanda was going to come back and completely disrupt Josie's life, no worrying if his job was too many hours or if he was doing enough as a parent, no stressing about Christmas and getting all the little details down. There was no disappointment in his sister or irritation at their mother or loneliness at doing all of this alone or—

The hand tapping his shoulder startled him so much he missed a step, which sucked because he was going fast enough for the treadmill to throw him *hard* against the console and slam his shoulder with enough force to bruise. The rebound threw him backward and he was seizing hold of the handrails so he could stabilize and press the stop button when a long-fingered hand darted in front of him and pushed the stop button for him. Hank grabbed hold of the handrails and steadied himself, panting and furious, and turned around ready to unload his temper and his pain and found himself face to face with the one person he *hadn't* been running from.

"Justin?" he asked, his temper skating the fine edge, and Justin grimaced.

"I'm sorry, Mr. Calder—I really am. But Josie has to go potty, and company policy says that her guardian has to take her. We're not allowed to."

Oh. "Oh." God, he felt dumb. "Of course."

Suddenly Justin—who had shown some clear-headedness turning off the treadmill—started shaking his hands and trilling, and Henry was *not* in the mood.

"Ohmigah omigah omigah! Mr. Calder—you're *bleeding*!"

Hank looked down at his aching arm and saw that Justin was right. "Fuck," he said succinctly. "Fuck. Just… hell. Okay. Let me get Josie to the bathroom. I'll get some Band-Aids or—"

"Don't worry about it," Justin assured him, flapping his wrist airily. Hank had picked the treadmill closest to the wall, and Justin grabbed a disinfectant bottle, paper towel, and poly gloves from the little alcove made just for that purpose. As he spoke, he put on the gloves and wiped the console that had taken a chunk of Hank's skin. "I've got the supplies, you just get your little princess to the potty before we have *lots* of things to clean up, okay?"

Hank grunted, sort of impressed by Justin's competence and the triceps flexing as he worked, and Justin turned to him, furrowing his brow. "*Okay?*"

Deep breath. The kid was doing his job. It wasn't his fault Hank hadn't been laid in a year and a half. "Okay," Hank said mildly. "Proceed."

Justin smiled, like he'd won something, and Hank followed him down past the weight machines to the daycare room again. There was a tiny little bathroom adjoining the playroom, and Hank walked Josie over to it as fast as he could.

"Wait outside!" Josie ordered, and Hank nodded.

"Right."

He stood outside and listened to her tinkle, and Justin approached him. His hands were already encased in the poly gloves, and he had a first aid kit open on the tiny kid-size table.

"This really isn't nece—"

"Oh, of course it is," Justin said, a playful inflection in his voice. "Besides! We're trained to do this and everything. I've been *dying* for someone to bleed on my watch, just so I could doctor them up and prove I can! How else am I going to get my merit badge?"

Hank allowed a brief laugh to escape. "I have no idea," he said, and then, calling behind him into the bathroom, "Josie, angel, how you doing in there?"

"I have to go number two!" she called back, and Hank looked at the clock and sighed. So much for his workout or his cool down or working out any of the anxiety that had built up in his muscles over the—

"Ouch!" he cried, pulled out of that death spiral of frustration by the sudden sting at his arm.

"Sorry!" Justin apologized brightly. He was dabbing at the cut on Hank's arm with a cotton ball and some hydrogen peroxide, a look of concentration on his face.

Hank grunted. He didn't want to be a baby.

"So," Justin said, setting the cotton ball down on the absurdly small table next to them, alongside the rest of the first aid kit, "why don't you want to take her to see Santa?" He picked up another cotton ball then and smeared some antibiotic ointment on it, and his attention on those things were what let Hank answer.

"I'm dying for her to see Santa," he said, more sincerely than he thought possible. "But the social worker is coming on Monday to give me full custody, and her bed is coming on Saturday. I want it to look like *her room*, so it's perfect." Justin smeared the ointment delicately on his arm, and Hank sighed. "She needs permanent. And that's—"

"Ohmigah! That's *way* more important than Santa!" Justin said, and Hank turned to him, surprised.

"I know but—"

"I can *totally* see why you'd want to do that more! Why can't you just tell her that? She's a smart girl, I'm sure she'd understand."

"Uncle Hank!" Josie called imperiously. "Are you still there?"

"Right here, Bunny!"

"Mommy likes to sing when I'm in the potty so I don't get scared."

Hank met gazes with Justin, who grimaced a bit, and then Hank launched into something Hank and Amanda's mother had played almost constantly when they'd been kids.

"*I'm on top of the world looking down on creation—*" And then Josie's voice interrupted in command.

"*Christmas* music, Uncle Hank!"

Hank closed his eyes. "*Deck the halls with boughs of holly—*"

"*Tra la la la la,*" Justin chimed in, smiling encouragingly. Hank smiled back, grateful for the moral support, and they continued.

"*La la, la la.*"

Justin bandaged his arm as they kept singing. They made it through the entire song by the time she was ready to go—after needing some help with the cleanup, of course. Hank figured that there was nothing more guaranteed to let you know where you stood in the order of the world than a four year old bending over the potty waiting for you to wipe her behind.

When he was done, he left her in the gym childcare office for a moment to run and get his stuff from his locker. It was close to seven o'clock, and the locker room was completely empty, which was a good thing. Hank was in the process of pulling a spare pair of sweats over his workout shorts when Justin stuck his head in.

"Who's with Josie?" Hank asked. When he'd left, Justin had been the only adult in the room and—

"Don't panic, cowboy!" Justin said, rolling his eyes and waving his hand. "Jackie's in there—you know, my supervisor? I had something to ask you!" His wrist never stiffened up, did it? But Hank remembered those long, artistic hands working steadily on the cut on his arm and figured that Justin was good at pulling in the swish when he needed to.

"I'm sorry," Hank muttered, struggling with getting his pants over his shoe. "I didn't mean to—"

"Don't worry about it." Justin rolled his eyes again. "I get that you don't like me, but I've got a plan."

"For what?" Hank asked, giving up on the shoe. He sat down, toed the shoe off and yanked it through the elastic opening of the sweats while Justin finished speaking.

"If you like," Justin said helpfully, "I can come get Josie on Saturday and bring her in with me. I just cleared it with Jackie and…"

Hank took a deep breath, not wanting to be indebted to him anymore, *especially* because that thing, that drama thing, was still there, grating against Hank's teeth. Justin must have seen his refusal because he just kept talking faster like that was going to get him his way.

"…and don't say no because you're worried about her, because I'm totally certified in *everything*, and I'm getting a liberal studies degree and units in child development so I can do CPR *and* teach her the alphabet and—"

It was time to inject some sanity.

"Why?" Hank asked bluntly. "It's nice of you. It really is, but why?"

Justin shrugged and smiled, looking embarrassed and eager and everything. "Well, because I like kids, Silly! If I didn't like kids, I'd be studying something that made me more money, like banking, right?"

"I like kids!" Hank heard his voice pitch up embarrassingly. God. He should turn in his employee card as Loan Officer at Wells Fargo for that voice crack.

"I know, I know," Justin placated, holding his hands out. "But, you know, you have to be the responsible parent, and I get that and it's really great! But I can be the fun Uncle Justin, and she can see Santa! Please?"

Hank let out a sigh. He *was* the fun Uncle Justin right now. At the moment, he was Hank's best ally.

"Yeah," Hank told him, getting his clothes situated. He stood up so he could get to the inside of his gym bag. "Here. I'll get you my address—"

"Oh, I can get that from the computer or find it on my phone…"

Hank felt his eyes bulge out, and Justin backtracked at warp speed.

"…and that would be totally illegal so of *course* I wouldn't do that, so go ahead and write that down for me, 'kay?"

"Thank you," Hank said belatedly as he was writing down his info. Justin had his phone out and was punching the numbers into it briskly, and Hank envied him. He was pretty sure he didn't have many friends at the moment because of his antiquated texting skills, and he kept losing people's numbers. "She… *we* really appreciate this."

Justin grinned so widely his eyes almost squinched shut. "I'm happy to help."

There was a moment, then, an awkward one, and Hank felt compelled to be truthful.

"I don't 'don't like you'," he said, putting his pea coat on over his workout clothes. His skin was still clammy from the sweat he'd built up and not been allowed to wash off.

Justin had moved closer to get his address, and when Hank turned around from his locker, he saw that Justin was right in front of him, looking up at Hank's six-foot-three-inch height from his own much shorter build. His eyes were open and blue, and Hank could see the places in his hair where his gel was starting to break down. Justin had apparently put in a long day too.

"Sure you do," Justin said. "You think I'm a big ol' flaming 'mo, and you're way too butch to have anything to do with me, and you don't think I should be hanging out with your niece and generally you wish my entire people would fall off the face of the earth." He did the rolling eyes, twitching hips, and limp-wristed thing all in conjunction, and, Hank had to admit, it was one hell of a show.

He hated to put a stop to it.

"I'm gay, moron." He swung his duffel bag over his shoulder and paused for a moment to admire Justin's sweet little heart shaped face, open jaw, bulging eyes and all. God, he was pretty. It was a shame about that whole other problem.

"Wait a minute!" Justin said, reaching up to grab Hank's arm and stop him. He must have remembered at the last moment that Hank had actually hurt himself, because his grip on Hank's shoulder was surprisingly gentle.

Hank turned around with a long-suffering sigh.

"What?" he asked. The one thing that had been getting him through this day had been his workout. That had been cut short, and he apparently had a commitment with this... *person* in his future, and he was hanging onto his patience with a very, very fine thread.

Still, he couldn't help but hear the naked hurt in Justin's voice when he spoke next, and yeah. He felt like shit.

"But, if you don't have a problem with gay people, why do you always seem like..." Justin was waving his hands and trying to find the right words, and Hank realized he'd have to put the guy out of his misery. Justin was still wearing the company uniform, and he really had been nothing but professional.

"Look, I'm sorry if I've been a complete dick," he said, and looking at Justin's helplessness and his kindness, he realized he meant it, too. "I am. It's not the gay, Justin—it's the drama. I mean, people like you are fun to be around, right up until they let you down. I totally appreciate the help with Josie, and I'm going to take you up on it, because, I'll admit it, I'm desperate, but...." His head was starting to ache, and he hoped the rolls of cookie dough he had in the refrigerator had enough sugar to counteract that little problem. Maybe the coffee drinks he had in the fridge would help too.

"But what?" Justin asked, curiosity apparently warring with the hurt. He was worrying his lower lip, and it was becoming sort of succulent and red, and Hank realized he'd wandered off in the middle of his sentence.

"But what? Oh." He flushed. "I guess I just mean, I can't count on you, that's all. Believe me. I've lived through drama. At the end of the day, it just gets you tired."

Justin just looked at him, his eyes dark with hurt, his mouth opening and closing, and Hank felt that curious sense of needing to make him feel better.

"It's like turkeys," he said, out of the blue, and Justin blinked.

"Turkeys?"

"Yeah! Turkeys in the snow." Hank sighed and set his gym bag down. "See, turkeys are like the drama queens of the animal world. They freak out at any little thing, but they ignore all the really important things. So, you put a bunch of turkeys in a pen, and let a fox in there, and they look at him and think, 'Hey! It's a fox! So the hell what?' Which is bad because the fox is *eating* the turkeys, right? But these same turkeys see a snowflake, and they're like, 'Omigodomigodomigod', and they run around the pen just freaking out, until they trample the other turkeys in the pen, and they hurt them too."

Justin was starting to giggle, and Hank closed his eyes, realizing that he'd sort of flapped his arms and made "Omigodomigodomigod" sound a lot like "gobble gobble gobble."

"Oh no," Hank said, sighing and hating himself a lot.

"Oh yes!" Justin crowed.

"No, you didn't get the point—"

"Oh, I totally did!" Justin was laughing and Hank grabbed his workout bag again and slung it over his shoulder.

"No, no, no, no—" He said, trying to get out of the locker room before he had to hear Justin say it.

"Omigah, Mr. Calder! You sounded totally *gay*!"

Hank sighed and just kept right on walking. "Yeah," he muttered, "I totally know." This sent Justin into another paroxysm of laughter, which Hank heard rattling around in his head for the rest of the interminable night.

HOME. FINALLY. Mac and cheese, rolling out the refrigerated cookie dough and cutting shapes, icing them, quick bath, bedtime a half an hour too late.

Josie was happy rolling out the cookies, but unhappy with the icing. It wasn't perfect, wasn't pretty, wasn't shiny. Hank had bought the sprinkle things, and that helped, but generally, there was whininess and dissatisfaction about the entire affair.

"You don't know anything!" she shouted at him when he told her that he thought her Christmas tree was the prettiest. "It's ugly! Mom says the best Christmas trees have pink!"

Hank swallowed back a tightness in his throat that felt embarrassingly like tears. He remembered Amanda saying that exact thing when she was seven or eight. How wonderful that she'd taught it to her four-year-old daughter, and then gone off and left that kid in the hands of Hank, who had liked Christmas trees best when they were in the house a week before Christmas and not the night before.

"Yeah, I get it," he said, his throat raw. "Your mommy knows best. You know, Josie, all this great stuff your mom knows might carry a little more weight if she was *here.*"

Josie had started to cry then, helplessly, and Hank picked her up and carried her to the bathroom, and held her—crying—while he ran water and bubbles in the tub. He undressed her—still crying—and set her in the water, soaping her hair and rinsing her off, and the whole time, her mouth was open as a low, pulsing wail was striated out, and Hank couldn't think of a damned thing to make it go away.

She finally stopped and was down to sniffles and deep, shuddery breaths when he had her dried off and in her nightgown and in her bed.

"I hate this bed," she told him. "It's too big."

"I hate it too," he told her, because it was a reminder of all the ways in which he was ill-equipped for fatherhood at this particular moment in his life. It was meant to be a guest bedroom/den, so he had the bed and bookshelves and a desk and a laptop—all of the things a little girl *didn't* want in her room. The bookshelves had big, thick, boring books on finance, and the walls were a stark white. There had been a beautiful, boldly colored print of two naked male torsos—no butt-crack, no peen, but very obviously non-hetero. Hank had taken it down before Josie even entered the room. The blank wall just sort of stared at them now, and Hank wiped his cheek with the back of his hand without thinking, and remembered his plan for Saturday.

Saturday, they would make this room better. They would. And now, thanks to the kindness of one very swishy, sweet-faced twink, that would be a whole lot easier.

"Are you crying, Uncle Hank?"

Hank shook his head no, because crying meant drama, and he absolutely, positively *refused to do fucking drama.* Not right now.

"No, Bunny. I'm just ready for a shower right now." One of the first things he'd gone and bought her was one of those squishy fleece blankets, the kind that were impossibly plush and soft. This one had a pink rabbit on it, realistically done, in spite of the color, with the ears at helicopter position. It sat on top of the white comforter on Josie's bed— yet another thing Hank was planning to change in two days.

"Sleep tight, angel," he said, and bent to give her a kiss on the cheek. She turned unexpectedly and kissed him on the lips instead, and brought her tiny hand up to his own wet cheek.

"I'm sorry I made you cry," she said in a small voice, and he shut his eyes really tight.

"Grownups get tired," he told her, weary from his knees to his navel and all points north, south, and in between. "I…" He tried to keep his voice steady. "I was really looking forward to that workout, you know?"

"I'm sorry," she said, her voice even smaller, and he hugged her tight.

"It's okay. We'll try for a better day tomorrow."

"Can we make more cookies?"

Sure, since I think I may eat half of them tonight. "Yeah. That's a plan."

"Are you going to work out tomorrow?"

"Yeah."

"Good. I can see Justin. He's nice."

Hank had heard this a dozen times before, but this was the first time his entire heart was in it when he said, "Yeah. Yeah, he really is. We'll see him tomorrow. Good night."

He escaped then, practically running to the shower. He turned the water on, hot and full, and left his clothes in a puddle as he stripped and jumped in. He hadn't even soaped his hair before the day caught up with him, and the frustration and the frantic, palm-sweating, heart-pounding fear that somehow *he was doing it wrong.*

His body was jerking, his face contorted, his breath coming in gasps before his brain fully caught up to the fact that he was blubbering like a little kid, but once his brain caught up? Game over. He was lost, brain disengaged, while the stress and the panic and the disappointment of the past few months caught up with him, and he cried in the shower like he hadn't done since his break-up with his first boyfriend.

NONE OF THE HEARTBREAK

HE WAS feeling much better by the time Saturday morning rolled around. He'd actually gotten in a long workout on Friday for one thing, and he brought his running shoes and his sweats to work on Thursday for another, and managed twenty minutes of exercise during lunch. He thought he might start doing that a couple of days a week—it helped take off some of the day's stress when he couldn't make it to the gym.

Friday night, when he'd dropped Josie off in the gym's daycare, he was actually disappointed to see that Justin wasn't there. When he'd asked Jackie, the supervisor, the girl had winked at Josie and told them that Justin was helping to get ready for S-A-N-T-A. After Josie went off to play with the dollhouse, she'd told Hank that Justin had needed the night off to study for finals, and Hank felt stupid. He was a nice kid, but surely, Justin was entitled to a life of his own, right?

But that didn't change the fact that his stomach was distinctly fluttery on Saturday morning. It took him a while to identify the feeling, and unfortunately, when the cause surfaced, it was in a particularly uncomfortable way.

He'd gotten Josie all ready, and she was sitting in the living room with the few toys she'd had when she'd arrived and a couple more that he'd bought her since. If he left the cartoons on with the volume low, she'd start singing to the dolls. He loved that sound—Amanda used to do the same thing when he was watching her.

He'd just finished his first cup of coffee when Alan and Keith showed up. Alan breezed by him in the entryway without even saying hello.

"Hi, Hank," Keith said, embarrassed, and Hank grimaced and nodded. "Hi, Keith."

"Stop sucking face and get me a beer!" Alan snapped, and Hank grunted, looking to see if Josie had heard. She hadn't—small blessings.

"There is no beer in this job," Hank said evenly, and Alan made that little whining sound that Hank deplored so much. Of course, when they'd been together, Hank had found it adorable. That had changed when Hank had walked into their apartment and heard him making it with Keith buried to the hilt up his backside. Poor Keith. Alan had hidden the pictures and told him it was his apartment alone. Keith wasn't that bright, but he'd been mortified. Well, that was okay—now it was Keith and Alan's apartment. Hank had been coming home early to tell Alan about his big promotion at the bank they worked at—and now Hank was Alan's boss.

They'd had to settle into an angry détente—jobs in the financial world were hard to come by these days, and neither of them wanted to look for a new position. So Hank made the teller schedule and did the counts and Alan made snide comments about Hank buying his suits from a funeral home, used. Hank's raise was enough for him to make a down payment on the house, so moving out was timely, and it was all copacetic—or, at least for Hank, drama free.

And it worked out well when Alan wanted to take an extra day off for Thanksgiving. Hank had a teller with a new baby who needed the hours, but requisitioning for overtime was a pain in the ass, and not the kind Hank used to give Alan, either. This had been Hank's compromise—come over, break down the bedroom, paint it, and help him decorate it. Three strong men could do it in eight hours, when it would take Hank all weekend by himself.

Of course the downside was working with Alan.

"What do you mean, no beer?" Alan asked, curling up his lip. He had a small pretty face, and a slight build—a born in the butt bottom, as he liked to say—as well as blond hair that he could grow fashionably long. (Hank had tried to grow his thick, brown hair long in college, when they'd been dating. Gel, blow-dryer, it didn't matter—more than two inches of length, and Hank had what they'd called back in the '70s, a "'fro." It was not a good look for him.)

"No beer," Hank repeated. "I've been a little too busy to have a beer lately, is that okay with you? Now here, let me show you what I need done." He took the guys back to the bedroom and explained the situation—he'd stripped the bed that morning when Josie had been eating her cereal, and he had Alan and Keith on their way to his garage with the mattress when Justin came knocking at the door.

He answered it, hot and breathless, and startled enough to smile warmly when he saw Justin there, fidgeting, wearing his trademark Cal-Fit jacket.

"Come in," Hank said, gesturing. "Geez, Justin, aren't you cold?"

Justin had just opened his mouth to answer when Josie saw him, and unlike Alan and Keith, Justin was *not* to be ignored.

"*Justin!*" she squealed, and came running across the living room through the entryway. "You came! Hank said you'd come, but you weren't there last night so I thought you might be gone. People go sometimes. But you're *not,* and we're going to see Santa, right?"

Justin squatted down and hugged her, and talked to her from that level, earning Hank's eternal appreciation.

"Of course we're going to go see Santa. And then, if it's okay with your Uncle Hank, we're meeting my sister-in-law with her kids at Chuck E. Cheese, and you can play there. Do you want to do that?"

Josie's face lit up. "Oh *yes!*" She turned to Hank. "Can I go, Uncle Hank? Can I? Oh, please? Mommy never took me because she said it was 'spensive, and I've never been!'"

Hank cringed at the thought of Chuck E. Cheese—oh hells, the lights, the noise, the giant rat, the crappy pizza… and then he looked at Justin, squatting in his entry way and smiling like he knew *exactly* what Hank was thinking. Hank saw that smile, the slightly crooked front two teeth, how his cheeks dimpled up, the way his blue eyes crinkled in the corners, and his stomach got even more fluttery. He had the sudden realization that *Justin* was taking her to the dreaded faux-pizza den of the six-foot rat, and *Hank* was going to be completely in the clear.

Oh geez, it was enough to make a guy fall a little in love, right there.

"Of course you can, Bunny," he said, smiling back at Justin and feeling a little shell-shocked. "I'll just go get some money for games and things."

"No, Mr. Calder. That's all right!" Justin stood and put his hand on Hank's arm as Hank was turning around.

It wasn't Hank's sore arm, and he didn't flutter or grab too hard, but suddenly the two of them stopped still and looked at Justin's chilled red fingers on Hank's bicep. Hank shivered, and covered the hand with his own, and turned back around, smiling hesitantly.

"You're a college student, Justin, and you're doing a really wonderful thing here. Please let me pay for her games."

Justin nodded, and Hank wasn't imagining it—a dull red settled under his eyes and across his high cheekbones.

"Thanks, Mr. Calder," Justin said quietly. "I appreciate it."

"Well, *hel-lo* gorgeous!"

Both of them jerked when Alan came in from the garage through the kitchen entrance, Keith at his heels.

"Here, Bunny," Hank said, bending down to heft Josie into his arms. "Let's go get some money for Justin and a bag of clothes for you, just in case, okay?" One of his first lessons about having a little girl was that little girls had accidents. If Josie was going to be gone for more than a few hours, an extra change of clothes was very, very necessary. He looked up to where Alan and Keith were zeroing in on Justin and smiled apologetically.

"Justin, this is Alan and Keith. They're helping me out with the bed. Alan and Keith, this is Justin. Don't talk to him, don't touch him, and if you have to communicate, do it in Morse code with your bulging eyeballs, are we clear?"

He scowled in particular at Alan, who rolled his eyes and said, "Touch—*ee!*" and Hank decided this whole thing would go best if it went quickly.

"Okay, Bunny," he muttered, "let's work fast, because I'm telling you, Alan works faster."

Josie, encouraged by the triple threat of Justin, Santa, and Chuck E. Cheese, wasted no time at all in helping to pick out her clothes as well as Lisa, her very bestest most special doll. They were back in the entryway no more than three minutes after they'd left.

Alan was already holding Justin's arm companionably as he and Keith laughed about something. To his credit, Justin looked like he was trying to escape.

"Alan, hands off before I break your fingers." The words sounded mild, but Alan let go quickly with a sniff.

"Jesus, Henry, you're the one who always says you don't like drama!"

"Well, you're the one causing it. Go start breaking down the bookcases. Set them up in the garage and move the books. I need to call to see if the delivery is on time." With that he transferred Josie from his arms to Justin's, and then gave Justin the bag. "Okay, I've got an extra set of clothes, her health insurance card—it's Kaiser—and one of those little school ID cards, and I know you have my phone number and—"

"It's okay, Henry," Justin said, laughing. "It's fine. Remember— I've done this before!"

Hank flushed, and then he realized that Justin had called him Henry, not Hank or Mr. Calder, and he caught his breath again and looked into those dark blue eyes.

Justin winked at him. "Henry," he said again, with inflection, "I do know how to deal without the drama, okay? Now give your Uncle Hank a kiss, Josie-bunny, and we can leave."

Josie pursed her lips dutifully, and Hank went in for the kiss—and blew a bubble on them instead. Josie broke into a cackle of glee, and that's the sound she was making as Justin turned around and took her out the door.

Hank turned around to Alan and Keith—who hadn't left yet—and scowled.

"You two are, under no circumstances, ever, to touch the babysitter. You are not to talk to him, not to molest him, not to lure him over to pervert central with free beer. You are not to show him your etchings, and I swear to heaven, Alan you asshole, if you so much as fondle his shirt, I will fire you."

Alan winked. "Now, now, Henry. You know if you do that, you'll probably lose your job too!"

Hank looked at Keith, who was watching the two of them with the avidity of a tennis enthusiast at Wimbledon, and then grabbed Alan's arm and frog-marched him down the hall. "Excuse us, Keith," he called back, "I need to talk to him a minute."

They got to Josie's room and Hank pinned his ex-boyfriend to the wall with a glare. "Alan, you're right. I may not be able to fire you without losing my job, but if you so much as talk dirty to that boy, I will do worse than fire you."

Alan rolled his eyes in disbelief.

"You doubt that? I guarantee, if you touch a hair on his sweet twinkie little head, I will personally tell every person you are screwing about the other four people you are screwing, including your little experiment in bisexuality, Julie."

Alan's mouth had dropped open. "How in the hell—"

"Do you think you're the only one who likes drama, Alan? I swear to God, you can't take a piss at work without someone walking into the bathroom and spilling all the business you never wanted to know." Well, technically, he'd been in the stall, so he'd been doing more than taking a piss, but the point was, he'd overheard plenty—most of it from Alan himself.

Alan's eyes narrowed and his lip curled. "God, you just can't *stand* the idea of anyone else having fun, can you? Just have to go make the whole rest of the world as goddamned Puritan as you are!"

Hank grunted. "The Puritans weren't big on treating people decent, Alan. Find another comparison, but leave me, and my niece, and my niece's babysitter out of it. Now you're the one who wanted the day off, and I'm the one who has to deal with the paperwork. You want to make that happen? Move your scrawny uncomfortable ass."

Alan gasped and held his hand to his mouth like *that* was the most offensive thing about the conversation, and Hank ignored him and started shuttling books.

THEY DID it. He was ready to strangle Alan (and have Keith canonized!) by the time they were done, but when Alan and Keith left—Alan actually too tired to bitch, and Keith *very* grateful for both the day off to visit his parents before Christmas *and* the pizza and beer Hank had bought—the room was done.

Hank was in there shutting the window, which had been left open to get rid of some of the paint smell, when there was a knock on the door. He practically ran down the hall, he was so excited to see what Josie would think about it. They'd painted one wall pink and all of the trim in the room lavender, and although they'd left the other four walls white, Hank had put up posters of Disney princesses and Bubble Guppies and Dora the Explorer all over, but that wasn't the best part. The best part was the day bed—the kind that looked like a long couch and had a little trundle cot that slid underneath—that was all set up in the corner. Hank had ordered it in lavender and also bought a pink comforter with a white eyelet sham with matching pillowcases and pillow shams and even a little canopy.

That bed looked like an iced party cake and Hank was dying, *dying* for her to see it, so she could know that she had a home in Hank's little house, and that she could stay there as long as she wanted.

He threw the front door open, as excited as he'd ever been about Christmas, only to find her asleep over Justin's shoulder, so exhausted she was leaving a little puddle of drool on the shoulder of his thin company windbreaker.

Hank was so disappointed it felt like he shrank.

"Here," he said softly, "I'll take her."

Justin shook his head. "Let me put her down, Henry. Odds are better she won't wake up that way."

Hank didn't protest that he wanted her to wake up, because that had happened once, when he'd gotten her from Mrs. Watson's daycare *really* late, and at 1:00 a.m. that night, when she'd finally dropped off to sleep, he'd sworn never ever again.

He gestured Justin down the hall instead, turning on the hall light as Justin walked into what was obviously her bedroom, so Justin wouldn't have to turn on the pink tiffany lamp that Hank had installed on the new white bookshelves. He slipped into the darkened room as Justin pulled back the comforter with his free hand, and then laid the limp little body down on the clean pink sheets. Justin was very careful then, taking off her shoes and her coat, and leaving her in her second set of clothes—stretch pants and a T-shirt, which were damned close to pajamas—before pulling the blankets up and tucking them under her chin.

Hank bent down and gave her a quick kiss on the cheek before she could wake up and then followed him out of the room into the hallway.

"Well, I—" Justin started to say, and then Hank said, "Thank you so much for—" and then they both stopped and looked at each other bashfully in the middle of the hallway. Finally Hank reminded himself that he was the older of the two of them, and it was his job to break the ice.

"We have real pizza," he said hopefully. "And beer, that is, if you're… uhm, you know. Twenty-one yet. And if not I've got milk. But, would you—"

Justin brightened while he was talking, like the light that made him Justin from the inside had been flipped on.

"I'd totally love to!" he said, keeping his voice quiet, even if his gestures started to get a little loud. "And don't worry, Henry, I turned twenty-one in November, so you're totally safe. Not corrupting a minor or anything."

Hank had been leading him down the hall and he turned around and looked at him sharply over that. Justin returned the look cheekily, and Hank turned back around, resolute.

"Why 'Henry'?" he asked as they got to the kitchen, and Justin didn't miss a beat.

"Because Mr. Calder's too formal, and that other guy called you 'Henry' and it pissed me off."

Hank was in the kitchen by now, and he turned slightly, looking at Justin wryly. "Well, people do that when you've got history. The only two people to call me 'Henry' have been Alan and my mother." And his sister, but he wasn't going to mention that.

"And now me," Justin said, waggling his eyebrows.

Hank had no choice but to laugh. He reached into the refrigerator and pulled out two microbrews. "I've got pizza, if you like. Slightly higher quality than Chuck E. Cheese."

"Please?" Justin begged, holding his hands up like a puppy dog. "Please please please please *pleeeze!* I'm *dying* for something to wipe the taste of Chuck E. Cheese pizza outta my gullet... I'd mug your mother for a decent piece of pizza!"

Ah, gods, laughter, quiet laughter. It really was a luxury. "Don't mug my mother," Hank said, the chuckles freeing something inside him. He handed Justin the plate with the last five pieces on it and added, "She never had money for pizza."

"Now tha's a cwyin shame," Justin said through a full mouth. He closed his eyes for a blissful moment and chewed. After he swallowed he said, "Omigah—is that Mountain Mike's? Us broke college students *never* eat at Mountain Mike's!" He took another bite, his face lit up and happy in total ecstasy over the pizza. For a moment, Hank let himself bask in the pleasure of a completely happy human being.

"Come sit in the living room if you like," Hank said. He moved across the little hallway and pulled the coffee table in front of the brown corduroy couch, getting two coasters and a placemat from the compartment underneath for the beers. He took the recliner and put his coaster on the end table next to it. He had one of those little organizers on the arm of the recliner, and had just pulled out the remote when Justin came in and settled down.

"No, no," Justin said hurriedly. "Don't turn the TV on. Let's talk."

Hank paused midclick and wondered what his expression must have been. He didn't have to wonder long.

"*Ohmygah! Jeeez*us, Henry! I'm not going to torture you with tongs! I just get distracted by anything pretty, and I'm more in the mood to be distracted by you!"

Henry looked at him. "Because I'm not pretty?" It was more for clarification than because he was fishing for compliments, and he was unprepared for the adult, predatory look to cross Justin's baby face.

"You're plenty pretty, Hank. But right now, I'm more interested in your mind."

Hank snorted. "That's a switch."

"We're not all like your... whatever that was... Alan."

"We're?" Hank asked, flummoxed for a moment.

"Us drama queens," Justin said with a wicked grin. "We're not all like your friend, ex-friend… okay, what *is* he to you? Cause whatever it is, I don't see it!"

Henry took a swig of his beer and swiveled the recliner so he could see Justin instead of the television. "He *was* my boyfriend. My first serious one, actually." Sigh. "More serious for me than him I guess."

"What makes you say that?" Justin took a dainty bite of his new slice of pizza, as if to make up for stuffing his face from the last one, and washed it down with a sip of beer.

"Finding him in bed with someone else," Hank said. He was, he realized, walking a difficult balance between trying not to be a dick and trying not to spill his guts on the floor. Nobody liked guts with their pizza—talk about unappetizing!

"Nice. Did you really find him in bed? Because you hear that all the time, but you gotta think, like, sometimes, you just catch one guy walking out of the apartment, and then there's confession time, or, you know, you see a kiss or—"

"Alan was in our bed, screaming 'Fuck me harder with that thing!' and Keith was behind him, doing what Alan said." Hank had to admit, he did get a perverse pleasure out of watching Justin try very, very hard not to spit pizza out all over his plate. When Justin had mastered himself, and after he'd knocked back another swallow of beer, he cocked his head thoughtfully.

"That was a lot of drama," he said, and Hank found himself looking into a pair of surprisingly intense blue eyes.

"Yeah, well, I've seen worse," he admitted.

"Mm…" This time Justin was eating thoughtfully, and Hank supposed he was enjoying the hell out of just watching this guy eat. It was like every mouthful was a different mood. He swallowed, and Hank was sure another question was coming. He was wrong.

"My mom's the dramatic one in my family," Justin said, smiling. "She can turn any moment into a joke or a reason to laugh. My dad likes to play practical jokes—stupid ones, like pulling down your pants if you're wearing them too low or playing hide and go seek when you've been reading and you're not sure if anyone's in the house. They do this haunted house every year for Halloween—it's huge, and scary, and the louder the music the better. It always scares the hell out of the neighborhood kids, so my sister Brenna and I are the last two left at home, and we always have to go meet the little ones Josie's age and take them by the hand and show them how it's not as scary as they think." Justin laughed softly. "There's this one little girl on our block—red hair, blue eyes, freckles, cute as hell and a bossy little shit, too. This last year she left her older brother at the sidewalk with their mom and stalked up to our porch all resolute and everything—she's like five, right? And she's got her little pumpkin in front of her, and she's a little witch with a black hat, and she's frickin' adorable, right?" Justin's shoulders went back, and he clutched his pizza plate in front of him like a little girl clutching a handbag. He widened his eyes and pursed his mouth to a little girl's kewpie doll pucker, right down to making his rather lush lower lip tremble, and Hank started to laugh.

Justin kept going. "Anyway, she gets almost up to us, and the lights start going and the ghost drops from the tree and the big cackle comes out of the sound effects machine, and she doesn't scream, she just turns right around and stalks back to mom and her brother, saying, 'I'm not old enough! I'm not old enough! I'm not old enough! You go!'" And now he mimicked her shoulders and her posture and Hank had this image of this pudgy five year old, being absolutely in control at the same time she was frightened to death.

By this time he was laughing so hard he could barely breathe, and as he wiped his eyes and calmed down his breathing, he saw that Justin was grinning wickedly, chuckling through another bite of pizza.

"That's awesome," Hank breathed, still coming down. "I can totally see her. How'd her older brother take it?"

Justin grinned some more. "Oh, Kaden's all about the science of the thing. I swear, he's like, eight, right, and he's like, 'Evelyn, I told you that at our age we're too imaginative to confront a manifestation of our fears!'"

"Oh get out! No way an eight year old said that!"

"No, I swear! This kid is something else. Their mom just stands back and listens to them talk and crosses her eyes. She's a trip—she's perfectly willing to let them amuse the hell out of her. I love it!"

Hank sobered a little, still feeling the release of laughing so hard. "Yeah, kids are a trip. I always wanted them, you know? Alan wasn't so excited, but I always knew I was going to have some someday." And he remembered Josie, sleeping soundly down the hall. "I wasn't exactly planning on it being quite so soon," he said, his voice quiet and thoughtful. "I don't regret it, but, well, it caught me off guard."

Justin nodded, and set down the empty plate of pizza, then drained his beer. "What happened?"

"Would you like another beer?" Hank asked, making to stand up. "Here, I'll get your plate for you and get us another round."

"I'd mostly like for you to not dodge the question," Justin said, and unlike when he was telling the story, his entire body was absolutely still, waiting, like Hank was a feral cat and Justin was going to gentle him into submission.

"Well, I'll get us another beer anyway." Hank stood up and took Justin's plate as well as the placemat and everything else into the kitchen. "They're the last two in the fridge. No, no, don't get up. Get comfy, turn on the television—I'll just be a moment."

Justin sighed behind him. As he cleared the living room, he heard Justin on his cell phone, telling someone not to wait up for him. When Hank returned, after rinsing off the plate and wiping off the placemat and putting them in the rack to dry, Justin was sliding the phone back in his pocket.

"My mom," Justin said, neither apologetic nor sheepish. "She worries if I don't let her know I'm okay. She figured I'd be late. I told her we'd probably end up talking after I brought Josie back."

Hank handed him the opened beer, surprised. "You knew we'd—"

"Well, I've been crushing on you for months, thinking you were straight. No way I was going to let you go without at least a little conversation!" Justin was smiling again, inviting Hank to share the joke, but Hank couldn't. Months? Months, and Hank had just pushed him away, dismissed him, because he liked to move his hands a lot. It didn't speak well of Hank, that was for—

"You're feeling all guilty, aren't you?" Justin asked, that wicked grin still in place.

"No!" Hank lied.

"Of course you are—look at you. Your house is totally neat; you do everything by the book. I mean, you had a placemat for pizza on the coffee table for Pete's sake! Yup. Little bit of raging-queen-o-phobia, and you're all freakin' out on yourself for not being a better person. I can read the signs."

Damn. And now Justin had made Hank smile again. Hank took a drink of his newly cold beer. He needed to change the subject.

"Do your parents know?" he asked randomly, and Justin blinked. Good. For once *he* was surprised.

"That I'm gay?"

"Yeah."

Justin shook his head. "Nope!"

Hank snickered hard enough to spit out his beer. "The hell they don't!"

Justin laughed. "Well, we haven't officially had the talk, how's that?"

Well, Hank hadn't had "the talk" until college either. "Why not?"

"I don't know. I guess there's no reason to yet. Nobody serious yet, no reason to rock their world."

Hank nodded. "Yeah."

"Did you have the talk?" Justin asked, and Hank looked despairingly at his beer. The beer was full, the pizza was cleaned up, and he hadn't heard a peep out of Josie in the last hour. It wasn't even like the memory was that bad.

"It was anticlimactic," he said with another swig of his beer. "No drama, nothing to talk about."

"Well, tell me anyway." Justin toed off his trendy little lace-less sneakers and curled his feet up under his bottom, then leaned on the arm of the couch, propping his chin up on his hand. He looked sweet and defenseless sitting there, and Hank found that he trusted that complete lack of defense. For all his drama, there was nothing about Justin that Hank couldn't see right in front of him.

"Okay," Hank said, leaning forward moodily and resting his forearms on his knees, holding his beer between his palms. "Here's the thing. Alan and I were going to move in together—find an apartment and everything—so we could stop having to listen to his roommate have sex when she thought we were gone. So I came home to tell my mom that I was gay, I was moving out, and all those sleepovers hadn't been just to watch movies, and as we get there, my sister Amanda hauls ass out of the house screaming, 'Because you're a bitch and I hate you!'"

Justin squeezed his eyes shut and then opened them again wide. "And you said there wasn't going to be any drama."

"Yeah, well not on our part. For once, Alan kept his mouth shut, and we go into the kitchen. Mom's cracking open a new bottle of whiskey and pouring herself a giant glass, and she looks up at me and says, 'Yeah, what?'"

"Oh dear."

"Yeah. Anyway, Mom's sort of formidable—big woman, wide shoulders, don't-fuck-with-me jaw—and she scared the holy hell out of Alan, and he reached for my hand and I squeezed it to let him know it was all right. And Mom, she just raises her eyebrows, plonks down on the kitchen chair, and starts downing the whiskey like it was iced tea."

"What'd she say?"

"Well, first I said, 'Mom, this is Alan, my boyfriend, we're moving in together,' or, you know, something to that effect, and then Mom polishes off her giant glass of alcohol and says, 'Fucking lovely. You're gay, your sister's pregnant, and I'm moving to fucking Reno. Feel free to send me a postcard, Henry, I'll be really happy to hear from you.'"

Justin was scrubbing his face with his hands by then. "Oh, Henry, I'm so sorry."

Hank shrugged. "What for? It didn't matter. She was still my mother. She'd just had enough of Amanda, that was all. Mandy's boyfriend was a real loser, and Mom dared to ask—just ask, mind you—if maybe raising a baby alone was more than a high school senior could manage, but Mandy was freaking stubborn. Mom apparently had been planning the move for months. She'd sprung it on Mandy that morning, and Mandy came back with 'I'm pregnant' and then…." He shrugged.

"Then you walked in, and your little bomb wasn't hardly a fart in the wind."

Hank laughed a little and shrugged. "Drama," he said pragmatically. "Like I said, it's overrated."

"Mmm…" Justin said, but it wasn't a dissenting sound. "I hear you—but you know little girls like some drama, right?"

Hank thought of Josie, fast asleep in her new room. "Yeah," he sighed. "I know."

"So, you and, uhm, Santa—you've got the hookup? Christmas *is* in three weeks, you know."

Hank had to laugh. "You mean the house not being decorated? Yeah. Well, I'm taking Monday off. The social worker is coming at nine, I'm dropping Josie off at daycare after that, and then it's all about Christmas shopping. I figured when that was done, I'd get Josie early and we could decorate."

"Are you getting a tree?" Justin asked, his expression avid, and Hank could tell he was excited about this just because it was Christmas.

"Tomorrow," Hank said, smiling. "I was going to go to a lot with Josie." He hesitated, and then asked shyly, "Did you want to come?"

Justin's smile was so damned bashful Hank almost wiggled in his seat. "Very much, but I work tomorrow." Justin perked up. "I'm off Monday, though! I've got a final at nine, but I can meet you back here in time to go Christmas shopping. Can we do that? Then I can come back and help you decorate."

Hank laughed, because Justin had just invited himself over and insinuated himself into Hank's plans and his day and his life, and Hank had no impetus to say no.

In fact...

"Hey," he said shyly, "do you, uhm, want to see what I was thinking about getting for her?"

Justin sat up perkily and nodded with so much force his hair flopped back and forth off his forehead. "Yeah! Yeah—absolutely."

Hank got off the seductively comfortable recliner and yawned outrageously. "I'm sorry—I didn't realize that was coming. I hope—I mean, I know you called your mom and everything, and you're welcome to stay later, I just...." He flushed. "I don't want you to stay here if you're bored or anything."

Justin's smile was sweet and wicked. "Well, Hank, it's not like you're my first sleepover."

"Oh?"

"Yes. My best friend Shelia in high school used to have me over all the time."

Hank made the time honored fishhook gesture, to indicate that Justin had caught him fair and square; then he walked around to the other side of the coffee table so he could get into the locked drawer next to the place mats. He felt Justin's presence there acutely, and just as he'd jimmied the drawer open (the lock had long ago ceased to be functional) he felt a tentative hand on his backside.

There were not enough letters in the language to describe the sound that came out of his mouth.

"You like?" Justin asked, and Hank pulled in a breath that felt like water.

"I'd be lying if I said no," he confessed, thinking he should move. Justin's hand got a little more personal, curling around Hank's cheek and squeezing, and Hank let his breath out on a little grunt. "But." He swallowed. "See, Josie really loves you, and if you decide this is a bad idea and disappear…." Justin's hand slid away, the fingertips lingering for a moment.

"I get it," Justin said, his good humor intact. "Drama."

Hank grabbed the stacks of marked up toy catalog in the drawer and crab-walked away, moving to the less personal space of the recliner.

"I appreciate it," he mumbled, unable to look Justin in the eyes. Then Justin giggled, and he had no choice. "What?"

Again, that wicked look from that gamine face. "You act like I'm not going to try again, Henry. Look, I may be relatively inexperienced, but I'm not giving up after one grope!"

"But I'm a *dick*!"

Justin said "pfft" and waved his hand. "And I'm a drama queen. I mean, I've been behaving, but you and I both know I'm gonna snap sometime soon and you're going to have to decide if I'm worth all that trouble!" He smiled, wiggled his shoulders, and crossed his legs before placing his clasped hands on his knee. "We're just going to hope that by then, I'll have made myself indispensable enough that you'll decide I really am."

Hank couldn't help it. In fact, he was coming to realize that he could *never* help it around Justin. He laughed.

"Okay, drama queen," he said, smiling with everything in his body. "Are you gay enough to shop for a four-year old girl?" He offered Justin the catalog from the coffee table.

"*Omigah! Are* you really getting her *that*? Of *course* I can shop for *that*!" Justin was fawning over the picture that Hank had marked, and Hank didn't have the heart to tell him that his drama queen was already rearing its pretty little head.

"Well, I want to see it in the store first," Hank said, chewing on his lip a little with uncertainty. "You know, sometimes the pictures look so awesome, but you see it in real life and it's just tacky. But I figure if we go check it out on Monday, if they don't have some of the stuff I want in the store, we can get it online."

Justin nodded his head, looking suitably impressed. "But that's not the only thing, right? I mean, I know, all little girls want one of *these*!" And with that, he pointed out a little plastic vanity table that Hank hadn't seen at all.

They stayed up half the night. They picked out toys to check out at the store for Josie, raided the cupboard for Ho-Hos (which Hank kept in the back, for those really, really bad days), talked about workout regimens and Justin's plans when he finished college. They giggled over old crushes and bad mistakes—Justin's first boyfriend who was now married, with the second child pending, or Hank's first blowjob, given in a movie theater and discovered by a *very* unimpressed usher. ("So you *still* can't go to that Regal in Natomas?" Justin asked, and Hank had to admit that no, he was still blacklisted.)

Hank didn't remember when he stopped talking, but he woke up around three in the morning because the hand under his chin gave out and he fell sideways. He looked to see Justin stretched out on the couch, his head resting uncomfortably on the arm, which was a surefire way to fuck up your neck. Hank went to the closet and got a spare pillow and an afghan, and came back to make the poor guy more comfortable. He covered Justin up to his chin with the afghan, trying hard not to look at his plump lips and the fading freckles on his cheeks, and then shoved his arm under the surprisingly solid shoulders and slid the pillow under his head. He pulled back for a moment and was arrested by the open eyes, blinking sleepily at him.

"Aren't you going to kiss me goodnight, Prince Charming?" Justin slurred, and Hank was just tired enough, just happy enough from the best evening he'd had in he couldn't remember when, to place what he thought was going to be a chaste peck on Justin's oh-so-kissable mouth.

Justin opened for him, though, and Hank slid into his waiting, wet mouth with ease and heat, and a surprising, gut-wrenching hunger. He slid his hands up to frame Justin's face, and Justin took his position on the bottom and took over, clasping Hank's forearms with urgency. Hank finally pulled back, panting, and rested his forehead against Justin's; he was trying not to start groping the guy under his shirt.

"Oh, thank God," Justin breathed. "I'd built that up so big in my head, I was starting to doubt it could live up to that picture."

Hank pushed his next breath out on a laugh. "That was a total and complete surprise," he said. "You could knock me over with a feather." Justin kneading his swollen groin was unexpected enough to make him stand up and yelp.

"But first you'd have to pound nails with your penis." Justin smirked, but his eyes were closing in spite of his smile. "Night, Henry. I told you I'd try again."

Hank very carefully maneuvered his hips out of Justin's reach and bent down and kissed his forehead. "Night, Justin," he said softly. "I'm sort of hoping you'll keep on trying."

Justin giggled a little, even as Hank turned off the lamp and left him sleeping in the darkened room.

Prima Donnas and Princesses

JOSIE WOKE him up early enough that he sat up in bed, disoriented, still wearing the Henley shirt and the sweats he'd had on when he'd kissed Justin goodnight.

"Uncle Hank!" she told him, her eyes wide and her jaw jutting out like she was angry, "Somebody *highbacked* my room!"

Hank blinked a good five or six times and finally figured out what she talking about. "Don't you like your highbacked room?" he asked. What time was it? It took him a moment to make sense of the numbers on the clock, and when he did, he fell back against his pillows, squinting against the light coming from her hallway. "Great googly-moogly, angel—it's five in the morning! You usually sleep until seven!"

"The smell woke me up," Josie said, her cheeks scrunched. "The color is pretty, but I *don't* like the smell!"

Oh hells. The smell. "It'll go away in a few days. It's the paint, Josie. Is that the only thing you don't like, or can I go back to sleep now?"

"Why did you change my bedroom?" she asked, and Hank rolled to his side and looked at her.

"Because you hated the bed, and you didn't feel like you had a place and I just wanted you to like living here." Oh God. Now *he* was whining.

"I never had my own bed before," she confessed. "I used to sleep with Mommy."

Hank sighed, wondering if Justin had already gone. Probably. Hank dimly remembered him setting his phone's alarm before they'd both fallen asleep talking.

"Do you want to climb in with me?" he asked, beyond proprieties, and Josie nodded.

"Can you hug me too?" she asked, her voice tiny. "I rode the motorcycle ride lots yesterday, and I keep thinking I'm still moving."

Hank grunted and scooted over. "Yeah," he sighed, caving in. "Go ahead."

"No, Uncle Hank," she told him. "Closer. Mommy let me hold her hand."

So Hank did, wrapping his arm around her little chest and holding her tight, like nothing was going to get her, and she raised her little hands to pat his hand where it lay. In a few hours, he'd deal with his disappointment that she didn't love her room, but right now, he forgot about what he was supposed to do according to the good book of parenting, and went with what made her happy. It was like Justin, he thought muzzily as he dropped back into sleep. That much spontaneous human happiness just could *not* be a bad thing.

AFTER THEY got the Christmas tree, they set it up in the corner of the living room. Josie was surprisingly willing to put off decorating until Justin came over, which was probably the only reason Hank had the fortitude to wait.

After that, they spent the day quietly: grocery shopping, doing laundry, cooking some mac and cheese and a crock pot of soup to put in little containers in the refrigerator, the better to eat during the week. In the afternoon Hank made some more cookies and let her put the sprinkles on again, and she didn't complain. After she washed her hands, Hank heard her talking to herself in the bedroom. When he peeked in, she was sitting cross-legged on her new bed, playing with her dolls. It wasn't loud or dramatic, but it *was* extremely, almost painfully gratifying. Yes. Hank had *finally* done something right.

In the evening, after dinner and a bath, he pulled her onto his lap and turned on a Christmas special (*Shrek The Halls,* of all things) and they sat and watched it together. Her eyelids started to droop (and, for that matter, so did his) when she said a curious thing.

"You're like Shrek, Uncle Hank."

"Yeah?"

"All grumpy sometimes. And Justin's like Donkey."

Hank laughed like she wanted him to. "Shrek's a nicer guy with his Donkey," he conceded. He'd been thinking about Justin all day. The sound of his laughter, his animated voice, all of the flamboyance and, face it, *fun* had filled in all the quiet moments, whether he'd been there or not.

Hank wondered if a day like this one—peaceful and relaxed and perfect—might not be even better if Justin would be there to laugh in all the empty spots.

"Yeah," Josie said, her head drooping on his shoulder. "Justin could be like Mommy, and be fun. And you could be Uncle Hank, and be safe."

Hank opened his eyes. Safe wasn't really a dirty word, was it? Hank had grown up with not particularly safe—his mother had worked and he'd been the one getting Amanda dressed and walking her to school. There had not always been enough to eat, and sometimes a place to sleep hadn't always been a lock, either. His mother had tried—every day, she'd tried—but she had ended up dour and grim. Her drama tended toward the cynical, and sarcasm had been her armor against disappointment.

Fun and safe. It was like a super-hero duo, right?

Hank was falling asleep with Josie too, but still, he waited until the special was over before he picked her up in her Dora the Explorer pajamas and put her to bed.

"Think you can sleep here all night, Bunny?" he asked, tucking her new comforter under her chin.

"As soon as it feels like mine," she mumbled. But she didn't crawl into his bed that night, so that must have been progress, right?

THE NEXT day, as he fidgeted under the gimlet eye of the social worker, he hung on to that.

"So she has her own room and her own bed," the social worker said, ticking things off handily on a triplicate form. "And your job at the bank has checked out—you're doing really well financially."

She glared at him and, given the grim financial climate, Hank managed a sheepish sort of smile back.

"You really are," the social worker said, cocking her head. "So the judge is going to want to know why the mother couldn't stay here?"

Hank looked desperately at Josie (who was playing on her bed again, ignoring the social worker in spite of her repeated attempts to get Josie to talk) and gave a nod to get the woman out of the room.

She was a short Hispanic woman in her fifties, and Hank got the impression that nobody had given her a damned thing. Ever. Not even for her birthday. Well, Hank had grown up through birthdays like that too, and the one thing that he'd given himself was the promise that when *he* got to be the grown up, he would have it all together, and he'd done okay that way. No boyfriend check on his list, but other than that, he had the job, he had the kid, he had the house, and he was barely twenty-six. This woman could damned well cut him a break by not bringing up the "big drama" that he and Josie had tacitly agreed not to talk about.

They got out to the hallway and the woman said, "Okay, so *why* didn't you offer this sweet setup to your sister?"

Hank glowered. "Because Amanda didn't ask, okay? There was no asking, there was only leaving. Do you think if she'd asked, I would have said no?"

Mrs. Ramirez fluffed her dyed black hair and raised a sculpted eyebrow. "So why wouldn't she stay here?"

Hank sighed. "I like rules," he said, feeling like a six-foot three-inch dick. "I like knowing where my next paycheck is coming from, and having the dishes washed after they're dirty. I like going to bed around the same time every night and knowing the people in my life are going to be right where I left them when I wake up."

Now both eyebrows were up. "That sounds like a perfect environment for a child."

"Well, it was for the four-year-old," he said shortly. "I think the twenty-year-old was tired of those rules, and so she did what lots of children do and ran away."

Mrs. Ramirez nodded. "Fair enough. So, you want to make this situation permanent?"

Hank's heart gave an excruciatingly awkward lurch in his chest. "Yes," he confessed. "I really love having her here." He gestured vaguely back toward Josie. "We found a really nice daycare lady—Mrs. Watson, her name's on the paperwork. I spent all Saturday remodeling her room, and I've adjusted my workout so the gym childcare guy is the one she really loves. I've started going running on my lunch hour so I don't have to go to the gym so much when he's not there. I've added her to my health insurance and she's had a dentist appointment and a checkup and I just... I *really* like having her here. It's hard—harder than anything I thought I'd do. I can see why Amanda bailed. But I don't want to bail. I want Josie to know her people are right where she left them when she wakes up."

Mrs. Ramirez nodded some more and made some more checks on her list. Then she asked, "So, is there a *missus* Uncle Hank in the future?"

Hank grimaced. He couldn't lie about this. Hell, he couldn't lie about *anything,* as that giddy, delirious night of truth with Justin had proven. But he certainly couldn't lie about this.

"Uhm, there might be *mister* Uncle Hank in the future," he said, looking her gay in the eye.

She nodded, not even batting a thickly gooped eyelash. "Have there been a lot of Mister Uncle Hank's in the past?" she asked. "The judge is going to ask."

Hank thought. How long ago was Alan? "My last boyfriend was a year and a half ago," he said frankly. "I don't do random hook-ups, so it's been a long dry spell—"

"Any water in the future?" she asked, not even quirking her lipsticked mouth. Geez, what did it take to get this woman to smile? Admittedly, Hank wasn't a laugh riot, but *she* was the one to crack the joke!

"Uhm," he said, wondering if she needed to know about Justin. At that moment there was a knock at the door and Hank looked at his watch. Wait, he wasn't running late, right? He excused himself and opened the door, and Justin was standing there with a box of doughnuts.

"He-ey," he said, grinning as he swished in. "My final was a *breeze*, and I wasn't sure if you'd be back yet so I thought I'd check and here you are! My sister got some doughnuts from this place—ohmygah, you've *got* to taste these! They're… they're *decadence* in a pink…."

Justin petered off as he set the pink doughnut box on Hank's kitchen table. Hank was staring at him, torn between joy, because he was *really* happy to see him, and horror, because Mrs. Ramirez was *not* cracking any smiles.

"Uhm, Justin?" Hank said, taking a few steps toward him. "This is Mrs. Ramirez, the social worker. She's running a little late this morning. Mrs. Ramirez, this is Justin, he's—"

"Your rain man, isn't he?"

Justin raised an eyebrow. "I beg your pardon?"

"His first boyfriend after a long dry spell," Mrs. Ramirez said.

"Well, I'm still sort of interviewing for the job," Justin said, grinning at her now that he understood. "Would you like a doughnut? They are to *die* for!"

Mrs. Ramirez sent a pointed look at Hank, who had offered her a cup of coffee, which she apparently didn't drink. "I'd love one," she said, reaching into the box. She chose a French cruller and took a bite, then closed her eyes. When she opened them, she was glaring at Hank all over again.

"You should give this boy the job for the doughnuts alone. I'll tell the judge this is a nice, stable home, and you all have a Merry Christmas."

With that, she looked around the house. "You *are* going to decorate, aren't you? You've only got three weeks!"

"Oh yes," Justin said, smiling at her and handing her a napkin—the icing was thick and flaking off onto her bright gold and black blazer. "Tonight—it's going to be a thing." He reached into the pocket of his windbreaker. "I even brought music!" he said, pulling out two CDs that looked freshly burned.

Hank realized that he was just standing there, stupidly, looking at Justin like his last best hope, and with that, he closed the final distance between them and took the CDs out of his hands.

"That's a perfect idea," he said softly, wishing they were the only two people in the room. Justin turned to him, radiating that absolute good will, and Hank ignored Mrs. Ramirez and the second disappearing doughnut, and kissed Justin on a chilly cheek, his lips actually tingling for something more. "Thank you," Hank said sincerely. "Do you want to go get Josie ready while I close this up?"

Justin's smile was bright and white and brilliant as the sun. "Oh Josie!" he called, before breaking off eye contact with Hank and trotting down the hall. "Are you ready to go to the babysitter's?"

"*Justin!*" Josie squealed, as she rocketed out of her new bedroom and right into Justin's arms.

"He's something else," Mrs. Ramirez said, and for the first time all morning, Hank detected a little bit of warmth in her voice.

"You have no idea," Hank said, finally tearing his eyes off the two of them, chattering away in some secret kid language that Justin spoke fluently. "Now what do I have to sign to make sure she gets to stay here as long as she wants?"

SIGNING THE papers took a while, so Hank cleared it with childcare and let Justin take Josie to Mrs. Watson's in Hank's car. By the time Mrs. Ramirez left, Justin was pulling back into the driveway, and Hank walked out of his house with a feeling of relief. Six hours to go shopping, and then back to decorate the tree, and it was all, *all* in Justin's company.

Oh God. He hoped he didn't screw this up.

Justin rolled down the window. "Can I drive to the mall?" he asked. "I gotta tell you, Henry, this thing is *sweet* compared to that piece of crap I drive!"

Hank had to laugh at Justin's battered blue Ford Neon parked in front of his house by the curb. "Knock yourself out," he said, settling down in the passenger's seat. "But I have to tell you, it's not nearly as much fun as my Mustang."

"Ohmygah, you had a *Mustang!*"

The way Justin said it made Hank feel like he was an old superhero. *Like ohmygah, you were able to fly?*

"Yeah—it was a recent model, though." Because everyone knew the old restored ones were the best.

"So why'd you get rid of it?"

"I needed something sensible for Josie."

Justin grunted as he turned left on Madison, heading for the freeway.

"We're not going to Sunrise?" Hank was surprised—Sunrise Mall was the closest and the least crowded of the three major shopping networks in the area.

"When we have the Galleria?" Justin asked with a huff, and Hank suppressed a groan.

"Oh God," he whined, "the crowds and the—"

"Oh yes, Henry. There's gonna be drama. Get over it. I *love* the Galleria at Christmas."

"I get lost," Hank confessed. "I can never find my way around in the parking garage and—"

"Well, it's lucky you have me." They were at a light and Justin cast a flirtatious glance to his right. "I shall be your guide through the fields of frantic holiday shoppers. You will come to depend on me. I'll be your Sherpa through the human mountain, your faithful Saint Bernard, guiding you through the shopping Alps, your Strider, hauling your poor hobbit ass through the perils of Middle Earth—"

"My Gollum, prepared to dump my hobbit ass in the volcano," Hank finished, although it was hard because he was fighting laughter with every word.

"No-oo!" Justin protested. "I would *never* dump your ass in a volcano." He gave one of those giggly smiles, the kind that was all teeth, and that popped his cheeks so close to his eyes that they got all squinchy. "I need to grope it first!"

Hank's laughter cut off with a swallow, and heat swept his body. Justin pulled his chin back into what Hank was thinking of as his meerkat pose, even though he kept two hands on the wheel.

"You're thinking about it right now, aren't you," Justin asked, waggling his eyebrows.

"I… uhm… oh God." Hank fought the temptation to put his face in his hands, and instead stared out the window. There was something about the gray skies of December that made the foothills look featureless as they drove to Roseville. But beyond that, Hank could see the mountains, and they'd always seemed to promise something great, something grand and perfect and magnificent. Hank had never questioned why his mother had moved to Reno—he'd only questioned why he'd chosen to remain in the valley.

"How long's it been, Henry?"

"A year and a half." Somehow, with his eyes focused on the mountains, that didn't sound so pathetic.

"You know, I, uhm, haven't gotten much past second base, right? A year and a half, a total butt-virgin—it'll be very Sweet Valley High."

Hank tried not to choke on his tongue. "God, you're making a lot of assumptions," he said when he'd recovered, and Justin thumped him on the back a couple of times to make sure he was done coughing.

"No, no," Justin said, and although his smile was more low key, it was still there. "See, you don't get it. I mean, I've worked at the gym for two years, right? And I saw you from afar, and… man, do you have *any* idea how hot you are?"

Could Justin hear him swallow? How about the screeching, rusty gears in Hank's head, could he hear those too? "Uhm…"

"I mean, you've got that whole 'Don't touch me' thing going, but from afar, I've got to tell you, you starred in a lot of pornographic dreams, Henry. And suddenly you show up with this little girl, and anybody could see you were struggling. But I see parents and kids all the time, and I've got to tell you, you're one of the good ones. You keep your patience— and man, when a kid's got all the baggage Josie's got, that's not easy. I thought if she said 'But Mommy never did *tha-at!*' one more time, you were going to crack a tooth, you were grinding your jaw so hard. But you didn't. And maybe you can't see it, but she's happier already. It's only been a couple of months, but *I* can see that she's happier. And I love kids, so you went from my 'worship from afar' to my 'dream guy', even though you were a dick, and I thought you were straight."

"I'm sorry about being a dick," Henry mumbled, embarrassed down to his toes.

"But see? Then you got all human on me the other night, and it's official. I'm there, Henry. I'm… I'm in the United States of Henry right now. I'm ready for the Henry *lifestyle.* And I know you've only gotten your toes wet in Lake Justin right now, but I want you to come in, take a swim, and build your house out here, okay?"

Hank was torn between laughing and hyperventilating, and he couldn't seem to get a handle on either. Then Justin, eyes still on the road, put his hand on Hank's knee, and the world slowed down, spun a little saner, became more a manageable, gravity driving mass and less a broken gyroscope on the edge of the abyss.

Hank covered that hand with his own. "You don't have any gloves," he croaked, because it was cold and Justin's hand was icy.

"Yeah, well, I wasn't planning on baring my soul to you. Some of that's flop sweat."

Hank laughed a little and squeezed. "It was a good speech. No flopping. I'm still in the car."

"Good, Henry. It's your car."

"You're a really good human being, and I wasn't very nice. And now I'm worried about hurting you. I'm sort of a selfish bastard—"

"Bullshit. Start over."

"I *am* worried about hurting you."

"Let's have us some sex, Henry, and then you can worry."

"Are you saying it won't hurt if we don't have sex?" Because as awesome as Justin's hand felt in his own right now, that was really, really tempting. Pain was drama. Drama was overrated.

"No," Justin said, his voice gentle. "I'm saying that if we don't have sex, this relationship *will* hurt, because it *is* a relationship. I've been dreaming about your kiss for two days, Henry. Don't let me down because your chicken heart suddenly thinks we're going too fast. Like I said, I can't go too fast. I'm already there."

Oh God, so am I. Hank thought it, but he didn't say it. He didn't let go of Justin's hand until Justin needed it to steer, either.

"HMM…." JUSTIN said a half hour later as they tooled through Toys "R" Us. "I can see why you wanted to see it for real. This close it's sort of…." They both looked at the item Hank had picked out in the catalogue and at all of the accessories that were chained to the display board too.

"Cheap," Hank said grimly. "It's cheap. It's going to fall a—"

"*Ohmygah! Ohmygah ohmygah ohmygah!*" Justin had disappeared to the end of the aisle, and he was… vibrating there, his feet dancing in place and his hands flapping up and down so quickly they blurred. "No, no, no, no, no,… Come *here*, Henry! You need to *see* this!" And that last part was superfluous because of *course* Hank was going to go over there—if nothing else because it looked like he was having a seizure and Hank might be needed to hold his head or something.

"Oh." Hank looked at it and could swear he saw a shining light from above beaming down upon it. It was just the display light, but still.

"*That* is the best damned dollhouse I have ever seen," he said, ignoring the fact that he had never really looked at a dollhouse until this point in his life. It was immaterial. The house itself was made of wood, but it was sized to accommodate everything from Barbie dolls to Bratz, although Hank was pretty partial to the smaller, detailed wooden dolls that came with it. He looked up from his gift trance and was disoriented for a moment, because Justin had disappeared again. Before Hank could even look around for him, he came back, pushing the cart through the crowded store with all the aplomb of a Maharajah in the Imperial Bazaar.

"Here we go," Justin said, squatting down and pulling out the first dollhouse on the shelf—and then setting it aside.

"What are you doing?" Hank asked. He loved this gift. He wanted to hold it to his chest and hiss at anybody who came to touch it. Well, maybe he'd let Justin touch it. And Josie of course. Definitely Josie. But seriously, only the three of them. That was the circle of dollhouse trust. Anyone else was not invited.

"We don't want the first one," Justin said logically. "It's been picked up and looked at and fondled and rattled. We want the second or third one on the shelf—and here you are, my little beauty, come to Uncle Justin!"

Justin straightened triumphantly, and Hank had never seen a more beautiful heart than the one Justin wore out for anyone to see in his smile.

"Okay, we've got the house. Now the—"

"And we want this one, and this one, and this one—" Justin was already picking out the accessories; Hank had to act fast or get left in the dust!

"You want a big brother doll?" That was a little out of Josie's detail range, wasn't it?

"It's an Uncle Justin doll. And see here? It's an Uncle Hank doll. He's even got your scowl."

"Well, Uncle Justin has nothing near your smile," Hank said without thinking, and his reward was that same smile, amped to the brightness scale of a solar flare, softened only by shining blue eyes.

"You like my smile?" Justin asked wistfully, and Hank nodded, suddenly tongue-tied.

"Very much," he said, gnawing on his lower lip out of sheer shyness.

If Justin hadn't stood on tiptoe and kissed him right then, in the middle of Toys "R" Us, Hank might have been blind for life. But that was okay. It was a very nice kiss.

THEY CLEANED out Toys "R" Us. Well, not exactly, there were a lot of toys, and the *boys* side of the store was definitely untouched (although Hank set his eye on a set of three Nerf air-soft pistols to give Justin, because he thought those looked like fun) but generally, after the triumph of the dollhouse, they'd gone a little nuts.

Everything.

Hank wanted to buy her *everything*.

He had not forgotten his common sense, though, and he did draw the line about ten gifts before Justin would have, but Hank figured that if he was tired *shopping* for the gifts, then Josie would be tired *opening* them on Christmas day.

"But…" Justin whined as they cleared checkout. "What are we going to look for now?"

Hank grinned at him, suddenly feeling like a kid playing hooky.

"Anything we want!" he said, surprised, and Justin giggled.

And then they went shopping.

Oh, it was fun. They didn't actually buy much, but they wandered into almost every store, picking things up and commenting and cracking random, juvenile jokes, revealing hidden things about each other just by talking. Hank learned that Justin had failed algebra twice, until his father just started feeding him answers to get him through, and that a complete helplessness with math was one of the reasons he wanted to teach the very young children instead of the older ones. He learned that Justin had one older sister still at home (which he'd known) and two older brothers who were still in the area (which he had surmised) and that his parents had set up a very nice, very adult agreement about letting him live at home.

"I've got enough saved to move out," Justin said, "but I like knowing someone will worry about me when I come home. Does that make me immature?"

"No," Hank said. "That makes you human."

Justin dragged him kicking and screaming into a woman's bath shop, only to spray Hank with all of the scents in their men's line, to see which one would smell best.

"Justin," Hank whined. "I've got Earth on my left wrist, Sky on my right wrist, and Ocean on my chest," because Justin had missed, "what are you putting on me now?"

"Oak," Justin said absently, spraying Hank's neck and hitting his mark this time. "Now shut up. I'm trying to smell." He closed his eyes and stood on tip-toes, and inhaled, his nose *very* close to Hank's neck. "Mm…" he said dreamily. "*That's* your smell."

Hank blushed and bumbled backwards, almost running over the woman behind him, who did not look amused. "Do you have a smell?" he asked, flustered, and Justin smiled wickedly.

"I'm all about Sky, baby, cause that's where Oak is reaching for."

Hank's lips quirked sideways. "Unless they're burying their roots in Earth's firmament," he said, and Justin set the tester down and burst into giggles.

"Let's get out of here, big guy, before you make any more puns and hurt yourself."

And off they went. They bought some extra ornaments and garlands in their next stop, and then went and got Josie from Mrs. Watson's, who was so excited she reminded Hank of Justin.

"Oh boy! Oh boy! Is Justin gonna decorate with us? Oh is he, Uncle Hank?"

After a short dinner, they jumped into the fray, letting Josie hang most of the ornaments below waist level. She ran to one or the other of them before each ornament, so they could examine it and tell her it was perfect, and then she placed it very carefully on the tree. Hank tended to prefer the Hallmark ornaments—his childhood trees had been filled with hand-me-downs and homemade—but this year, he was particularly proud to put a candy cane made of beads front and center. Josie had made it in daycare.

Justin held her up so she could put the star on the top and then string tinsel garlands all around the living room, and Hank put a nail in the front door to hang the new wreath on. When he was done with that, he disappeared into the kitchen to make cocoa and came back, setting it on the coasters on the coffee table, and looking around.

"It's wonderful," he pronounced, and Josie ran to give him a completely unsolicited, delighted hug.

And then to ask him if she could watch *Shrek* again after her bath, which he'd forgotten about.

But finally she was bathed and full of hot chocolate and her teeth were brushed, and Hank had read her one story and Justin had sung her a Christmas song in his sweet tenor, and she was fast, fast asleep.

Hank came out of her bedroom to find Justin in the kitchen, cleaning up.

And fell very much in love. Again.

He moved behind that compact, vital body, placed his hands on Justin's hips and started to kiss the back of his neck. Justin gasped and put the pot he was washing down in the sink, and simply leaned back into Hank's arms and allowed him to....

To kiss him, his neck, his back, his ears, his jaw, his shoulders....

To touch him, his chest, his face, his stomach, his arms, his throat....

To *feel* him, pressed up against Hank's front, a willing, warm human being who was moaning breathlessly and grinding back against Hank as he breathed, touched, and pillaged the young man who had come bouncing into his life and who showed no inclination of leaving.

"You have to promise me something," Hank whispered, and Justin moaned in return. "You have to promise me that no matter how this goes, you'll smile at me tomorrow morning, okay? I'm starting to depend on that smile. I need to see it when we leave the house."

"Deal."

Hank grabbed his shoulders and turned him around and took his mouth savagely, his breath sobbing in his throat when Justin matched him for urgency. He shoved his hands down the back of Justin's jeans and pulled up his shirt, dying to feel bare skin, and was gratified when Justin did the same thing. Justin's hands were warm and still a little damp, but Hank didn't care. Skin-on-skin, after so long, it was *amazing.*

Justin panted and bucked his hips forward, then pulled back from the kiss and leaned his head on Hank's shoulder. "Please tell me your door locks."

"Yes," Hank breathed back, reaching into Justin's jeans and grabbing twin handfuls of taut yet squishy backside. "But we need to unlock it and get dressed when we're done."

"Deal." And then they were kissing, and Hank was walking Justin backwards to the bedroom, leaving the dishes in the sink and turning off lights as they went.

The kiss didn't stop when they got to the bedroom, but it did get interrupted as Hank pulled off Justin's bright green sweater and the red T-shirt underneath it. Justin obviously used the gym too, but his muscles were smaller, more compact, and his chest had maybe three hairs on it.

"Does this mean," Hank asked, kissing down Justin's pec, "that I'm cradle robbing?"

"Yeah, Henry." Justin tipped his head back and appeared to enjoy every one of Hank's perfectly placed kisses down the center of his chest. "They changed the age of consent to read 'age of chest hair'."

Hank pulled away to snicker at him, and Justin knotted his fingers in Hank's short hair and pushed him back to placing kisses on Justin's nearly smooth chest. "If you suck on my nipple, I may come in my pants," Justin promised, and Hank went for it, to see if that could really happen.

It was a near thing. Justin's über-responsive body bucked under his mouth, and his grip tightened to the point of pain in Hank's hair, so Hank moved to the next nipple to tease some more before shucking Justin's pants and boxers in one go, and moving straight for ground zero.

"Henry," Justin whined, struggling to get his pants and his shoes off at the same time so he could lie back on the bed. "Jeez, just give it a little bit of a—" His shoes finally landed with a plop, along with his jeans, and Hank pushed him back on the bed and took Justin's entire length into his mouth with one hungry shove.

"*Ohmygah!*" Justin breathed, and Henry tightened his lips and pulled back, tasting skin, sweat, soap, and then pushing forward again as far down as he could go. Justin pounded the mattress in the sweet pain of almost instant arousal, and started to jerk hard. Hank hadn't done this in a while—he took Justin's cock in his fist and held tight, then clamped his mouth over the widely flared head and teased with his tongue, letting Justin thrust as hard and as fast and as wildly and—"*Ohmygah omygah omygah… fuck!*"

He surged forward and Hank swallowed, wanting all of it in his mouth, down his throat, the salty, the bitter, the surprisingly sweet, and Justin kept thrusting until every last bit of it was shot. When Justin made a sound of discomfort, Hank let go of his cock and pushed himself up onto the mattress, still hard and aching but content for a moment to just touch and see the first man he'd had in his bed in too long a time. He didn't look Justin in the eyes, not yet. First he danced his fingertips across thighs—there was some fur on those, and black hair at Justin's groin, proving that yes, in fact, Justin did have body hair. From the thighs, he stuck his tongue out and caught the edges of Justin's oblique muscles and traced up while Justin held himself, quivering, and tried, Hank could tell, not to fall apart and giggle.

Hank moved to his side and tried to give him a hickey, and Justin lost the battle, curling up defensively and giggling like a little kid.

"Ohmygah, *Henry*! Way to kill a mood!" he said, still laughing, and Hank slid up to put his head on the pillow next to him and pulled Justin, giggles and all, into his arms. He dropped little kisses in Justin's silky and enviably straight black hair, on his temple, on his cheek, and then, as the giggles stilled, on his mouth. Justin opened his mouth and returned the kiss and Hank made a sort of desperate sound and ground his still-aching groin.

"What do you want?" Justin asked, tucking his hands under Hank's shirt and sweater, and Hank closed his eyes and shuddered.

"Just touch me," he begged. "Just…"

"Yeah," Justin whispered. "Here, Henry, let's take your clothes off."

There was some scrambling and some breathless giggling but in a few moments, Hank was naked and lying on the sheets across from Justin, who pressed a kiss on his mouth and then scooted closer and wrapped his arms and legs around Hank's body, just pulling him into a full-length, skin-on-skin embrace that left Hank shuddering.

"C'mere," Justin whispered against his neck, even though Hank was solid in his arms and they couldn't get any closer without penetration. Hank didn't want that, though. He found he was clinging to Justin, aroused—*painfully* aroused—but needing Justin's skin, and his kindness and his joy with every fiber, atom, skin cell, particle, electron, platelet and neuron in his body. "Shh...."

Justin stroked his back and his sides and even his backside, and when Hank's hips started to buck, he slid his hand between their bodies and grasped Hank's cock. He stroked jerkily because there was no room for anything else, but Hank was so primed, so high off the thrill of being touched, that Justin's stuttering, inexpert touch was all he needed.

He climaxed hard, the hot come spurting between them. His vision went black, the orgasm convulsing him into Justin's arms until he huddled there, still shaking.

Justin held him, nothing delicate or fragile in his touch at all, until Hank got hold of himself and tried to pull back, if nothing else, to restore his dignity.

Justin's embrace only grew tighter.

"Stay," he whispered. "It's okay. I've got you."

Hank wanted to laugh. It was ludicrous, wasn't it? Hank was the banker; Justin was the fun guy the kids loved. Hank had the house; Justin lived with his parents. Hank took care of Josie like he'd taken care of Amanda, and Justin... oh God. He was taking care of Hank. He was. He was clutching Hank right up next to him, naked and vulnerable and unafraid in a way Hank had never been.

Hank found himself breathing shakily into the hollow of Justin's neck, taking everything he had to offer.

HE WASN'T aware of the moment he managed to pull himself together, but it came. He drew back a little and yanked the comforter over the two of them to their chins. Justin laughed and pulled it over their heads and looked at him in the light shining through the deep gold comforter, and Hank blinked back, relieved that he was Hank again because he'd felt a little lost as Henry.

"That was good," Justin whispered, and Hank smiled and nodded, feeling excited like a kid at Christmas.

"That was *wonderful*."

"Want to do it again?"

For a moment he almost said no, they had to go to sleep, they both worked in the morning blah blah blah blah. Of course then it hit him;

he had *Justin,* and he was *naked,* and he was in *Hank's bed*, horny, and ready for a (hopefully slower) second round.

Common sense reasserted itself in a hurry.

"Oh God, yes," he said, closing in for a kiss, and Justin's laughing mouth opened for him and their secret hiding place from all the scary things in the world kept them safe while they made love again.

DRAMA

CHRISTMAS EVE loomed in four days, and Hank was waiting for the other shoe to drop.

It had to, right?

He'd just been so damned happy.

Yes—work, Josie, clean the house, repeat daily as necessary—all of that was still there. But, like he'd imagined, having Justin to fill the quiet places in all that routine also filled the empty places in Hank. Having him spend the night—quite a lot of them, for two weeks—well, damn.

Hank could *never* remember waking up every morning and being so incredibly grateful.

Josie had woken up that first night that Justin slept over and tiptoed into Hank's room. (He'd expected this—they were both chastely dressed in sleep shorts and T-shirts by then.) Hank had walked her back to her own this night, but she'd seen Justin, still sleeping, on the other side of the bed.

"Will he be here in the morning?" she'd asked, as he pulled the covers up to her chin.

"Yes," Hank said, not doubting it for a moment.

"Good," she yawned. "I can sleep if he's going to be here."

Hank had no idea how that worked, but as he'd gone back to bed and pulled Justin against him, he'd thought blearily that it was probably just magic.

So TWO weeks later, the biggest thing he was stressing about was what to get Justin for Christmas. He'd gone back to the bath shop and bought Sky—the entire line, bath scrub, body spray, shaving cream, mansturizer, the works! But it didn't seem enough. Although it was personal, maybe the most personal thing he'd ever bought for a man (Alan had preferred gift certificates and DVDs) it just didn't encompass all of the good things, all of the hope and the joy and the *oxygen* that Justin had brought into his life.

So when Hank sat down at his desk after his lunchtime run, the question of whether gloves were lame as a gift and a worry about taping the *Charlie Brown Christmas* special on television that night were the only two things on his mind.

And then his desk phone rang and his world ended.

"Henry! How ya doin', big brother? How's my baby girl?"

Hank had heard about a person's "bowels turning to ice," but even though he'd been in a car wreck when he was seventeen, he'd never had it happen to *him*.

Until now.

He almost hung up the phone, but like social niceties, cowardice wasn't his strong suit either.

"Hello, Amanda," he said, pulling out the files he'd been planning to review and a pen and pretending like this was any other office call. "You couldn't use my cell phone?"

"Didn't want you to hang up on me," she said impishly. "You can't turn the office phone off!" No one had ever said she was stupid.

"Yes, well, only cowards run away," he said coldly and was not surprised to hear her gasp.

"That's not fair, Henry! I was desperate!"

"You were tired!" he snapped back. "And I totally would have helped you out, but you didn't ask for that, did you! You just..." his voice threatened to shake and break and he took a deep breath. "You abandoned your child, and you were just lucky you left her with me, because Josie's in a good place now. I'm just waiting to see what fresh hell you've got waiting for your daughter now."

"Henry! Don't be mean to me! I want to come back!"

"Why?" Hank lashed out, hating himself but unable to stop. "So you can dress her up like a doll and parade her in front of your friends? So you can *leave her alone* while you go to the movies? Yeah, Amanda— she told me about that. She told me that you snuck out while she was sleeping, and she told me about different men every morning."

"God, the kid's a freakin' narc!" Amanda whined, and Hank took a deep breath and tried to control himself. This... this *blame* thing wasn't going to help the situation. Besides that, his voice was rising, and his co-workers were eyeballing him and, *dammit*, he didn't like drama!

"What did you need, Amanda?" Hank asked, because that had to be the only reason she called, right?

"I just…" Amanda's voice dropped. "I just wanted to see her, that's all," she said. "I… I was passing through town and I wanted to wish her a Merry Christmas. Is that so freakin' bad?"

Oh hells. "No," he said shortly, running his fingers through his hair. No. It wasn't. Amanda was young, and it was Christmas, and it wasn't so freakin' bad to want to see your family at Christmas. "Are you going to try to take her from me?" he asked, surprised when he said it, shocked at how close this fear was to the surface.

"I wouldn't mind if she wanted to come with me!" Amanda said excitedly. "I've got this sweet setup in Lincoln now, and my boyfriend says he likes kids and wouldn't mind her. My best friend lives in the same complex and we've got a pool and—"

"Please," he said, his voice tinny and echoing in his ears. "Please rethink that," he said when he could get his breath. "The social worker just okayed her for my house, and we've got a routine and a daycare worker and…." Oh God. Justin and Josie, they were… they were his home and his everything. She couldn't just swoop in and take half his everything, could she? "I fixed up her room and we've got plans for Christmas.*" No, oh please, Amanda, I gave you all my toys when we were kids, I fed you, I walked you home from school, and I never wanted anything, being your family was enough. Please don't take this thing, this one thing, away from me when it's so close to all I ever wanted.*

"Oh Henry!" Amanda laughed. "God, you're so uptight! She's a kid! She'll be fine wherever she is. Some television, some McDonald's, she's all good!"

"Right," Hank said bitterly. "Because God knows we both turned out just fine!"

There was a wounded silence on the other end of the line, and then Amanda inhaled. Hank recognized that inhale—it was the sound Amanda made right before she dug her heels in.

"I'll be there tonight. I'll let you know if I'm taking her with me then."

Amanda hung up and Hank was left at his work desk, shivering, trying to tell himself that those were *not* tears burning tightly in the back of his throat.

Suddenly he wanted Justin. He *needed* Justin. He told his supervisor that he was not feeling well and excused himself from his afternoon, then made a beeline for the gym.

When he got there, he flashed his ID and went straight back to the gym daycare, so focused on talking to Justin that he actually stopped short when he heard Justin's voice come out of an empty workout classroom to his left.

He didn't sound happy.

"Justin! Baby!" came a female voice that Hank dimly identified as Justin's supervisor. "You've got to calm down. It sounds like things are going great—I don't know what your problem is!"

"You don't get it, Jackie!" Justin wailed, and as Hank backed up and leaned against the wall, the better to eavesdrop, just hearing his voice—even distraught—eased something in Hank's chest and slowed his heartbeat. Justin charmed children, small animals, grim social workers, and Hank. Surely, Justin would find a way to convince Amanda that Josie needed to stay with him, stay with *them,* so this warm, almost painfully gratifying sensation of home didn't need to evaporate like sweat after a run.

"What don't I get? He's a nice guy, he likes children—hell, he *has* one built in—and I've seen him look at you. I think he sort of worships you. It's weird. What's the problem?"

"He doesn't like drama," Justin said, and Hank grimaced. Well, he'd made *that* clear, hadn't he? "And I want to bring him home. *Home.* You've met my mother! She'll call in the whole family and they'll grill him and I'll be coming out too and there will be tears and... *drama!* And... I... I don't want to scare him off, but... it's so stupid." Justin's voice broke a little. "I just want to bring him home for *Christmas.*"

Hank found himself laughing a little—not from Justin's misery, because he was pretty sure he could put an end to that—but from Justin's enthusiasm. The way his voice broke on "Christmas," the way his enthusiasm had to be measured in joules and not degrees. Oh God, how had Hank made it? How had he made it through the first week of parenthood, through his whole adult life thus far, without knowing Justin?

He opened the door then and stepped inside. "Hey, Jackie," he said, smiling a little, "can Justin and I have a minute?"

She was a wide-hipped, buxom girl with corkscrewed brown hair, and she nodded, looking grateful. "You guys have fifteen minutes before the next class, 'kay?" With that, she shouldered her way out into the hallway, leaving Hank and Justin alone.

Hank opened his arms and gestured with his hands and Justin flew into his chest and sniffled. Hank clung to him, kissing his temple and fighting back a smile in the wake of his obvious misery.

"You heard everything?" Justin asked after a moment and Hank nodded.

"Uhm-hm."

"I'm sorry."

"It's okay, drama queen, you didn't scare me off."

"No?" Justin looked up at him hopefully, and Hank shook his head.

"No. But I do have a request."

Justin's wide blue eyes were shiny and his lashes were spiked with tears as he looked up and nodded. It was an appealing look—helpless and vulnerable like that—but Hank knew better. Justin was plenty strong.

Hank kissed his forehead. "Tell your mom that you're gay first, and *then* ask if Josie and I can come to Christmas Eve dinner."

Justin wrinkled his forehead. "But—"

"Yeah, I know Alan and I did it that way. But I needed the hand, because my mom wasn't exactly the warmest person, and I never felt safe. Not even with Alan. The whole reason he agreed to come was because he didn't think I had the balls to do it. Not with mom. Not with anyone, really," he said, and he knew that would hurt Justin, but he didn't know how to make it not. He held Justin a little tighter. "I'm working on that part, okay?"

Justin nodded.

"If your parents are the people you've told me about—the people who made *you*—you don't need me for this. But I need to know I'm not walking Josie into Drama Kitchen on a holiday, okay?"

Justin choked on a hiccup. "Oh. Oh God. *Ohmygah!* You're right! I'm so stupid! I didn't even think! I was just thinking about you and I didn't even think about Josie ohmygah ohmygah ohmygah—I'm so *sorry!*"

Hank closed his eyes really tight and kissed him, thinking their ten minutes were about up. "Justin, you're a total drama queen, and I love you. You're wonderful," he stated. "Josie needs you in her life. So do I." Oh God, he made it sound like they were going into battle or something. But he couldn't help it. He needed to call the social worker and he needed to get himself all ready to talk to his baby sister and to make a case for her letting her baby stay with him.

He pulled away and backed up. "I, uhm, I'm not going to be coming to the gym tonight—"

"Are we still on for later?" Justin asked, instantly upset, and Hank hesitated. "What? I'm not good enough to come over anymore? Didn't you just say 'I lo…'. *Omygah!* You *did!* You *did* say the *L* word, and now you're running away?"

Hank backed up; he knew he was leaving Justin confused as hell, but he felt powerless to do this any other way. All his railing against drama, how was he supposed to let Justin see him falling apart like a lost child if Amanda stole their little girl?

"Call me when your shift's over," he said, reaching behind him for the handle. "We'll talk then, okay? You're perfect, and don't forget to ask your mom about Christmas Eve." And with that he fled, leaving Justin gaping after him, aware that he hadn't told Justin why he was there in the first place.

THE NEXT few hours were agony.

He called the social worker from in front of the daycare lady's house. Mrs. Ramirez once again confirmed what he'd known, which was that Amanda had every right in the world to come sweep Josie out of his home.

"Can I get her to sign something that makes that not possible?" he asked, and Mrs. Ramirez sniffed.

"We do have papers where a parent agrees to relinquish custody. Odds are good she could overturn it if she changes her mind, but in the meantime—"

"It'll take her a while to change her mind. Can she sign them today?"

There was a sigh over the phone and Hank almost imagined Mrs. Ramirez felt a little bit of pity for him. "Now Mr. Calder, you know we don't work that fast. But if you like, we can start drawing them up, then the next time you see your sister, we can see about doing that."

Hank thought about screaming, but he didn't. That was drama neither of them needed. "Okay, then. Let's draw up something legal, and yeah. If Amanda doesn't… if we can, we can get her to sign them."

He clicked off then and went in to get Josie. He'd promised her a chance to make decorations tonight, and he figured since there was no gym and he was off a little early, he could make good on that promise even if Amanda came and took her away, and there were no more promises ever.

Melodramatic, Henry. Don't be melodramatic.

They made little drums out of felt and toilet paper rolls, and then they made wreaths with little bows using beads and pipe cleaners. When they were done with that, they moved on to foamies, and he helped her decorate little picture frames. He pulled out the pictures he'd had taken at Sears with her and painstakingly glued them to the back of the frames.

"Now who do we want to give these to?" he asked, forcing himself to look at them dispassionately. He'd had them taken in November, and she had sat so stiffly in his arms. He'd had an idea that if they had a picture up on the mantelpiece, she'd believe that this place, his house, was where she belonged.

"Mrs. Watson," Josie said eagerly, and Hank thanked Heaven for good daycare services, and set that one aside.

"Good. Who else?"

"Cee Cee—she's the girl with the black hair at Mrs. Watson's."

"Very nice. Who else?"

"Justin—Justin will want one, right?"

Hank nodded. "Yeah. Exactly. Justin would *really* want one." If Amanda took Josie, Justin would probably cry his eyes out over that picture—but he'd still want it. God, Justin was so much braver than Hank was.

"Good," Josie said, putting an extra sticker on Justin's frame. "We should have new pictures taken, with you and me and Justin, and then we could give one to Mommy."

Hank wondered if his lungs could freeze, right along with his bowels. "You think your mom would like one of those?"

"Yes. Then she could see our family. She'd be happy, to see our family."

Hank nodded, and the ice spread to his whole body. He was numb, he thought gratefully. He was numb, and he'd just do this. He had her help make dinner—omelets tonight, and she got to pour in the egg mixture and sprinkle the cheese and the spinach and the tomatoes, and then she spooned sour cream on top of both the omelets on the plate. He set her at the table on her booster seat, and sat kitty corner to her, like he had for the last three months. When Justin ate with them, he sat on her other side. For a moment, a bare moment, Hank wished he'd invited Justin over, had *begged* him to come over, in fact, so he could have that one memory of the two of them at his dinner table, but he blocked that thought out before it could level him.

Decorations, dinner, bath, television, book, song, bed. It was their routine, and it was soothing, and Hank couldn't live every goddamned second in a state of freaking out. When bedtime rolled around, he put her to bed with a hug and a kiss. He looked around her room, wondering if he should have packed her clothes, and then it hit him.

Nine o'clock, and Amanda wasn't here. Maybe she wasn't coming?

"Is Justin coming over?" Josie asked sleepily, and he bent down and kissed her one more time.

"Maybe," he said, and for the first time that evening, the little ice skin that had congealed over his heart chipped large, and he had to take a deep breath to keep everything from spilling out onto the shoulders of a very small, and at this moment, very *content* little girl. "He had something to do when he got off work, but he said he was going to try."

"Good," Josie whispered. "Tell him 'night for me."

"Night, Bunny. Love you."

"Love you too," she whispered, and even though she said it a lot, almost every night, he promised himself he'd never forget that she did.

He went out into the living room afterward, and stood, at a loss. All set for drama and none had arrived. He pulled out his phone to call Justin when he heard a creak on the porch and then, sniffing, smelled cigarette smoke.

Very quietly he opened his front door and went outside.

Amanda was sitting on the bench out on his front porch, and judging by the butts in the empty coffee cup at her side, she'd been there for quite some time.

"Jesus, Amanda! It's freezing out here!" It was, in fact, dank and foggy and damp. He wasn't wearing a coat and he shoved his hands in his khaki pockets in basic reaction.

"I'd noticed," she said softly, inhaling. She lifted her shoe and stubbed the butt out on the sole, then dropped it in the coffee cup, breathing out smoke while she did so. Hank looked at her, trying to radiate disapproval, but it was hard. She had blond hair and brown eyes, just like Josie, but her hair was straight and Josie's was starting to curl, like Hank's did.

"Why didn't you come in?" he asked, and she shrugged.

"You two, you had your thing. I saw you, right? Sitting on the couch, watching television, reading, bath time. All that shit you used to do for me, except you were... hell, ten, right?"

"Yeah."

She was wearing jeans and an old denim jacket with a pink hooded sweatshirt underneath it. When she looked up at him, he could almost imagine that she was a child again and he was taking care of her this time, and not her daughter.

"I knew, right?" she said, looking at him, her eyes filling. She wiped them with the back of her hand and just kept talking, her voice roughened by grief and cigarettes. "I knew when I brought her here that you'd take care of her—"

"I could have taken care of you too," he said, and she half-laughed.

"Yeah, well, Henry, I don't seem to do really well with that."

He sighed and leaned against the house, shoving his hands deeper inside his pockets. "I'd noticed."

"You didn't tell her I was coming, did you?" It was a question, and Hank had to answer, when he'd been putting off the answer even for himself.

"No."

"Why?"

"Because I really hoped you wouldn't show up."

She sighed and pulled up her knee so she could rest her chin on it. "My boyfriend would take her in you know. We could have a really cute little family."

"Yeah?"

"But he wants, like, a kid of his own. I don't know if I could do both kids." She shuddered, and he did too. But he couldn't make her stop smoking or take care of herself or make her take birth control. He could only do a small set of things to make his world work. His job, Josie, taking care of the house. And Justin.

"I want custody," he said, ignoring her little hurt gasp. "Legal custody." His voice broke a little. "All I thought of all day was you coming here and taking her away, and I can't do that, Amanda. I've been a stand-up guy. I've done right by you. All I want is just a promise that you won't take her away from me."

"You can't make me do that!" she snapped, standing up, and he shook his head, not looking at her so he could talk.

"I know I can't. But next time you come by, I'll have papers for you to sign anyway. Think about it, Amanda. It won't be hanging over your head like a broken promise. You give me custody, and next time, you can come in the house, and you won't have to feel bad. She won't expect anything of you, she'll just be happy to see you."

"Yeah?" Amanda asked, her voice uncertain, and Hank looked up quickly into brown eyes so very like his own. "She'll be happy to see me?"

"Ecstatic," Hank said, his voice raspy. "She'd be thrilled to see you now."

Amanda shook her head. "I couldn't," she said. Now her voice broke too, and he could see what this visit had cost her, and how high the price had been of *not* knocking on his door. "You think I don't remember, Henry. You think I'm not grateful. But I remember. I remember how you made a home when Mom couldn't. I saw you doing the same things with my little girl and I thought, 'Yeah. That's why I brought her here.' And suddenly it seemed like the best thing I'd ever done."

"She has her own room." Hank wiped his eyes across his sweatshirt. "It's pink, with purple trim—"

"Like cake icing," she said, smiling a little. It had been the room she'd always wanted. It was how he knew how to decorate it.

"Yeah."

She nodded and threw herself into his arms unexpectedly, smelling like coffee and cigarettes, and not like little girl at all. He hugged her back.

"Take care of her, okay?"

"I promise."

"I'll come back after Christmas, maybe, and sign those papers."

He half-sobbed into her shoulder, the relief making him weak, and Amanda pulled away from him, wiping her eyes some more. A pair of headlights paused at the end of Hank's driveway, and Hank looked up to see Justin's old Dodge Neon parking behind Hank's practical Hybrid, instead of next to it.

"Who's that?" Amanda asked with a small frown.

"My boyfriend. He adores Josie."

Amanda half laughed and then backed away. "Well, I'm gonna leave before this goes all drama queen on me." She looked into Hank's eyes again and nodded. "Bye, big brother. See you 'round."

She trotted off the porch and hopped into her battered gray Corolla, barely waiting for Justin to get across the driveway before she backed out. Hank found that his knees weren't working right, and he slid into the porch bench like warm Jell-O.

"Who was that?" Justin asked, his nose wrinkled at the smell of cigarettes. "And jeez, Henry, why'd you let her turn this place into an ashtray?"

Hank took a few minutes before answering—long enough for Justin to stop and get a good look at him, and then to come closer and wipe off Hank's cheeks with his thumbs.

"Your face is freezing, Henry," Justin said softly. "Want to come inside?"

Hank shook his head. "Did I ever tell you about the day Josie came to stay with me?" he asked.

"No."

It wasn't that long ago, it really wasn't, but Hank felt like a whole other person now.

"See, Amanda had her, and every so often she'd call up on Josie's birthday or before holidays, and Mom and I would meet her somewhere and celebrate. We never knew when her number would change or when her cell phone would be working, so after a while, we just stopped calling, and started to depend on those random phone calls. And then we went for like, three months, with no Amanda, no Josie—Mom and I were getting worried, but we had no way to track them down, and then, the day after Josie's birthday in October, they just showed up on my porch."

Justin was still standing in front of him, so Hank took advantage of that and wrapped his arms around Justin's thighs so he could rest his face against Justin's middle. Justin stroked his hair, and Hank relaxed into him—and kept on talking.

"So they get here, and I'm happy, but I'm nagging too. Where've they been, is Amanda smoking again, why didn't she call—you know, all that big brother bullshit that just makes Amanda skittish as all hell, but I get them inside, and give Josie the birthday present I bought in the hope that I'd see her. Josie says she's hungry, so I start cooking up some hot dogs, right? And while I'm getting the pot out and filling it with water, Amanda says, 'Going out for a smoke, Henry'!"

Hank laughed a little into Justin's windbreaker. Justin was shivering by now, but Hank couldn't stop telling the story long enough to get up and get them inside.

"And?" Justin prompted into the silence, and Hank shivered this time.

"And that was it," he said. "That was it. I spent my time playing with Josie and the doll, and then the hot dogs are done, and I get Josie a plate. I go outside to tell Amanda that I've got lunch, such as it is, and all of Josie's clothes are on the porch, and Amanda is gone. She'd parked on the curb that time. I didn't even hear her start the car."

"And that was the last you heard from her—"

Hank nodded. "Until she called me this afternoon and showed up on my porch."

Justin jerked back from him suddenly, and Hank couldn't blame him. "Oh. My. *God. Henry!* You *knew*? There I was blubbering about my own petty bullshit problems and you *knew*!"

Henry sat there and looked up at him, feeling like a little kid. "Don't be mad," he begged, closing his eyes. "I just... I couldn't. It was your drama, and it was sweet, and you were worried about your family and I didn't want to take that away. But you see? You see why I didn't want the drama at first, right? Because if something so... so *quiet* could totally turn my life upside down, I was just fucking terrified of real drama. Just scared to death that it would rip me apart and just leave me in little bleeding pieces, right?"

Justin's expression softened and he came closer. He tried to put his hands on Hank's shoulders but Hank was too agitated; he shot up from the bench, forcing Justin to take a step back while he got this out, laid it into the world so maybe the moonlight could kill it.

"So when I heard your meltdown this afternoon, it was like... it was like wonderful," Hank said. "Because there you were, and everything in you was there for me to see, and it was okay. It didn't hurt. I could help you fix it and it made me happy. So I started thinking about those turkeys in the snow, remember?"

Justin nodded, mutely, and Hank wondered if maybe he wasn't going to be the one who was too crazy to keep. "So, they freaked out with the snowflakes and hurt each other, but... but that wasn't the deadliest thing. The deadliest thing was the quiet stuff, the fox that didn't make any noise. With you, I'll always know where you stand. God, baby, you make a lot of noise, and I sort of love that about you, is that okay? Is that—"

Justin then did something Hank didn't expect—he grabbed Hank's arms and pulled Hank's mouth down for a kiss. Hank opened his mouth and tasted salt, and realized that here he was, the anti-drama queen, and he was the one crying and freezing on his porch, and maybe he should know better.

But Justin was wrapping his strong arms around his shoulders and pulling him in for a hug, and Hank thought that maybe he should wait until he stopped shaking to change anything.

"I love you too, Henry," Justin said, and Hank rested his wet cheek in Justin's straight, soft hair, and wondered if he could pull himself together enough to get them inside.

Eventually.

Eventually they got inside and Hank showed Justin the pictures and told him about the plan to have one taken of the three of them.

Eventually Justin told Hank about telling his mother and father the big "secret."

"So what'd they say?" Hank asked, fixing them some coffee laced with chocolate to warm them up since they were both still cold.

Justin looked aggrieved. "Would you believe it? My mother said, 'Wait—haven't you told us this already?' and Dad said, 'No, dear, we just imagined he did.'"

Hank found himself laughing as he handed Justin his mug. "Classic," he said, loving that story. "So, are Josie and I still invited to dinner?"

"Yup," Justin said, nodding. "In fact, Mom was in seventh heaven. She was like '*Ohmygah!* Instant grandchild!' You may become her favorite son."

"I doubt it. But good. I look forward to Christmas with her." They settled into the living room, and Justin brought up the Big Bad and Hank blessed him for it.

"So, your sister. She didn't even come in?"

Hank breathed out. "No," he said. "But she may come back after Christmas to sign some custody papers for me."

Justin sighed. "Henry, you know I'm still a little pissed, right?"

Hank studied his coffee. "I'm sorry."

"You should be! Going through all that alone. Hurts my fucking feelings, you know that, right?"

"I'm sorry," Hank said again. He looked up and clasped Justin's hand, and for a moment they were silent. "We had history," Hank said after a pause. "There was stuff that... that I needed to say to my baby sister, that's all. Next time, I swear. If it involves Josie or involves us, you'll be in the know."

"That's not good enough," Justin snapped, and Hank jerked back, startled. "Not just if it involves Josie or involves me—what if it hurts *you*, do you understand that? You're a *mess*, Henry Calder. Not the kind that drives off and leaves a kid, no, but look at you—you knew this *all day* and you didn't *talk* to me?" Justin set his coffee down on the table without a coaster, which was good because he was starting to gesture and Hank was worried he'd scald himself. At no time did he release Hank's hand, though, and that was a better thing.

"What if she'd taken her?" Hank asked. He set his coffee down too, because his hands were getting slick with sweat just thinking about it.

"Yeah, Henry!" Justin let go of his hand long enough to turn around and face him on the couch. "What if your sister had come and taken her away! What about that? You didn't even tell me to come over after! What would you have done if I'd called? Were you just going to tough it out like a frickin' man?"

Hank couldn't look at him. "I am sort of a frickin man," he said, and Justin slugged him hard in the arm. "Ouch!" Hank whined, rubbing the tender spot, and Justin shook his hand out and yelped.

"God, that sucks! Bitch-slapping is totally underrated!"

"Well, don't do it!" Hank snapped, taking Justin's hand in his and rubbing the wrist to make sure there was no permanent damage.

"Well, you were being stupid! I totally care about you—I want to be the guy who throws the pity party and the guy who rides clean up. No 'toughing it out on my own' bullshit—next time your world is going to fall apart, *tell* me!"

Hank stopped massaging Justin's wrist and looked up to meet his eyes instead. "Okay," he said quietly. "I promise."

"I take that seriously, Henry."

"I do too."

Justin nodded. "I'm going to live. Can you come over here and kiss me now? I want to skip the preliminaries and get you in bed now. I sort of kind of need to touch you."

Hank all but tackled him as he sat. They barely made it to the bedroom, and when Hank climaxed into Justin's eager mouth, he had to bite his palm because he was afraid he'd wake Josie with the sound he wanted to make.

When they were done, and Justin was where Justin needed to be, with his head on Hank's shoulder and his hand gliding across Hank's chest, Hank played with his hair and drifted in and out of sleep.

He must have dreamt a little, too, because the next morning, waking up with Justin's arm around his waist and Josie's usual request (demand!) for breakfast, he felt like he had glimpsed the future.

Nothing specific, really—just the basics.

He'd seen Christmas Eve, meeting Justin's parents, and being hugged within an inch of his life. Justin's mother had adopted Josie on sight, and suddenly Josie had a happy, smiling woman to look to, to maybe grow into, with some love and care to help.

He'd seen Christmas morning, after he and Justin had spent all night wrapping gifts and stacking them under the Christmas tree. Josie had been happy and excited and delighted and joyful, and she'd squealed and shrieked and all of the little girl things that Hank had always wanted for Amanda, but he'd never been able to give.

He'd seen beyond that, to a New Year's Eve in Justin's arms, and a Valentine's dinner when he asked Justin to move in.

He'd seen beyond that, even to Josie's first day of school and volunteering in her class and hearing her tell him about her day, and even beyond *that* to being in the audience with Josie when they watched Justin get his degree.

He'd seen an entire lifetime in those magic glimpses in and out of sleep, and it was filled with laughter and sadness and joy and disappointment—and, by necessity, drama.

He slept that night secure in the knowledge that he was proud to be part of the human play.

❄ *AMY LANE* ❄
GOING UP!

To anyone who has ever watched an old movie,
and wanted to live in it. And to Mate, who watches old movies.

GROUND FLOOR

*ONCE UPON a time, there was a prince who lived in a tower. He had
been born to a king and a queen in the kingdom of San Francisco, and
he was raised by nannies and boarding schools. He was a good child.
He did everything he was told. He never questioned his world, and his
rebellions, on the whole, were very, very small.*

*He worked hard, earned his law degree, and made a life defending
the weak and downtrodden, while he enjoyed a privileged life atop the
tallest tower of the kingdom.*

*But although there was no snow in his kingdom, there were chilly
bay breezes, and they left his heart cold, oh, so very cold....*

ZACH DRISCOLL sipped his champagne and looked around him. His
parents' annual Christmas party seemed to be in full swing: the chandelier
was dusted, the galleria ballroom glittered with tasteful silver decorations,
and his secretary, Leah, was flirting with the up-and-coming young president
of the local chamber of commerce.

Fortunately for Leah's fun, she didn't know he was gay.

Zach knew Angelo Fitzsimmons was gay—but Angelo didn't know
Zach knew. It was a sad fact that Zach owed pretty much every decent
sexual encounter he'd ever had to a flier on "escort services" that Angelo
had left in a bathroom stall when Zach was still in college.

Zach figured that if the firm was discreet enough for Angelo with
his budding political career, it was discreet enough for a union lawyer
who only showed up to these things for his parents.

Oh, and speaking of....

"She's charming, Zach. It's about time you settled down and brought
a date to one of our parties."

"Hi, Mother," he said, pursing his lips in a really horrible
approximation of a smile. "We're not dating. She's my secretary—she
does a really good job. I figured she deserved a perk."

"So you brought your secretary to a fundraiser?" His mother.... God. She looked forty, was closer to sixty-five, and could ooze disdain with a few choice words. Right now, she needed a little sponging off at the edges.

Zach looked over at Leah, who was wearing a red crushed-velveteen dress that left one shoulder bare and sported gold spangles up the split sides. Her dusky skin and sturdy, wide-hipped body looked lush and sensual under that textured fabric, and he only wished he could appreciate that. She'd dyed her hair Christmas red to match, worn gold bangles in her updo, and was currently trying to teach Angelo the Harlem shuffle.

"Yes," he said, smiling a little. He didn't joke with Leah, or get too personal with her, but he sure did admire the hell out of her. She'd started off the job wearing black suits and black shoes, and had kept her normally straight black hair cut short and practical. In the past three years since he'd started the firm and hired five more lawyers and three more paralegals, she had, one tiny bit at a time, let little bits of the real Leah shine through.

First it was fuchsia or lime-colored shirts under her business suit. Then it was fan*tastic* shoes to match the shirts.

Then it was suits to match the shoes.

Then it was hair to match the whole shebang.

And while her wardrobe expanded, her sarcasm also began to expand in depth, breadth, and sheer breathtaking scope. "What, you didn't finish that file before it's due, Mr. Driscoll? I'm suspecting you stopped to take a crap sometime this weekend—shame on you!"

Zach hadn't known how to respond at first. He'd never been proficient in sarcasm, or in any of the more salient social skills such as conversation, eye contact, or generally wanting to get to know his fellow human beings. He'd simply grunted and walked into his office, wondering what to say.

But over the last six months, that sarcasm had started to feel like overtures of friendship. When he'd gotten the invitation to the party stressing the need for a plus-one, he told Leah he'd spring for the dress, and, well, there they were.

"Do you think that's appropriate?" his mother asked, not smiling at all, and Zach watched Angelo actually grace Leah with a real smile, one that didn't seem as constipated and as cramped as Zach felt most of the time.

"I think something needed to happen," he said quietly. "And she's having a lovely time."

Some flashes went off, and Zach figured that moment exhausted his family time for the rest of the year as his mother stood up and left. Zach watched Leah dance like she was Cinderfuckingella (her word, when he'd given her the credit card) and then he looked up into the windows that surrounded the high ceiling of the ballroom. It was raining, and in the cutting silver light from the galleria, the rain looked like slivers of crystal. Like wishing stars.

I wish a prince would rescue me, he thought, half in whimsy and half in despair. Silly wish, right? His parents were rich, and he was a lawyer. Wasn't he the prince? *Okay, then. I wish a knight would rescue the prince in the tower.*

In the distance he heard Leah laugh like a kid in a playground, and he went to tell her that he'd leave her the town car and take a cab home. He knew enough about fairy tales to know that the knight in shining armor never really did show up at the ball.

ZACH LIVED in the penthouse because his dad owned the building. It was that easy.

Of course, law school at Stanford hadn't been that easy, establishing his own practice hadn't been easy, and keeping his relationships to the guys from the escort service wasn't particularly easy on him either.

But Zach had always been good at putting a slick face on things.

He got up in the morning and put on his wool suit—and in San Francisco, it was always a wool suit—with his bright patent leather shoes and his crispy starched collars and hundred-dollar ties. He shaved and slicked back his dark hair, made sure his eyebrows were tweezed and his face was moisturized, and generally ensured he looked and smelled like a man who could protect your future.

He'd been the same way as a kid, except he hadn't had to tweeze his eyebrows.

When he was a kid, his father and mother had insisted on hygiene, and so had his nannies, but the resulting behaviors were neat, orderly habits of mind and he wasn't going to discard them just because there was a sort of echoing, vaultlike quality to all of his childhood memories.

And he figured, after that childhood, living in the nice penthouse of Driscoll Towers in the middle of downtown was a perk. He'd take what he could get. Hiding his sex life from his parents wasn't such a big price to pay, and really? They lived in a mansion down on the peninsula, so about an hour of commute time separated them from him and the guy he'd paid to leave before midnight. Not that there were that many of *those,* but a guy had to be touched, right? That wasn't so bad, to be touched?

But certainly not in an express elevator in the middle of a soulless January.

Which was currently breaking down. The cab lurched to a halt between the nineteenth and twentieth floor, and then, just as Zach was hitting the button for maintenance, it dropped half a floor and the doors opened.

Zach got out of the elevator on the nineteenth floor, absolutely bemused. He didn't even know the express elevator could *open* in this part of the complex. He got out and turned around, seeing there was a bank of elevator doors instead of just the one like he was used to. He thought, *Hunh?* but hit the button to the hopefully *working* elevator, and got in when the doors opened.

The elevator stopped at the fifteenth floor, to let in a teenage girl in bright-pink spandex with a matching iPod who ignored him, and then at the fourteenth floor, where the doors opened and then started to shut again.

"Wait! Wait! I didn't think it was going to open so soon!" The guy was running, and Zach was in the back corner behind the teenager, so he couldn't stop the doors either. The kid—he looked like a kid—who stopped the doors and opened them again, wore cowboy boots and leather chaps and a pink-striped oxford shirt and a really revoltingly large fake-Stetson hat. He had kind of a long neck, a really prominent jaw, a smattering of freckles still on his cheeks, and teeth that barely escaped being bucked.

And curly yellow-brown hair.

And really blue eyes.

And not an ounce of embarrassment for skating in through the door at the last minute, stumbling past the girl and pitching into Zach's arms.

"Sorry 'bout that!" he burbled, straightening himself and then straightening his hat. He arranged a scuffed leather satchel over his hip, and got a tighter hold on the peacoat he'd obviously brought to ward against the cold San Francisco morning. The doors were still open, because sometimes they did that, and the staff complained about it going slow and the tenants said things about it being haunted by the ghost of the bachelor who had died on the twenty-second floor and who had been so lonely his cat had eaten his face.

Zach pretended none of that was actually happening because even though he didn't own a cat, he didn't want to think of his face being eaten. So he didn't think about his face being eaten. He just scooted around the teenaged girl, leaned forward and pressed the "close" key, and mumbled, "No problem" so the boy didn't think it was totally okay to go rocketing into a stranger's arms.

"Yeah, well, I'm still sorry," the kid said, tilting his hat up. Zach had no choice. He looked up from the control board into those plasma-blue eyes, and the kid grinned. He had the slightest space between his teeth, which made Zach think that maybe his parents hadn't had good health insurance, and that made him feel bad.

All his own teeth were capped, because six years of braces hadn't been enough and his smile had been... well, it was perfect now, and that's what mattered.

"That's okay," he said, a little more clearly, and he quirked his lips up for good measure. "Uhm, going on a round-up?"

The guy's face split into a grin. "Substitute teaching in seventh grade. They didn't give me a cattle prod so I figured this would have to do."

"That's... you do that *voluntarily?*" The thought of facing a battalion of sugar-crazed grunion made Zach's well-worked abdomen muscles roll tightly. "You don't look old enough to be in *college!*"

He laughed. Not a polite "you just insulted me so I'm brushing this off" laugh, but a full-stomached laugh, like what Zach had just said was really fucking funny.

"I'm twenty-six!"

Ding!

The elevator opened into the lobby then, and Zach watched the boy—guy, man, crap—stride off into the shiny, fogless day, struggling into his battered peacoat as he went.

Zach followed him, feeling bemused. He didn't see which way the guy turned, and so he went his usual right, because it was twelve blocks to his office building and he walked it every day, wielding his briefcase like a weapon against the hordes on the crowded sidewalk. The bay wind scalpeled its way through his wool trench coat, but he didn't let that stop him, and he didn't resort to huddling and blowing on his hands, either. He just kept up that same relentless pace that allowed him to push his law firm into success, that allowed him to gut school districts and corporations that tried to treat their employees like crap, and that allowed him to subvert every desire he'd ever had for a warm and comfortable life in favor of the thing his parents had decided he should have instead.

He strode into his office with an expressionless face, because that's how he always walked through his office.

Leah smiled brightly at him like she did every day.

"Hello, Mr. Driscoll, are we having a good day, Mr. Driscoll, I have your coffee waiting for you, Mr. Driscoll, all of your appointments are on your computer, Mr. Driscoll—"

Her perky sarcasm usually washed over him like acid rain. After those first conservative months, Zach had come to treasure the punk rock diva who couldn't sing, who wore matching lime-green Converses with her lime-green-and-black suit, and who harangued Zach about his lack of personal life like she had a right.

Her job performance was *spectacular.*

And she thought she was funny.

Usually Zach tolerated her, but today, as he was walking through the lobby, he had a thought of her in her Christmas dress, flirting with a man just to see him smile, and then a vision of a sort of geeky-looking teacher, dressing up to impress middle schoolers he might never see again.

It was an awful lot of effort to go to, this effort to make people respond to you, wasn't it?

He turned to her and spared her a brief smile. "Thank you, Leah—I definitely appreciate the coffee."

Leah's mouth dropped and her stunned silence actually made him a little sad. Jesus, Zach—way to fail Humanity 101.

Maybe tomorrow, he'd bring her dessert coffee and nut bread. She really did try hard, didn't she?

HE LEFT a little early the next day to get the coffee and the nut bread, and even though the elevator was still broken down and he had to sidestep at the nineteenth floor again, he was disappointed not to see his substitute teacher/cowboy on the way down.

But Leah brightened up so much with the coffee that he thought maybe it was worth it. After all, he *worked* with Leah every day. This other guy he didn't know from a monkey in the subway.

Anyway, he kept getting off on the nineteenth floor, whether or not the haunted elevator of the guy on twenty-two with the cat-eaten face worked or not, but it didn't seem to matter. He didn't see Mr. Cowboy Substitute Teacher the next day, or the next, but on Friday, when he decided that he could be five minutes late and still bring Leah her coffee, *that's* when Mr. Cowboy Substitute Teacher slid in at the bell.

But he wasn't wearing his cowboy outfit anymore.

He was wearing a three-piece suit instead, and for a moment Zach felt absurdly disappointed. He saw suits every day.

Then he noticed that Mr. Cowboy's Adam's apple bobbed nervously above the collar of his suit, and that his arms were too long for the obviously off-the-rack ensemble, and that his shirt was a little rumpled and that his tie was off-kilter.

This wasn't his normal attire, now was it?

"Your tie is crooked," he said softly, after getting a nervous, flop-sweat smile from the man next to him.

"Oh fuck!"

Zack snapped his head back, because the obscenity was violent, and, well, unexpected. Mr. Cowboy dropped his satchel and his coat at his feet and started fiddling with his tie. "Crap crap crap crap... dammit. I need this freaking job!"

Zach didn't even know he was doing it until he did it. "Here, hold this."

Mr. Cowboy grabbed his briefcase from his outstretched hand, and Zach moved in, squaring the knot and adjusting the whole works until it rested neatly at his throat. Cowboy looked up at him—he was about four inches shorter than Zach—with implicit trust, and Zach kept his breathing even and focused exclusively on the tie and not on the little bits of stubble that Cowboy had missed when he'd been shaving, or at the rainy smell of body wash, or the fact that his breath was freshly scrubbed with mint toothpaste. When he was done, he stepped back, still not making contact with those limpid blue eyes, and smoothed his palms against Cowboy's bony shoulders, then turned him around and did it again.

The door dinged, and Zach took his briefcase back, and then walked away while Cowboy scrambled for all of the stuff left in the bottom of the elevator car.

"Thanks!" he squeaked, and Zach turned around in time to watch him narrowly slide out of the elevator before the doors closed.

"Good luck," Zach said. He felt something unfamiliar stretch his cheeks, but it wasn't until the wind hit his teeth that he remembered what it was.

When he gave Leah her coffee, he felt it again. When he was telling his latest client—a gay man who had been fired from his office temp job on some bullshit excuse—that they had the company over a barrel and he could have the settlement and new job of his choosing, he felt it again.

He was *smiling.*

ZACH DIDN'T see Mr. Cowboy (or was it Mr. Teacher?) that evening, but since he worked very long hours, he assumed he wouldn't anyway. Instead, he went to the gym to work out, stopped at a take-out place for dinner, and sat in front of his television, mindlessly wondering if he should call the escort service he sometimes used just so he could have a man *pretend* to like him.

He couldn't make himself do it. He kept imagining that Adam's apple bobbing, and the total vulnerability of that slender neck. Poor guy. Looking for a job in this city must suck. Putting himself out there like that.

He was so brave.

Hiring a rent boy just seemed like the height of cowardice after that.

HE STARTED setting his alarm and crossing his fingers. When he left *exactly at that moment,* his odds of seeing Teacher-baby (which sounded so much better than Mister anything, because the boy's limpid blue eyes were just too… yum) increased dramatically.

He left at *that moment* as often as possible.

On Wednesday he was rewarded. Teacher-baby slid into the elevator, followed by a voice screaming across the hallway.

"Sean! Wait!"

"Dammit, Wendy, I'm late!" He held out an arm though, and kept the elevator from closing. Today he was dressed in jeans and a nice button-down shirt with a sweater over it. If he had to hazard a guess, Zach would guess he was subbing again today—those weren't the clothes you wore to a new job.

"Todd wants you to get coffee when you come back!"

The girl running down the hallway in her T-shirt and underwear was incredibly pretty. Elfin, delicate, around five seven, with a short cap of dyed-ruby hair, an oval face with a pert little chin and matching nose, and obviously green contacts.

"Does he have money? It's his turn, and I'm just as broke as he is!"

"Yeah, we all are." She sighed and held out a hand with a crumpled five in it. "Here—you and me will get it today—again—and Toby and Chris can get it next week. Todd and Katie are up for it after that." She batted her eyelashes appealingly. "Please, Sean? I know you got it last time, but we all need the stuff, okay?"

Sean sighed and took the money, shoving it into the pocket of his jeans. "Yeah, okay. Go back inside before some pervert ogles your ass."

She turned to him before she left and grinned. "That would be *awesome!*" And then disappeared down the hall.

Zach blinked. "That is a *lot* of people." He had a penthouse apartment—it took up a quarter of the floor, and it was just him. The other apartments were an eighth of that size, with—

"Six," Sean (his name was Sean!) confirmed. "Yeah, but prices here—man, they're steep, you know?"

Zach had sort of known, but now it was more personal. "Yeah," he said. He didn't ask why someone would want to live in the city when it was so expensive—who wouldn't? "How do you all fit?"

"Toby and Chris in their own bedroom, since they're a couple, the girls and me in a king size in the other bedroom, and Todd the straight guy on the hide-a-bed in the living room. Don't tell Mr. Driscoll, right?" Sean smiled and winked.

Zach found himself smiling back, because… well, because. "Will the new job help?" he asked, and Sean's face fell.

"Didn't get it," he murmured. "It was a Catholic school—they have morality clauses. I sort of violate them just by my very existence."

Zach wanted to roar in outrage, or, at the very least, go sue the crap out of someone, but he knew it was legal. Church-run schools had the right.

"Good luck on the next one," he said gently, and Sean looked up and smiled.

"That's really sweet," he said.

Zach found it suddenly hard to breathe, and his mouth went dry, and he was caught up in the idea that the only thing sweet in the world was that oh-*dayum* smile but the smile faded and—

Ding!

The elevator door opened and it was time to go. This time Sean left first, but before he walked out the glass doors from the lobby to the street, he turned and offered a tentative smile and a wave.

Zach waved back. That whole stretchy-face/cold-cheek thing lasted until he got to work and everything!

"SHAKESPEARE?" ZACH asked politely.

Sean wore peasant garb today—drawstring pants, a doublet, the floppy hat and everything. He grinned.

"Romeo & Juliet, eighth grade. I get them for a week!"

"That sounds…." Zach couldn't do it. "Awful," he apologized. "But I'm glad *someone* enjoys eighth grade."

"Well, it's a lot easier when you practice," Sean said with a wink. "Besides—I've got all this theatre stuff, and I'm teaching them English/History—I mean, it feels like the whole reason I hauled this stuff around with me, you know?"

Zach didn't know—he'd been on the debate team. But he nodded anyway. "The teaching thing—you really like?"

Sean nodded and Zach was treated to *that* smile—all teeth and dimples and a ducked head that sort of asked forgiveness for that much joy. "It's like being the most popular kid in the class. Eighth graders never had it so good!"

Zach hadn't been particularly popular. He'd kept his head down and his grades good, and had ignored the girls who thought the valedictorian was some sort of trophy.

"I wouldn't know," he said quietly, and Sean's long, mobile face suddenly assumed a look of compassion that Zach was entirely uncomfortable with.

Ding!

Saved by the bell!

"VAUDEVILLE?" BECAUSE really, he couldn't believe even a public school would let a guy teach in drag.

Sean didn't smile back. The fulminating look he sent Zach *should* have shut Zach up for life, but.... *God,* he was so cute. Even in heavy bordello make-up and a saloon-girl-style purple velvet dress. "Singing telegrams," he replied sourly. "They were hiring."

Zack held in the smile, because he could tell Sean was *not* in the mood. "And, uhm, you had Mae West in your costume trunk."

Sean flashed a reluctant dimple. "No—this is Katie's. She's in theater too."

"So, the, uhm, ankle boots?" They were leather, with a slight heel, and Zach really couldn't tell if they were feminine or masculine and he was rewarded by a full-out Sean smile—the kind that he'd started to treasure.

"No, those are mine. I wear them clubbing—you like?"

"Yeah," Zach said gravely. He inclined his head. "They're very unisex."

Sean rolled his eyes. "They're gayer than gay—but it was a nice try."

Ding!

"After you," Zach said, bowing slightly and gesturing for the "lady" to precede him.

Sean wrinkled his nose and shook his head—and smiled. "Thank you, kind sir," he said, his voice as dry as I-5 in the summer.

Zach had to admit, as he watched Sean struggle into his peacoat and wrap a scarf around his neck before he hit the glass door out of the lobby—the dress sure did nice things for his behind.

Ground Floor

"Who is she?" Leah asked tartly, getting her now customary coffee. This time, Zach had brought six scones, and told her to share the goods with the other office assistants in the firm.

"I'm sorry?"

"It's *someone.* You've been actually—that thing on your face, the one that still shows through your five-o-clock shadow. I've been seeing it a lot in the morning. Who is she?"

"There is no she," he said quietly, and he kept his voice uninflected. "Actually, that *does* remind me. Remember the Christmas party?"

"Where I got to be your plus one and drink champagne and eat foie gras? Yeah—why? Your dad having another fundraiser?"

Zach nodded. "Do you have a favorite department store?"

Leah's smile was blissful. "Oh yay! Shopping on the firm's expense account—I *love* this job!"

Leah's Christmas dress really had been worth buying—he wanted to see her happy.

"Well good," he said soberly. "We want to keep you here."

Suddenly her eyes narrowed. "No, seriously, why aren't you taking *her* to this thing?"

Zach's face heated. "Honestly, Leah, the only person I see in the mornings is a male substitute teacher who likes to play dress up. My father would not approve."

"Wait a minute…."

Zach increased his pace to his office, the better to throw himself in and slam the door, but he heard Leah's feet clacking behind him with absolutely no dignity at all in her platform spikes, and she was in the doorway to his office as he turned around to shut the door.

"I've been asking the wrong question!" she burst out as soon as the door closed. "I should have been asking who is *he!*"

Zach swallowed. "My father would not approve," he said again, his throat dry.

"You mean your running-for-a-Republican-office father who doesn't approve of you being a union lawyer!"

"He approves of the second word," Zach said, and Leah rolled her eyes.

"Look, Mr. Driscoll—"

"You know, you can call me Zach," he said. He didn't have any real friends. He had coworkers and cocktail-party friends and his father's political friends—but not one person in his entire life had ever actually asked him who he'd want to *really* take to a party.

Leah looked surprised—and justifiably so. She'd been working there for three years. She'd called him "Mr. Driscoll" when they'd walked arm in arm to his father's fundraiser.

But then, sexual harassment had never been further off the table before.

"Okay," she said simply. "Zach. You don't even know? What's the worst your father could do?"

Zach swallowed. He didn't know. "I had this train set when I was a kid," he said, thinking. "It was great. One of those wooden ones—I must have gotten a new train and new tracks for every birthday and every Christmas for like, five years. And then, I turned... I don't know. Ten? And I woke up Christmas morning and I thought I was going to get another train—there'd been an engine I wanted and me and the nanny had rewired the train for it, and—anyway, I woke up and ran to the nursery where the Christmas tree was, with the train around the bottom, right?"

It was the longest, most personal thing he'd ever said to anyone, and he was talking to his secretary. She nodded, barely, because her mouth was open and she probably couldn't say anything until she thought to close it.

"And the train was gone. Dad decided I was too old for it, so the train was gone, and I had a laptop with learning software under the tree."

Leah closed her mouth with a snap. "That's the saddest fucking thing I've ever heard in my life," she said, appalled.

Zach shrugged. "I've heard sadder," he said frankly, thinking of the nurse who'd gotten fired because she'd gained weight. "The point isn't the sad."

"Oh the hell it *isn't*—"

"The point is that I don't know what he'll do," Zach said evenly, because that *was* the point. "He has an idea of what the world should be like, and I don't know what he'll do to make that work."

Leah swallowed. "What *can* he do?" she asked, narrowing her eyes.

Zach shrugged. "You, uhm, ever wonder why we get a nice office building doing union law when the rest of the building is all corporate law and high-priced media attorneys?"

"Oh."

"And, you know, my *own* apartment is sort of awesome."

"And all your employees get discounts," she said numbly, and Zach nodded, thinking about six people in an apartment, struggling with rent.

"Yes, yes you do."

"Oh," she said again.

"Oh," he repeated quietly. "So, uhm, enjoy your shopping trip. The party is in three weeks."

Leah took two steps toward the door, and then turned around. "You, uhm, well, maybe not a month ago, but now, you know I'd move, right? To see you smile every morning like you have been."

Zach shrugged, and managed a small smile from that reserve of all those moments in the elevator. "I promise, I won't stop bringing coffee."

She sighed and left, and he got to his day's business.

HE TOLD himself that he'd have to be content with visions of Sean in the mornings. From floor fourteen to floor one, he had a relationship with someone funny, quirky, kind, smart, and surprising.

It was almost a perfect relationship, really. Except that the more times Sean came galloping down the hall begging Zach or someone else to hold the elevator, the more Zach felt like he was missing something in the greeting. A simple kiss, a peck on the cheek, a pat on the arm or the shoulder—shouldn't he be getting in on some of that?

He had to keep reminding himself that the relationship didn't really exist.

IT WAS hard. Two weeks after the Mae West dress the entire world was strewn with red paper hearts and doilies, and Sean blew his mind.

"Oh my God." Zach's eyes were so big he could feel them drying out.

"Don't say it," Sean warned him, but his eyes were twinkling under the big blonde bouffant wig he was wearing.

"I *know* you're not teaching today," Zach said, seriously, and Sean's mock seriousness started to dissolve under blush-highlighted dimples.

"Don't say it," he warned, the giggles threatening as Zach took in the entire ensemble. Flesh-colored leotard and tights, giant white diaper, golden halo, little wings, and a quiver full of valentines.

"Cupid!" Zach burst out before clapping his hand over his mouth.

Sean nodded, smiling so wide his makeup flaked and crinkled around his eyes. "I'm…." Sean nodded some more and Zach blurted out, "Fucking *adorable*!" at the same time Sean said, "Cuter than hell!" They were both still laughing when the doors opened.

Ding!

"So," LEAH said when Zach brought her coffee and pink-iced lemon cake slices. "What was he wearing today?"

Zach closed his eyes and his face split into a grin. "He was *Cupid*!"

"Oh my God!"

The entire rest of the day was sort of tinted pink.

ZACH WAS late home that night per usual, but as the elevator doors were closing he heard a familiar voice.

"Hold the elevator! Oh, hi!"

Zach smiled at Sean, relieved that he was back in his street clothes. It was cold outside, and while cute, the whole Cupid thing had to have gotten old after a bit.

"Hi," he said quietly. "No date tonight?"

"Party at my apartment!" Sean said, holding up a case of cheap beer. "And a date *there*."

Zach's heart crumbled quietly into his ribcage. "Really? You have a date?"

Sean rolled his eyes in embarrassment. "Well, it was actually a customer. I delivered an apology telegram, and he tore it up. And then asked me what *I* was doing. I figured why not—if we don't work out, *someone* at the party is going to make his day better, right?"

Little fragments of heart began to reassemble themselves in Zach's chest. "That's sweet."

Shrug. "Well, it's a stupid day. I mean, I'm almost glad I didn't sub today. The kids—like in middle school—maybe 15 percent of them have a good day. The rest of them are just on the shitty side of the popularity scale, you know? As adults, I think it's better to go out and get plastered than to try to find the perfect lay."

Zach had to laugh. "I think that's a good policy," he said, pursing his mouth and trying to look sage. "Have a nice evening."

The door opened for Sean's floor, and Sean took a step out of the elevator. The doors started to close and he held out a hand and turned around.

"You, uhm, you wouldn't want to come to the party too, would you?"

Zach swallowed. "That's really nice of you to ask," he said sincerely. "I have work to do at home though."

Sean shrugged, and Zach had to tell himself that the gesture wasn't wistful. "Next time?" He actually sounded hopeful, and Zach found himself promising something he shouldn't have, even though he really wanted to promise it anyway.

"Absolutely," he said, nodding. "I'd love to come next time."

After all, what were the odds he'd actually meet Sean at the elevator at night again, right?

SEAN STOOD in the lobby when Zach arrived three nights of the next week. For a brief, wild moment, Zach entertained the idea that Sean was actually *waiting* for him, but that couldn't be right, could it?

"Your, uh, friend didn't work out?" Zach asked tentatively, the first night he found Sean in the lobby waiting for the car.

"Not for me!" Sean said brightly as the elevator arrived. "But someone else at the party got lucky, so it's all good. I told you— Valentine's Day hook-ups never work. No skin off my nose."

Zach noticed that Sean's nose was a little freckled and a little pink every day. "Good," he said. "Because you don't have a lot to spare."

"Ouch!" Sean hammed, clutching his chest as they got in the car.

Zach chuckled, because he was clearly not all that put out.

"What about you?" Sean asked. "Get all your work done?"

Zach thought about the files he had in his briefcase and shook his head. "No. Never. My work is *always* waiting for me to finish it."

Sean grimaced. "Wow—is that the pain that comes with the suit?"

Shrug. "That's what comes from being the boss."

Ding!

Sean turned and waved on his way out.

THE NIGHT after that, they shared the cab with five other people, smashed against the mirrored back, close enough for Zach to smell his body wash again. It had changed—now it smelled like oak. Zach sort of preferred the last one, but really? The skin beneath the soap was all he cared about.

At the "ding" for Sean's floor, Zach waved his briefcase like a weapon and said, "Out of his way, folks, he's got to get out!" As the doors closed on him, Zach could swear Sean was executing a little bow.

THE NIGHT of the benefit, Zach actually met him on the way out of the lobby, as Sean was walking in.

"Oh my God!"

Zach stopped in the middle of the doors and looked at him, startled. "What? Do I have a stain? A hole? A wrinkle?"

"That's a *tux*! That's an Armani tux! Where the hell are you going?"

Zach grimaced. "A benefit for my father," he said. "My secretary is my plus one." He wasn't sure why he added that. Maybe he didn't want Sean to think he was going on a date, which was stupid, because he'd already consigned the man to his own love life, right?

"Wait," Sean said blankly. "A benefit? For your father?"

Oh. Oh hell. "Yeah. Uhm, Gordon Driscoll." He smiled greenly, and watched as Sean's mouth dropped open. A gaggle of people approached: a woman with a poodle, and the two stockbrokers who shared the top floor with Zach.

Zach stepped out of the elevator and let them step on, and Sean just stood there as the elevator doors closed, looking at him like he'd kicked his dog.

"You're Gordon Driscoll's son?" Sean said, sounding hurt.

"Zach." Zach extended a hopeful hand. "Uhm, pleased to meet you."

Sean's hand was clammy in his, and Zach's heart once again crumbled into powder. He wondered how many times it was going to do that before it just blew away like dust.

"I, uhm, promise, I'd never tell my dad how many people live in your apartment," Zach said for the sake of saying something. "He charges too much anyway."

"Gordon Driscoll, the Republican candidate for state assembly." Sean was still making sure Zach was related to a douchebag, apparently, and Zach sighed.

"I never vote for him, if that helps."

Sean let go of his hand abruptly. "Wait—what do you do for a living? You said you were the boss?"

"Union lawyer," Zach told him. Sean's hurt was starting to penetrate his chest. Maybe this would help, right? He was a good guy, right? "If, uhm, you know, anyone ever gives you crap about being a gay teacher, you, uhm, well, know where to find me."

Sean didn't respond. His blue eyes were still huge and Zach was seized by the sudden urge to kiss him, right there, and say, "I'm just as human as you are!" but that would be silly, right? What purpose would it serve?

He saw his town car pull up to the front of the building and sighed when his driver got out and started walking toward the lobby.

"I'm sorry I disappointed you," he said at last, and then turned toward the driver. He wanted to turn and look back to see if Sean had snapped out of it, if he'd smiled yet or recovered his humor, or remembered that they'd laughed together several times in the past two months, but he couldn't.

God. It was hard enough already.

THE BENEFIT was held in a library galleria, with an indoor fountain and great windows looking out onto the San Francisco night. It was a glorious venue, something that needed a costume and quiet humor to appreciate.

Which made him think of Sean the minute he walked into the reception with Leah on his arm.

He proceeded to get quietly, devastatingly drunk. Leah honed in on his mood, and instead of getting charmingly tipsy, she made sure his glass was always filled with top shelf vodka and cranberry juice, and that he never had to talk to someone alone.

At the end of the benefit, his father walked up to him, looking hale and distinguished. His hair was silver instead of sable, but his eyes were still the warm brown Zach's were, and his handshake was hearty.

"Good to see you here, Zach," he said genially, but Zach wasn't feeling genial.

"Did I have a choice?" he asked bleakly, and Gordon blinked.

"Well, this is what you do for family, isn't it?" Gordon's aide came up to his elbow and murmured something in his ear, and Zach raised ironic eyebrows.

"Yeah, Dad—every family meets four times a year at political fundraisers. It's in all the sitcoms."

Leah tugged on his sleeve. "Uhm, Zach? I don't think this is a good night for this."

"Well," Gordon said, annoyance lacing his voice, "if you'd like to visit more often, your mother would be happy to see you. Have Leah make an appointment with her secretary, but I think we're usually available for Sunday brunch."

"Yeah but that's when all good boys sleep in with their b—" Zach had his mouth open to say it. He was going to by God finish that sentence and say Sunday brunch was when good boys slept in with their boyfriends, even though he didn't have one—but Leah grabbed his sleeve in earnest this time and he managed to turn his bleary attention toward her.

"Not tonight," she said quietly. "I don't know what got into you, but this is not the mood you need to go about this, okay?"

"If you'll excuse me," Gordon said smoothly, and he shook his son's hand again and left without looking back.

The arrow of memory suddenly pierced his alcohol haze, and he was abruptly miserable.

"He found out who I am," Zach mumbled, wanting to cry. Did he know Leah well enough to cry on her? She was wearing a new black dress with rhinestones up the sides, and one sturdy brown shoulder exposed. She'd obviously come prepared to have a good time on the company dime, and he'd just gotten drunk for the first time since his freshman year in college.

"Elevator boy?" she asked, but Zach couldn't talk about it anymore.

"I didn't tell you that your dress is fabulous," he said with dignity. "And I think I need to go."

"I'll take you home," she said, and her wide face was suddenly so kind he thought he really *would* cry. She patted his cheek and smiled, and none of her usual sarcasm was in the gesture or in her sweet brown eyes. God, he owed this woman a raise.

WHEN HE woke up the next morning to find her on his couch, wearing his sweats, he thought that maybe a raise wouldn't be good enough.

"Fuuuuck!" he groaned, stumbling into the living room in his boxer shorts. She stretched and yawned and looked out his bay window onto the city below.

"Damn, this is some view," she muttered. "If I woke up to this every morning, I'd be singing like a fucking bird!"

"No singing!" he pleaded. He kept the painkillers by the coffee, and right now he needed both.

"Water first," Leah directed, scrambling out of the blankets on the couch and rushing into his kitchen to take over and boss him around. "My God. Have you never been drunk before?"

"Why are you still singing?" he groaned, resting his head on the counter and wrapping his arms around it. "Why are you singing and why is the sun stabbing my brain and why do I feel like shoe gum?"

"Because you drank enough vodka to fund an entire Russian coup," she muttered. "Jesus—you almost told your father you were gay, do you know that?"

"You're lying," he mumbled. "I don't even tell *myself* I'm gay."

"Well, you apparently do now, because I don't think I've seen a more serious broken heart in my entire life."

Oh God. Oh *God.* Zach felt actual tears starting. "He wouldn't even look at me," he mumbled. "Just for who I am."

"Well, it probably took him by surprise," Leah said kindly. She poked at him until he took his arms from around his head and stood up. "Here. Motrin and water. You'll feel better. Or you'll throw up. Either way you'll feel better."

He took the Motrin and drank the entire glass of ice water.

And then he threw up.

And then Leah made him take more Motrin with more ice water. And added soda crackers with it.

That he kept down.

And *then* he felt better.

And then?

Well, he took a shower, brushed his teeth and dressed, but Leah insisted that he only dress in sweats. "You have an *amazing* entertainment center," she said thoughtfully when he emerged from his room with wet, uncombed hair and in his old college sweatshirt. "Come, sit next to me and let us explore."

He felt a reluctant smile on his face. "What are we exploring?"

"Bruckheimer movies," she said with decision. "We can see Alcatraz from here—I think we need to watch *The Rock.*" Sure enough, it was on Netflix, and she made him watch the whole thing. She fixed him instant oatmeal, because it was the only thing he had in the cupboards and then ordered take-out delivered for lunch. And besides that all she did was sit on his couch, lean on his arm, and talk about how Nicholas Cage had made a mockery of his career. They watched *Con Air* and *Ghost Rider* to prove it.

Sometime between *The Rock* and *Con Air,* he actually started talking. And then he started listening.

He found out that Leah Chambers was from Hawaii, and that he couldn't really pronounce her real name. He found out that she roomed with another girl who was a librarian, and that they both mourned their love lives but really didn't want anything to change about them right now. He learned that she had six nieces and two nephews and that she sent them gifts *every* month, and that during her vacation over Christmas she went back to Hawaii, and had *every* year since he hired her.

And he told her about Sean.

He told her about the freckles and the blond curls and the funny costumes and the umpteen roommates. He told her about the ankle boots and the way he'd brought a stranger into his Valentine's Day party in the hopes that *someone* would have a happy evening.

"Why didn't you go?" she asked. "When he asked you, why didn't you go?"

He sighed and leaned against the arm of the couch, and to his surprise she leaned on him. "Are we snuggling yet?" he asked fuzzily. "Isn't there some sort of rule about when two people can snuggle?"

"Yes. We've known each other for three years. We've met the requirements." She poked him in the ribs with fingernails that had recently undergone a bright-red manicure. "Answer the question."

"Because I don't do anything," he said after a moment. "I work and I come home. And when I get lonely I pay for sex."

"Ew," she said, wrinkling her nose.

"And you're the only person alive who knows that," he told her grumpily. "So if that gets around the office—"

"I'll hire the assassin myself."

He didn't believe she'd do that, but he was, at this moment, too hungover and too heartbroken to care. "Anyway, I don't do anything. I wouldn't be a lot of fun at a party, because all I've got is work, and a lot of that is confidential."

She dug her flat little chin into his bicep until he looked at her.

"What?"

"Well, for starters, you do a good impression of big, bad boss—I never knew you were an overgrown eighth grader. I'm proud of you for that, by the way, because it's a lot more likable than big, bad boss. And for finishers, Jenn and I are going to Golden Gate Park next weekend to play Frisbee and visit the Exploratorium. Do you want to come with us?"

He was planning to say no. It was absolutely on the tip of his tongue. And then he thought about that look on Sean's face, the utter disappointment in the person he'd thought he'd been talking to.

Maybe Zach could be a better person.

"Yeah, okay," he mumbled.

Leah took pity on him then and pressed play on the remote. He fell asleep in the middle of *Con Air* and didn't wake up until *Ghost Rider,* and after that Leah bid him a reluctant good-bye.

Yeah, he could have given her a raise, but it wouldn't have been enough. Frisbee in Golden Gate Park was a much better payback for a day spent teaching him how to nurse a broken heart.

Two Elevators,
Passing in the Night

ZACH MADE a concentrated effort to leave early after that, and to take the express elevator all the way down. He had to leave early to get his secretary and one friend her coffee in the morning and still get to work on time. It was the only way. It was a conscious decision, made fully aware of the consequences, but still, that didn't stop him from flinching every time the car passed the fourteenth floor.

One of the plusses of leaving early was that he found himself in the elevator with Jace and Quent a lot. He hadn't known their names until then, but they were the day-traders who shared the penthouse floor with him. Jace was the obsessive one who left early and apparently made them power walk through the San Francisco streets, and Quent, his goateed partner with the warm brown eyes, was the talker. Apparently, poker was their religion, and after they'd met for nearly three weeks, Zach was even invited to worship.

"Seriously, Jace—we could always use another man!" Quent said as the elevator began its descent.

Jace flicked steel-blue eyes over Zach's face and dismissed the idea. "He'll get eaten alive. He's got a worse poker face than you. *Look* at those eyes."

Quent shrugged apologetically, but Zach didn't mind if his partner was an ass. They were better company than no one on the long trip down, and they were so obviously in love with each other he didn't have to worry about stupid, heartbreaking attachments finding purchase in thin air.

Frisbee in Golden Gate Park turned out to be wonderful. Jenn was a chubby girl with waist-length blonde hair and an absolutely filthy mouth. Zach wasn't sure what to do with her at first—he hadn't even told dirty jokes in the eighth grade, but he liked watching Leah laugh, so eventually he stopped clenching every time she said something like "that old fucktard can go eat a bag of dicks!"

About three weeks after the benefit, right when he was getting used to living without hope or color, he got home one Friday evening and was getting on the elevator just when Sean was getting out.

Sean was dressed nicely—slacks and a sweater, with the familiar peacoat and bright-red scarf over his arm, and there was a stocky, powerfully built man in a suit standing behind him with a hand in the small of his back.

Sean and Zach stared at each other for a minute, and Zach figured this was it. The moment his heart really did blow away, and he didn't have to worry about it anymore. Except that couldn't be right because it was thundering in his ears.

"Hi," he said, feeling lame.

"Hi," Sean said, his sand-colored brows puckering in the middle. "I haven't seen you in a while."

"Luck of the elevator," Zach lied, and Sean nodded like that had to be the case and Zach couldn't have possibly been avoiding him. That was enough for Zach—this sucked; this hurt horribly. This right here was the reason a flirtation on an elevator was the closest he'd come to a real relationship since he'd gone down on his roommate in college.

"Well, you know, maybe the elevator can stop avoiding me," Sean said, and he was the one who sounded put out.

"Well, maybe it could stop pretending I have the plague," Zach said sharply.

"Well *maybe*—" and Sean's mouth was quirking up, like he knew this was a silly conversation to be having right now, and Zach was *dying* for his response, when the man behind him spoke up.

"Sean, we're going to be late. These tickets were expensive!"

Sean grimaced at Zach and then turned toward his date. "Yeah, sorry." The elevator was still standing there, open, and Zach moved toward it automatically. He turned around at the last minute, before the doors started to close, and saw that Sean had turned around too.

"So, see you around?" Sean said hopefully, and Zach smiled.

"Yeah. Yeah. See you around."

HE DIDN'T want to completely ditch Quent and Jace—he'd started to feel like they might be friends too, like Leah and Jenn, and seriously, how had he lived for thirty-three years without friends? So he compromised.

He left early two days a week and took the express all the way down, and then left a little late three days a week and switched elevators at the nineteenth floor. He managed to catch his friends on the two days (because apparently Jace was made out of clockwork parts and would never be late, rushed, or anything but perfectly attired) and maybe, once or twice a week, Sean managed to make it into the elevator on time.

It was just enough to feed Zach's quiet obsession with him.

He saw Sean dressed in his Renaissance gear three times—apparently *Romeo and Juliet* was big in middle schools in the spring. He saw him dressed as a 1950s biker once—S.E. Hinton was also big in middle schools—with his blond hair slicked back and only a highly lacquered cluster of curls allowed to escape out the front. Zach also saw him dressed as a WWI soldier, because some sadist made eighth graders read *All's Quiet on the Western Front,* and *Jesus,* didn't those kids deserve a good laugh after that!

And Zach saw him on the last day of school, ebullient because the teacher who had been gone for the second half of the semester and given him access to the job had filed for a two-year leave of absence, and Sean could count on being able to pay his bills.

"So, what are you going to do for the summer?" Zach asked. He racked his brains, wondering if they had an internship or a gopher position or if they had the budget for a guy to go get coffee or—

"Theater tech!" Sean said gleefully. "I don't get to dress up, but Katie has me signed up for three shows—the money's not great, but it'll keep me in Top Ramen until August!"

"School starts in August?" Appalling. Absolutely appalling—at least private schools waited until after Labor Day!

"Yup. Two months of theater, and suddenly I'll be a real boy!"

"You're the most real thing in my life," Zach blurted, and the sudden silence was worse than hot coals and pincers. They weren't even alone in the elevator. This was supposed to be a Jace and Quent day—and the little old lady with the poodle was there too. But the elevator had died at the nineteenth floor, and they'd all hopped into the next car, and suddenly, hey, Jace and Quent and old-lady-with-dog, meet Sean. The only one who cared, actually, was Zach. The rest of them had listened to Sean and Zach's banter with half an ear, probably submerged in the white noise of their own thoughts.

"Oh," Sean said, like the entire world made sense to him right then.

Ding!

The doors opened and the little old lady with the poodle got out, and Jace and Quent went after her. Quent turned an anxious glance behind him and Jace grabbed his arm, hissing, "Leave him alone!" before dragging his boyfriend into the San Francisco morning.

"I, uhm…." Zach stopped the door from closing and gestured for Sean to precede him. He followed him out of the elevator and prayed, just prayed that he would keep walking through the glass doors and into the city. Zach realized he didn't even know which direction Sean usually turned. He always slowed his steps just enough to make sure their time in the elevator was their only time.

Sean didn't do that this time. He waited for Zach to come out and walked shoulder to shoulder with him.

"You were early today," Zach said into the silence.

"Yeah."

"I usually come down with Jace and Quent, or I come down with you."

"So you choose?" They were at the glass doors now, and Zach, again, gestured him to go first.

"I have to hop at the nineteenth floor to see you. And I made friends," Zach said with dignity. Then, because it was honest. "But, I, uhm, I still like it when I see you in the morning."

They got outside and Sean angled his shoulders left, toward the Muni stop probably, while Zach's office building was right. They paused, awkwardly, and foot-traffic swirled around them on the crowded sidewalk.

"I'll, uhm, see you in August," Zach said, trying not to sound wistful.

Sean turned toward him fully, lifted himself up and kissed his cheek.

Time stopped. The *world* stopped. There was only Sean's rain forest smell, his warmth, the freckles across his nose, and the feel of his soft lips on the arch of Zach's cheekbone.

"We're having a party tonight," Sean said. "Apartment 1409. Beer is always appreciated."

Then he turned and time zoomed him away to be lost in the crowd, and, *dammit,* Zach didn't even have a chance to tell him that he had an event that night to attend for his family, and that he couldn't get out of it.

He made a stop on his way home anyway, and on his way down, while dressed in his tux and everything, he stopped at the fourteenth floor.

He hesitated before knocking on the door, but while he was standing there a couple came up behind him.

They were young—Sean's age—and dressed casually. The young man had nice jeans and a dress-up shirt, and the young woman wore a pretty summer dress in lime and turquoise. Her hair was platinum blonde, and if she hadn't been wearing bright-green contacts, he never would have recognized her as Sean's roommate.

"Uhm, Wendy?" he said hesitantly, and her eyes widened in recognition.

"Yeah, uhm…. Yeah. You're the guy—the one from the elevator Sean's obsessed with. What can I do for you?"

Zach fought off the urge to dance—obsessed with? Really? Because Zach planned his entire *day* around thirty seconds in the elevator. "Here—uhm, Sean invited me, but I didn't have a chance to tell him I couldn't make it." He thrust the two six-packs of expensive microbrew beer at Wendy and her date, and gave a nervous little head bob. "Tell him it sounds like fun though!"

And with that he turned and fled for the elevator.

He'd just gotten in and the doors were starting to close when he heard his name. Sean was running for the elevator full tilt, and Zach put his arm against the doors and let him in.

They closed behind Sean who laughed slightly and moved to the back of the elevator to lean against the mirror with Zach. He was wearing jeans and a dress shirt in black and red. It looked *horrible* with his complexion, and Zach thought that Sean should get his friend Wendy to help him with his clothes.

"You couldn't make it," Sean said, sounding breathless and disappointed.

"I'm overdressed anyway," Zach pointed out.

"It was such a good gesture." Sean pouted. "You couldn't blow off one fundraiser?"

"Not this one," Zach said, turning his head sideways and smiling at Sean from under his lashes. "It's the one that might get me evicted."

"I'd hate for you to get evicted," Sean said, but he was looking at Zach, his blue eyes wide and hopeful, and his voice lacked conviction. "I'd never see you again."

"You know, there's these things called cell—"

Ding!

Neither of them moved.

"You keep wearing tuxedos and going places without me," Sean complained, and now he sounded breathless for a whole other reason.

"I hate tuxedos." They were standing so close. Sean must have downed a beer or two, but his breath wasn't unpleasant—just hoppy. He smelled a little sweaty so he'd probably been dancing—Zach would bet Sean was an atrocious dancer, because he moved like he was made of elbows, but Zach still wanted to see it happen.

"Then change into jeans and come to my party," Sean begged plaintively.

This time Zach leaned into the kiss, and their lips met softly for a minute. He pulled away. "Someday," he said softly, "I'm going to take you to one of these. I'll buy you a tuxedo, and pick out your tie. I'll escort you in and we can dance."

Sean's laugh was almost more sober than Zach's dreamy voice. "I'd settle for having you come to my flat for a beer."

"That too."

"Are you guys getting out?"

Zach pulled himself back to the present and sighed. "I will see you around," he said softly, and Sean shook his head.

"God, I hope so."

He walked out and the irritated father, bemused mother, and baby in a stroller all crowded in.

The door closed behind him.

Ding!

GOLDEN GATE Park at night, even in the summer, was cold. He'd forgotten his scarf in his tizzy about the beer, and the breeze blowing through the amphitheater could have frozen the nads off an ice wizard. After the cellist performed (and Zach hoped they found a way to heat her and to keep her instrument from reacting to the salt air, because *dayum*, whose idea was this?) Zach found one of the gas-powered heat lamps. He huddled under it, wished heartily for Leah's tipsy company, nursed his gratis mug of coffee (in a new insulated mug with his father's face on it, no less!) and waited for the obligatory fly-by.

It took a half-an-hour for his parents to work their way around the reception and get to him. He almost hated it worse when his mother was there—her smile seemed genuine, but he was never really sure with her.

"Zach, darling—why didn't you sit with us?" she asked, taking his hands in hers and going in to kiss his cheek. Her dress was a sort of sequined taffeta, and it whispered loudly when she leaned. She turned at the last moment so that the flash of the camera could blind them both and Zach turned back to her and tried to make his five minutes count.

"Because I got here late," he said truthfully. Only by a few moments, really, but he hadn't wanted to put his parents out. "I had to talk to a friend before I left. You've been unavailable for brunch."

"I'm sorry, darling," his mother said, moueing sweetly for the camera. "The last few months have been a whirlwind—it looks like your father actually has a shot this time!"

"Which is why I wanted to talk to you," Zach said, and suddenly his father wanted in the conversation.

"Why—are you finally interested in helping with the campaign?" He shook his son's hand and smiled as the camera went off. It was like they didn't even have to think about it—every reaction went with a pose. Well, let's see what pose they chose for this.

"No, actually. I, uhm, I wanted to talk to you about something personal, but you never got back to me, so I thought I'd warn you in case it hit the news, which it might do since you didn't want to talk to me personally."

Uh-oh. That got his parents' attention. "Mr. Crosby, could you leave us a moment?"

Gordon Driscoll dismissed his aide, and the man—short, balding, fortyish and invisible—ushered the photographer away as he went.

"What have you done?" his mother asked, her matronly smile all but gone.

"Nothing. But I'd really like to go out on a date, and given that I'm gay, and with you two, it's actually a meet-the-press moment."

There was a sudden moment of shock, and Zach hopped up and down on his toes. Suddenly he wished he'd brought Leah, because she would have been *so* proud of that.

"You're not gay," his father told him dismissively.

"Yes, yes I am."

"But you date women!" his mother protested.

"Name one!"

They both stopped, mouths slightly open, eyes wide.

"But—but your father's campaign…." his mother sputtered. "How could you do this to him!"

"I can't wait for your campaign to clear so I can get laid!" Zach snapped, and he was loud enough for most of the beautiful people in the expensive clothes to turn around to see what the fuss was about.

"What do you want from us?" his father asked coldly. "You come here, in a public venue and—"

Okay. Well, at least Zach knew what to expect. "All I want to know," he said, interrupting, "is if I need to move either my residence or my business. And I need to know if my employees lose their discount if they rent from one of your properties. *They* need to know, as soon as possible, so there's that too. Have your lawyers contact me. But tell them to watch their language, because if you try to make this about the gay, I'll fight and I'll fight ugly."

And with that he bowed slightly and turned around and walked away.

"YOU DID *what*?"

He grimaced at Leah, and scrubbed his face with his hands. Leah was scanning the papers that had just been delivered complete with vellum envelope and gold seal, and he knew what they said, because the lawyers had called him on a Sunday and told him what they said. While his father *couldn't* evict him or change his rent or even refuse to renew his lease for the apartment, the same did not go for the business address, and Zach was going to have to spend his next month frantically tracking down a new building that his firm could afford, and then moving four years of accrued stuff from one building to the other.

"I outed myself to my family?" Zach said, wrinkling his nose. "I'm sorry?"

Leah tapped a foot encased in a frighteningly bright-fuchsia-and-gold pump, and scraped her fingers through her lime-colored hair. "Wow. *Wow.* I mean, I thought you were kidding. I mean—I mean, you go to those benefits, and everyone's so pretty, and there's champagne in a fucking fountain—I had no idea!"

Zach shrugged, telling himself it didn't hurt. It couldn't hurt. Why would it hurt? If he had to be penciled into his parents' schedule to out himself, odds were good they weren't close.

"Well, you know. I guess the train really was a fair assessment of them," he said, and tried not to let his voice shake. "But, I'm sorry it had to be *here*. Here is all of you guys. At least if it was just me, I could find my own damned apartment." His apartment really was huge, he thought dismally. He could use a smaller apartment.

"Why don't you move?" Leah asked, and Zach gave her a weak smile, unsupported by his heart.

"I like the view."

She sighed and moved close enough to pat his cheek. "Well, good. Because I think you just went to a whole lot of time and expense to make that view your personal property, baby. And Jenn's gonna be pissed, because she was enjoying the hell out of Frisbee too."

Zach's smile grew sounder, even if it was still crooked. "You know," he said meditatively, "I haven't been to Monterey since I was a kid. Before dad started running for office, we had a cottage off of Pebble Beach. I really loved it there. Maybe, we get this done, you, me, Jenn, we drive down to Monterey and spend a weekend. Watch whales, play on the beach—just, you know."

"Get out of the city and go somewhere fun?" Leah said, and because they were in his office—his nice, big, important looking office with the dark-paneled wood and the cream-colored carpeting—she could give him a brief peck on the cheek. He was getting used to that from her. He was getting used to having friends. He was even getting used to the idea that Sean might want to see him sometime out of the elevator.

"Yeah," he said with dignity. "Go be somewhere outside the box."

"Good," she said. "I think you've been in that box for way too long."

He wasn't sure how he would have made it through the next two months without her.

The first month sucked hard enough—he had to find the new space, make a bid, secure the loan, all while servicing his clients, whom he absolutely *couldn't* let down. How could he look at the teacher with four kids who'd had her schedule completely rearranged when she was on pregnancy leave and tell her that she wasn't important enough to fight for? How about the gay teacher who'd been let go midsemester because a student had walked in on him during his prep period while he was talking on the phone to his husband about who was going to pick the dog up from the veterinarian, and who suddenly found himself charged with unprofessional conduct for exposing his personal life? What about the strict old battleax whose students had decided to sabotage her career by refusing to take her STAR tests, simply because she refused to be bought?

Zach had grown up with privilege, but he'd never had anyone to fight for him. Now, as he fought for his business in a way he didn't know he'd ever had the guts to, he realized how proud he was to fight for people who didn't get enough as it was.

And, in the middle of this, he had to tell his staff why they were moving.

Since more than one of his employees was not only from the LGBT community, but *actively* in the community, he was pretty sure nobody at the firm was going to shun the boss for being gay.

But explaining that Daddy was just that much of a douche bag was humiliating.

Oddly enough, Leah helped with that too—but probably not in any way she'd planned.

On the first day of unpaid overtime, when the whole office was in packing the least-necessary stuff and preparing to move it, he called them all in to explain why exactly they'd lost their lease on the pricey commercial building they occupied now, and why they were moving to something a lot less opulent—and for some of them, a lot farther away.

"I've heard the rumors," he said apologetically, because Leah had been the one to pass the rumors up to him. "You're worried about mismanagement; you're worried about missing funds. The truth is, we were in this building on the sufferance of my father—I'm Gordon Driscoll's kid, and he owns the building. I just came out to my parents—"

The smattering of applause surprised him, but he managed to bow through his blush anyway.

"—and their response was to revoke my business lease. Fortunately, the language around your discounts for those of you who are renting from a Driscoll property is not affected—believe me, that was the first thing I looked for, since I rent from him too." Polite laughter, and some exchanged glances of relief. "Anyway—I'm sorry my personal life—"

"What personal life?" Edward, the first lawyer he'd ever hired, said from the back. Edward was a nice guy, with long Midwestern features, dark hair, and blue eyes, who was also wild for his college professor boyfriend, and had a way of being kind when clients were more hysterical than helpful.

"Well, yeah, that was sort of the point," Zach said, and the laughter, again, was helpful. "Anyway—"

And that was when he saw the cash changing hands, most of it ending up with Leah.

"You had a pool on me?" he asked, amused. "You had inside information!"

Leah smirked. They were all in jeans today, but hers were lime green. Her T-shirt was fuchsia. "Yeah, but the pool started before you and me got tight. *And* I waited until you came out to the office yourself to collect, so karmically, I'm good." He grinned at her, loving all of her color and vibrancy. When he thought of his life earlier this year, it had been all charcoal gray, like his suits, but color and motion—that was attractive. It's why he loved... uhm....

"It's only karmically good if you get lunch today," he decided before he could finish that thought, and suddenly he really *was* everyone's favorite boss. Leah's included.

HE SAW Sean that night, for the first time in a month since the benefit at Golden Gate Park. God, had he really been that busy?

He must have been, getting up early, coming home at midnight, and now, here they were, on a Saturday night, both of them staggering in around eleven. Zach still had on the jeans and old college sweatshirt he'd worn while packing, his hair was mussed, and he was well aware the circles under his eyes were dark and deep. So *Zach* was still tired from being a workaholic, but he couldn't be sure where Sean had been.

"I worked a late show," Sean said, as they hit the lobby together. It was like he'd read Zach's mind. "What the hell happened to you?"

Zach smiled, almost giddy to see him after their last trip in the elevator. "Work," he said serenely. "I didn't get evicted, but my whole office had to move to... crap. I forget the address. It's down by Brannan somewhere. I'll remember when all our letterhead changes. Jesus. I need to get Leah right on that."

Leah would be happy to change their letterhead and stationery— he just needed to remember to ask. He smiled at Sean beatifically as he leaned against the back of the elevator, and he was so tired, his eyes drifted shut between the ground floor and....

Ding!

His eyes flew open. "We're here?" he whined, and knew it for a whine. "Fourteenth floor already? Damn. Damn. I haven't seen you in a *month.* I just wanted to…. God. I'm sorry. We can ride the elevator again later," he promised. "I swear. I'll be witty. I will. I'll make you want to talk to me. Just not today." Oh, hell. He'd been a *rock* over the last month. He'd been a *pillar* of grown-up fortitude and "we're fighting the good fight!" rhetoric, but, dammit, the whole time, when he'd been coming out to his parents, when he'd been dealing with the paperwork asking him to vacate—and the hurt that came from knowing his father's political career really *was* more important than his own son—he'd been promising himself, what?

"You were going to be my dessert," he said soberly.

Sean's eyes widened. His mouth quirked up a little too, and he shook his head while he guided Zach out of the main elevator and over to the express elevator. He hit the "door closed" button and positioned Zach a little more closely to him. "You are either really stoned, or you're dog tired. I'm going to vote on the second one, since I haven't seen you for a month."

"We had to move," Zach said, watching as the numbers on the readout went up, and Sean was still in the car with him. Wow. He'd had dreams about this. They'd been going up, up, up, and they would end up in bed, right?

But no. That's probably not what was going to happen. Not tonight. Tonight he smelled like sweat and he couldn't keep two thoughts in his silly little head.

"Move? Why?"

Sean looped his arm more tightly around Zach's shoulders, and it was warm and friendly and Zach leaned into it, not thinking about passion or kissing or anything but that he needed a warm and friendly arm.

"Because I came out to my father, and he can't evict me, or even raise the rent from *here,* but the office space—that contract was worded differently. *That* they could revoke. And they did. And now it's all about how to keep my employees employed and my clients from exploding and…. God. You smell good." He lowered his head and buried his nose into Sean's neck, and inhaled. Yup, he was back to the rainy body soap again.

"You should wear this kind always," he said into Sean's neck. "*Always.* I want to smell this on you forever."

Sean chuckled and it was such a warm sound, Zach wanted to just pull it over his head and around his toes and huddle in it.

There was a "ding," muffled by the heat of Sean's body and the hollow of his neck and Sean pulled on his shoulders.

"C'mon, big guy, let's go."

Zach allowed himself to be guided out of the elevator, and then he looked up and sort of leaned right to his door. He fumbled in his pocket for his key and when he pulled it out, Sean took it from him gently and opened his door.

Zach thought it would be over then, and he yearned rather wistfully for a kiss at the door, but Sean had other ideas. That warm arm wrapped around his shoulders again, and he was being guided through the darkened apartment.

"Holy Christ, would you look at that view!" Sean breathed, and Zach could only look at Sean's lean profile, with the bony jaw and the bobbing Adam's apple, and freckles you could almost see in the moonlight.

"'S awesome," he agreed soberly.

Sean turned toward him and rolled his eyes. "*You* are a crackup like this. I think getting you drunk would be like giving a cat catnip—we could laugh for hours."

"And then I'd go down on you and then I'd throw up!" Because Zach remembered that much from college.

Sean cackled. "Well, maybe not get you drunk if you're going to go down on me, 'kay?"

"I'm probably not good at blowjobs," Zach apologized. He felt like he owed full disclosure. "Not enough practice."

Sean steered him into the bedroom and shook his head in wonder. "Well that is a sin I'd like to correct—some other time."

"Of course. You have to get back in the elevator and go away. Always with you, it's the going away."

"Here, sit down on this pristinely made bed. God, it's a nice place, but everything's black and gray. Doesn't anybody live here?"

Zach felt the bed under his bottom, and then Sean knelt at his feet and unlaced his shoes. Zach ran his fingers through Sean's hair, because it was there, and this was his dream and it was something he wanted to do.

"No," Zach said softly as his tennis shoes were popped off. "Nobody lives here. Not even me. Whee!" Because there went his socks, and his feet felt *wonderful* free.

"Now stand up and we'll get your pants and sweatshirt," Sean mumbled, but something was wrong with his voice.

Zach did what he said, and allowed himself to be undressed down to his boxers and T-shirt like a child. "You sound sad. I don't like it when you're sad. I wanted to *make* a job for you, out of thin air. Did you know that?"

Sean pulled back the covers and nudged him into bed, pulling the black comforter up to his ears. "That's sweet, my prince in the tower, but real life doesn't work like that."

"Someday I'll figure out what that's like," Zach mumbled. Anything, he wanted to say *anything* to keep Sean there, one more minute, in his bedroom, talking in the dark.

"What what's like?" The bed sank next to him and Zach felt delicate fingers stroking through his hair.

"Real life."

"You're the one who relocated your entire office to come out of the closet. You tell me."

"Lonely," Zach mumbled, feeling tearful and a little broken.

"Sh...." He didn't imagine Sean's kiss on his forehead, did he? "You're exhausted, buddy. Time to sleep."

"But I'll wake up, and you'll be gone, like a dream."

There was a sigh, and some violent rustling next to him. "Scoot over."

Zach did, and Sean lay down on top of the comforter next to him, wearing his boxers and T-shirt. "I've got an early matinee," Sean said softly. His phone glowed softly as he set an alarm on it. "I've got to be up at seven."

Zach buried his nose in Sean's neck and murmured, "Thank you."

"You know, you *do* know where I live," Sean said softly.

"That's not how it works," Zach said, feeling loopy. "The prince in the tower needs rescuing. The peasant on the fourteenth floor has it all figured out on his own."

Soft laughter ruffled Zach's hair. "True. And, I gotta admit, the tower has a lot more privacy."

"Mmhm...."

Oh, the things Zach wanted to do with all the privacy....

And on that note he fell asleep.

HE WOKE up alone, but there was a piece of his old company letterhead next to his pillow, probably from a pad he kept in the kitchen.

See you in the elevator, sweet prince. When your life is settled, maybe I can visit your tower again.

Sean Mallory

He looked at the note and smiled.

Sean Mallory.

Very carefully, before he took a shower and brushed his teeth or anything, he folded that piece of paper up and put it in his wallet, behind his driver's license. Sean Mallory, Apartment 1409.

That right there was real.

IT TOOK another month before his life was settled again. Then, one morning, he stepped outside his door and watched Jace and Quent disappear into the elevator, and realized that, oh *hell* yes, it was mid-to-late August, school might have started, and he might actually see Sean today.

His heart pounded while he waited for the elevator to return, and when the door opened....

Sean stepped out and right into his arms.

"Ohmygod!"

And then he didn't have anything to say, because Sean's mouth was on his, and his lips were soft and his tongue was sweeping in and....

Sean pulled back and grinned. "You're a terrible kisser. I've waited for that for *months,* and that's all you've got for me?"

"Uhm... I'm surprised. How would you fix it? I'm surprised!"

Sean went to step back, but some weird constriction thing happened to Zach's arms, and he wasn't letting go. Sean's wicked expression, the kind with the arched eyebrows, sobered, became gentle, and he nuzzled Zach's cheek and this time, when he stepped back, Zach let him go.

"I'll give you kissing lessons later. Right now, we're both running late."

"So, lessons—that implies I'll get more kissing, right?"

"You are so *not* suave and sophisticated, you know that?"

"I'm aware. So, kissing?"

Sean laughed, grabbed his hand, and pushed the down button. "I've got an in-service today—let me not be the slacker who gets there last, okay?"

"So school hasn't started yet?"

"Monday—why?"

Zach shifted a little, uncomfortable about asking, but not wanting this moment to end. "See, my secretary Leah and her roommate Jenn— we were meeting for Frisbee on Saturdays, but I screwed that up with the whole 'hey, let's move the office in an insane amount of time!' and I offered to make it up by taking them to Monterey for two days, like, Friday through Sunday, and it wouldn't be a sex thing, seriously, it would be a date thing, not that I—" He stopped babbling and closed his eyes because he wasn't sure if that look in Sean's eyes was pity or fear, but he was pretty sure it was no.

Sean kissed him and pulled back, and he had to open his eyes to see whether that was no or not.

It was still no, but the genuine regret sort of helped.

"I'm never going to get everything done in time," Sean said, shrugging. "I mean, I know you don't teach, but, it's like, we get two paid days to do a week's worth for work, and I haven't taught this class from beginning and there's *so* much I need to—"

Ding!

Zach nodded, and gestured for him to leave first, but Sean didn't move.

"I love that you asked me," he said helplessly. "I just—"

"I get it," Zach said quietly. "I defend teachers all the time. Your hours are insane. I forgot, that's all." He glanced up, and people he didn't know and didn't recognize were waiting to get on the elevator. "C'mon. We can talk in the lobby."

They walked out of the elevator and stepped to the side.

"Our timing!" Sean muttered ruefully. "It... it sucks. It does. But I'm... I'm *dying* to give you kissing lessons, and...."

"And we've got to go."

Sean looked down for a moment, and Zach followed his gaze.

And squeezed their twined fingers, surprised, because clasping Sean's hand felt like the most natural thing in the world.

Sean pulled their hands up and kissed his knuckles. "I will see you next week," he said quietly. "Wait for me on the fourteenth floor, and we can go down together."

Zach grinned. "Yeah. It's dating by elevator!"

Sean's entire face went slack for a minute, and his eyes went heavy-lidded, and his hand shook in Zach's. "That... that is my smile," he said breathlessly. "Promise, you won't smile like that for anyone but me."

Zach didn't have any words for that. He had no frame of reference for being possessed. No understanding of what it meant to be desired wholly for himself. His lips parted, and he looked helplessly at the blue-eyed boy who had done this to him.

Sean let out an impatient whine, said, "Those eyes... *dammit, I've got to go!*" and kissed Zach's knuckles before turning around and running out the double lobby doors.

Zach watched him go, and then turned and followed, turning right instead of left because his office was still that way, and walking the extra four blocks in a daze.

MONTEREY WAS gorgeous—even if he and the girls weren't staying on Pebble Beach. He told Leah and Jenn it was his treat, so he rented a suite for two days at a hotel on the waterfront, and listening to the two of them ooh and ahh over the view was totally worth the expense.

"Holy fucking Jesus," Jenn muttered as they stood at the window and looked out over the ocean. "I can't even believe this funky bullshit. Leah, you have the best boss *ever.*"

Zach smiled quietly at her, and was the sudden recipient of a squishy, chubby, bubbly hug.

"You look like we squashed your kittens, baby. This was supposed to be a *fun* trip!"

Zach didn't know what to do with that much hugging. He stroked her blonde hair awkwardly and went to step away, and found Leah behind him, her arms wrapped around his waist.

"You didn't talk the whole way down," she mumbled against his back.

"I'm not exactly Mr. Personality in the best of times," he said, ducking his head.

"Yeah, but Zach!" Leah moved around him but her arms stayed firmly planted at his ribs.

"God you're short," he said, wondering how he'd managed to work with her for three years and live without the hugs and the companionship and the crude sense of humor and the best friend who made him laugh.

"Why didn't you ask the guy to come?" Jenn asked, squinting at him. Yeah, she looked like a plump little Persian kitten, but she was sort of damned smart. "I mean, yeah, we didn't want to hear mansex, but if you're treating to a suite and a trip to the aquarium—that's almost, I don't know, a college trip right there."

Zach shrugged and tried to extricate himself. "He couldn't make it," he said, trying not to drown in self-pity. There were sea lions barking outside. *Sea lions.* Which, of course, they had in San Francisco, but somehow they were better in Monterey. And some of the best food in the world being served around them. Again, they had that in San Francisco, but Monterey also had the aquarium, which, as far as he could see, hadn't gotten less fun since he'd been there in high school. And the ocean, which, well, he saw every day, but it was better when it was out another window.

"Wait." Leah backed up. "I didn't know you asked him?"

Work was still a little nuts from the move. They had actually not had time to do more than establish a time for when they'd meet to get the rental car before work had been out and they'd both been hurrying home to pack.

"Yeah. Well. It was this morning. He…." Zach smiled in memory. "He rode the elevator up to meet me."

"So the fuck what?" Jenn asked, and Leah smacked her in the arm.

"So! That's *huge.* That's… that's… that's… breaking outside the code of elevators! Oh, Zach! I'm so happy for you!"

Zach beamed at her, because she understood. "I… well, he's starting school next week, and it's a new job, and he's so excited. I just really… I don't know." He sighed. "I need a gesture."

Leah grinned. "A romantic gesture?"

Zach smiled quietly back. "Yeah!"

Jenn rolled her eyes. "I would be more impressed if you showed up at his place with a condom and said, 'I'm sick of this shit with the elevators already.'"

Leah shook her head. "No. Jenn, hon, he wants something that lasts longer than it takes for the jizz to cool."

Zach backed away, cheeks flaming. "You guys…. God. Unpack. Dress. Jesus, let's go eat."

Jenn looked the three of them up and down—they were all wearing jeans and sweatshirts and tennis shoes—and she shook her head. "Baby, I love that you think we're the kind of girls who dress for dinner, but after that drive? Maybe you should just take us to a bar."

The Crown and Anchor sat in downtown Monterey, and they didn't mind jeans.

"This is swank," Jenn said, "but not intimidating. I approve."

"I like the big brass plates everywhere," Leah said. "And the dark beams with the white walls. It's a lot like the pubs in England."

Zach looked at her, surprised. Hawaii seemed far enough away. "You've been to England?"

"Yeah, summer trip to Europe, you?"

"Same." He lost himself in his menu then, thinking about travelling with Sean, because he'd probably memorize all of the facts on the menu for his students, and he'd probably be looking for costumes and....

And he'd probably be just as wonderful in a restaurant as he was thirty seconds a day on the elevator.

He was probably even better.

"Zach? Hello, *Zach*—aren't you going to order?"

Zach looked up from his menu and said, "Sean. I want one of those."

Jenn and Leah groaned. "He'll have the bangers and mash," Leah told the bemused waiter. "And we'll have a beer!"

But that right then was when Zach knew—knew for *sure*—that he was going to have to step outside of the box for good.

MONDAY MORNING, he got up early enough to brew coffee into the new thermos he'd bought. Hopelessly dorky, it sported "World's Greatest Teacher" written on the front, and a cartoon featuring a freckled, woebegone guy with a briefcase, a stack of papers, and, of course, a thermos of coffee. They'd stopped in Gilroy and picked up some cherries and melons on the way home from the beach, and he chopped up some of that and put it in a plastic cup, and added a fork and a little bit of packaged biscotti.

And then he made a sandwich and added carrots and a small bag of chips, all of which he'd picked up on the way home the night before.

When it was all assembled (and the coffee was still brewing) he got dressed, grabbed his briefcase, and put the whole works in a little basket that he tried desperately to balance.

The little hop from elevator to elevator at the nineteenth floor felt so smooth by this time, he'd forgotten that he was supposed to have an express elevator from the top floors to the bottom all along. (He hoped that one guy's ghost wasn't opposed to that, and that he'd forgiven his cats.) The doors opened at the fourteenth floor, and he checked his watch—he was about five minutes early, which was perfect.

He'd never realized that walking through a door was terrifying.

And, oh hell, someone he'd never seen before opened it—a tiny man in a bright-blue paisley shirt and red jeans stared blankly at him through fashionably thick-rimmed glasses.

"Uhm, Sean—?"

"*Sean! Prince Charming is here with coffee, get your ass in gear!*"

Zach's hands started shaking from sheer nerves. "The entire fourteenth floor heard you."

"Oh calm down!" With a little swish of his hand, the guy gestured Zach inside the apartment of chaos. Zach's basket threatened to tumble, but the little man rescued it deftly. He peered into the mass of people moving, dressing, and (in one case) folding the hide-a-bed with deft movements. "Sean!" he snapped. "Man, stop mugging my boyfriend for toast, your guy here brought you breakfast. And *lunch*! Now get him out of here before we scare the shit out of him."

Suddenly five sets of eyes were turned toward Zach, and Zach tried to take inventory. Wendy was in the middle of fastening her bra, and she gave a little head bob before resuming dressing from the pile of clothes that sat on a battered recliner. The other girl—taller than Wendy but no less thin, with brown hair—actually had a bra on, and even slacks, but she was shirtless and in the process of putting one arm in a dress shirt while using her other hand to slip on a very practical black pump. The straight guy (he had to be; he was at the hide-a-bed) and was wearing boxers, and, well, yeah, he was decked to the nines with muscles and a hairy chest and a nice ass, but he had sort of a vacant expression in his eyes that indicated a complete lack of self-awareness.

And there, by the toast, was Sean, next to a shorter—but still taller than his boyfriend!—man who was wearing a Japanese silk robe and bunny slippers.

Sean turned to Zach with a dreamy expression and said, "You brought coffee? And fruit? And biscotti? Oh my God—*marry me!*"

"Okay," Zach said, completely overwhelmed. "Sure. I'll be just outside." And then he made his escape, closed the door behind him, and leaned against it with a thundering heart.

Oh hell. Talk about a madhouse! He... he couldn't. All those *people,* all in that tiny space, and they all….

"Hey!" The door opened behind him, and Zach moved enough to let Sean out. Sean had his satchel over his shoulder and the little gift basket in his hand. "You brought me coffee! And everything—that's *awesome*! Don't bail!"

"People," Zach said numbly. "You have more friends in that room than I've had in my entire life."

"Ohmygod!" Sean muttered. "It's like dating Rapunzel!"

That actually cheered Zach up. "Hey, we *are* dating. Excellent. Are you ready to go?"

"You made lunch too—and the bag matches the mug!"

Zach grinned, calming down a little from being faced with all of those people. "I did. I got them when we were shopping in Monterey— but my friends helped me pick them out."

"See! You have friends!" Sean nudged him with an elbow and took a sip of his coffee. "Mm… that's good, but, uhm, really sweet."

"Too sweet?" Zach asked anxiously. Oh no. He made dessert coffee for someone who liked it black! The horror!

"I like it this way, but I'll get fat really quick."

Zach turned a little in the hallway as they waited for the elevator. Sean was wearing jeans, a black sport coat, and a neatly pressed white shirt with a thin red tie.

"You look great," he said quietly, feeling privileged to be in on the ground floor of this outfit. "But your tie is crooked." He set his briefcase down and straightened Sean's tie and collar, and paused, his hands on Sean's collar. Sean's hands were full of his gift basket, so Zach did all the work, leaning forward and kissing him softly.

When he pulled back, they both smiled into each other's eyes for a moment. "You're going to do great," Zach said, and Sean grinned.

"You already made it a good day!"

Ding!

ZACH BROUGHT him coffee every morning that week. After that initial shock, he got used to knocking on the door and walking into various stages of chaos (the worst being when Sean's alarm had failed to go off and the entire household was naked *and* running in six different directions. Zach had simply shouted "I've got your lunch and coffee!" and then sat down in the corridor until Sean emerged.)

Sean hadn't been wearing anything exciting—just his basic teaching suit—but as he'd emerged from his apartment every morning, the smile on his face to see Zach waiting for him—*that* had been pure magic.

On Friday morning, the elevator opened to the lobby with Sean in full cry about his students, and the ones who were already troublemakers and the ones who were terrifyingly smart, and it wasn't until the traitorous "Ding!" that they both realized that, per their usual custom, their time together was at an end.

Zach—as usual—gestured Sean ahead of him, but once they cleared the elevator, Sean turned around.

"This can't be the end for the week," he said, smiling, and Zach shrugged.

"It's Friday—I'm usually late on Friday."

"How late?" Sean's eyes were anxious, and Zach ducked his head shyly.

"After I work out and everything, around nine or ten."

Sean's face lit up. "Make it nine thirty," he said, taking charge, and Zach blushed.

"Should I come get you?" He dreaded thinking about that apartment in the evenings, but he'd do it.

"If you need to," Sean said, and then he captured the back of Zach's head with his hand and kissed him, hard and deep enough to make Zach open his mouth and moan, then pulled back. "You're a little better at kissing, but we still need to work on it."

Zach nodded dumbly, and he swallowed, knowing what this meant, but so, so ready for it. "I could really use more kissing lessons," he said, hoping.

Sean's smile was sweet, and it pulled up at the corner. "Well, I'd be willing to tutor you after hours." He kissed Zach pertly and then pulled away. "But first, our day awaits."

Zach almost skipped to work.

"And here's your coffee," he sang, putting Leah's coffee and croissants on her desk. "And what do you have waiting for me?"

Leah looked at him apologetically and gestured to his office. Three people sat there, two middle-aged women in tears and a thin-faced young man looking close to tears himself. "Zach, it's bad."

Zach blinked. "Bad. Explain bad."

"They run the school's GSA. The kids asked for a list of books they could read—these guys got a list of books from their local YA librarian, and the parents complained. Bam! Yesterday morning, they get taken out of their classrooms."

Zach blinked. "That's...."

"Heinous. Yeah, I know. But there's three of them, and Edward doesn't get here for another hour. It's you and them. I've rescheduled most of your stuff until Monday, and I'll get Lori here to mind the phones while I go in and take notes, but baby, we're talking a two-hour interview and all the shit that comes after."

Zach sighed. "Well, enjoy your coffee," he murmured grimly. "I'm going to go get pissed off."

Leah surprised him with a giggle. "*That's* something. You know? A year ago, I would have said you don't have it in you, but now? Kick ass and take names, kemosabe—I'll just watch you work."

And work he did. He interviewed and investigated and assigned and deposed—and, of course, dealt with the things he'd already planned on doing that day.

By the time seven o'clock rolled around, he realized he wasn't going to be able to make it to the gym.

By the time nine o'clock rolled around, he realized that he needed to shove all of his briefs in his briefcase and take them home.

The thought was depressing.

"Goddammit," he muttered. "I finally have someone waiting for me, and I have to bring my work home for the weekend?"

"Wait!" Leah had just stuck her head in—probably to say goodnight, and to have him walk her out to her bus stop. "You've got someone waiting for you?"

"Maybe," Zach muttered, grabbing his coat and his scarf from the rack in the corner. "I brought him coffee every morning—I was... you know... sort of hoping...."

"For a real date." Leah practically crowed. "Excellent—well, text him and tell him you're on your way."

Zach's pained expression made her bang her head on the doorframe.

"Okay—so, how long have you known him?"

"Shut up," he murmured.

"And you've actually kissed him—you told me that."

"Several times."

"You know his last name."

"Mallory."

Leah sighed. "Zach…." she whined. "Please tell me you'll get his phone number this weekend?"

Zach found his smile. "I think, if nothing else, that could be arranged."

HE WAS not so sure though as he hurried into his building and realized it was, oh hell! Nine forty-five. God, let Sean still be awake, please let him be still awake, please let him be….

Sitting on the bench next to the elevator, wearing yoga pants and a long-sleeved baseball shirt, leaning against the wall with his eyes closed.

Zach had to draw a little nearer, just to make sure it was him.

"Sean?" he said softly, and Sean's eyes remained closed but the corners of his mouth turned up.

"Someone had a late night," he murmured.

"I didn't even make it to the gym."

Sean's eyes opened, and he regarded Zach from only a few inches distance. "What happened?"

"We'll talk about it later," Zach told him. He placed a very careful kiss on Sean's cheek. "Right now, do you want to come up and… uhm… I've got movies! Or, uhm, a soda. Or… coffee. I've got coffee and biscotti! Or…."

"Sex, Zach," Sean said soberly. "I think we can skip the preliminaries. We need to have sex."

Zach felt color wash his face. "Maybe more kissing lessons," he said, hoping. "And, you know. Phone numbers?"

Sean's eyes narrowed wickedly. "Okay. That's a deal. Phone numbers in the elevator. Kissing lessons in the living room. Sex in the bedroom. We've got this locked. Now let me up, and we can make it happen."

Zach backed up and offered him a hand, and Sean took it—and used the leverage to launch himself at Zach. Their mouths met, melded, and time ceased to exist, as did the rules of physics.

The elevator dinged, and Sean steered them inside, pressed the button for floor thirty, and the kiss went on.

THE TOWER FLOOR

ZACH DIDN'T see if there were people in that elevator or not. Everything was a haze except Sean's mouth on his, and the quietly murmured instructions.

"It's a dialog," Sean said. "See?" He pressed his mouth against Zach's and Zach opened in response. Sean pulled back and breathed, "Good, now listen to this next one." And then he touched his tongue to the edge of Zach's lips and Zach drove his tongue into Sean's mouth like a deep-core drill trying to strike oil.

Zach half expected Sean to correct his form or punctuate his tongue work or something but Sean went boneless in his arms, opened his mouth, and melted against the back of the elevator. Zach tasted *everything*— tongue, teeth, tonsils—and then pulled back, touched Sean's lips and then moved in a little deeper and then accepted the quest of his tongue and sucked on it gently and released it and teased his lips some more. There was no coming up for air, there was only Sean, who tasted like coffee and magic and unicorns and knights in geeky armor and some sort of gravy he'd had for dinner.

Sean's hands slid down the back of Zach's slacks and squeezed, and Zach whimpered and buried his face in Sean's neck.

"Lesson over," Sean whispered. "You kiss like a Shakespeare sonnet."

"It's not dialog," Zach apologized.

"Nope." Sean's hands were squeezy and intimate on Zach's backside. "'Sheer poetry, ah!'"

Zach shuddered, and while one hand was still clutching his briefcase, the other hand was sort of mauling its way under Sean's shirt. "I have no idea what that means."

Sean growled into Zach's mouth and the kiss was on again, except this time Zach got a good handful of Sean's backside, and it felt *so* good in his hand. Sean whined a little and ground up against Zach's thigh, and Zach had a sudden flash of the obvious: *That's his cock. And it's getting hard. And I'm going to see it, and touch it, and taste it and ***!*

Zach's brain sort of shorted out after that, and his briefcase hit the floor. Now he had *two* handfuls of Sean's ass, and that magic thing in the yoga pants was getting harder and grinding closer and—

Ding!

He couldn't seem to stop kissing Sean.

"Zach…. Zach—"

A little smack on the top of his head snapped him out of it. He pulled back from Sean and they both regarded each other stupidly. Sean's pupils were blown and his breath was coming like a sprinter's at the line.

"Huh?" Zach said, looking around. Jace regarded him over Sean's shoulder, his steel-blue eyes sardonic and unamused.

"If you two don't get out of the elevator and down the hall, you're going to get evicted for indecent exposure."

"Jace!" Quent protested.

"Their hands are *still* in each other's pants," Jace snapped. "I'm doing them a service." Then the irritated stockbroker turned back to Zach and literally grabbed him by the collar and pulled him back. "Get out your key, Romeo, and go kiss yourself an entire play—just do it *out of the elevator.*"

Zach grabbed his briefcase in embarrassment, and was fumbling around in his pocket for his key when Sean grabbed his arm and started hauling him down the hall. "Bye fellas!" he burbled. "Have a nice evening!"

"Not as nice as yours!" Quent called, and the last thing Zach heard as he opened his door was Jace growling, "Wanna bet?"

Sean chuckled and the two of them fell through the door and the rest of the world was forgotten.

Sean—oh wow. Taste and taste and taste and it didn't get old or awkward or weird, it was just… kissing him was like eating chocolate and raspberries—it shouldn't have to stop. And Sean's hands—his presumptuous, forward, filthy-minded hands!

First they were fumbling with Zach's fly, then they were pushing his slacks down to his thighs and then they were shoving his suit jacket off his shoulders and, between kisses, nibbles, breathless little cries, unbuttoning his shirt.

Zach managed to pull back and gasp, "The bedroom. There's condoms in the bedroom."

Sean pulled back and looked at him suspiciously. "Yeah, Zach, but how *old* are those condoms."

Zach flushed. "I, uhm, bought them this week."

"Cause the other ones were… c'mon. Fess up."

Zach looked into that ordinary, beautiful, freckled face with the riot of hair and the windburned nose, and actually felt like he *could* fess up, to everything.

"Expired," Zach mumbled, because it really had been that long since he'd even called up the escort service to allay the loneliness.

Sean nodded then, and kissed his forehead. "Okay then. A little slower. We're going to do this a little slower."

Zach whined and did his own filthy-minded exploration of Sean's backside with his hands. "Fast first!" he begged. "Slower later!"

Sean reached behind him and grabbed Zach's hands firmly, hauling them out of his pants and pinning them to Zach's sides. "Go get undressed," he ordered softly. "Down to wherever your courage fails you. Get the condoms out and ready on the dressing table, and the lube too, but don't get too disappointed if we don't get that far. You and me, we're going to have us a long, meaningful body conversation tonight, and I have waited too long to rush it."

Zach swallowed, some of his urgency fading. "Undress?"

"I'll be right in," Sean murmured, kissing him quickly.

Sean must have remembered where the guest bathroom was, because he disappeared in there, and Zach picked his jacket off the ground, left his briefcase where it was, and pulled his pants up so he could shuffle into his bedroom.

He felt a little better after he hung up his suit jacket and his pants, and he managed to unbutton his dress shirt and take off his tie without any nerves whatsoever.

But down to his tank—that's where his nerves failed him, and while he managed to take it off with shaking hands, he was huddled under the comforter, looking balefully at the supplies on top of the nightstand when Sean came out of the bathroom.

Naked.

Zach stopped huddling, and actually propped himself on an elbow to check him out.

Sean grinned and gestured to himself suggestively. He didn't work out—he had a little tummy, and his chest was narrow. He wasn't fat— just soft—and Zach thought about how real he'd felt under Zach's hands.

"See?" Sean said, still grinning. "One-hundred percent red-blooded gay man. Right here. No preservatives or additives, just—"

"Just you. Get in bed, okay? You promised me dialog."

"Dialog?"

"Repartee, banter, an exchange of quips—"

"Oh hey! Look who's getting all teacherly and shit!" Sean got close to the bed and reached down to feather his fingertips along Zach's jaw. "Why are you so worried? You're the one who's buffed and toned and—"

Zach captured his hand. "Do you have any idea what you mean to me? How important you are? How much I need to touch someone who's real?"

Sean knelt on the mattress and captured his mouth. Zach accepted the first sally, and replied. He listened with the opening of his mouth and his touches along Sean's back, and replied with a leg thrown over a slender, naked thigh, and arching into Sean's aroused body, so they could continue the conversation.

The dialog whispered when Sean kissed along his neck and down his chest, and exploded into babble when Sean's swollen pink mouth closed around his nipple. When Sean's soft hands pushed Zach's boxers down his thighs and grasped Zach's cock, they were no longer bantering; they were negotiating for the territory of Zach's soul.

Sean's mouth closed over Zach's erect flesh, and Zach conceded the conversation with a shout, with begging, breathless sobs, broken syllables of raw need.

Sean responded with tenderness, with firm touches, with increased pressure where it was needed, and Zach ended the conversation, spilling his soul in his lover's mouth.

Silence, hushed and reverent, filled the darkness.

Zach threaded shaking fingers through Sean's hair, and Sean rested his cheek on Zach's upper thigh and gazed up at him with sober eyes.

Sean captured Zach's hand and squeezed.

"You didn't… uhm, I mean, well…."

Sean shook his head then, squinting inscrutably. "We have so many more things to talk about," he said quietly. "This conversation is going to take way longer than a night."

Zach nodded and tried a shaky smile. His eyes burned absurdly and he closed them and returned the pressure of Sean's fingers.

"Could you come up and kiss me, then?" he begged. "I... I don't even know what to say anymore."

"A kiss is good. I think kisses are where all good things start."

Zach closed his eyes and accepted the kiss, accepted the taste of his come on Sean's tongue, and all he had to return was that acceptance, that willingness to be himself and only himself for the man who had just made love to him in what had once been a cold and lonely bed.

The kiss ended, and Sean lay next to him, rubbing the hard muscles in his chest and the planes of his stomach. Zach took the tacit invitation and started to explore Sean's body with tentative touches as well.

"That was wonderful," Zach breathed, and Sean nodded.

"Your hands are still shaking."

Zach's hand stilled the tentative petting of the soft oblique muscle of Sean's stomach. He watched curiously and saw that Sean was right.

"I've... it's uhm...."

"Zach, you're the loneliest person I've ever met."

Zach shrunk in on himself in mortification. "I wasn't a minute ago," he muttered, trying to turn his back.

Sean stopped him with a quiet hand. "Come back here. C'mon, I won't bite." Zach rolled back and Sean opened his arms for him. Zach found himself cuddled up to that narrow chest with a few silky chest hairs peeping out, which Zach petted when Sean began to talk.

"My parents are still stupid sickly in love, you know," Sean told him, and Zach didn't even have to make listening noises, because suddenly, oh gift of gifts, Sean's life story was spilled out before him like treasures for Zach to sort through.

His parents were still in love and living in Sacramento, and he had two younger sisters and a brother who was still in high school.

"They're both retired, right? So Timothy gets dragged everywhere—I think he barely attends school, but his test scores are *phenomenal,* so he can go almost anywhere he wants. Of course, mom and dad can't really afford anywhere, so it's probably going to be state college, but he'll do amazing, like he always does. And the girls are both getting their degrees in humanities and teaching, because it's like, the family curse, you know? Some families do business, some are cops, ours are teachers. I picked middle school because I can teach almost anything, and I like being busy.

So, every year we meet at home for Christmas, and my parents invite our significant others and we pick on each other and eat way too much and help mom with the dishes and tell her all about our personal lives and try not to let them give us money."

"Sounds happy," Zach whispered.

"We are. I missed them so bad when I went away to school. I called three times a week and about drove my mom crazy with e-mails and pictures. But eventually I really started to love it here, and I met Chris and Toby, and we all moved in together and then when my student loans ran out, we recruited Wendy, Katie, and Todd. And I dated a few guys for more than a month and partied a lot, and had just about decided I was ready to date like a grown-up when this really nice guy smiled at me on an elevator, and that was pretty much it."

"Why?" Zach asked, thinking about the guy with the play tickets in a hurry. "You had other offers."

Sean kissed the back of his neck and the edge of his shoulder blade, and Zach's breath hitched and he pushed backward just to feel Sean's curly pubic hair and his growing erection.

"Because I was ready to feel something important," Sean murmured. "And that's just how you looked at me."

"Yes." Zach's hips started to undulate all on their own. "That's exactly how I felt."

Sean's hands smoothed down his chest, stopping to tweak at his nipples and then centering at ground zero. "So," he purred in Zach's ear, "tell me about yourself."

"Nungh...." Zach thrust into Sean's fist, and Sean sighed.

"It's a good thing this part of the convo has it going on," he murmured, and then he proceeded to... well, just proceeded. He stroked Zach until he was crazy again, and then, boldly and without apology, propped Zach's foot up so his bottom was accessible. His fingers, slick and probing, were a surprise at first, and Zach made a shocked sort of sound.

"You've never bottomed?" Sean asked, stretching him gently.

"No," Zach told him, pushing back onto his fingers because it felt so good.

"You're practically a romantic trope, you're so needy," Sean murmured. "Why haven't you ever bottomed?"

And Zach was so mindless, so drunk on touch and conversation, that he actually told the truth. "Rent boys don't usually top," he murmured, and for a terrible second Sean's hands actually stopped on his body. "Oh hell."

"No," Sean said, sounding like he was making a resolution. His hands resumed, the one soft and probing and the other hard and insistent. "Here, hold that for a minute," and he placed Zach's hand on his own cock while he fumbled with the condom from the nightstand. Zach knew his own body well, and he loved it when his crown was squeezed between the circle of his thumb and forefinger. He listened to Sean's noises with the wrapper and the condom with only half an ear, and concentrated on the white light that centered at his penis and radiated out.

"Don't come yet!" Sean admonished, and there was a sudden pressure at Zach's entrance. Zach let out a little grunt and then… just sat still. Sean pressed forward and waited, waited, waited, and Zach's body did an extraordinary thing. It stretched, and for a moment it radiated a sharp pain, and then… then… it stretched some more, and Sean let out a great sigh right in Zach's ear.

"Oh…."

"Good?" Sean panted. Zach felt sweat smearing on his back when Sean wiped his forehead, so he knew this wasn't easy.

"Yes. Yes… it's… oh… oh yeah… move a little more. A little more. God… yes. A… *harder.*"

Sean's breathless laugh tickled his ear. "Oh *now* you're vocal." And that was the last thing he said for a while with actual words in it.

Give and take—this kind of sex brought it to a whole new level. Sean gave and Zach took, then Zach thrust back and Sean took and again and again and again. A shift in position had Zach facedown in the mattress and Sean thrusting into him like a jackhammer while one or both of them started screaming *"Yes, God yes, hell yes, ohmygod don't fucking stop!"*

Sean's frantic spasms in his body were Zach's only warning that Sean was close, and he groaned, desperate for his own edge, then grabbed himself and squeezed.

The pulses of come against the sheets splashed wet and hot on his stomach, and Sean fell against him, clammy with sweat.

"Wow." Sean didn't say anything after that for a while. Just panted and crushed Zach into the mattress. Zach took it, like he'd taken the invasion of his body and the whole other human being in his bed.

Like it was a miracle.

"Yeah," Zach said against the darkness in front of his eyes. He was taking inventory. Everything either tingled, ached pleasurably, or was shaking too hard to tell. Little puckers danced across his back as Sean peppered his back with tiny kisses.

Sean pulled the hair back from his ear so he could place a kiss against the outer hollow, whispered, "How you doing?"

"I... uhm...." Oh no. His voice shook. His voice shook, and his eyes burned more and could he be any more of an idiot?

"Hey," Sean whispered. "Hey, what's wrong?" Sean rolled off of him, and his absence from Zach's body almost hurt. While he was deftly dealing with the condom, Zach rolled on his side, away from Sean and toward the wall.

"It was great," he said, feeling all sorts of desolation. "It was... I can't believe... I mean...." He couldn't explain it. He couldn't. It was like his entire life, he'd thought he knew what breathing was, what pleasurable meant, what human connection could be.

He was wrong. So, so far off the mark, so far short of what the world was about. He couldn't stop the shivers that swept him, and it wasn't until Sean plastered himself along his back that he was able to breathe again.

Sean's kisses along his neck centered him. "You've never done that for real before," he deduced.

"An orgasm is an orgasm," Zach said tonelessly. "I've seen enough of them on TV."

"C'mon, Zach, look at me."

Zach sighed and rolled over, staring fixedly at Sean's chest. Escorts didn't have chests like that, he thought. They waxed and worked out, and their muscles were spectacular. They didn't have imperfections like a soft waist or loose pecs or a little patch of hair in the middle. Tentatively he reached up and stroked Sean's little patch of hair.

"What's wrong?" Sean asked, and Zach met his eyes—sort of. His whole face was blurry, and it was dark, but he was pretty sure he was focusing in the right place.

"This is new," he said shakily.

"What is? Sex? Been around awhile." The words were flip, but the voice was soft, and kind. Sean wiped under his eyes with gentle thumbs.

"Happy. I'm happy. I've lived my whole life and not known what this feels like."

Sean kissed him, and pulled back. "That's awful," he said, a little hitch in his voice. "We're going to have to fix that."

"Yeah?"

Sean kissed him again, and Zach opened his mouth and let that warmth fill him.

"Yeah."

AT FIRST, Zach thought Sean meant for the rest of the weekend, which was pretty awesome. They stayed in bed for two days, getting out only to change the sheets, shower, and order takeout, but basically? They stayed wrapped up in each other. Zach fed on Sean's family stories like magic beans fed on water, and felt his soul grow stronger, less tenuous and wishful.

Zach still had to work—but then, so did Sean. Sunday afternoon, he ran down to his apartment and came back with his outfit for the next morning and his satchel of papers to grade, and for a couple of hours, they sat at the kitchen table and worked quietly, reaching out to touch each other every now and then.

Zach had never worked with anyone like that. Not in grade school, not in college, not even in law school where group work had been part of the norm.

He was just happy to be there, in the same room, while Sean wiggled in his seat, ate all his apples and crackers, and worked in furious grading spurts followed by lots of pacing.

Finally, Sean put the last stack of papers back in his satchel and walked behind Zach, leaning over his shoulders and nuzzling his ear.

"Zach?"

"Yeah?"

"You gonna be late tomorrow?"

"Seven, probably. I was going to work out. Want to come with?"

Sean grinned at him. "I don't have a membership."

"I could get you one," Zach said earnestly, and Sean kissed his cheek.

"Maybe after school settles, I'll take you up on that. How 'bout this. You work out and come get me when you get home."

Zach was sitting at the table in the open kitchenette. All he had to do was reach behind him to his pen drawer and pull out the little ring of keys.

"Here," he said, pushing the spare into Sean's hand. "Come in if you like—enjoy the quiet."

Sean looked at the keys and then looked at him. "Can I bring a friend or two? Wendy or Kate might appreciate the quiet too!"

Zach nodded. "Yeah. Yeah." He looked sightlessly at his computer and leaned his head against Sean's arm. "It will be nice to have someone home when I get home, I think," he admitted.

Sean kissed his cheek, and then his jaw, and then down his neck. "We'll try to make sure that happens a lot," he promised.

And then, wonder of wonders, he proceeded to keep that promise, without any signs of wavering, forever.

Zach didn't *know* it would be forever at first. He and Sean assumed it would be just what it sounded like.

A day.

A week.

A month.

And it was.

But August turned into September, and Sean moved more and more of his things into Zach's apartment, until the only thing of his down in 1409 was the hide-a-bed, but he figured he'd let Todd keep that.

September turned into October, and Sean's costumes came out again. He and Zach went down the express elevator every day with Jace and Quent, and in the last week of October, he wore a mummy costume, a Dracula costume, a pirate costume, a race-car driver costume, and a train engineer costume.

That last one made Zach quiet for the entire day, and after the Halloween party at 1409—which Zach dragged Leah and Jenn to as well—Zach told Sean about trains, and how much he loved them, and how they'd disappeared from his life.

And Sean had made love to him while wearing his conductor's hat until Zach smiled and stole it and wore it for the rest of the night—and nothing else.

October turned into November, and Zach dragged Sean to the gym, and to Frisbee with Leah and Jenn, and to the Thanksgiving benefit dinner that his firm gave for their clients and that he let Leah organize because she loved it.

Zach dressed him up in a tuxedo and got him a new haircut and gave him a diamond tie clip, all so he could see his boy look like the prince Zach knew him to be.

He looked good, and he charmed pretty much the entire company in that suit.

Then they went home and Zach charmed him out of it.

Zach topped that night, and the feeling, the trust, of being allowed inside another human being's body, inside his heart, left Zach breathless and thrilled. It took them hours to come down from the high of it, and this time, Sean's eyes watered, and Zach discovered what it meant to be kind to someone naked and vulnerable in his arms.

It was terrifying, a responsibility Zach would never take for granted, a gift he would never cede back.

November became Thanksgiving, and they hosted Sean's friends and Zach's friends and Sean's sisters. Zach's apartment, now dressed with Sean's tchotchkes and his movie posters and his bizarre statuette collection from various movies and his bright, cheap comforters of which he owned seven, seemed warm and welcoming.

It was a good place to have prime rib (because Sean hated turkey) and stuffing (because Leah loved stuffing and brought some to prove it) and wine and whatever anyone else felt like bringing, and they ended up watching *Mary Poppins* of all things on Zach's big screen as the entire lot of them lay about with distended stomachs and blurry vision from too much wine.

It was a good place for Sean to ask Zach to accompany him to his parents' house over Christmas break, and a good place for Zach to ask Sean to stay with him for all of the nights forever.

It was a good place for all of these things, but in the end, it was not the place they wanted to stay.

Zach's lease was ironclad—he didn't have to leave unless he wanted to. His one reason to stay had been Sean.

They moved the first week of December, from the penthouse flat to a second floor condo on La Portola, some place where Sean could have a cat and Zach could keep a car, and neither of them would ever have to ride in an elevator again.

It was less pricey than the penthouse, and not nearly as privileged, but Zach had spent thirty-four years paying for that privilege with his soul.

He had his soul back now—he figured the privilege could go to someone else.

His parents didn't say anything when he resigned his lease, but something must have thawed. Two days before Christmas Eve, after Zach drove his spiffy new Mercedes home to get Sean and their suitcases for the trip to Sacramento, he checked the mail.

"Hey, look," he said over his shoulder. Sean was bouncing around in the entryway, after having locked all the doors. He'd dressed warmly in his peacoat, with a gaudy fleece hat that his sister had made him on top of his head and around his ears.

"I'm looking at the night getting older is what I'm looking at!" Sean complained. "Let's get out of here before the fog gets any worse!"

"Well seriously—it's an invite for my parents' party—look, it must have gotten lost after we moved. I think it's been all around the city." The vellum envelope was battered, marked, and redirected almost to tatters.

"Mm." Sean's ebullience fizzled away for a moment, and he abruptly stood looking over Zach's shoulder, his arms around Zach's waist. "Is that something you wanted to do?"

Zach smiled a little, and remembered the year before.

Someone please save me.

"Are you kidding?" he asked, leaning forward and capturing Sean's mouth in a kiss. "You're my knight in shining armor—you *saved* me from all of this. I'd have to be nuts to think about going back!"

Sean rolled his eyes. "I'm your knight in shining armor?" he asked dubiously.

"Yes," Zach said, eyes dancing.

"And I saved you from your life in the tower?"

"Absolutely."

"So, was the elevator my charging steed or my magic carpet or my—"

"I didn't say it was a perfect metaphor!" Zach laughed. He threw the invitation away in the receptacle by the entryway.

"Was it my magic portal to your world, you know, like Rapunzel's hair, except, your elevator?"

"I have no idea. Do you have our bags?"

"Absolutely, my prince. Do you have our charging steed?"

Zach shook his head. "I've seen you dressed in shining armor," he said threateningly. "I have pictures to prove it."

Sean laughed and wrapped his arms around Zach's waist and pulled him in for a solid kiss. "C'mon, my prince. Let's get on the charging steed and go have adventures in a neighboring kingdom, and you never have to go back in the tower again."

Zach clung to him, secure and happy as he could never remember being. "Do you promise?"

"It is my solemn vow, my Christmas wager, my—"

Zach shushed him with a kiss. Over Sean's shoulder, he could see the Bay Bridge, lit up in Christmas colors and flickering playfully. Yes, they would leave their little kingdom and visit another, and he would still be safe. He'd never have to return to the tower again.

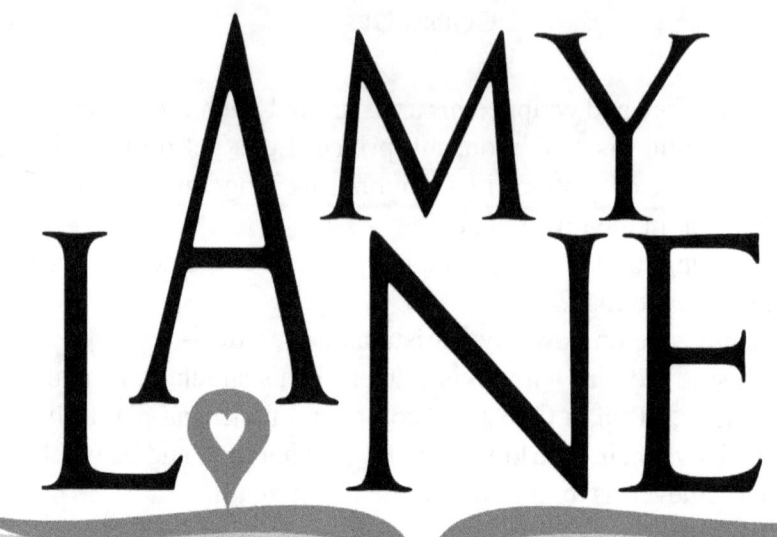

Choose your Lane to love!

Yellow

Amy Lane Lite
Light Contemporary Romance

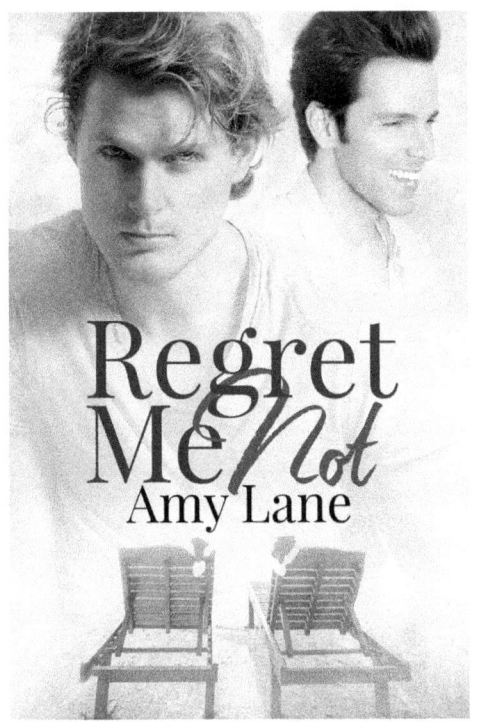

Pierce Atwater used to think he was a knight in shining armor, but then his life fell to crap. Now he has no job, no wife, no life—and is so full of self-pity he can't even be decent to the one family member he's still speaking to. He heads for Florida, where he's got a month to pull his head out of his ass before he ruins his little sister's Christmas.

Harold Justice Lombard the Fifth is at his own crossroads—he can keep being Hal, massage therapist in training, flamboyant and irrepressible to the bones, or he can let his parents rule his life. Hal takes one look at Pierce and decides they're fellow unicorns out to make the world a better place. Pierce can't reject Hal's overtures of friendship, in spite of his misgivings about being too old and too pissed off to make a good friend.

As they experience everything from existential Looney Tunes to eternal trips to Target, Pierce becomes more dependent on Hal's optimism to get him through the day. When Hal starts getting him through the nights too, Pierce must look inside for the knight he used to be—before Christmas becomes a doomsday deadline of heartbreak instead of a celebration of love.

AMY LANE is a mother of two grown kids, two half-grown kids, two small dogs, and half-a-clowder of cats. A compulsive knitter who writes because she can't silence the voices in her head, she adores fur-babies, knitting socks, and hawt menz, and she dislikes moths, cat boxes, and knuckleheaded macspazzmatrons. She is rarely found cooking, cleaning, or doing domestic chores, but she has been known to knit up an emergency hat/blanket/pair of socks for any occasion whatsoever or sometimes for no reason at all. Her award-winning writing has three flavors: twisty-purple alternative universe, angsty-orange contemporary, and sunshine-yellow happy. By necessity, she has learned to type like the wind. She's been married for twenty-five-plus years to her beloved Mate and still believes in Twu Wuv, with a capital Twu and a capital Wuv, and she doesn't see any reason at all for that to change.

Website: www.greenshill.com
Blog: www.writerslane.blogspot.com
Email: amylane@greenshill.com
Facebook: www.facebook.com/amy.lane.167
Twitter: @amymaclane

www.ingramcontent.com/pod-product-compliance
Lightning Source LLC
Chambersburg PA
CBHW070051030726
47506CB00002B/431